"Tell me? Please? I'll do anything." She reached across the table and took my hand.

"You have to make me a promise," I said.

"Anything." She squeezed my hand.

"Swear to me you won't try this ritual except as a last resort. And if it turns out to be the only answer, promise me that you'll always act in the interest of Zumorda and its people."

Praise for OF FIRE AND STARS:

"A powerful and exquisite love story."
—*Publishers Weekly* (starred review)

"Reminiscent of the kinds of fantasy books I loved when I was a young teenager, tales of princess angst, horses, and the blossoming of reluctant love. This book is bold enough to create a world that moves beyond the prejudices we are still fighting in our real world."
—Caitlyn Paxson, NPR

"A deeply romantic, bold, and nuanced fantasy. You will be captivated by Denna and Mare and their star-crossed love for each other."
—Malinda Lo, author of *Ash* and *Huntress*

"Lovely. A worthy debut that succeeds as both an adventure and a romance." —ALA *Booklist*

"Murder, mayhem, magic, romance—and horses. A romantic fantasy that will appeal to those who appreciate character-driven novels."
—*Kirkus Reviews*

"I devoured *Of Fire and Stars* in two sittings; it's a delightful debut, full of all the things I like best in a fantasy story, including not one but two wonderful heroines. I'm looking forward to seeing what Audrey does in the future!" —Mercedes Lackey, *New York Times* bestselling author of over 125 books, including the Valdemar series

"Coulthursts's debut is an absolute delight; I loved seeing these smart, fierce princesses fall in captivating, slow-burn love as they investigate political assassinations and unravel magical conspiracies."
—Corinne Duyvis, author of *Otherbound* and *On the Edge of Gone*

"Romantic, compelling, and bursting with fascinating characters, *Of Fire and Stars* is the fantasy novel we've all been waiting for."
—Amy Tintera, author of *Ruined*

"A slow-burn love story about two unique, brave, and endearing young women."—*VOYA*

INKMISTRESS

Also by Audrey Coulthurst

Of Fire and Stars

Of Ice and Shadows

AUDREY COULTHURST

INKMISTRESS

BALZER + BRAY
An Imprint of HarperCollins*Publishers*

Balzer + Bray is an imprint of HarperCollins Publishers.

Inkmistress
Copyright © 2018 by Audrey Coulthurst
Map © 2016, 2018 by Jordan Saia

www.epicreads.com

ISBN 978-0-06-243329-9

Typography by Torborg Davern
18 19 20 21 22 PC/LSCH 10 9 8 7 6 5 4 3 2 1

First paperback edition, 2019

For Casi, the one who taught me about love

THE NORTHERN KINGDOMS

HAVEMONT

OSMA

MT. VERITY

SPIRE CITY

ZIR CANYON

FAIRLOUGH

Northport Province

CIRALIS

COROVJA

Nax Province

ALMENDORN

ORZAI

LAKE VIERI

MYNARIA

LYRRA

PORT OF
KINGS

Queenswood
Province

ZUMORDA

VALENKO

DUVEY

TAMERS FOREST

AMALSKA

NOBROSKA

Trindor Province

KARTASHA

PORT JIRAE

TRINDOR CANAL

SONNENBORNE

 CHAPTER 1

WHEN OUR STORY BEGAN, I THOUGHT I KNEW LOVE.

Love was a mind that moved quickly from one thought to the next, eyes an inimitable blue that lay somewhere between morning glories and glaciers, and a hand that tugged me along as we raced laughing through the woods. Love was the way she buried her hands in my hair and I lost mine in the dark waves of hers, and how she kissed me until we fell in a hot tangle atop the blankets in the back of the cave I called home. Love was the warmth kindled by her touch, lingering in me long after the first snow fell and she had gone for the winter.

Love was what would bring her back to me in spring—and spring had finally begun to wake.

I braided my hair and wound it into a coiled knot, then pulled on my heavy fur-lined boots studded with nails for traction. My satchel hung on a hook beside the door, already packed with supplies to collect ingredients for my tinctures. A gentle wind nudged at the mouth of my cave, no longer carrying the weighty smell of ice and snow, but that of the earth beneath it. My heart quickened with the promise it held, not just of spring, but of her.

Invasya. My Ina.

The long nights of winter had left me forlorn, but soon Ina and other mortals from the village at the base of my mountain would visit with goods to exchange for the potions I brewed to heal them or help their sorrows slip away. The frozen waterfall that had left the bridge slick with ice would dissolve into a muddy rush of snowmelt. Winds strong enough to blow even the most seasoned climbers off the narrow path would ease, gusting from the west instead of the north, pushing away the clouds banked up against the peaks. Even if the villagers were wary of me and my gifts, I looked forward to having others to talk to, instead of singing to myself as I cooked or crafted, or whispering questions only to have them snatched away by the wind, unanswered. Visits from the villagers eased the constant ache left by the death of Miriel, the mortal herbalist who had been my mentor.

"May your death be free of life's sorrows," I murmured. Grumpy and exacting as Miriel had been, three years after she'd died, I still missed her. Her absence made me long even more fiercely for things I'd never had, like feasts of summer's bounty shared with family and friends, or the intimacy of stories told to children in whispers beside the hearth before bed.

Now that she was gone, I often had to remind myself that I belonged on the mountain, alone. Anytime I'd spoken of wanting a family, or living in the village, Miriel had reiterated why I couldn't.

Miriel claimed that when my father, the wind god, had abandoned me to her as a baby, she claimed the earth god spoke to her and gave very clear instructions that I was never to leave. We could go to the village only under the most necessary circumstances, like helping with births or tending wounded livestock. If mortals found out about the magic that could be performed with my blood, they'd hunt me like an animal. Amalska needed an herbalist, I needed training in potion making to understand the magic in my blood, and the gods had chosen this place for me. Truth had been one of the pillars of Miriel's vows to the earth god, so I knew she'd been honest.

As I grew up, I discovered why it was best I'd mostly been kept apart from others. When mortal children scraped their knees, red flowers didn't bloom where they bled into the earth. They didn't have magic Sight that revealed the glow of life in everything alive on the mountain. When the wind whispered through the trees, they didn't hear music that could be made into melodies sung for the gods. Their blood couldn't be enchanted to bestow powers on people. And those were just incidental side effects of my true gift—the one I'd been told never to use or reveal. Secrecy made it a burden, yet another thing that isolated me.

I fastened my wool cloak beneath my throat and tossed the satchel across my shoulder, picking up the lightweight staff I'd need for stability as I traversed the mountain. Outside, sunlight filtered through snowy pine branches overhead to dapple the ground in shifting patterns. The snow drip-dropping from the trees had the quality of thousands of muted bells, a song of welcome for the sun. A breeze nipped at my cheeks. The gusts were a gift from my father—his promise of warmer weather soon to come.

"Thank you," I whispered to the wind, smiling as it caressed my face. Though we had never spoken directly, sometimes the wind god's touch and the reminders of his presence were all that kept me from being paralyzed by my own loneliness. I sketched his symbol in the air and walked out into the bright morning, following a trail around the side of the mountain. Along my path, clusters of crocus buds pushed out of patches of fresh brown earth that had finally surfaced from beneath the snow.

Halfway up the trail, a white wing flashed over the edge of a bluff high above—the dragon who lived on my mountain had awakened. After a few more flaps and stretches, her wings steadied and she settled into position to sun herself. A shiver passed through me despite the warmth of my cloak. The dragon and I had an uneasy coexistence. We stayed out of each other's way, though I sometimes left the unusable parts of my kills in places I knew she'd find them. Feeding her was better than feeding the vultures, especially if it increased the chances that she'd leave me and the villagers alone.

Eventually the trail cut to the north near a cliff where snow lay banked in drifts and a frozen stream had created layered icicles down the side. Water now carved through the ice, slowly beginning to open the creek's spring path down the mountain. With the help of my staff, I stepped carefully over the trickle of water, walking alongside the snowdrifts until they grew smaller—a subtle indication that secrets lay hidden nearby.

I pushed through the snow to follow the face of the cliff, tracing my hand along the stone until it grew hot under my palm, and then I blew on the warmest spot until a crevice opened in the wake of my breath. Heat enveloped me as I sidestepped through the fissure into a hidden cave. A spring gurgled in the back, filling the air with haze. Weak light filtered in from holes and cracks high above, and all around me, fire flowers grew thick and wild in every color, alive with magic, the heart of every blossom a spark in the dim.

The flowers reached for me as I paced through the cave. I trod carefully so as not to crush any blossoms beneath my boots and ran my fingers gently over their petals, feeling the life pulsing in each one. My Sight allowed me as a demigod to sense the life force and magic in everything on the mountain when I chose to look. The red blossoms burned my fingers a little, and the orange and yellow blooms tickled like summer sunlight. The blue was cool to the touch as the snow outside. But I always harvested the purple first. There were the fewest of them, all clustered at the edge of the spring.

I knelt before a purple flower in full bloom and whispered a request of it, telling it of the tincture it would become if it sacrificed itself to me. I took out my silver knife and asked permission to cut it free, but it turned its sparkling face away.

I nodded in respect and turned to the next, and when I asked, it bent its stem into my hand. The touch of the purple petals against my arm made my head spin a little, helping me temporarily forget the hollow ache of loneliness deep in my stomach.

"Thank you," I said, and sliced the stem. As soon as the stalk was cut, the spark in the center of the flower fizzled out. Even without the flame at its heart, the blossom remained more vibrant than anything that bloomed outside the cave—the purple as rich as the indigo sky just after a summer sunset. I tucked the flower into my basket and smeared a bit of balm over the severed stem.

I asked for a few blossoms of each color, harvesting them and then tucking them into the narrow wooden boxes in my satchel. I took my time, making sure all the plants were healthy and strong. A soft peace came over me with the ritual. Sometimes I felt more kinship with the fire flowers than people. Like me, these flowers lived in seclusion, hidden away from the world. To help mortals, their lives ended sooner—as would mine if I used my true gift.

After emerging from the cave, I shivered in the cooler air and whispered the crack in the mountain closed again. I should have taken advantage of the warmer weather to go to the lake for the water I needed to complete my tinctures, but I still had time. Waiting a few more days or even a week would ensure that the ice had begun to melt. Instead, I hiked back to the south. I couldn't resist checking for signs that the path to the village had begun to clear.

Farther down the mountain, the trees grew closer together and the snow deeper in the shadows beneath them. I slogged through until I reached the vista, a rocky outcropping that ended in a cliff. Thin clouds hung in the trees like veils on either side of the valley. I froze at the tree line, caught between hope and fear.

A person stood with their back to me, looking down at the valley, waiting.

 CHAPTER 2

NO ONE SHOULD HAVE BEEN ABLE TO MAKE IT UP THE mountain so early. Last time I checked, the path had been buried in snow so thick as to make it invisible, the bridge near the waterfall still encased in ice. But one sole person might have tried to reach me, and this was where I'd told her to meet me when spring came.

"Ina?" I asked.

She turned as I emerged from the trees, pulling down the hood of an indigo cloak that fluttered around her boots in the breeze.

"Asra," she said, her face lighting up.

Feelings that had lain dormant in me all winter rose as though they had wings.

"You're back!" I rushed over to throw my arms around her.

We hugged and laughed breathlessly for a few moments, and when we pulled apart, I finally let myself look at her. Ina had changed since last summer. She was taller and a little more chiseled in the cheekbones, even more beautiful. The memories of her I'd held close for moons didn't do justice to the sight of her straight nose, long flat eyebrows, and the barest hint of a cleft in her chin—the place I used to sometimes put my thumb before I pulled her in for a kiss. Her eyes were the same bottomless blue I remembered, and I never wanted to come up for air.

"Hello, you," she said. The gentle tone of her voice made a flush rise into my cheeks.

Before I could speak, she pressed a kiss to my lips. Suddenly my insides were in my toes and my head was lost among the stars, all the words I'd saved for her through the dark nights of winter forgotten.

"I came as soon as I could," she said. "I've hardly been able to think of anything else."

"Me either," I said, and fell into her arms again. My stomach fluttered like the wings of a butterfly. With the way she made me feel, sometimes I thought she was as magical as the fire flowers. All winter I'd been incomplete, and now I was whole. She gave me hope that I didn't have to be alone forever, that maybe I could have a place in the community by her side now that Miriel was no longer here to forbid it.

"Why did you come so early? It can't have been safe." I examined her for any signs of harm, but she looked as radiant as ever.

"It was a hard winter." She gestured to the valley.

Far below us, dozens of snow-covered A-frame rooftops poked up on either side of the river, barely visible but for the wisps of smoke rising from their chimneys. On the opposite side of the valley, where the hills were gentler than the sheer cliffs we stood upon, spots of scorched earth dotted the hillside like a disease.

Funeral pyres. Sorrow made a lump rise in my throat. Through the winter I had occasionally smelled smoke, and I had seen one or two pyres on my other trips down to the vista. A few funerals was a normal number for a village of Amalska's size, but with fog hovering in the valley most mornings, I hadn't been able to see how many there were until now. What made it worse was that more probably lingered under the most recent dusting of snow.

"There are so many," I said, my voice nearly breaking. Those were people whose care had been entrusted to me. Unknowingly, I had failed them.

"We lost half the village to fever in the last two moons," Ina said softly. The strained expression on her face gave away how keenly she felt the deaths.

"No!" That had to be as many as a hundred people. She must have lost friends. Maybe even relatives. A wave of guilt followed. "Is your family all right?"

"For now. They've been helping tend the sick, though, so who knows how much longer their luck will hold. We ran out of your tinctures almost eight weeks ago. And of course it's been impossible to get up here until now. We tried, but one climber broke his leg and another fell to his death near the ice falls. We gave up after that." Ina's shoulders sagged.

"Eight weeks?" I was horrified. Even in the case of disease, the villagers should have had plenty of medicines to last the winter. Miriel and I had never left them undersupplied, even in years of weak harvest when they had little to offer in trade.

Guilt tasted bitter in my mouth. I should have moved to the valley last summer, but memories of Miriel's warnings had held me back. When her time to meet the shadow god had drawn near, I'd pleaded with Miriel to give her blessing for me to join the villagers. If I moved there, I could help deliver babies born out of season, or get access to herbs that bloomed earlier down there than on our mountain. She refused to hear of it, reminding me that the gods had ordained my place in the world and that I needed to be wary of mortals. They would discover my gifts, she said. They would hurt me to help themselves.

But now all I knew was that my obedience had led to the death of half the village.

Ina nodded. "As if that wasn't bad enough, half a moon ago we received a messenger pigeon from farther south with a report of bandits. Raiders barely waited for the ground to thaw before they attacked one of the villages north of Kartasha."

"That doesn't make sense," I said. Bandits were a summer problem. They traveled when the roads were clear and produce or livestock was easy to steal, not when the snow had barely melted and the nanny goats hadn't even birthed their kids.

"My parents released a pigeon to the king in hopes of getting some support to fend them off if they come north. His reply said, 'The crown does not currently have enough resources to support communities not in immediate danger.'" Her expression darkened. "I suppose the fact that our village is on a trade route only open in summer makes us less important. Or worse, dispensable."

I squeezed her arm gently. "All communities matter. No one is dispensable."

"You may believe that, but apparently the king doesn't. The crown has done very little to quell banditry in the south these last few years. It's gotten bad enough that I've been working on my own plans to do something about it if I'm elected elder."

Her words worried me. Last year's harvest had been a good one. Oversupplied with food and short on fighting bodies, a village decimated by fever would make a tempting target. If Ina's parents had told him the whole story, why hadn't he sent help?

"I can at least give you some potions for any who are still ill. Come home with me?" I extended my arm.

"Of course," she said. She fell into step beside me, took my hand and gave it a squeeze, but then she let go.

Last summer, she'd hardly let go of me at all. But then again, it had taken time for us to grow close, and perhaps we needed time again. Ina had never been afraid of me as so many of the other villagers were, but she had been visiting the mountain daily for almost a moon before her curiosity about me shifted into something else. I would never forget that night.

We'd been sitting by the bank of a creek that murmured its soft music to us in the dark. I had been telling her the names of all the constellations I knew, from the huntress and her arrow guiding travelers north to the war steed in the west galloping his way across the sky with the seasons. Our conversation had eventually turned to more personal things, and she told me her deepest fear—that she would fail to take the place of her parents as an elder—and I revealed to her my secret—that I wasn't mortal. After my admission, her fingertips brushed my cheek. I turned to her, surprised, and her mouth found mine—as gentle and inevitable as the way twilight shifts into darkness, her lips still sweet from the plums we'd eaten after dinner.

That had been the first night she stayed with me. I still trembled to think of it, the newness, the way she'd touched me and I her, the awkwardness that quickly fell away as we figured out how our bodies fitted against each other. We'd kissed until we couldn't keep our eyes open, and in the morning I laughed watching her try to find everything she needed to make a meal to break our fast, stubbornly refusing to let me help. Her passion and determination were as addictive to me now as they had been then.

"Will you stay awhile?" I couldn't bear the thought of her leaving yet, not with the heaviness of the news she'd brought with her.

She grinned at me sidelong as we walked up the path toward my cave. "I hoped you'd ask."

When we got home, she sat down on one of the cushions in front of the hearth and took down her hair, unbraiding it until the black waves fell loose around her shoulders. I could hardly stop staring at her long enough to unpack my satchel and carefully stow my fresh picks in the deepest part of the cave, where they'd stay cool and preserved until I was ready to brew tinctures. I'd have to go to the lake for water to make more, but at least I could send Ina home with what remained of last year's batch.

Ina patted the cushion beside her. Longing bloomed in my chest, burning more brightly than any of the blossoms I'd picked on the mountain. I walked over as though in a trance. How could one human girl hold so much power over a demigod?

"I missed you every day," Ina said as I sat down.

"Did you?" I asked, and the look in her eyes made me forget what my mouth was for or how my limbs worked or what a thought was shaped like.

"Come closer and I'll show you how much," Ina whispered, her voice sweet as cream and honey.

When her warm lips touched mine, I remembered exactly what my mouth was for. The dark cloud of my worries and guilt temporarily receded as her closeness comforted me. She undressed me in front of the hearth, trailing hungry kisses down my neck until desire crashed through me in waves. We retreated to the back of the cave and spent the next hour rediscovering each other, charting new paths across each other's bodies until they became familiar once again.

Afterward, I lay beneath thick piles of blankets as Ina ran her fingers through my hair, my worries creeping back in. It was mid-afternoon and already my eyelids were growing heavy. Yet I couldn't afford to sleep, not now, not when the people of Amalska needed me.

"I should get those tinctures ready for you. You'll need to leave before the sun gets close to the hills." Emptiness crept in at the thought of her departure.

"Yes. My parents are under the impression that I'm out meditating and asking the spirit god for guidance. I didn't tell them I was coming up here."

"But what if something had happened?" I sat up. Her audacity shocked me.

Ina propped herself up on an elbow. "I told a friend where I went just in case. I might get a scolding from my parents, but they'll be grateful for the tinctures. Besides, I wanted to see you." She put a warm hand on my back, drawing shapes until gooseflesh rose on my arms.

I couldn't help a small smile. "You shouldn't disobey them. They already disapproved of how much time you spent up here last summer."

"Bah," Ina said. "I never heard you complaining."

"Of course not," I said. I wanted to tell her that no moment with her was wasted—that I loved her—but I bit back the words before they could escape. We had problems to deal with first. If we could make it to summer, banish the fever, and find a way to hold off the bandits . . . then there might be room for declarations and promises. I hoped there would be.

"Do your parents have a plan for handling the bandits if they attack?" I asked. I needed to be prepared if they expected me to play a role.

"They want to join forces with the nearby villages, like Nobrosk and Duvey. Once the fever has passed, they're planning to invite some of them to help protect Amalska. We have land and goods to offer them in exchange, and stopping the bandits before they get farther north would benefit the other villages, too."

"But what do you have to offer that isn't already being traded?" It didn't sound like enough. Many of the mountain villages shared or exchanged resources already.

Ina's expression became guarded in a way I'd never seen before. Nervousness prickled across my skin like the bite of a stinging nettle.

"There's one other thing." She lay down on her back, staring up at the uneven rock of the ceiling.

An uncomfortable silence built between us. I pulled the covers tightly around myself as if they might shield me from whatever she was going to say.

"My parents want me to get married this summer," she said. "To a boy from Nobrosk."

 CHAPTER 3

WITH INA'S WORDS MY HEART FROZE IN MY CHEST.

"I came to tell you as soon as I could," she said, as though it would help. "His name is Garen. His manifest is a stag." Her hesitant expression held none of the sorrow or disgust I would have liked to see. I didn't know how to absorb her words.

"Oh," I said, the only response I could manage. We'd never really talked about boys. Before Ina had entered my life, I'd nursed a hopeless crush or two on handsome hunters who had come to me and Miriel for tinctures—but ever since Ina I'd had no desire for anyone else.

"He arrived with the last fall caravan and stayed the winter. He's the son of Nobrosk's elders. My parents are pleased by the thought of a match that will facilitate trade and help defend us from the bandits." She spoke the words with a familiarity that made it sound as though her fate was already decided.

My stomach clenched. All winter I had waited for her. For weeks I'd been making plans for the things we could do when the weather warmed again. An entire shelf in the back of my cave was devoted to the gifts for her I'd crafted to stay busy during our time apart—a polished bowl made of burled wood, honey hazelnut candy, and intricately braided deer-hide sandals.

Now I saw our future together vanishing more quickly than the melting snow.

"What do you think of him?" I asked, hoping that part of why she'd come was to escape, to tell me there was no one she loved more than me—to ask me to save her.

"Well, he has the grace of his manifest. He's been quite respectful of my parents . . . and of me." She glanced at me as though looking for permission to go on.

I kept my face in a mask that belied the churning in my stomach.

"He seems kind. And gentle," she said. The words stole my breath in spite of her careful tone. There hadn't been any promises between us at the end of last summer, but I never expected this. Hadn't she just run back into my arms? My bed? How could she do that and now be telling me this? Already I could picture her on the arm of a handsome boy on her wedding day, a wreath of summer flowers in her hair. Jealousy consumed me as I imagined them taking their vows, sealing them with a kiss, building a family together that I had no place in.

"But how can you marry if you haven't found your own manifest?" I asked, my voice hollow. I couldn't sense the presence of a second soul inside her. Though she was seventeen winters old like me, she still needed to come of age as Zumordan mortals did, by forming a permanent magical bond with an animal. After the manifestation ritual and the blessing of whichever god oversaw it, she would forever be able to take the shape of that one animal at will. Manifesting would bring her fully into adulthood and make her suitable to become an elder someday—something she'd always wanted.

It would also make her eligible to marry.

"Well . . . they said they'll accept the betrothal anyway, upon the condition that I manifest in time for a midsummer wedding. But that's the other reason I'm here. I hoped you might know a way to help me find it now," she said tentatively.

I looked away, upset. How could she ask me this? She should have told me right away, not pretended things were the same between us. Not reminded me what she could make me feel before asking for favors that might take her away from me forever.

"Please," she added when I didn't respond.

"How do you expect me to do that?" I scoffed, pulling on my clothes and striding over to the fireplace to add another split log.

"I don't know. A potion? A spell? There must be something. My parents have had me fast and meditate. Make offerings to every god. And of course last summer I was supposed to be searching the mountain for my manifest, seeking the ear of the gods, but there were other things . . ." She trailed off, distress in her voice.

I remembered those "other things" all too well. I had known she was supposed to be spending the summer in search of her manifest, but back then it hadn't seemed important, not when we were alone, not when she lay beside me, tracing patterns over my bare skin.

"I need to think." Emotions rolled through me too quickly to name.

"I'm sorry, Asra. I know it's a lot to ask. But I don't know what else to do." Fabric rustled as Ina pulled on her clothes, fingers deftly retying the laces on the sides of her gray woolen overdress. She followed me to the kitchen, taking a seat on one of the crude chairs at the dining table.

I knew of only one way Ina had not tried to seek and take her manifest, an arcane ritual that Miriel had told me about during one of her many lectures on the dangers of mixing blood and magic.

That lesson had been a warning, not a suggestion.

I cast a glance at Ina, whose brow furrowed as though she felt some kind of pain.

"Are you all right?" I asked. Even with the mess she'd laid at my feet, I couldn't stand to see her suffer.

"My stomach is a little upset." She spoke softly. "I haven't eaten since before I started the climb up here."

"I'll get you something to settle it." I sighed. It was no wonder her stomach hurt with all the problems weighing on her. I removed a half loaf of dense oat bread from the oven where I kept it, and pulled away the waxed cotton wrap. My hands shook a little as I cut a thick slice, making the knife slip. I jerked my hand away and stuck my finger in my mouth, dread rising until I was sure I tasted no blood. Gratitude washed through me when my tongue touched only the jagged edge of a fingernail I must have nicked with the blade. It might have been fitting if I bled, thanks to the news Ina had brought me, but it also wasn't safe. Unless I bled with purpose and gave direction to the magic in my blood, anything could happen.

Sometimes the blood magic seethed inside me as if seeking a way to escape, like it was unsatisfied with the smaller purposes for which I used it. Enhancing tinctures didn't seem to be enough to satisfy the power, and I hadn't practiced any greater enchantments since Miriel passed; they required a guiding hand and a willing host. Now I had no one trusted or skilled enough to paint with my blood to lend them my Sight, shielding, or ability to borrow magic from other living things.

Without using those powers, sometimes I felt like my blood was begging me to write with it—the one thing I'd sworn never to do again.

The memory of what I had done that one time twisted inside me like a blade, even now. Though it had been eight years since I took up the quill to use my true gift, I still feared the power. I knew without having to test it that I could still dictate the future or the past by writing in my blood.

Sometimes I felt the threads of fate twisting around me, tempting me to shape them into something different, but the price was too high: dictating the future made me age more rapidly, and changing the past could only be done at the expense of my life. Given the hundreds of years I was meant to live as a demigod, it was impossible to know how much each word I wrote in blood cost me, but I remembered too well the agony of time being stripped away from my life.

No one but Miriel knew I was a bloodscribe. Not even Ina.

I passed Ina the bread on a plate with a jar of honey and some butter and sat down across from her, my own stomach now uneasy, too.

"Please, Asra. If there's anything you can do, it would mean so much. Our village might depend on this." The desperate note in Ina's voice tugged at the part of me that would do anything for her.

But it wasn't my place to interfere. Manifests belonged to the gods. They were the only powerful magic the gods granted to mortals other than the monarch.

"Have you settled on the animal you wish to take? Or have the gods provided any guidance at all?" I asked. In a kingdom where the throne was always won by combat to the death, strength mattered, even in small settlements like Amalska. Village elders—and our monarch—always manifested as creatures that inspired respect. Or fear. Usually both. Affinities for certain animals or gods seemed to often run in families, as much gifts of blood as choice.

"I tried the bear, like my father, and the puma, like my mother, but I don't feel an affinity for them—or anything else—no matter what I try," she said, her voice nearly breaking with frustration.

"Then they must not be the right animals," I said. We'd already discussed this the summer before, though she hadn't been as anxious about it then.

"I know they're not. I've prayed to all the gods, but none of them have spoken to me or sent me any signs. I have so many plans for our village, so many things I want to do if I'm able to earn elder status." She spread the butter on her bread with such force she almost tore a hole through it.

"Like marry a boy you barely know?" I said, my tone flat. I thought I mattered to her more than that. In the dark of winter nights, I had even occasionally let myself dream of asking for her hand and building a family, perhaps taking in orphans from our own or other villages since I couldn't have children of my own, thanks to my hybrid nature.

"You know I never thought about marriage. Mostly I want to

protect and grow our village. Maybe if my animal form is powerful enough, we won't have to make the alliance with Nobrosk. Maybe there will be enough of us to fight off the bandits ourselves." Her voice rose with hope.

I looked up. Was she saying what I thought she was?

"And will you still marry Garen, if it isn't necessary?" I asked. I shouldn't have let my willingness to help her depend on it when the remaining lives in the village might be at stake, but I needed the answer.

"Perhaps not," she said, setting down the remains of her bread and taking my hand. Her slender fingers wove together with mine, her touch and her words filling me with uncertainty. I couldn't tell what she wanted. Maybe she didn't even know.

"I'm going to need some time to think about all this," I said. Her return had brought light back to my life and just as quickly plunged me into deeper darkness.

"Of course. I'll appreciate anything you can do. You've always been so good to me, and I wanted to ask someone I trusted, someone who might have other ideas besides telling me to pray or fast or go outside naked and howl with the wolves." She rolled her eyes.

"Surely no one suggested that." My mouth twitched in the barest hint of a smile.

"I just want to have a say over my own future. If I don't manifest, I'll never be able to become an elder. I won't be able to do anything to protect Amalska from bandits. I can't watch my family and my village suffer." Passion darkened the sapphire of her eyes.

I knew what she meant, because my protectiveness of her was equally fierce. I also understood what it was like to want a choice over one's own future—not that I'd ever had one. It was fairly rare for someone not to manifest eventually, but she was definitely overdue.

"I'm not sure there's anything I can do," I said. It wasn't entirely true, but I didn't want to give her false hope. Besides the arcane ritual Miriel had told me about, I knew only one other way to help Ina; I could dictate her fate and write her manifestation in my blood. The thought made me shudder.

"I should go before it gets much colder," Ina said, her voice gentle. "I'll come back soon. I want every moment with you I can get. At least until I manifest . . . if that ever happens."

"And if you don't?" I asked, my voice hardly more than a whisper.

"I don't know. Perhaps I'll take up sewing undergarments, like the last girl in our village who failed to manifest," she said. Her smile didn't quite reach her eyes. As always, she took a lighthearted tone when she most wanted to hide her fear. My heart ached. She cared for her people and deserved whatever life she wanted.

Last summer she'd told me about her ambitions for Amalska—a multi-village midsummer trade festival, a better network of messengers for winter, and ideas about how we might export lake ice to the south or even into the kingdom of Mynaria in the west. She was too bold and passionate to be content on the outskirts of town, relegated to second-class citizenry without a manifest.

I packed a canvas bag for her, carefully wrapping the tinctures in cloth to protect them.

"Garen must return to Nobrosk with my answer to his proposal as soon as the roads clear," Ina said as she pulled on her indigo cloak.

"That can't be more than another week or two," I said, feeling faint. Snow would melt sooner in the valley than it did up here. I needed to buy myself a little more time. "Promise me you won't make a decision before the next community meeting. Come back before then and I'll have some ideas about how to help you."

"Oh, thank you, Asra!" Ina rushed over and threw her arms around me.

I took a breath, catching a whiff of lavender that lingered in her hair—dried lavender I'd given her when she told me how much trouble she had falling asleep most nights. The painful familiarity of it deepened my confusion. Did she share any of my hopes for the future, or did she only want my help to forge her own way without me?

Once the sun had set and the winds grew biting and sharp, her loss felt colder to me than ever before. If I did nothing, she could be cast out for failing to manifest, but if I helped her, it might lead to her marrying someone else. I didn't know what to do. At least if I tried to help, perhaps there would be more choices for her—and a chance for us. She belonged with me, didn't she? She could become a village elder with me by her side. She didn't need to marry Garen—not if I could find a better way to protect the village, not if we could find a better reason for Nobrosk to support Amalska. A common enemy should have been enough.

Either way, I had less than a week until the community meeting to figure out what I was able and willing to do for her.

CHAPTER 4

IN CONTRAST WITH MY TROUBLED MOOD, THE GOOD weather held for the next few days. Necessity demanded I trek to the lake. I preferred its water for my tinctures, as it was much easier to purify than melted snow or the muddy creeks just beginning to flow. Also, the lake carried history in its depths, memories of the mountain far deeper and more enduring than the streams that came and went with the seasons. I loved the lake. If I hadn't known my father to be the wind god, I might have wondered if the parent who'd given me life was one of the genderfluid gods—water or spirit. Their fluid natures might have explained the magical gifts that made fate so malleable in my hands.

Only a few wispy clouds overhead hinted that winter might not yet be done. Life stirred all around as I traversed the mountain. Pine trees pondered the bursts of fresh green needles that would soon adorn their branches. Animals stirred in their nests and dens.

Beneath the dirt and snow, bulbs released their first shoots, pulsing with life I could feel but not yet see. Still, spring felt more like a curse than a promise if the coming summer wouldn't be like the last.

I checked the vista on my way out, hoping against reason that Ina would be waiting for me again. But I found it empty. All I saw was a fresh funeral pyre in the valley sending a thin coil of black smoke up into the sky. With a pang of sadness, I sketched the symbol of the shadow god and whispered a prayer. I still had important duties, and potion work seemed like the only thing I had control over now. My options for how to help Ina hung over me, each one feeling increasingly impossible. The deeper I dug in search of a reason she should be with me instead of Garen, the more empty my hands came up. I couldn't give her normalcy. I couldn't bear my own children—a fact that devastated me anytime I dwelled on it for more than a few heartbeats.

Nuts and dried berries in my belt pouch made for a lean breakfast as I crossed the mountainside toward the lake. Even as I ate, my stomach growled at the prospects spring would bring, like fresh hare roasted with salt and honey and spices, or fiddlehead ferns sautéed in butter brought to me from the village. On the north face of the mountain, snow still obscured deep gullies that cut through the land, but I knew the ridges and ravines of the mountain like I knew the contours of my own hands.

As I crested the last part of the summit, the expanse of the frozen lake glittered below. I picked my way down to the shore and knelt beside the lake. Water gently lapped at the lacy gray ice falling apart near the edge. Beneath the frigid surface I drew a variation on the water god's symbol to clear the mud and ice from a patch of water. I dipped jars in to capture some and stopped them with corks. Once my satchel was repacked, I had everything I needed to brew my next batch of potions—just in time to see ominous clouds gathering over the western peaks.

I raced back to my cave, arriving as the first wet flakes of snow began to fall. The wind whooshed wordlessly outside, souring my mood. If this was my father's answer to the vespers I'd sung to him, I wasn't impressed. Ina was down in the valley with Garen. I was on the mountain, alone. The thought of things remaining that way for the foreseeable future made me ill all over again. I hadn't known true loneliness until I met Ina—until I knew what it was to want someone beside me always.

I put on a kettle filled with the lake water I'd gathered, and laid out my supplies close to the fire: empty vials, the blue fire flowers, small sachets of dried peppermint and black elderflowers I'd picked last summer, and finally the thin silver knife I used for all my magic work. Candles completed my preparations, arranged in a semicircle, as much for light as to invite the blessing of the fire god. I settled on the worn fabric of my wool-stuffed cushion, crossing my legs beneath me before closing my eyes and letting the outside world disappear.

I reached inside myself to the deep, dark place where magic swirled like a black river winding through my soul, peaceful and boundless as a night sky filled with glimmering stars. Warmth blossomed in my chest and swept through my veins, suffusing my body with magic, accompanied by the sudden, fierce longing to pick up the knife to set my blood free and put quill to paper. The magic begged me to write something, to shape the future into something better, though I knew every word would cause me pain. As always, I could not give in to the temptation. Only the gift of healing was mine to give.

When I opened my eyes, everything glowed in my Sight, living things surrounded by soft auras, and magical things, like the fire flowers and my silver knife, far brighter. I could use the Sight any time and often caught glimpses of it at the edges of my vision, but it was never as bright or clear as when I performed a magical ritual.

I placed a peppermint and elderflower sachet in each jar and poured boiling water in them to steep, sketching the symbols of the water, fire, and earth gods over each one to acknowledge their contributions. While the infusions darkened and cooled, I carefully plucked the lambent tubelike petals from each blue fire flower, the ones closest to the centers where the sparks at their hearts had once burned. They left soft trails of glittering dust on my fingertips.

After I pulled the sachets from the jars and squeezed them against the sides with the blade of my knife, the petals went in, seven for each container. From within myself I called forth a tendril of magic that I released into each vial, sketching the symbols of the spirit god and shadow god, who between the two of them held the powers of life and death. Finally, I asked my father to bless each one, for his cleansing air to sweep away any impurities laid before him. Each potion came to life, the fire flower petals dissipating into pinpoints of light that hung in the liquid like motes of dust in a summer sunbeam.

I stopped up each bottle with a piece of cork and lined them up with the others in the cabinet closest to the hearth, where the temperature would keep them from freezing at night.

Not certain if the storm might prevent Ina's timely return, I considered going down the mountain myself. Then Miriel's words of warning rose in my mind as they always did. If mortals knew the extent of my powers, they might try to manipulate or harm me to get what they wanted. Miriel's favorite cautionary tale was about a demigod daughter of earth whose bones sprouted apple tree branches if they were left untended. The demigod had been cared for at one of the earth god's temples, until a mortal lord caught wind of her extraordinary ability and abducted her. He put her in his garden and drove stakes through her arms and legs to espalier her like an ordinary shrub. Eventually her own growth swallowed her, encasing her in wood. It was said that when pressing an ear against the enormous tree, one could hear her weeping even as her branches bore the most exquisite fruit.

I packed and unpacked my satchel a few times, not sure what to do. If anyone died because I was too cowardly to go down to the village, those deaths would be on my hands. But as I made the final decision and reached for my cloak, Ina's voice called from the mouth of my cave.

"Are you home?" she asked, slightly out of breath. My heart sped up at the sound of her voice. It was as if my thoughts had made her appear before me.

"Come in," I called.

Ina's cheeks were rosy from the mountain wind, her boots wet from trudging through the slush. A smile was on my lips before any thought could enter my mind.

"Can I set my boots by the fire?" she asked.

"Of course," I said. After all this time, there wasn't any need for her to ask permission, but I loved that she did. She had always been thoughtful about how she behaved in my space. I held out my hand. She smiled and gave her cloak to me. The things that went unspoken and the small familiarities we had with each other made me long for the contentment I'd felt with her last summer. It wasn't the same with her manifest and betrothal hanging over us.

"How is the village?" I asked.

She sat down at my table while I put on the kettle. "The tinctures you gave me last week helped. No one else has fallen ill since then, and the only person we lost had already been sick for some time. I expect there to be a lot of gratitude shared when the community gathers tomorrow for the weekly tithe." She sounded so much more optimistic than she had before.

Relief washed through me, a soothing balm to all my fears. "I'm so glad. I have more you can take when you leave." It was convenient that she had come, but I was almost disappointed that I didn't have reason to break the rules and make the journey to the village. Some dark part of me wanted to get a look at Garen. I trusted her, but he was an unknown—one of which I was very skeptical.

"I brought you something," she said, interrupting my brooding thoughts.

"Oh?" I said, joining her at the table.

From her pocket she produced a black silk ribbon threaded through a flat piece of silver carved into the shape of a rearing dragon.

My breath caught. Wrap bracelets were given only as courting gifts. I'd often thought of making one for her but couldn't risk her parents seeing it when they didn't know about our relationship. It wouldn't be easy to convince them to accept our love, not when they had such big dreams for their daughter. "It's beautiful," I said, and extended my wrist for her to tie it on. This had to indicate I meant more to her than the boy her parents expected her to marry.

Her fingers made swift work of it, dancing over my skin with the lightness of feathers.

"Thank you," I said. I loved how it pressed on my skin like a promise.

"I knew it was meant for you from the moment I saw it." She leaned across the table and kissed me, teasing the edge of the ribbon with her fingers to send tingles up my arm.

"Where did you get it?" I asked. There weren't any metalworkers in Amalska.

"Garen gave me a few. His parents are silversmiths." She shrugged.

"I'll get the tea," I said, turning so my face couldn't give away that the gift had suddenly soured for me. Even if Ina loved me, she clearly meant more to Garen than a marriage of convenience for their villages. He wouldn't have given her a gift like this otherwise, and if he'd arrived last fall carrying bracelets, he'd known he planned to court someone. I couldn't figure out if I should be flattered that she gave a courting gift to me or upset that it was a hand-me-down from another suitor. Her seeming indifference about it gave me heart, but why did she tolerate his courtship at all if it wasn't what she wanted? It must have been her parents' expectations and her desire to help the village. Ina wasn't someone to suffer anything that annoyed her. I wanted to ask her what it all meant, but what if I didn't like the answer?

I dropped herb sachets into two thick mugs and poured the hot water over them, then made one last trip to the cabinets for some honey to satisfy Ina's insatiable love of sweets.

"Have you thought about whether you might be able to help with my manifest?" she asked, spooning honey into her tea until the liquid rose dangerously close to the top of the mug.

I nodded reluctantly. The thought of giving her the knowledge she needed to manifest in the old way frightened me. The ritual did not include a vow to one of the Six Gods or the customary oath to serve the monarch. Sharing the information with her could be interpreted as treason. But the king had chosen not to help us, so now we had to take care of ourselves. Besides, knowing that Garen was courting Ina made everything feel more pressing.

"Tell me? Please? I'll do anything." She reached across the table and took my hand.

"You have to make me a promise," I said.

"Anything." She squeezed my hand.

"Swear to me you won't try this ritual except as a last resort. And if it turns out to be the only answer, promise me that you'll always act in the interest of Zumorda and its people." It wasn't too much to ask.

"Of course." She nodded, her expression serious. "Nothing is more important to me than Amalska and my family. It's why I hope to become an elder."

I sat back on my stool and took a deep breath. "Miriel told me about an old way to take a manifest, used ages ago before manifests or the monarchy were bound to the Six. The ritual is one of blood, not to be taken lightly. If something goes wrong, you could die. You can't try this unless there is no other way."

Ina set down her tea and leaned forward. She had always liked dark stories and tall tales. Her favorite was the legend of the griffin queen, a Zumordan monarch who had somehow taken two manifests—an eagle and a lion. Sometimes she appeared as one of the manifests, other times both at once to strike terror into her enemies. She'd made short work of the badger king and his champions. I hoped Ina would understand that what I was about to tell her was no parable. If she attempted to manifest in the old way, she would be taking her life in her hands. I didn't even know if it would work.

Instead of asking one of the gods to send her manifest animal to her, she'd have to call it herself. She'd have to bind the creature with her own blood instead of asking the gods to seal the union and bless her as she merged with it. I explained the details as she listened with a serious expression on her face.

"You mean this ritual doesn't include an oath to the Six?" Ina asked. "What would I be bound to, then, besides the animal?"

"I'm not entirely sure, but my guess would be the land itself. Life itself. The magic that ebbs and flows all around us," I said. It was the best assumption I could make based on what Miriel had told me and my Sight revealed to me about manifests.

"The magic you can see as a demigod?" Ina's eyes widened.

I nodded slowly. The spark of excitement in her eyes worried me. Blood magic should never be taken lightly. I knew that better than anyone.

"If I succeed, would there be any consequences to having this different kind of manifest?" She frowned, concerned.

I thought for a moment. "I doubt anyone would be able to tell, not unless they could see magic. So another demigod. Or the king, if he can borrow that ability from the gods." I wasn't sure what the boar king's geas with the spirit god allowed him to do.

"I think it's safe to say the king will never visit Amalska. He can't even be bothered to send any help to villages this far south. If he had, we wouldn't be in this situation in the first place." She muttered a curse under her breath.

"I know," I said. "But please, Ina . . . understand that the blood rite could kill you if it goes wrong. If that happened, I could never forgive myself." Fear consumed me at the thought of losing her.

She met my eyes. "I know that manifestation should happen in its own time, but I'm not sure how much longer I can wait. There are so many others expecting me to take a position of leadership soon. I need to be able to live up to those expectations."

"There's a lot of pressure on you," I acknowledged. "But what do you truly want?"

"I don't know," she said, tracing her finger around the edge of her mug. "I want to do what's right for my community, and my parents think that means marrying Garen, but I'm not sure. I feel like I'd be more certain about everything if I had my manifest."

Disappointment swelled in my breast. I wanted her to be sure about me, if nothing else. "You've always said you want to be a leader, but there might be other ways to achieve that than marrying. Ways that allow you more autonomy."

"You're so good to me," she said. "That's what I love about you. You always want the best for me and to let me find my own path." Her eyes brimmed with warmth.

"I care about you. That's all," I said. The words were far too small.

The truth was that I was selfish. I wanted her to be free to choose me. I wanted some hope of a future for us, no matter how fleeting it was in the face of my much longer life. I wanted the best for her, but I wanted to *be* the best thing for her.

"I care about you, too." She reached across the table and traced her fingertips over the back of my hand. The knot between my shoulder blades eased a little. I needed to have faith that everything would work out as it was meant to.

After our tea was gone, we retreated to bed. I lost all sense of time as words became far less important than the spells woven and stories told by her hands on my skin. Afterward we went deeper into the mountain to soak in the hot spring of my bathing chamber, but by the time we emerged warm and hungry, it was to howling wind.

"Listen," I said. Outside, pine boughs finally free of snow hissed against one another with every gust. "The trail won't be safe."

"I didn't want to go home anyway." Ina smiled, and brushed a lock of hair from my cheek. "Is it all right if I stay? My parents won't mind. They'd rather I be safe. I'll have to leave early in the morning to be back in time for the community meeting—if the wind has died down."

"Of course," I said.

I wanted her to stay until the snow melted.

Until the flowers bloomed.

Until the leaves fell.

Until the winter returned again.

I wanted her always.

So we passed the evening talking, sharing a meal of spiced boar stew with juniper and a dessert of cherry preserves spread on thick slices of butter cake she'd brought. Long after night fell, when our conversations finally gave way to yawning, I brewed her some chamomile and valerian tea, rubbed her pillow with lavender, and gently stroked her hair until her eyelids grew heavy.

"You're everything that's good in my world," she mumbled, kissing my fingers just before she drifted off. My love for her almost drowned me in that moment. But once her breathing grew soft and even, I lay awake, troubled.

Miriel had never told me if blood manifests worked differently from gods-blessed ones. Could some evidence of the ritual disqualify Ina from becoming an elder? Worse, what if my darkest fears came true and she died trying it? I would be to blame.

If I got over my cowardice, I could prevent Ina from having to perform the blood rite at all. Would it hurt to use my true gift one time to bring hope and happiness to someone I loved and trusted? To help the village I was put here to protect? I couldn't stand by and do nothing.

Perhaps the effects on me wouldn't be severe if I helped along the process of Ina finding her manifest rather than dramatically changing the future. It would hurt, but not as much as it would wound me to see Ina suffer. The smaller workings I'd done with Miriel by using a little of my blood to intensify tinctures or to temporarily bestow some of my powers on her had never had dire consequences. There had been fevers, some minor aches, but not the agony of that one time I'd written the future.

I got up, lit a single candle from the embers of the fire, and quietly padded to the kitchen to gather the few things I needed—my silver knife, a tincture made from the hearts of midnight thistles, an inkwell, a quill, and a blank piece of vellum. I spread them out on my worktable. My candle sent flickering shadows dancing over the worn wood.

My heart pounded in my ears, but I pushed away my fear and pricked my finger with the silver knife. There was a difference in the way I bled knowing that it would be used to write, like magic slipped out from beneath my skin in a way that could not be replenished. I squeezed my finger and let the blood drip into the inkwell, then stirred in the thistle tincture to keep it from coagulating.

I hesitated, anxiety twisting in my belly. Surely nothing too bad would happen this time—I was only helping the girl I loved. I was doing something for the people of Amalska, those I'd sworn to protect. A deep breath steadied me, and then I dipped my pen into the ink. I chose my words sparingly, because every letter would pull at my mortality, drawing me back into the dust we would all one day become.

I didn't ask for much—only one small thing that would give Ina her freedom, even as I wished with all my heart for her to choose me instead of Garen.

Ina will find her manifest tomorrow.

Sweat broke out on my brow before the last word was finished. When I set down my quill and released the magic, it felt like a bent tree branch snapping back in my face. Several minutes later, I finally found the strength to put everything away in spite of my shaking hands.

I eventually crawled back into bed, keeping my distance from Ina so as not to disturb her rest. My bones ached no matter what position I tried. Still, it didn't hurt as much as it had the last time, perhaps because I was older now and had no growing left to do. It was just the slow ache of time passing more quickly than it should, the fever of my life burning out more quickly.

The sweating and aches subsided after a while, and I finally fell into a deep sleep.

But I woke not to a morning breeze, or the soft touch of Ina's hands and her kiss good-bye, but to smoke that smelled of death.

CHAPTER 5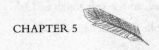

INA AND I STUMBLED OUT INTO THE FOREST AS QUICKLY as we could, coughing all the while. Though a plume of smoke blotted out the exact location of the sun, the temperature told me that we'd overslept.

"Something feels wrong," I said. In my Sight the life in the valley ebbed away, a soft counterpoint to the violence of the flames. The absence of life was a wound in the landscape, a dim spot where once there had been brightness.

"No!" Ina took off down the trail toward the vista, sliding though the mud and slush.

I raced after her, coughing, not certain whether smoke or fear stole more of my breath. Ina skidded to a halt at the edge of the cliff. Seconds later, she fell to her knees on the rocky ground, screaming.

Shifting clouds of smoke blew away to reveal the valley in flames. The largest building in Amalska had already been reduced to scorched bones—the hall where the entire town must have gathered this morning for the community meeting. A train of eight large wagons dotted the main road of the village, the first one already trundling out of town.

Bandits.

They must have raided at daybreak. It was already almost over.

I caught the edge of Ina's cloak as she leaped to her feet and tried to bolt for the trail.

"Stop," I cried. "There's nothing we can do!" If we went to the village now, we'd only be targets, whether for the chaos of the flames or the cruelty of the bandits. I didn't want to make the long climb down before we were certain all of them had left and another wave would not be coming.

She fought me for only a moment, until the last of the meeting hall collapsed, sending a dark cloud of smoke bursting into the sky. No one who had been in that building could have survived. We sank back to the ground and huddled together, our eyes blurring with tears.

If only we had wakened sooner. If only there had been some way to stop the bandits.

The shadow god had surely taken the village.

"I hate him." She choked out the words. "He could have sent fighters. He could have done something. Anything! Why didn't he help us?"

I didn't have to ask to know she spoke of the boar king. She was right. He should have been able to help. What was the point of having a monarch with powerful magic at his disposal if he didn't use it to protect his people?

I murmured words of comfort to her, knowing they were empty but sure that silence would be worse. She clung to me until the last of the bandits' carts departed with their spoils, just as the sun hit its height in the sky, glowing an angry red through the haze.

"I have to go back," she said after the wagons had disappeared into the pass. "Someone must have survived. My parents . . . they knew this could happen. They planned for this. There are places they could have hidden."

My stomach twisted. I couldn't tell her the truth: Amalska was a dead place. Normally the valley was bright with life, softly glowing in my Sight, the villagers' mortal magic and manifests resonating with mine like a distant echo. Now I sensed nothing—only a void.

"I'll come with you," I said. Miriel's rules about me staying away from the villagers were meaningless now.

I followed Ina down the trail, my heart leaping into my throat every time her step faltered near the edge or the wind whipped at our backs. I racked my mind for words of comfort she might need when faced with the destruction below, but what comfort are words to someone who has lost everything? I had lost everything, too. Without the village, I no longer had a purpose. My dreams of ever being part of the community had burned as surely as everything else. All I had left was Ina. I had to protect her, to keep her close.

The flames had already begun to dwindle by the time we reached the valley floor, though a column of smoke still rose from the meeting hall. The houses surrounding it had also burned, leaving little but charred rubble and the reek of blackened flesh behind. The muddy river tumbled through town in a song of sorrow. I shivered in spite of the mild afternoon air. In the face of this destruction, it felt more like a cruelty than a kindness.

Ina ran toward her parents' house, which still stood intact on the near side of the river. I knew we'd find it empty. I stepped through the door she'd left hanging open. The house still smelled like a home. A place where at any moment smiling people might come through the door, eager to share a meal and their hopes for the coming spring. My throat tightened until I could barely breathe. The most important things in the world—a family and a home—had been taken from Ina.

Though the bandits had left the kitchen untidy in their haste to take anything useful, a kettle of water still stood ready to be heated. Dough sat rising in a warm spot next to the oven, overflowing from its dish and collapsing upon itself. Ina rushed through the four small rooms, even checking the loft, her breathing fast, her hands trembling. I helped her push aside a shelf that covered a trapdoor in the floor, but a lantern shone down into the secret cavern illuminated only shelves of preserves, spices, and dried meat. I retreated to the front door and watched helplessly as she began to come to terms with what I already knew. They were gone. Everyone had been at the meeting hall for the weekly tithe.

After closing the trapdoor, she fell into my arms.

"How could this happen?" She sobbed into my shoulder.

I held her wordlessly, my heart breaking. What were we going to do now?

"Maybe they got away," she said, her head jerking up. "Someone else will know. Someone must have survived." She pulled away and took off out the door.

Wide, muddy wagon-wheel tracks showed that the bandits had

continued north, no doubt headed for the next city on the trade route. I trailed behind as Ina hurried among the other houses of the village, which were silent in the way that only dead things are. She combed through people's homes in a panic. Objects the bandits hadn't taken littered the rooms—everything from books to wool-stuffed sleeping mats to barrels of pickling vinegar.

Waves of horror crashed through me as we approached the meeting hall. Burned corpses littered the ground, bodies twisted into unnatural configurations where they had fallen. I choked on the stench of charred meat and scorched hair. Not a single body showed signs of life. Ina stopped over one and covered her face with her hands. Her breath came shallowly.

Resting over the corpse's exposed organs lay a silver belt buckle tarnished by fire—an intricate design of looping branches and leaves framing a leaping stag.

I numbly led Ina away from Garen's body.

By the time the sun had begun to edge toward the western hills, it was clear that the bandits had left no one and nothing. Our desperate search for survivors ended in front of the smoldering remains of the meeting hall. In the fading twilight, I could now barely make out the outlines of bodies amidst the rubble. Ina crumpled onto a stone bench chiseled into aspects of all Six Gods—fire, wind, earth, water, shadow, and spirit. Not one of them had watched over Amalska today.

"What did my people do to deserve this?" she asked, her voice hollow.

I tried to say more, to offer her some explanation, but the words caught in my throat. My chest felt like it was caving in. No potion could bring back the dead. I couldn't rewrite the past without sacrificing my life, and there were no guarantees it would even go right. Miriel's loss ached more keenly than ever. Perhaps she would have known what to do.

Images of the villagers I'd known and loved raced through my mind—an older couple who had always brought me honey candies when I was still a child; a young woman whose breech baby I'd helped Miriel deliver one stormy autumn night; and most of all the children, who hid behind their parents, cautiously peeking at the "witch" while their parents bartered with me for tinctures at the vista. I dropped to my knees, taking perverse satisfaction in the discomfort of the chilly mud and the cold that seeped into my bones.

After a while, Ina knelt and bowed her head alongside me. I spoke the prayer of the shadow god over and over, but it brought no solace. Even as I stole melodies from the wind and the water to sing vespers of comfort, the hole of loss continued to deepen. I stayed in place even as my knees grew stiff, even as the breeze grew cold and biting when the sun slowly sank over the hills. When it finally touched the tips of the mountains, the hazy sky turned red as blood. Shadows closed in on us.

Ina did not speak until the first stars glimmered in the sky, barely visible through the clearing smoke.

"I can't let them die in vain," she said. "I know what to do." The certainty in her voice was cool and detached, a turnabout from her earlier tears.

A spark of fear kindled in my stomach.

"What?" I said, my voice coming out like a croak.

"My manifest will be my revenge." Ina got up and walked off

with purpose, leaving me to clamber to my feet on unsteady legs.

"Wait!" I called, but she had already disappeared into the night. Though I had spent most of my life alone on the mountain, somehow the solitude of this moment was more total, the shadows darker, the sky more empty. Embers glowed in the rubble, still sending up tendrils of smoke that scratched at my nose and throat.

"Ina!" I called.

Only the distant hoot of an owl answered me as dread climbed up my spine with clawed hands.

I hurried through the town, shouting Ina's name. Then something pulled at me—a strengthening current of magic, insistent and deep. The flow of power tugged me nearly all the way back to the base of the trail leading up my mountain.

Up ahead, a flame guttered in the wind.

Ina had lit a candle to begin the summoning of her manifest. She sat on a rocky expanse of ground, chanting over the flame. Power gathered around her like a whirlpool. This was the old manifest, the blood rite, and it was too late to stop her now. If I interrupted the ritual, it could backfire on her and irreparably damage her mind and soul.

"No," I whispered, anguish strangling my voice. When I'd written her manifest in my blood, this wasn't what I'd imagined.

Her eyes were closed, her cheeks pale. She shouldn't have attempted to do something like this with her emotions running so high. It required strength and serenity to summon an animal and merge with its spirit, even if she had been doing it with a god to guide her. By the time I reached her, she had disappeared into a trance. The flickering candle flame reflected in the glassy darkness of her dilated eyes.

Power unspooled from her, reaching tendrils far into the sky and up the mountain. My hands shook, though whether with cold or fear I was no longer certain. The only certain thing was the way the wind rushed past my cheeks and whipped at my hair, yet the flame of her summoning candle steadied.

Ina's eyes slowly began to focus again as something appeared out of the darkness. It gathered before her like living smoke. Huge white wings fluttered into view, followed by serpentine eyes that caught and reflected the candle flame in their icy depths.

She had called the dragon.

She would die.

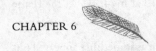

CHAPTER 6

INA STOOD AND FACED THE DRAGON UNAFRAID, EVEN though it towered over her with feral hunger in its gaze. This wasn't a quiet serpent still lazy with winter torpor. It was a predator as wild and angry as Ina herself. Unlike a normal manifest, in which a person peacefully invited a creature to share her life, the blood rite had brought the dragon ready for a fight. It snapped at Ina with fangs as long as my forearm, but she ducked nimbly out of the way and drew a knife from her belt. Then she screamed a wordless challenge to the beast.

It roared in defiance, flames pluming from its mouth into the nearby treetops. Cinders rained over us as pine needles sizzled into ash, caught and scattered by the wind. I scurried behind a nearby boulder, choking on smoke and fear.

The dragon circled Ina, then bit at her again. She didn't even flinch. That kind of confident recklessness would get her killed.

Panic crashed through me in drowning waves. I had to do something.

"Ina!" I called to her, but the wind tore the word out of my mouth. Only the beast heard, pausing to fix me with a stare as cold as the heart of winter. I stood frozen for what felt like an eternity but must have been only a heartbeat.

Ina took her advantage.

She hastily swiped her knife over the palm of her hand, then caught the dragon on one cheek with her blade. The creature hissed as she pressed her bleeding hand to the side of its jaw. Magic shimmered in the air around them, called by the blood and the summoning to lock them both in place. The dragon's hiss dissipated into the wind.

"No!" I shouted, even though it was far too late. If she ended the ritual now, the dragon would turn on her.

Terror consumed me. She was all I had left.

Ina chanted,

"I gift you my blood so that I may serve my kingdom.
I take your blood so that I may be more than myself.
My heart is your heart.
My life is your life.
Until the blood of us both is but memory and dust.
Together, we take a new name.
Together, we rise as one."

My horror intensified with every word she spoke. This was my fault. I had given her the rite and written it in my blood. Everything I wrote had come true, even the unspoken intention behind the words.

Ina would never marry Garen, because he was dead.

The dragon closed its eyes and bowed before Ina, lowering its head nearly to the ground in submission. She wiped away the blood from its face as tenderly as a mother might smooth away a child's tears. Then she ran her hand over one of the pearlescent horns jutting from its neck, gently exploring the contours of the spikes down its spine. The dragon quieted and softened under her touch, a low thrum rising from its throat.

Tears glistened on Ina's cheeks, and though every fiber of me twisted with fear for her and horror for what I'd done, I sensed that her tears were not only those of loss, but also relief. She had finally found her manifest, the creature that answered something in her. Yet the price had been everything she had ever loved. It wasn't supposed to happen this way. Would she still have bonded with the dragon if I hadn't interfered?

She lay down beside the creature, fitting herself beneath a milky wing. Her body seemed to elongate and pale, magic enveloping them until I could no longer see where the dragon ended and she began. The girl merged with the dragon, and then the beast stood up with a new spark of intelligence in her eyes. The manifestation was complete.

I tried to calm my breathing, convince my heart to ease its pace. There wasn't anything I could do to change this now.

Ina unfurled her white wings and fluttered them as though testing the air. The taut skin over her wing bones shimmered like it was dusted with silver. Then she took to the sky, awkwardly at first but quickly learning the ways of her new form. I ran after her as she flew back toward the village, even though it was foolish to try to keep up as she circled and swept and dove overhead with the grace of a heron.

It did not take her long to tire, and soon she winged back down to earth, landing clumsily near me. My heart raced. How much of the girl I loved was left in the creature she had become? As if to answer, she slowly folded in on herself, magic blurring the edges of the dragon's form until it shrank into Ina's familiar body.

When the transformation was complete, she fell to her knees. A deep scratch adorned her face from cheekbone to jawline. The injury she'd inflicted upon the dragon now belonged to her.

"Ina?" I said tentatively, stepping closer on trembling legs. "Are you all right?"

She staggered to her feet and met my frightened stare, but her eyes no longer looked quite like those I recognized as Ina's. They were darker. Colder.

"It hurts," she said, her voice small. "No one told me how much it would hurt."

I didn't know if she meant the ritual itself or everything that had led her to this point. Perhaps both. In my Sight she glowed with the intensity of an open flame. I touched her arm, and even through the fabric of her cloak I could feel the heat of her skin. If there had ever been any doubt before about the permanent presence of the dragon within her, that touch dispelled it. She burned with the dragon's magic, an amount of power and presence that a body her size should not have been able to contain. I withdrew my hand, trying not to let the shock register on my face. I had never heard of anyone taking a dragon as a manifest.

"Did I hurt you?" Her lip quivered.

I shook my head as tears stung my eyes. What had I done?

"I don't . . . I don't feel well." She staggered to a stone bench and sat down for a moment before retching into the ashes of the burned house behind it.

"Recovering from your first manifestation takes time," I said, collecting myself. She needed me. I placed a hand softly on her back. "It will be a while before you're comfortable in your new skin." I tried to find more words of reassurance, but my worries silenced me. If it was difficult to recover from manifesting as a deer or a rabbit or a mouse, how much worse would it be to recover from the dragon? They outlived humans by hundreds of years. Who knew how it would affect Ina to constantly carry that with her, especially without the protection of the gods?

"I don't have time, but I do have what I need," she said. Her voice carried a detached confidence that unsettled me.

"You should rest. Why don't you come back to my cave? There are tinctures I can make to help ease the pain. And something for that cut, too." My voice came out pleading.

Something savage flashed in her eyes.

"I don't want to ease the pain. Pain is my reminder that those who killed my people must pay." The cruelty in her voice terrified me. I clutched fistfuls of my cloak to keep my hands from shaking.

"But it could take days, weeks even, before your manifest settles—especially without a god to guide you through this!" A note of panic crept into my voice.

"It doesn't matter if it settles, as long as those bastards die. This form has given me everything I could possibly need to destroy them." She rubbed her thumb and forefinger together and a spark popped from between them.

My eyes widened.

She tried it again, and this time a flame sputtered at the end of her finger and then died.

"Seems I've acquired more than a manifest," she said with wonder.

I was speechless. I had never heard of anything like this. Performing the blood rite and bonding with the dragon had given her the kind of access to magic that only a demigod or a monarch should have. I didn't know if it was the creature or the ritual. Mortals were meant to be able to draw on enough magic to take a manifest, but not to wield it like kings. How would she learn to use it without the guidance of a god?

What had I done?

"I promised I would take care of the village. Avenging their deaths is all I can still do for the people I love." She paused. "Loved. The people I loved."

She let go of her human form, her limbs elongating back into those of the dragon.

"Stop! Please don't do this!" I said, my voice cracking. While the rite hadn't killed her, overextending herself so shortly after taking her manifest might. She couldn't possibly be thinking clearly after all that had happened today. If she managed to kill the bandits, how would she feel later with all that blood on her hands? This wasn't the Ina I knew.

"There are other ways to seek justice. More death isn't the

answer. It never is. This isn't you, Ina. The girl I love is passionate, and gentle, and kind. Please—" I begged.

Her transformation faltered, and she slipped back into fully human form. It would take time for her manifest to settle and for her to be able to change shape as easily as breathing. For most mortals it took at least a few moons. With no guidance from a god, it would certainly take longer.

"I can do anything now, and I won't let you stop me." She gritted her teeth, and finally her clothes reshaped into scales as she fully transfigured.

"No!" I ran after her as she launched into the sky, my heart beating a staccato rhythm.

She flew away without looking back, a moonlit silhouette against the smoke and stars.

I collapsed to the ground, sobs and shivers racking my body. I couldn't believe she'd left me so easily. I had never been more alone, and I had only myself to blame. One wish, one hope, one sentence in blood had killed everyone I was supposed to watch over.

Because of me, Ina had become a monster.

 CHAPTER 7

I STAGGERED THROUGH THE VILLAGE, HALF BLIND with grief and fear, trying to climb out from beneath the weight of my guilt. Something tripped me on the path back toward the mountain. A closer look revealed it to be the remains of a small person. Probably a child. Tears burned down my cheeks. Half of me wanted to lie down on the ground and die with those I should have kept safe.

Only one thing kept me moving—I had to stop Ina while the newness of her manifest would still slow her down. Once she was at full strength, she'd be nearly unstoppable. If I caught up with her, I could make tinctures to soothe her grief and the pain of her manifestation before she did something she'd regret. That was one thing I could do with confidence. None of this would have happened if I hadn't selfishly decided to try to determine her fate.

I had to stop her before anyone else died because of me.

I raced up the trail back to my cave and packed my satchel with my silver knife, some food, the journal of potions and enchantments Miriel had passed to me, and as many herb sachets as I could carry. I tried not to think about what it meant to venture away from my mountain for the first time, or what cities might be like, or what might await me in parts of the kingdom I'd never expected to see. If I dwelled on those things too long, I wouldn't be able to make myself go.

By the time I worked my way back down, the trail had already grown perilously slick. The town, dark and lifeless, still smelled of cinders and burned flesh. No one would be here to greet me when I returned. My throat tightened and my eyes stung. All I had ever wanted was for people to care about me, and to one day join the community here. My chance for that was gone.

Icy wind whipped through the valley as I followed the trade road, and it sounded like my father's voice saying, *Don't go, don't go.* But I had to. Peaks loomed on either side, blotting out the stars. If I didn't catch up to Ina by moonset, it would be impossible to see a thing in the inky darkness.

I increased my pace as if I could outrun my grief. If I told Ina that I had written this into being, she wouldn't dirty her hands with the blood of the bandits. She'd know it was my fault. She might hate me for what I'd done, but at least she wouldn't have to live with the kind of guilt I did.

The deep ruts left by the bandits' heavily burdened wagons were easy to track. I followed them doggedly, knowing they couldn't have gone far before camping for the night. Where I found the bandits, I would find Ina. She had to have taken her human form at some point; she would want to conserve her strength if she planned on attacking them as a dragon. I just hoped I could catch up with her before she did.

As I rounded the far side of the mountain, a row of torches finally glowed in the distance. I could barely make out the camp except to see that the bandits had settled in a blind canyon surrounded by high cliffs. It would be easy to defend from any attackers coming from the road. Unfortunately, it was also the perfect trap in which to be cornered by a dragon.

I reached for the magic around me, extending my Sight. I didn't call out to Ina lest the bandits had sentries around their camp. My Sight revealed a bright, silvery presence glimmering in the woods, luminous with magic, moving through the trees like a ghost.

It had to be Ina.

I ran toward her. Before I caught up, she emerged from the trees, already taking the shape of the dragon.

"Ina!" I shouted, throwing caution away.

Again, her transformation was slow and uncertain, but the determined way she moved made it clear that it didn't matter to her if she died doing this.

The first scream came as the sky lit up with dragon fire.

"No!" I was too late. I hastily sketched my father's symbol in the air for protection and guidance.

Ina moved through the air beautiful as the moonlight and deadly as the wrath of a god. Flame burst from her jaws as she ignited wagons like kindling. Animals tore free of their tethers and people poured out of tents to scatter in every direction, but the canyon had them trapped. Trees crackled with flame, showering sparks over the bandits' camp. The few who had escaped the blaze raced for the road, but Ina picked them off from above as though it was a game.

She swooped down and cracked open a man's head with her jaws like a walnut. His blood painted the dirty snow. Another she picked up in her talons and dropped from high above the treetops, his body crumpling into an unnatural shape on the road. She threw a woman against a tree, and a short, broken branch low on the trunk skewered her through the stomach. Some tried to escape by taking their manifests, but Ina caught them with ease. She shook a manifested goat the way a dog might snap the neck of a squirrel and snatched up a goose as though he were no more than a fly.

They all died screaming.

Eventually the chaos ceased, and Ina glided down to the road and folded her wings. She tipped her silvery nose to the wind, smelling for anyone she might have missed. Tree branches still crackled with flames and whispered to the wind, but now they spoke only of death.

I stood frozen with horror. How much of Ina was still the girl I loved, and how much was the creature she'd taken as her manifest?

I had done this. I was responsible.

I crept through the woods with my heart in my throat until I got close enough to see the rise and fall of Ina's sides heaving. Though the dragon's gaze was keen as ever, she hung her head in exhaustion, her white scales streaked with blood. My chest constricted. In spite of all those Ina had killed, it still wounded me to see her hurting.

Assured that none of the bandits remained alive, she folded in on herself until she was once more a girl, and then set about the practical business of raiding the less damaged bodies for useful things. The dragon must have changed her. This ruthless, efficient person was not the same one I loved. Fires cast deep, flickering shadows all across the road, the heat of them palpable even from a distance. With the bloody corpses all around, it was exactly like what I imagined one of the Six Hells must be like.

"Ina!" I said, barely able to find my voice.

Her head snapped up. "Don't come any closer." In the flickering light of the burning trees, her eyes deepened to sapphire as she fixed me with the cold stare of the dragon.

"Please listen. It's my fault this happened. My power—" I started.

"You'd take the blame for the sky being blue and the tendency of snow to come in the winter if you thought that it might make someone feel better about it," she said. Her expression finally softened a tiny bit. "This wasn't your fault."

"But it is," I said. "I have to explain—"

She doubled over, breathing heavily, then retched into the slush along the side of the road. To my horror, the vomit glistened red in the firelight as it melted through the snow. She must have swallowed enough blood to make her sick.

"Are you all right?" I stepped closer, hesitantly, clutching the strap of my satchel to keep my hands from trembling.

"I don't know." She spat another mouthful of blood and bile, then rolled her shoulders as if trying to become comfortable in her body again. "When I was the dragon, I felt invincible."

"But you're not," I said. The cut on her cheek still wept tears of blood. She must have torn it back open during the attack.

She shrugged. "What difference does it make? At least this form has given me what I need to see my family and my village avenged. It's all I have left to live for."

She'd already done that. What came next? Didn't I matter to her, too?

"I'm still here," I said, softly, already knowing it wouldn't be enough. I blinked away tears and ran my fingers over the ribbon on the bracelet she'd given me. "Doesn't that mean anything?"

"Of course." She looked away. "But everything is different now. I was supposed to take care of my village. I was going to build our town into a community so big the king couldn't ignore us. Now I'll never be Amalska's elder. I'll never be able to live in these mountains again, because all I see is empty space where my people were." Her voice held steady, but her eyes glistened.

I swallowed hard. "We could start over. Find a new place. Maybe the north? You always wanted to see Corovja. . . ." I needed to calm her and know her plans before I told her the truth.

An unsettling smile crept across her lips, and I swore I could see the dragon in her eyes again. "Yes. I do think I will go to Corovja. I thought killing these people who destroyed our village would satisfy me, but the only reason they succeeded was because the boar king refused to send us support or help." Her voice grew more savage. "A king who doesn't take responsibility for the people of his kingdom is no king of mine. He is the one at the root of this, and he will pay."

I stared at her, aghast. The boar king's guards would surely kill her before she got anywhere near him. I racked my mind for an argument that might dissuade her.

"There's still time to think about this, to seek justice some other way. Even if you challenged him for the crown according to tradition, you'd need a god to stand behind you. A geas like he has with the spirit god."

"Who said anything about challenging him traditionally? I don't have to wait for the first snow of next autumn. I could fly there right now and kill him before he wakes." The savage glee in her expression made me shudder involuntarily. She said it like it would be the easiest thing in the world, like it wouldn't take her days, if not weeks, to fly that far with her manifest so new.

As if an act of treason meant nothing.

As if taking life no longer carried any guilt.

As if the spirit god, ruler of emotions and the intangible, would let her touch the king even if she made it past his guards.

"He'd destroy you before you got within striking distance. Don't you remember how his last challenger died? The spirit god turned her mind against her body until she bled to death devouring the flesh from her own bones!" My voice rose to a fever pitch of desperation. My panic felt like a creature that was no longer under my control, writhing and twisting inside me, desperate to escape, impossible to soothe.

Ina hissed in frustration, more dragon than girl. She knew I was right. "Then I'll find another way to ensure he dies." Before I could argue any further, she was already struggling to take dragon form again, anger giving her another wave of strength to draw on.

"But I love you." I choked out the words. It was the only true thing I had left to cling to. The wind whipped over the lifeless road and a sob tore loose from my throat as my words were lost amidst the flapping of her wings as she took to the sky.

 CHAPTER 8

AFTER MY PRAYERS FOR THE DEAD WERE ALL SPOKEN, I forced myself to put one foot in front of the other, waiting to wake up from the nightmare. Eventually the smoke of the burning trees dissipated into a whisper on the breeze and dawn curled her pale fingertips over the horizon. I continued on for days, gathering what food I could from the forest, but taking very little in the way of rest. Every time I stopped somewhere for more than a few hours of restless sleep, I began to feel as though the ghosts I'd left behind were dragging their icy nails down my back.

All I could think of were the lives lost—babies I'd helped bring into the world now dead before their time, entire families charred to ashes, familiar faces reduced to cinders. In no way could I have ever failed my duties—or Miriel—more than I had by contributing to the destruction of the entire village. Stopping Ina was the only purpose I had left. She was all I had left of home, and I couldn't let her die trying to kill a monarch who wasn't to blame. Confessing the truth was all I could do.

Worst of all—even though I'd seen her kill without mercy, I still ached to feel her lips on mine again.

Traffic increased once the mountain road joined the main thoroughfare north just beyond the foothills, but I didn't dare try to beg a ride. The thought of interacting with strange people filled me with anxiety. I didn't know how to talk to them, or how long it might take them to figure out I didn't have a manifest. Would they shun me as they did other mortals without manifests, or might they suspect I was something more? I couldn't risk it. I envied riders their horses and humans their manifests, and without hesitation would have traded the power of my blood to take the shape of a deer or a common sparrow, anything that would have given me an option other than slogging along the road on foot. I kept the hood of my cloak up, fearful of what people might see when they looked at me. Did they see a witch? A demigod? Or only a girl, weak, hungry, and lost?

After the effort of killing the bandits and taking a new manifest, I assumed Ina would have to stop in the city of Valenko to rest and gather her strength, but not once did I see any sign of her—no white wings overhead, no shed scales or scorch marks anywhere alongside the road. Ina was far too clever to make herself obvious. My heart grew heavier each day that passed. So did the weight of all the death for which I was responsible. Even if I caught up to Ina and confessed the truth to stop her from doing any more damage, it still wouldn't make amends for the lives already lost.

Every evening I left the road and found a secluded place to say my prayers at sundown: a copse of spindly pine trees that shivered and swayed in the wind; a nook near a waterfall that surged with muddy snowmelt, so loud it drowned my words; an abandoned farmhouse, the remains of the stone structure covered in climbing vines.

I made my offerings to the gods by chanting vespers. With my eyes closed, I made monophonic songs of the most sorrowful melodies given to me by all that surrounded me on those lonely nights—the wind rushing through the trees, the lilt of water over rocks, the distant calls of night birds waking. The music allowed me to sink into my Sight, widening its reach, and I used it to search for any sign of Ina. All I sensed was a soft tug to the north, and when I opened my eyes, it was only ever to the same solitude and grief.

I crossed beneath the stone arch into the city of Valenko at midday almost half a moon after my departure from the mountain, feeling like a wild animal caged for the first time. Guardsmen stood sentry on either side of the road, wearing brown jerkins bound with wide triple-buckled belts of red leather. They had their weapons sheathed and bored expressions on their faces, but passing by them still made my skin crawl. I didn't like that violence might be required to keep order in this place.

As I wandered deeper into it, the city tore away the last threads of my connection to home. I had never seen so many people crowded so close together. Their skin ranged in tone from milky pale to dark brown and every shade in between. They lived stacked atop one another in stone buildings and shouted to their friends and neighbors across the cobbled streets. None of their business was quiet. Everyone seemed to be in a hurry to get to where they were going, knocking me out of the way if I didn't keep up speed. The warring smells of roasting meat, baking bread, and the dirty sludge trickling through the gutter alongside the road assaulted my nose. Every touch and sound felt like flames on my raw nerves.

I had no idea where to begin searching for Ina. I had never dreamed Valenko could be this big. In spite of Miriel's warnings to stay away from mortals in case they noticed I was something else, I felt more invisible than ever now that I was among them. I ducked down a narrow alley, trying to find a quieter street, only to be buffeted by the churning wings of an entire murder of manifested crows that burst out of nowhere. Every space in the city seemed to belong to someone or something, and territory was not something to be shared. I gave in to the flow of the crowd until the street opened up into a cobbled square. A communal fountain adorned the center, water spouting from the mouths of stone animals all along its length. I swallowed, my throat dry.

I wound my way through the crowd, some human, some animal, and a few mortals traveling stealthily in manifest form. Many of them were hungry, cold, or otherwise suffering, lean from a hard winter. The pressure of their woes made me feel as though I could barely breathe. Amalska had been so peaceful and the people's lives so easy by comparison—at least until the winter fever. Why wasn't it like that here? Had the king refused to help these people, too?

My hands shook as I hastily scrubbed off the dirt before cupping them to drink from the horse-shaped spout above me. After slaking my thirst, I traced the symbol of the water god beneath the surface of the fountain, hoping they might share some news of home, but I had traveled too far for the city aqueduct to have a direct connection to the lakes or streams of my mountain. Before I could open myself to the Sight to reach farther, a boy shoved me aside so that his pony could drink.

I fled from the square, nerves jangling even after the crowds grew thinner in the more residential part of town I'd entered. I needed to find somewhere quiet to think. Eager to escape the crush of people, I followed my Sight to a silent oasis amidst the bustle of the town. I stepped through a stone archway into what appeared to be a small park. Wooden buildings towered on three sides, faded shutters tightly closed.

A large tree with barren branches stood at the center of the area. I slumped beneath it and let my heart rate slow, grateful for the silence, then puzzled by it. Polished stone plaques lay on the ground all around me, and it dawned on me that it was not a park, but a place of rest for the dead. Miriel had mentioned that in cities sometimes the deceased were not given to fire, especially war heroes or the wealthy—those whom the crown chose to commemorate or who could pay for the privilege of being remembered. Amalskans scoffed at such ideas and told superstitious stories of the dead rising from their graves to pull bad children under the earth. Perhaps I should have been afraid, but after the chaos of the streets, the graveyard was a welcome haven. These people had been laid to rest in peace, unlike those who haunted me.

I closed my eyes and thought of home, of summer, of Ina. Of all the beauty in my world that I might never know again. The Sight came to me softly, bathing the graveyard in a gentle glow. There wasn't much to see in this peaceful place, just the barest hint of grass preparing to unfurl from beneath the earth.

Then I sensed a glimmer of familiar magic, like the flickering white of a dragon wing in my peripheral vision. Hope made me rise to my feet. I drew more heavily on the magic of the earth and that which existed inside me, widening the reach of my Sight. She had to be here somewhere. I sent out tendrils of my own power to seek anything that felt familiar or strong. Ina's magical gift and formidable manifest would make her stand out anywhere.

The magic led me to a narrow building several blocks north of the town square. The lintel bore no mark over the door, and the shutters were tightly latched. Someone inside glowed with energy, far more brightly than those with normal manifests. My pulse quickened. I crept around the side of the building into an alley hardly wider than the distance of my arms outstretched to either side, hoping to find a window with open shutters. I'd only gone a few steps when fists began to slam on the front entrance of the building.

"In the name of the king, open this door!" a commanding voice shouted.

I spooked like a frightened horse. The only place to go was farther into the alley, which dead-ended against a retaining wall. I scurried in and ducked behind a short flight of stone steps that led up to the recessed back entrance to the building.

I had barely settled into my hiding placce when the door above me burst open. Three hooded people sprinted into the alley to flee the building, knives appearing in their hands gracefully as if the weapons had been conjured by magic. I surged to my feet, hoping one of them was Ina, crushed with disappointment when I immediately knew from their gaits that they weren't. Before the three reached the end of the alley, they transformed into birds and parted ways over the roof.

I gathered my courage. If Ina was still in there, I had to know. No sooner had I taken one step onto the stairs than someone fell backward down them. He hit me hard, slamming us into the cobblestones and knocking the wind out of my lungs. Blood poured from his slashed throat, soaking through my cloak.

As soon as I caught my breath, I screamed.

He was definitely dead.

CHAPTER 9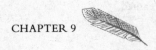

I WRITHED OUT FROM UNDERNEATH THE BODY, BACK-
ing away in horror to cower behind the stairs again. Two thin silver
blades were buried in his chest, one below the left collarbone and the
other just beneath where his throat had been cut. He wore the same
jerkin and red belts I'd seen on the city guardsmen at the city gate.

"They sure don't train guards like they used to," a woman said
from the doorway. A simple brown hood like the other three had
worn obscured her face. Somehow she didn't see me as she strode
down the stairs. With one fluid motion, she removed the blades
from the guardsman's corpse. A boy followed behind her, his hood
pulled up, but his hands bare. His skin was the rich dark brown of
the cattails that grew on the banks of the lake in summer. He stood
considerably taller than me, his jerkin hugging his broad shoulders
and well fitted down to his narrow waist.

The boy caught a glimpse of me and surprise flashed in his dark brown eyes. "Who're you?"

"Get them!" someone shouted, and three city guardsmen sprinted into the alley.

Without a word, the woman shifted into a bird of prey and swooped out of sight. One of the guardsmen changed into a crow and winged after her, though I doubted he had any chance of catching up.

The boy cursed under his breath. I expected him to manifest or fight, but instead he put up his hands.

"Help!" I finally managed to say, scrambling away until my back was pressed against the crumbling stone of the retaining wall. I clutched my satchel to my chest like a shield.

Unfortunately, help was not what the guards were there to offer.

A guard with hawkish features grabbed the boy. The other snatched me, twisting my arms painfully behind my back and fastening manacles around my wrists.

"You're under arrest for the slaughter of a city guardsman," he said.

"Please let go," I said, struggling against him in a way that only served to tighten his grip. "I didn't do anything—that guard fell on me. Someone else killed him!"

"Sure." The sharp-nosed man holding the boy sneered, eyeing the bloodstain on the front of my cloak. "The day a Nightswift isn't responsible for the closest dead body is the day I'll eat my boots for dinner. Finding a nest of you vipers on the heels of that double massacre in the mountains is about as surprising as snow in winter."

My fear doubled. News had traveled much faster than I had on foot. They knew about what had happened in Amalska and the slaughter of the bandits, but not who was responsible. How could they be blaming someone else already?

"What's a Nightswift?" I asked.

"Don't play stupid. We'll be the ones asking questions." His breath smelled like rotting garlic. The guard shoved me alongside their other captive. They yanked off the boy's hood to reveal an expression of inexplicable amusement. I couldn't help but admire his chiseled jawline and rounded nose, both held high in spite of our situation. His hair was cropped close on the back and sides and styled into spiraling twists on the top.

I shot a pleading look at the boy as the two men shoved us toward the exit from the alley. He knew it hadn't been me. Was he really going to let me take the fall for this?

The boy caught my eye and, when neither guard was looking, winked. A flush rose into my cheeks. Unless his good looks could somehow get us out of this situation, I couldn't afford to be impressed by him. The two guards dragged us down the street, people parting to let us pass.

"There's been a mistake," I tried again as we rounded a corner, heading right for a building with heavy iron bars on the windows. "I'm not from here. I was in the wrong place at the wrong time, just looking for my friend—"

"Quit flapping your maw, or I'll stuff a gag in it." My captor jerked the chain attached to my manacles, making my wrists smart.

"Makes ya wish we could hang 'em first and ask questions later, eh?" said the other.

"You two really should have gone after the other Swifts," the boy said, making eye contact with the guard holding me. "You would have caught them by now and come back with all the glory."

I braced myself, waiting for him to receive the same threats delivered to me. To my shock, the man stopped moving. The boy then twisted around to meet the eyes of his own captor.

"They have a secret meeting location. I can show you where it is," the boy continued. His voice sounded sweet as summer honey, almost cloying, but strangely seductive.

The hawkish guardsman looked at him, confused. Then his gaze unfocused.

"Maybe that's a good idea," the guard said.

I looked back and forth between them in shock. What was the boy doing?

"If you catch them all, you'll surely be the most decorated guardsmen in the city," the boy said.

"Yes," the man holding me agreed. "The king has put a high price on the heads of the Nightswifts."

"That's right. And the price will go up if it turns out they're responsible for the massacres, too. Anyone who uncovers who was behind that will surely be rewarded. Maybe a break from the tithe? Or even some additional lands? Free my hands, and I'll lead you to their meeting place." He smiled warmly, as though talking to friends rather than guards who had him in shackles.

To my astonishment, the guard removed his manacles. The boy massaged his wrists briefly, then grinned at me, revealing a dimple in one cheek. I stared at him, too shocked by what he'd done to offer up any kind of response.

"This way, fellows." His full lips remained in a smug grin. He walked ahead with a bounce in his step, as though we were simply going for a walk to the local alehouse. As it turned out, we were.

"The Nightswifts will reconvene here in an hour or so," the boy said. "Why don't you two sit and have a drink while you wait?"

The guardsmen behaved as though his suggestion was entirely reasonable. They started out complaining about their upcoming tithes to the crown, but three drinks later the two of them were guffawing over a joke about cows that didn't even make sense. I stayed quiet, hoping that there would be a way out at the end of this. We weren't close enough to an exit for me to bolt, and even if I did, the manacles would prove problematic. I also needed my satchel, which they'd shoved beneath the table. With my hands bound behind my back, there was no way I could reach it.

"When did you say the Swifts would be here?" Hawk-face slurred as the barmaid brought the guards their fifth round of brandy.

"Any minute. She and I should go out and meet them so they don't suspect you two are here," the boy said.

"Good idea!" The other guard slapped him on the back. They still both had that glassy look in their eyes that spoke of something more than intoxication.

Before I knew it, the guard beside me unlocked my manacles. "Go on then," he said. "Bring us the Swifts. You do the work and we'll take the glory."

The guardsmen raised their glasses in a sloppy toast. While they weren't paying attention, I pulled a tube of purple powder out of my shirt.

"Do you want to taste something special?" I asked.

Their gazes sharpened, and they both frowned. I glanced at the boy, alarmed. My words didn't work like his.

The boy jumped in to rescue me. "If you take off those red belts and have the special drink, the Nightswifts will mistake you two for the ones they're supposed to meet. The drink is the signal for them to approach."

I held my breath, terrified I'd broken the boy's sway over them.

"Oh!" Hawk-face said, his grin returning. "Of course."

He could have told them to walk off a bridge and it seemed as though they'd do it.

"You should remove your boots, too," the boy added. "That's customary procedure for a meeting with the Swifts."

"But where will we put them?" The guard set down his glass and squinted in confusion.

"There's an open window right behind you," the boy pointed out.

I bit my lip to hold in a laugh.

The two guardsmen giggled like naughty children, gleefully tossing their belts and boots out the open window as I added a pinch of purple powder to each of their drinks. Motes of light danced in their brandy, then faded, giving the liquid a faint pinkish hue. Someone yelled outside, apparently on the receiving end of a flying boot. I winced in sympathy, tucking the narrow vial back into its hiding place.

"We'll be right back. You two should have another round. On me." Out of nowhere, the boy produced a few coins and set them on the table.

The guards clinked glasses again and put back the last of their brandies, one raising his hand to flag down a server.

The boy glanced my way with another wink, and the dimple in his cheek appeared again. This time I couldn't help my slight smile back. Freedom was so close I could almost grasp it, and though I didn't know if I could trust this handsome person or his silver tongue, I was grateful he'd helped me instead of charming his own way out of the mess and leaving me to take the blame. He'd even made room for me to help him as soon as he knew I had something to offer.

"Let's go," the boy said, grabbing one of the guardsmen's cloaks and slinging it over his arm as he walked away from the table. He ambled toward the door as though he hadn't a worry in the world. I snatched my satchel and hurried after him, casting nervous glances behind me. The guards had already moved on to tunelessly slurring a song about their own greatness, much to the distress of the minstrel who was supposed to be the afternoon's entertainment.

"How did you do that?" I asked. I'd never encountered magic like his before.

"I'm very persuasive," he said with a smile. "What did you put in their drinks? I hope it wasn't poison. Believe it or not based on the company I keep, I'm not fond of killing people."

"Of course it's not poison. Let's just say they're going to get sleepy and then they're going to become very forgetful," I said. His warm eyes with their long, curling lashes made me want to trust him, but the guardsmen had, and that wasn't going to work out very well for them. I needed to stay wary.

"How forgetful?" he asked with barely contained glee.

"They won't remember anything." The purple fire-flower powder was potent stuff. They'd be lucky to recall their own names when they first woke up.

"Delightful!" He chortled and offered me the guardsman's cloak. "Here, I took this for you so you can dump the bloody one."

I accepted it, grateful for the gesture of kindness. "So why did you make them take off their boots?"

"I just thought it would be funny," he said, breaking into another grin.

An unexpected laugh burst out of me. After what had happened in Amalska, I thought I might never laugh again.

"Besides, it'll make it harder for them to come after us," he said, though it was clearly an afterthought.

We stepped out of the alehouse into the crisp afternoon air. The overcast sky was already beginning to fade—there couldn't be more than a few hours until sunset. Part of me wanted to latch onto him, to stay close to anyone who could make me forget my woes even for a second. But good feelings always begged to be chased. With Ina, love was the feeling I'd raced after with my whole heart, and love was what had led me into darkness. That love was the reason I'd tried to help her, and the cause of everything that had come after. Now I had to confess and atone to stop her from murdering the king. I had a job to do, and even if I hadn't, spending time laughing with a handsome boy was the last reprieve I deserved.

"Well, it was nice meeting you. Good luck with whatever trouble brought you down that alley." He turned to walk away with a casual wave.

"Thank you," I said. The longing to follow him rose up again, and I shoved it aside. His kindness had been pure luck—not something I could count on. I needed to get away before more city guardsmen turned up. Moreover, I needed to resume my search for Ina. A deep breath brought the Sight so I could look for her as I had before, but I had barely opened myself to it when light blinded me.

Even halfway down the street, almost gone from my line of sight, the boy burned with magic—just as brightly as I did.

CHAPTER 10

"WAIT!" I SLUNG MY SATCHEL OVER MY SHOULDER AND chased after him.

At the sound of my voice, the boy turned back, pausing for me to catch up. I ran to the end of the block. Standing in front of him, I barely knew how to put my question into words, much less ask it of a stranger.

"What are you?" I finally whispered. I'd never expected to meet another demigod. I couldn't help it—I reached out and touched his hand. A spark of invisible energy leaped between us, familiar and strange. We both jerked back in surprise.

"You're like me," he said, his eyes lighting up.

"My name is Asra," I said. I wanted to know him. I needed to.

"Phaldon," the boy said, "but I go by Hal."

He cast a furtive look around us, then offered his hand to me again. I stared at his tapered fingers, wanting to touch him, but a little bit afraid. I had never met another demigod before. I certainly hadn't thought it would be under these circumstances. I took his hand to shake it in a proper greeting, cautiously at first. When nothing happened, it almost disappointed me. Now that I knew it was there, I could feel his magic, but it didn't leap between us as it had the first time.

"Listen, I don't want to stay in one place long enough for the city guards to find us, especially if they figure out we're more than mortal. Walk with me?"

"All right," I said. I fell into step beside him. I had so many questions I barely knew where to start. "How did you get those guards to do what you wanted?"

"It's one of my gifts as a demigod," he said. "I'm . . . persuasive. To the point of compulsion if I make eye contact while I use the gift. But if I compel people for too long or to do something particularly irrational, it gives me a headache. The blinding sort. Takes hours, sometimes a day or more, to recover."

So that was why his voice was so sweet and his tongue so silver—and his gift had a cost, too. I was fascinated, and a little alarmed. Would his gift work on me? Did I need to fear that he'd try it? "Do you have any other abilities?"

"I can hear things far away." He inclined his head for a moment. "Right now the guardsmen three streets over are having a conversation about whose turn it is to take patrol in the Quova quarter. Nasty neighborhood."

"What else?" I asked.

"A few other things that aren't magical in nature. I'm handy. Locks, coin purses, the usual." He grinned impishly.

Something clicked in my mind. "The coins you put on the table before we left . . . those belonged to the guardsmen, didn't they?"

His smile widened. "You're clever. I like that in a person."

"And you're a thief," I said, raising an eyebrow.

"Only when the occasion requires it. I wouldn't take something from someone who didn't deserve its loss." He put on a lofty expression, but I somehow doubted he always acted for the greater good.

"Right," I said, not really in the mood or position to argue over his flimsy morals. Who was I to take positions on laws or morality when my actions had directly led to the destruction of an entire village and another subsequent massacre?

"What powers do you have?" he asked.

"I was apprenticed to an herbalist, so I'm good with potions and tinctures. I can see the magic in all living things, or enchanted objects. That's it." I wasn't going to destroy the first chance I'd had to speak to another demigod by telling him about my blood and its power to twist fate. He'd run for the hills before I could speak another word.

He tilted his head. "That's odd. Most of us have the Sight to some extent, though yours sounds more vivid than most. I've never heard of that being someone's only gift. My sister Nismae would be intrigued."

"Is she one of us as well?" I tried to ignore the twinge in my chest. The reminder that other people had families and communities might never cease to sting.

He shook his head. "No, Nismae is mortal—my half sister. A scholar. She spent years in Corovja researching magic and enchanted objects."

"She still does that now?" I asked. I wondered if she'd ever heard of a gift like mine.

"No, not exactly." He hesitated. "Nismae joined the Nightswifts to fund her education, then never left. It gave her more power than she would have had as a scholar alone."

"Who are the Nightswifts?" My frustration bubbled over. Everyone kept talking about them like I ought to know who they were.

Hal looked at me strangely. "You must live under a rock. The Nightswifts used to be the boar king's elite assassins. They took their new name when they split from the crown a couple of summers ago. Now the king has put a bounty on their heads."

No wonder the guards had been so eager to catch Nightswifts— they must have wanted the money for bringing them in.

"Why is there a bounty on them?" I asked.

"The boar king doesn't appreciate turncoats, and he doesn't want people with their knowledge and abilities freelancing. If they'll take money from anybody, it's only so long before some of the advisers and knowledge keepers he relies on become targets," Hal said.

"Will they come after you?" No matter how badly I wanted to know another demigod, that didn't sound like the kind of trouble I could risk.

"No, I don't think so. My sister is the one who worked for the crown, not me." He frowned a little, like there was some history there he didn't feel like explaining.

"So your sister was employed by the king as an assassin and now he's trying to kill her." I didn't like the sound of this.

"An assassin and a researcher," Hal corrected me. "Who better to track down rare and dangerous artifacts than someone who is an expert at stealth and killing? She loved her job until the king tried to have her killed." His voice was carefully neutral.

"What for?" I said, shocked. Why would the king turn against someone who loved what she did and was so useful to him?

"Nismae was researching a special artifact for him, some imaginary chunk of rock that supposedly grants eternal life—the Fatestone. When she got a few promising leads on its location, the king sent her on a suicide mission to try to dispose of her because she knew too much. I suppose he didn't trust her not to take it for herself. Needless to say, she survived. She took the rest of the Swifts and broke away from the crown. How have you not heard most of this already?" He cast a puzzled glance my way.

"I'm from a remote town in the mountains. We don't get much news in winter." Up on my mountain I had received less than most. Perhaps the elders in Amalska would have known, but they hadn't lived long enough to spread the word. Guilt made my stomach clench.

"Must be in the middle of nowhere. What do you do for fun all cut off from civilization? Have competitions to see who can build the best lewd snow sculpture? Surely that gets old a few moons into winter," he joked.

I gave him a withering look, but he only smiled in return.

With his jovial manner and rather unthreatening appearance, he didn't look like an assassin. Maybe that was intentional—he was certainly tall and strong enough to do some damage if the occasion required it. Still, my anxiety grew the more I found out. I had enough problems already. I didn't want to get involved in vendettas that put assassins at odds with kings.

All I wanted was to find Ina, stop her from killing the king, and then maybe start over somewhere new.

"Well, if you're a Nightswift, you might be able to help me. I'm looking for my friend. I thought I sensed her with you in that building when the guards attacked. Her name is *Invasya*. Dark brown hair, blue eyes . . ." Creamy skin. Soft lips. Hands that could melt me with the slightest touch.

Hal frowned. "I'm not actually a Nightswift, though I know a lot of them. Haven't ever seen or heard of your friend, though."

My heart sank. When I'd thought I sensed her in that building, maybe it was just the glow of his power all along. "What were the Nightswifts doing in Valenko, anyway? That's awfully far from Corovja."

Hal gave me an appraising look, as if deciding how much information he could safely share. "My sister is still looking for details about the Fatestone. She had reason to believe that its creator lived somewhere close to Valenko. We were trying to ferret out more information about him. Plus, there were those massacres south of here. The Nightswifts weren't involved, but she wanted to get a look at what they were being blamed for before anyone cleaned it up. The scene was straight out of a nightmare."

"That sounds like a terrible errand," I murmured. Tension coiled more tightly in my chest. I felt bad that someone else was being blamed for something that had started with me, but how could I talk about it to a stranger when I still couldn't think back on it without tremors racking my body? The horror of the bloody memories was stronger than my ability to speak of them.

He nodded, his eyes a little haunted.

"So why is your sister still looking for this artifact if she nearly got killed over it in the first place?" I asked.

"It's priceless, for one thing. And there would be no sweeter revenge for her than keeping it from the king," he said grimly.

"Hey! Hey, you!" someone shouted.

I looked over my shoulder. A city guardsman was jogging toward us, his short sword drawn.

Hal cursed, colorfully, and took off. If the guard had a swift manifest, we were doomed. I dashed after Hal, terrified of losing him. We raced through streets and alleys, my satchel slapping uncomfortably on my back.

Hal seemed to know where he was going as he wove through Valenko, always quickly shifting direction if he spotted a guard. We headed north, the sun drifting toward the horizon to our left, painting the buildings with yellow light fading into dusk. Lamplighters walked from block to block, igniting the gas lamps on each corner that would burn through the night.

"Slow down," I said, panting, after we'd finally gone several minutes without seeing a guardsman. "Please." After so many days of travel and so little food, keeping his brutal pace was impossible, and if he truly wanted to lose me in the city, I had no doubt he already would have done it.

He eased up to match my walk, bouncing on his toes as though the run had energized him. I eyed him balefully, and then looked at the sky. Stars had just begun to sparkle into life overhead, and never before had I been so grateful to see them. Until spending a day confined by the buildings of the city, I never knew how much I needed the vastness of the sky, the reassurance of empty space around me. Room to breathe. Room to live.

"We'll be out of town soon," he said. "Where are you going next?"

The truth was, I didn't know. "I need to find Ina. I suppose I'll spend the night outside town and then come back tomorrow to look for her."

Hal laughed. "You're the strangest person I've ever met."

"Why?" I bristled.

"Today a corpse fell on you, you dosed two city guardsmen, and now you want to march right back into the city where it all happened." He laughed again. "You might be more fearless than anyone I know, and that's saying a lot since I spend most of my time with the Swifts."

"I'm not fearless." I sighed, wishing I could explain the importance of finding Ina, but I couldn't trust someone I'd barely met with my darkest secret. "Honestly, I could use some company to keep me out of trouble for a change."

"Well, I'd be flattered to keep you company for a day if you'll have me," he said. "Though I hope you won't blame me if trouble finds us even outside the city."

"I doubt I can easily find more trouble than I already have," I grumbled. I was already in enough trouble to last a mortal lifetime. It seemed like a small risk to take to gain some temporary companionship—especially from another demigod. I wanted to know more about him. It didn't sound like he'd grown up in isolation, like me. What else might he know that I didn't?

"Never underestimate trouble," he replied.

I shrugged, though I wasn't sure he saw the gesture.

As we made our way closer to the edge of town, the taller build-ings gave way to single-story thatched cottages surrounded by low fences of stone. Chickens clucked from within their coops, already settled for the night. A mixture of wispy pines and bare deciduous trees dotted the yards, clotheslines strung every which way. Chil-dren played under them, waiting for their working parents, then greeting them with squeals and laughter as they returned.

My eyes welled. Amalska had once been like this. A place of family and love, if not always prosperity. A place of lives lived.

A place that I had destroyed, in spite of only ever wanting to be part of it.

"Are you all right?" Hal asked.

"Yes," I lied, hoping the falling darkness hid the agony that had to be clearly written on my face. "I miss home. I never thought I'd leave."

"Sometimes I wonder what it would be like to have a home to miss," he said, his carefree tone not matching the expression on his face. He took in our surroundings, his jaw tightening against some kind of emotion.

"But you have your sister. You have family," I said. I wondered how he could feel homeless with people who loved him in his life. I had never been close to anyone except Ina and Miriel, and both of them were lost to me now.

"Yes . . . but it isn't that simple."

I waited for him to elaborate, but instead we walked on in silence. I didn't want to drive him away by prying, so I pushed my questions down. He didn't owe me any explanations—not when we had only just met. We avoided the north road where guards might be patrolling, instead sneaking through a few yards and out into a farmer's orchard, grateful for the thin camouflage provided by the rows of naked trees. Word of our escape might not yet have reached the guards in this part of the city, but we'd already used up our luck for the day.

"Will that be a safe place to rest for the night?" I asked, pointing at a forest that appeared as little more than a jagged shadow on the east horizon beyond the orchard. I was eager to be back in a place that felt even half familiar. I wanted branches to shelter me.

Hal's expression was inscrutable in the dark, but his voice sounded uncertain. "The Tamers' territory begins where the farmland ends. They don't like trespassers, but if we stay near the edge, it will probably be all right. At least there's no way anyone from the city would take the risk of following us there."

"We don't have any better options, so let's go," I replied. There was no sense waiting until the middle of the night to find a place to settle. Exhaustion had caught up with me after our day on the run. I knew very little of the Tamers—only that they took Tamed animal companions instead of manifests and were dedicated to the preservation of nature. Their role in Zumorda was to protect the natural beauty and wildness of the kingdom, preventing cities from encroaching on their lands or upsetting the natural order.

We skirted the edge of the farm fields, heading toward the forest. The wind picked up and the night cooled, making the bare branches of the orchard trees click and the grass hiss. The time for my vespers had passed, but I began to hum a tune anyway, letting the melody drawn from everything around me help the place feel more familiar and safe.

"That tune," Hal whispered, his voice filled with wonder.

I stopped humming and mumbled an apology.

"Don't be sorry," he said. His fingers brushed my arm, and that spark of magic jumped between us again. "Are you the one I've heard singing?"

I froze, and Hal came to a stop beside me.

"Vespers," he continued. "For half a moon, every day at sundown I've heard the saddest, most beautiful songs."

"But how?" A strange feeling welled up, a muddle of fear and comfort. The gods might not have heard my prayers, but Hal had. It didn't make sense. I hadn't reached Valenko until today, and hadn't spent a night there when I would have sung my vespers.

"The gift of Farhearing is from my father, the wind god. It's the one thing his children all have in common," he explained. "Like your Sight, I have to open myself to it, but it's always there in the background. And someone as powerful as you? I could hear you from leagues away."

I stared at him numbly, trying to make sense of his words.

His father, the wind god.

My father.

"But . . . I can't hear things far away," I said, confused. If all Hal's siblings shared his gift, and I didn't have it . . . My thoughts raced like animals trying to take shelter before a storm. The wind god had left me with Miriel. He *had* to be my father, didn't he? I knew nothing of my mother, but I'd always had the wind to cling to as the place from which I'd come.

"Why would you be able to?" Hal asked. "It's a gift unique to children of the wind. I've been able to hear most of my siblings since I was small. Pretty confusing when you're a kid surrounded by mortals and they're convinced you have a lot of imaginary friends—never mind that your 'friends' always seem to know when a storm is about to blow in and helpfully give you a warning about it."

"That must have been hard," I said, still not quite able to process what he was telling me.

"Sometimes. But other times my siblings were there for me when no one else could be. I'm grateful for that. The wind's children have their families with them wherever they go."

"You're so lucky," I said, afraid my voice might crack. Everything around me was unraveling, even the last thing I thought was true.

"Except when I wish they'd shut up. One time, my sister Thendra spent a fortnight yelling at anyone with half an ear to the west because she was goosed off that the king of Mynaria had taken down some buildings with rooftops she relied on to get around his crown city. Never mind that there were twenty other ways to go—she just didn't like them. Bitter old cow. Learned some of my best insults from her," he said fondly.

"What about the wind god—your father—has he ever spoken to you?" I asked.

Hal looked at me like I was daft. "Of course not. The gods only speak to the king when he visits the Grand Temple, or to clerics who've sworn to a lifetime of service to them. You really must not get *any* information up in that mountain village of yours."

I frowned, remembering when the gods had spoken to me through Miriel and asked me to use my gift. Apparently that had been out of the ordinary, which made me think I'd best not tell him about it. Silence drew out between us as our boots padded over the spring-soft mulch beneath them.

"Which god do you belong to?" Hal finally asked.

"I don't know," I admitted. I had no seed of truth from which to grow my own story. I never had. Miriel didn't lie, which meant that the gods hadn't told her the truth about my parentage. By proxy, they had lied to *me*. A surge of anger accompanied the realization, so strong it nearly felled me. I fought it down, not wanting Hal to see me fall apart. I gripped the strap of my satchel like it might hold me together. "I was told the wind god was my father. That he brought me to my mountain."

He looked at me with pity in his expression. "No chance of it. You would have heard us ages ago, and if anyone had ever caught wind of your voice before those glorious vespers, you would have had all of us begging you to sing us to sleep every night."

Tears stung the corners of my eyes. I stared at the ground. The worst part was that I had always longed for what he described—to know what it was like to be wanted like that.

"Hey," Hal said. "I'm sorry. I had no idea . . ."

"It's not your fault." I sniffled. "Someone lied to me. I just wish I knew why."

"Well, I don't have any answers, but I can offer you this if you need something to hang on to." He held up his arm.

I hesitated only a moment before taking it, and like a gentleman he walked with me toward the trees. I swiped at my tears with my free hand, choking back the rest of my emotions. At this point it barely mattered who I was or where I'd come from. I ought to wait until I stopped Ina to worry about it, but still, it nagged at me, an impossible question to ignore. How was I supposed to start over somewhere new when I didn't even know who I was?

Miriel had seen to my childhood needs for food and education, but sometimes at night when I woke from nightmares, I had cried, wishing for someone to stroke my hair and sing me back to sleep. Was it from my mother that I'd inherited the brooding tendencies for which Miriel had frequently scolded me? Did I look like my father? Which of them had been a god? Maybe my mother had been a healer, or another cleric of the earth god like Miriel—a person who might be responsible for my gifts with herbs or the deep connection I felt to the land. Perhaps my father had given me my dark hair or hazel eyes. Either way, it was unlikely I'd ever find any answers now. The thought gutted me. I belonged to no one.

Hal tripped just as we entered the forest, startling me from my dark thoughts. I let go of him, and he stumbled a few paces away to brace himself on a large rock.

"What's wrong?" I asked. Anxiety rose again.

"I hoped it was just the darkness, but my vision is beginning to go. I must have overextended myself compelling those guardsmen." His words tripped over one another.

I cast nervous glances at him as we skirted the edge of the forest. I wanted to put more distance between us and Valenko before making camp. The dark color of his eyes and the dim moonlight made it hard to tell, but the deeper we got into the woods, the wider his pupils seemed to be.

Then he stopped, and gripped my arm with a shaky hand. "We're in trouble," he said.

"What? How?" I asked, looking around and seeing nothing but shifting branches cutting through shadows and moonbeams.

"They're coming," he said, leaning against a tree. "I hear them."

Before I could ask him what he meant, he collapsed to the ground, unconscious.

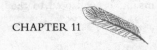

CHAPTER 11

I SANK TO MY KNEES BEHIND HAL AND SPOKE HIS NAME, but he didn't stir. Some small nocturnal creature rustled in the bushes nearby. I extended my Sight but sensed only the forest around us and the city glowing with life in the distance.

"Wake up," I whispered fervently. I didn't want to face whatever was coming alone. It had to be Tamers, or worse, city guards. Fighting wasn't my area of expertise. All I had in my satchel that could be used as a weapon was my silver knife or a handful of nightshade powder.

Then I remembered—if Hal had overextended his abilities, his collapse must be the result of a severe headache. I dug through my satchel, pulling out a vial of lavender oil and another of peppermint. I dabbed the lavender on his temples and held the peppermint under his nose. His head tipped to the side and a groan escaped his lips.

"Hal? Are you awake?" I put my hand on his forehead.

"Don't talk," he said. "Hurts." His eyes stayed closed.

I made a small noise of frustration. An unsympathetic part of me hissed in my ear, whispering at me to leave him. We didn't owe each other anything, really. He could take care of himself, even in this situation, even in this strange place. This couldn't be the first time overextending his gift had left him stranded. But the voice faded away as I looked at him lying there in pain. I couldn't repay him for helping me escape the city guards by leaving him unconscious in the middle of the woods, and I had to admit it would be easier and safer to stay with him out here than to go back to the city before morning.

My nerves jangled. I took off my cloak and laid it over Hal. The night air nipped at me like a familiar unkindness, the chill spreading gooseflesh up my arms. Prickles of fear followed close behind. At home on my mountain, my power had been the only thing I needed to be afraid of. Now, it seemed I might never know that kind of peace again. If a day lay ahead when I would once again feel as fearless as I had racing through the mountains in summer or as complete as I had lying with my head in Ina's lap, I couldn't see it ahead of me.

In these dark and lonely moments, did she think of me as I thought of her? All I wanted was to lie in her arms and for things to be as simple as they once were. I wanted to know who I was and where I belonged. The ache of missing her grew with the force of a landslide. It seemed like both yesterday and a lifetime ago that I'd brushed my fingers over her bare hip and kissed her lips, sweet from brandied fruit.

Hal whimpered, and I shook off the bittersweet memory.

I closed my eyes and tried to listen for danger, wishing more than ever that the lies told to me about my origin had been truth.

The gift of Farhearing would have served me well tonight. All I could hear was air whispering though the needles of the pines, and the bare branches of deciduous trees scraping together like skeletal hands that would forever be reaching.

When my ears gave me no information, I stood up and fell into the Sight, looking for other signs of life in the forest. Nothing. Frustrated and cold, I began to pace, hoping it would clear my head and keep me warm.

No more than three steps from Hal, a flame burst to life in front of me.

Fear sank its teeth into my neck. I yelped and scurried backward toward Hal as more torches lit all around. A dozen pairs of human eyes stared at us. The people surrounding us wore well-crafted clothing of leather from head to toe, the threat in their stances unmistakable.

Behind them, creatures emerged from the forest. A red fox peered from behind the legs of a lean boy, and two mice peeked out of the hoods of twin girls who stood side by side. Several dogs joined the circle, larger and more muscled than the ones the people of Amalska had kept to guard their herds. The dogs bared their sharp teeth, their growls a rumble that intensified the fright burning up what little energy I had left. A raccoon chittered from a tree branch overhead, and an owl winged out of the darkness to land on the padded shoulder of the woman who had lit the first torch.

She held up her hand and the animals went still. I swallowed hard. With their practical clothing and bonded animals by their sides, they had to be Tamers.

Why hadn't I been able to See them coming?

"Outsiders are not welcome here," the Tamer woman said, her eyes flashing in the torchlight. She flicked her wrist and a knife appeared in her hand.

"I'm so sorry. My friend fell ill as we were passing through. We were going to leave as soon as possible, but he collapsed," I said, deciding for now to omit the part where we'd been planning to spend the night in their forest to evade Valenko guardsmen.

My words had no effect on her steely gaze. She stepped closer, bringing the blade of her knife to my throat. I froze in fear. I could bleed a lot longer than a mortal before I died. Who knew what horrors I might write in desperation to escape that fate?

"Where are you from and what is your business in our lands?" the woman growled in my ear.

"I'm from the mountains near Amalska," I squeaked, fearful that the slightest movement would break the skin beneath her blade.

"And your friend, too?" She tilted her head toward Hal, her knife still steady on my throat.

"I don't know where he's from," I said, the words pouring out in a rush. "We only met today. Actually, we got in a bit of trouble in town. A Valenko guard got killed and the other guards thought we did it—"

"So you barely know him and you've been murdering people? Sounds like the start of a grand romance." The woman smiled, her white teeth bright and sharp. Her owl stared at me, unblinking.

I bit my lip. Everything I said was only getting us deeper into trouble. I wanted to explain that Hal was trustworthy, that he had saved my life, but she was right. I didn't know Hal. Not really. And citing our questionable escape from the guards as evidence of his trustworthiness probably wasn't going to win me any favors after I had all but incriminated us already. The Tamers notoriously despised people with manifests for upsetting the natural order, but I didn't know how they felt about those like me and Hal.

"Well, you're certainly more interesting than the usual trash we turn up. Elder Mukira can decide what to do with you," the huntress said.

Before I could respond, a pair of strong hands grabbed me. The woman removed her blade from my throat, and with a twist of her fingers, the knife vanished back to the unknown location from which it had come. The lean boy stepped forward, shoving a wad of dry cloth into my mouth and securing it with a strip of leather. His fox barked at his heels as though to encourage him. Panic made my knees weak. I tried to fight the people holding me, but the futility of that became immediately evident.

"Kaja, should we leave the boy?" a girl asked. Her dog sniffed around until he reached Hal's feet, then sat and let out a low bark. She pulled a long dagger out of Hal's boot and praised the dog.

I recoiled, causing the Tamer holding me to tighten his grip. How long had Hal been hiding that from me? A hunting knife was one thing, but that was a weapon. Had he been telling the truth when he said he wasn't a Nightswift? Maybe I couldn't trust him after all.

"Can't risk him coming after her when he wakes up," the leader said. "Samsha, Quari—you two carry the boy. I'll send Firva ahead." The owl launched from her shoulder and winged silently into the woods.

"Yes, Kaja," the twins said. Their mice vanished into their

hoods, and they snatched up Hal with remarkable strength for their size.

Another Tamer picked up my satchel, and the person holding me shoved me forward into the woods. I lumbered clumsily along while the others moved through the trees as silently as the fog, which slowly wound its way into the forest to smudge away the moon and stars.

I studied them as we walked, trying to figure out the secret to their invisibility in my Sight. Only after minutes of careful observation could I sense the subtle ways they wound the magic of the forest around themselves like camouflage. They made it look as natural as breathing.

In keeping with the Tamers' subtlety, I had no idea we were upon their camp until the wind shifted to blow from the north, bringing with it the scent of roasting meat. One of the scouts ahead whistled the melancholy song of a night bird. In the distance, hidden voices echoed her, the message traveling from tree to tree.

As we neared the cook fire, I coughed through the cloth in my mouth. Something was roasting over smoldering coals deep in a stone-lined pit—wild hog from the smell of it. Fat dripped from the meat, hissing as it struck the glowing embers. A few paces east of the pit, a sheer cliff jutted up abruptly. Moss and lichens clung to the gray rocks, barely visible in the light cast by the fire. The top of the bluff lay somewhere out of sight, obscured by the fog.

The hunters distributed themselves around the pit, tossing Hal on the ground like a sack of grain.

I looked around fearfully, my skittish gaze finally coming to rest on a short woman approaching us. She walked with a hitch in her step and an intricately carved cane in her right hand. A lynx slunk behind her, its spotted coat blending into the shadows. Firelight reflected in silver rings that adorned her ears from top to bottom. Though she stood short enough that I could easily see over her unruly thatch of white hair, she carried herself as though she was twice her height and half her age.

She came to a stop in front of me, fixing me with a pointed gaze. The hunters shoved me to my knees before her. The lynx stared at me, the tip of its stubby tail twitching.

"What did you drag in now, Kaja?" the woman asked, looking down at me with sharp humor in her green eyes.

"Trespassers, Elder. She had this with her." Kaja tossed my satchel at the woman's feet.

The elder bent down slowly and looked through my vials with interest. She held up one of the glass containers toward the light from the cooking pit. Luminous bits of fire flower glowed and sparkled as the liquid sloshed. Then she thumbed through my journal, eyebrows rising as she took in the careful script and detailed drawings in both my hand and Miriel's, pages upon pages filled with recipes for tinctures—and enchantments made with my blood.

"It's not often one of your kind visits our forest," Mukira said, tilting her head at me like a predator sizing up its kill.

"What do you mean?" I asked. I hoped she didn't know I was a demigod. I could have stolen the satchel or its contents.

She stepped forward and touched her staff to my shoulder. Magic coursed through me in a wave, and for a heartbeat I could feel the entire forest as though it were part of me. When she pulled it away, I gasped at the loss of connection.

"The gift runs in your blood," she said.

A chill danced down my back. She knew. Her ability to touch the forest's power must have let her sense my magic. I hoped she didn't know the other gifts my blood carried. I hugged my arms around myself as if I could somehow shield my secrets from her view.

"After decades of little more to do than hold off the human trash trying to cut down our forests to expand their cities, we seem to have a lot of trespassers this week. Interesting that two children of the gods should appear in our lands on the heels of a dragon." She stared at me appraisingly. "Tell me why I should let you live."

A dragon.

I surged to my feet, eliciting growls from the two closest dogs. "Is it a white dragon? When did you last see her?"

A surprised expression passed over the elder's face like a swift cloud through the night sky. "How do you know about our hunt?"

"I don't know about any hunt, but I'm looking for her. My—I mean, the white dragon. Does she have a scar on her left cheek?" I asked. Whatever they wanted, I would give it for them to reunite me with Ina.

Elder Mukira did not react, but the twin girls standing near Hal exchanged a knowing glance.

My pulse quickened.

It had to be Ina.

"Supposing it is the same dragon, what are you going to do to help us kill her? If that dragon stays and hunts in this forest for even a few weeks, it will destroy the order we've worked for generations to protect. Our lands cannot accommodate a predator of that size. We have enough problems with the city people pressing into our lands." Her eyes bored into me.

"If you let me and Hal go, I'll make sure she leaves your forest," I said, growing bolder. I couldn't let her kill Ina.

"And how do you intend to do that?" Mukira asked.

I didn't answer. Miriel had taught me the rules of bargaining. She who speaks last loses. We stared at each other until the others began to shift their weight, waiting for one of us to make a move.

"I suppose there's more than one way to gut a hare," Mukira finally mused. "I'm curious to see how you plan to reason with one of the wildest creatures alive, too dangerous even to Tame. So it shall be—but if you fail, both you and the boy die."

This was far more than I'd bargained for, and Mukira knew it, but I had no choice.

"As you say," I said, trying to ignore the way my stomach turned over with nerves.

Mukira kissed the top of her staff and then touched it to my left shoulder. A tingle of power danced through me as she sealed our bargain.

"So where is the dragon? Let me go and I'll talk to her now."

Mukira barked a short laugh. "Last we saw she crested the cursed cliff. It will have to wait until tomorrow."

"Cursed cliff?" I asked.

Mukira gestured skyward with her staff. "No one goes up to the top. If you can see the edge at all, you're already too close. At least once every few years, someone decides to try to conquer the winds and get into the Sanctum up there. In the heart of the

Sanctum lies a pool that can be used to see any place in our lands and to communicate with other tribes. We haven't been able to access it for generations, but the young and the foolish hope for the respect and glory that would come from reclaiming it. Every time, they die doing it—blown off the cliff and onto the rocks below."

"They couldn't have fallen?" I asked. It made sense that the winds might be stronger at a higher altitude, as they had often been on my mountain at home. However, there were plenty of trees up there to cut the wind. It didn't make sense.

Mukira shook her head. "The bodies are always found too far away from the edge. Anyway, come along. Tonight, we rest. Tomorrow, you hunt."

I didn't want to wait to search for Ina when I was so close, but arguing with Mukira wouldn't get me anywhere. I clung to what little hope I had. All I had to do was find Ina, tell her the truth, and stop her from killing the king. We could then grieve those we'd lost and start over somewhere new.

The elder turned to the two girls who had carried Hal through the forest. "Take him inside."

Their eyes betrayed some surprise, but they didn't question her orders.

Mukira dismissed Kaja and the other hunters with the wave of a hand, and they slipped away into the woods. As soon as they were out of sight they became as insubstantial as ghosts, as much a part of the forest as the trees.

"You, walk with me," Mukira said to me. "And stay where I can see you."

That was fine by me. I didn't trust her either.

We followed a path along the base of the cliff, leaving behind the fire pit and all signs of human life. Every sound in the forest seemed to carry secret meanings I couldn't decipher. Was that distant hoot the call of an owl, or another Tamer message?

The twin girls had almost left our line of sight completely when they turned toward the cliff and disappeared into an angled fissure in the rock. As we drew closer to where they'd gone, I yelped in surprise as Mukira's bony hand clamped around my wrist and pulled me through the pitch-dark zigzag entrance into the cave.

I gasped in awe when we emerged on the other side. This cavern was nothing like the humble place I had once called home. Hundreds of candles made from purified and dyed animal fat framed the room in a rainbow of colors. Natural columns that stretched from floor to ceiling had been intricately carved, making the room feel more like a temple than a living space.

"Come along," Mukira said, leading me deeper. We passed a fireplace with cushions scattered all around it, and Mukira's lynx trotted over to flop down on one, starting the serious business of grooming her graying whiskers.

In a small alcove at the back of the cavern, the hunters laid Hal on a bare cot, then left when Mukira dismissed them. I knelt by his side, already pulling the lavender and peppermint from my satchel. I dabbed a bit of each essential oil on a cloth and laid it carefully over his eyes.

"Do you expect him to wake up and make himself useful by morning?" Mukira asked.

"I hope so." Perhaps he could decipher what was going on with the wind at the top of the cliff. But the truth was that I had no idea what condition he'd be in the next day. We'd barely had time to get acquainted before he lost consciousness, putting us in a situation even worse than the one in which we'd met. Tomorrow he might choose to save himself and leave me behind, but I couldn't bring myself to do the same.

CHAPTER 12

A WIDE PAW BATTED AT MY CHEEK, ROUSING ME FROM restless sleep. I gently pushed the lynx aside. She gave me an affronted look and stalked off in the direction of the exit. Elder Mukira was nowhere to be seen, nor was anyone else. Though no sunlight penetrated the cave to help me determine the time, voices chattered unintelligibly outside and the smell of seared meat drifted into the cave. Morning had come.

"Hal," I whispered, rising to my knees to hover over him. He'd shifted during the night and now lay on his side. He opened his eyes slowly, taking a minute to focus them fully on my face.

"I knew you'd come through," he said, his voice a little scratchy. "Lovely accommodations you found. A bit rustic, mildly creepy . . . but they'll do."

"It's hardly the time to joke," I said, handing him the clay vessel of water one of the Tamers had brought us. All I could think about was finding Ina, and what might happen if I didn't succeed. She would try to kill the king. She would die—and I would be completely alone in the world.

He took a slow drink.

"Thank you for not leaving me," he said, and I recognized in the look he gave me that it meant more to him than words could communicate. Perhaps he'd been left before. Something broke in me as I remembered the feeling when Ina took to the sky, leaving me alone with the blood and chaos she'd strewn across the road.

I understood.

"So what trouble have you found now?" he asked with a half smile.

"The Tamers got us. I had to strike a bargain with them," I said, twisting one of the wool blankets in my hands. "I may have promised them we could find a dragon and get her to leave the forest in exchange for our freedom."

"Find a *what*?" Hal asked.

"Ina's manifest is a dragon." Telling someone felt strange. Manifests were not private business, but Ina the dragon was very different from Ina who had loved me in our long, quiet hours on the mountain. I didn't feel qualified to explain who or what she was now when I hardly had it figured out.

Hal groaned. "Start from the beginning."

I took a deep breath and cast a nervous glance toward the fissure in the wall that led outside. The absence of people in the cave didn't mean that no one was listening. Mukira's lynx stared at us from atop her cushion with a gaze far too keen for my liking. I whispered an explanation of everything else that had transpired after he collapsed, including the supposedly wind-cursed cliff.

"For the love of fewmets. I think my headache is coming back," he said.

"Oh no! Let me get you some peppermint—"

"I'm teasing, Asra." He laughed.

I glared at him. "That's not funny."

"On the bright side, if the Tamers' dogs eat us, my headache will be the least of our problems." He gave my shoulder a gentle squeeze.

His touch calmed me a little. "I'm afraid," I admitted. I didn't know how to be scared and not serious. It didn't seem possible. Each situation I found myself in seemed worse than the last, and my anxiety rose with every day I failed to find Ina. I wanted to go back to my quiet life in the mountains, where long, solitary winters were the hardest part of my life. They hadn't been so bad after all.

"Look at it this way—after we get out of here, this will make a great tale. What good is life if you don't have wild stories to tell when you're old?" He grinned again, making me wonder what stories he'd gathered before he met me. In spite of my better judgment, I wanted to know them. But first, I had to find a dragon.

"Between my Sight and your Farhearing, it could be fairly easy to find Ina. I don't know about the cursed cliff, but that's a mess to untangle once we get up there, I suppose," I said.

Hal frowned and rolled onto his back with a grimace. "I'm afraid I'm not going to be very useful to you. After the headaches, it usually takes most of a day for me to get my energy back. I doubt I'll make it far today. I certainly can't climb up a cliff."

My heart sank. "But can you Farhear? If you could send me in the right direction until I'm close enough to use my Sight . . . I think

I can find her. Then I just have to hope she'll listen to me." I didn't dare say more. If he knew the truth about what she'd already done—the violence of which she was capable—he might try to stop me. It scared me even more that part of me wanted him to. With no one left who cared, responsibility for my life and well-being was all my own.

Sometimes it was too heavy a burden to carry.

"I may not be able to scale a cliff, but I can listen for her. In the meantime, who do we have to charm to get some food?" Hal asked.

"I'll go find something," I said, grateful he'd changed the subject before digging too deeply into the history between me and Ina.

"Thank you." Hal nodded, his eyes already closing again. Even the short conversation had exhausted him.

Outside, I followed my nose and found the Tamers taking a communal breakfast farther north alongside the cliff. They sat in a scattered circle on rocks and logs, eating and laughing as they challenged one another to see whose Tamed animal would do the best trick for a scrap. Rather than hot oatmeal laden with fruit preserves, which was a common morning meal in Amalska, the Tamers started their day with meat. A woman and a man stood over a small but intense cook fire, searing thin strips of spiced venison over smooth river rocks pulled fresh from the embers. My mouth watered.

As I passed by clusters of Tamers, conversations among them silenced. I caught only bits and pieces—most of them were sharing tales of their hunts and of the latest city folk they'd managed to scare out of their woods. Instead of trying to talk to them, I took the plates of food they gave me back to the cave and ate in silence with Hal. The meat nearly melted in my mouth, tender from the quick sear. Hal ate even more greedily than I did, so much that I ended up giving him a few more pieces from my portion.

Afterward, Hal and I took turns scrubbing ourselves and our clothes clean in a hot spring deep in the mountains at Mukira's insistence. "You're no use at hunting if your prey can smell you coming," she'd said. Neither of us objected. The bath was a luxury we were all too grateful to have. When he saw me shivering in my damp shirt, Hal dried my clothes with a whirling gust of warm air beckoned by his fingers. We did our hair in companionable silence; I detangled and braided mine while he applied a thick, buttery cream to his and styled it back into the twists he'd been wearing before.

We emerged from the cave just as the sun peeked over the edge of the cliff at the apex of its journey across the sky. The hunters were already waiting to escort me and, I supposed, to bear witness to my failure if that came to pass. I half expected Kaja to be among them, but the Tamers accompanying us today were different, their animals diurnal. Mukira's lynx sat beside her in a patch of sunlight streaming down from above the cliff. Hal squinted and shaded his eyes even though it wasn't bright—another aftereffect of the headache, no doubt.

The hunters led us north along the base of the cliff until we reached a waterfall. The air smelled wet and green, and moss clung to the rocks just out of reach of the pounding water. As soon as our group stopped, Hal closed his eyes and tipped his face to the sky. Luminous mist danced through sunbeams streaking through the treetops, and a rainbow arched through the myriad droplets that broke and re-formed in the ever-changing light.

I bit my lower lip and waited, suddenly aware of every sound— the whisper of our cloaks as the breeze nudged against them, the distant crack of a twig under a person's boot, and the sharp bark of a coyote somewhere in the hills. I wished I could hold the world still for Hal and silence any potential distractions. Though he looked all right, if I dropped into my Sight, the glow of his magic was more dim than usual. He wasn't fully recovered.

"I Hear her," he finally said.

I exhaled a long breath. "Where?"

"It sounds like someone or something is splashing in the stream." Hal pointed up the waterfall. "But I also Hear something else. . . ." He furrowed his brow, then shook his head.

"How do we get to the top?" I asked Mukira.

Mukira considered her next words. The rushing of the waterfall hung in the silence between us, mist making my hair curl around my face.

"Your determination is impressive," she said at last. She hobbled toward the face of the cliff, deeper into the mist. Her lynx stayed back, huddled behind a rock where the water couldn't get to her.

"Asra, I don't like this," Hal said. "I Hear something else up there. Something like wind, but it sounds . . . wrong."

"What do you mean?" I asked.

"It's like a whispering voice, but I can't make out what it's saying. It sounds angry." He shook his head. "I'm sorry. My Hearing must be weaker than usual from the headache."

"The elder said the winds were strong up there. It must be that. I'll be all right." I said the words as much for myself as him, then followed Mukira. I'd spent enough time being afraid. If this was my chance to stop Ina from sacrificing herself in a misguided attempt to kill the boar king, I had to take it.

The elder stopped a few paces from the cliff. "A cave lies behind this part of the falls. Inside you'll find a tunnel that switches back all the way up to the top. It comes out in the trees, safe from the edge. Do not go near the cliff if you value your life. And if you can't reason with your dragon friend, know that we won't hesitate to shoot her."

"As you say," I said, wondering silently if falling off a cliff would kill me. Or was spilling my blood the only real danger if I fell? The rocks at the base of the waterfall were worn smooth from years of pounding water, but that didn't mean I could fall without bloodshed, and I had no idea what would happen if I did. Once I had scraped my hand on a sharp rock while gathering herbs and a tree had sprouted out of the stone, cracking it in half. A few years before that I had accidentally cut myself slicing turnips for stew, and any vegetable my blood touched withered into a desiccated husk.

If I fell off the cliff, broken bones might punch through my skin like those I'd once seen jutting out of a deer carcass at the bottom of a ravine. Perhaps magic would burst out of me, killing everyone in central Zumorda. I shuddered at the thought, and then pushed it away. I didn't have time to play out every disaster scenario in my mind. All that mattered was finding Ina and telling her the truth.

"I'll be back soon," I said, straightening my shoulders.

"Be careful," Hal said. "I didn't save you from those Valenko guardsmen so you could die falling off a cliff." This time I knew he was teasing me.

"Well, I didn't treat your headache and find you a place to sleep so I could die falling off a cliff, either," I retorted.

A smile tugged at his mouth, but the dark hollows under his eyes betrayed more of his true feelings. Exhaustion. Worry. If I failed, his life would be forfeit, too. He was in no shape to be able to use his gift to talk his way out of this one.

"A few hunters will wait here for you to return—at least until the sun hits the treetops to the west," Mukira said.

"I'll wait here too, if that's all right," Hal said.

Mukira shrugged. "Your fate is tied to hers, so why not?"

They didn't expect me to come back.

I entered the cave, which was every bit as dank as I expected. My chest constricted the instant the light from outside vanished. The stench of guano hit me, a reek that lingered even when I tried to hold my breath.

I sank into my Sight and used it to navigate the cave by picking up on the life within it. The perpetual presence of water made everything slick. Root formations and fungus lined the walls, and bats nested overhead, their sleep only mildly disturbed as I passed beneath them. Salamanders scurried away from me as I navigated the path, vanishing into cracks in the rock.

I crawled through sections of the passage too overgrown with roots to stand upright, and climbed up rugged stairs in the steeper portions nearly on my hands and knees. Water dripped onto my back, making me cringe with each drop. When I thought my legs might give out, I finally emerged. Sunlight filtered through willowy pine branches thinner than those back home. They rustled in a gentle breeze, but the wind was only a caress, nothing like the gales of doom the Tamers had described. Somewhere nearby the stream whooshed and gurgled as it raced toward the waterfall.

I saw no signs of Ina.

I sat down for a moment to catch my breath, relishing the

solitude. Pangs of longing for home cut through me with every heartbeat. There was something familiar as mountain honey about the way the sun struck my face and filled my soul. This was how the world was meant to be. Me, alone, only the sound of rushing water in my ears, sunlight streaming through the trees onto my face, the shadow tethered to my feet given time to shift over the course of the day. But today I couldn't afford to watch the shadows change or bask in the false sense of peace. Pining for a home that no longer existed wouldn't help me find Ina. If I wanted to start over, I needed to find her first.

I shook off the damp of the cave and walked through the forest, following the sound of water, but stopped cold when the trees suddenly gave way to an escarpment. A mixture of half-dead winter grass and new spring growth rippled and hissed in the wind like a warning. The stream cut shallowly through the grass in a wide, rocky expanse not far from where I stood. Past the rushing water and trembling grass, the cliff fell away into nothingness, the pine trees jutting into the sky like distant swords beyond it.

It was very beautiful for a cursed place.

I edged along the tree line, fearful of Mukira's warning that visibility of the cliff meant doom. Perhaps it was only Tamer superstition, or didn't affect demigods the same as mortals, but only a fool would take the chance. As I followed the tree line in the direction of the stream, the wind increased, whipping my cloak around my ankles. The area around the stream became rockier, and about ten paces ahead, a group of massive boulders jutted out of the land. Time-worn carvings decorated the rocks, shallow in some places and deep in others. That had to be where the entrance to the Sanctum lay.

Never even in the worst mountain storm had I felt the kind of wind that gripped me the moment I stepped away from the trees. It blew through me, cutting down to the bone. Sorrow swiftly followed it. No longer could I trust that the wind god was looking out for me. I had never belonged to him. I fought against the gale with stinging eyes, staggering from side to side until I got close enough to press myself against the boulders for stability.

On the other side of the rocks, sunlight glittered off the stream as the wind shattered the surface into a thousand gilded mirrors. I edged around until I could see all the way to the falls. The gusts seemed to ease for a moment as I took in the view, at the center of which was the person I'd walked leagues for, the girl who still held what pieces remained of my heart.

CHAPTER 13

MY NERVES JANGLED LIKE A CHOIR OF MIDWINTER
bells.

In a small hollow just a few paces below me, Ina sat on a rock
beside the stream, plaiting her dark hair while the water eddied
around her pale ankles. She finished the braid and began to coil it
at the nape of her neck, weaving in a thin strip of leather to tie it in
place. As another gust kicked up, she turned into the wind so that I
saw her in profile—the perfect straight nose, the sharp angle of her
jawline. Over the past few weeks, her scar had tightened to a red line
arching across her cheek like a bloody crescent moon. It only made
her beauty more fierce, the blue of her eyes more intense, the dark of
her hair and lashes more striking.

A day might never come when the sight of her didn't steal my
breath.

"Ina," I said. Her name came out suffused with longing.

Her head whipped around with serpentine speed.

"Asra!" She dried her legs hastily, slipping her feet into worn woolen socks and then her boots. One of the toes was beginning to come unstitched. She clambered over to where I stood, until the soft curves of her body arched within a hand's breadth of me. The wind whirled around us, our cloaks tangling with one another before we even touched.

I opened my arms and she stepped into them without hesitation. Relief flooded through me. The scent of spring hovered around her—cool mountain water and the verdant green of the soaproot shoots she'd used to wash her hair and bathe. My fear and worries slipped away as she melted into me like the softness of day turning to night, of darkness shifting back to dawn. The warmth of her against me brought back every moment we'd shared together with nothing between us at all. After all my fear, she was still my Ina, still the girl I knew, familiar in my arms. She would listen to reason. She had to.

"I'm glad you're here," she murmured. The hum of her words against my neck sent goose bumps racing down both my arms.

"Do you mean that?" I asked. Hope fluttered in my chest, fragile as a newly hatched butterfly. One minute she wanted me. The next she didn't. It had to be the trauma of everything that had passed since we left home—or perhaps the dragon, who might have felt differently about me than she did.

She released the embrace but kept hold of my hand as we scooted back around to the more sheltered side of the cluster of rocks, crouching low to hide from the worst of the wind.

"How did you find me?" She sounded nervous, not like the bold creature who had left an entire caravan of bandits nothing more than bloody smears on the road.

I cast an anxious glance toward the cliff. We were still within sight of it. "The people who live in the forest saw you."

"I'm glad you're safe." She ran her fingers over the ribbon of my courting bracelet, a small smile playing over her mouth. I wanted to kiss her.

"Not quite yet," I said. "I promised the Tamers I'd get you to leave their forest. They're worried about you upsetting the natural order. If I fail, they'll kill me."

Ina snorted. "They have no chance of killing you with me by your side. Besides, I don't plan to stay. It's hard to hunt as a dragon in these woods. Too many obstacles. We're mountain creatures, after all. But I'm so tired . . . I needed to rest. I still can't take dragon form for more than a few hours at a time—less if I'm flying for long periods. It should be at least a little easier by now."

"I'm sorry," I said. Guilt swirled through me. It had to be because she hadn't manifested traditionally. Even though I'd been the cause of it, I didn't know how to help her now.

"Oh, Asra." Ina rested her head on my shoulder. "You shouldn't have come after me. What if your death ends up on my hands, too?"

"I'm not dead, and it wouldn't be on your hands anyway," I said firmly. "This was my choice."

"I don't want to kill anyone else," she whispered, her voice barely audible.

"I know you don't." I squeezed her hand. Finally she was coming to her senses.

"Just the one. Just him." Her head snapped back up and her eyes took on a hint of wildness, the flash of the dragon within. "I would have flown straight to Corovja and killed him days ago if my manifest was settled, but it's taking time. Too much time."

I took a deep breath. So much for sensibleness. I had to talk her out of this before she got hurt wreaking vengeance on someone who hadn't earned it.

"Ina . . . there has to be another answer. The boar king didn't personally destroy our village. It could be moons before your manifest settles. You could take that time to find a way to protect others who are at risk of bandit attacks. Or figure out what future you want for yourself," I said. If I could just get her to slow down and think, surely she'd realize that the best course of action was to make a fresh start.

"But you and I could get revenge for what the king did to our home. We could stop him from doing it to anyone else ever again." She gestured widely to acknowledge the whole kingdom.

"But if you kill him, you'd be queen," I said. Had her determination for vengeance turned into a hunger for more power? Her justifications didn't add up.

She shrugged, but her eyes glimmered in a way that told me it wasn't the first time the idea had crossed her mind. "That can be decided after he's dead."

"Please don't do this. It's too dangerous. He's already got the Nightswifts plotting something against him. We don't need to get tangled up in that." My fear grew the longer we argued. She wasn't being reasonable.

Ina tilted her head. "Nightswifts?"

"Assassins who used to work for the king. I ran into some of them when I was looking for you in Valenko. Listen, I don't want harm to come to any other village, but you need to rest. Let's find somewhere to go that's safe and quiet where we can talk about this more," I said.

"If you don't want any other villages to be harmed, then don't let it happen. Help me kill him." The venom in her voice made me shiver.

What had happened in Amalska was inextricably tied up with the king and the crown for her, and I had let that happen. The time had come to tell her the truth. Whatever she decided to do from here, she had to do it with full knowledge of the role I had played in the fall of Amalska. I shoved down my desire for one more night beside her, one night to be comforted by her closeness before I had to risk letting her go.

I had always wanted impossible things.

This time, I could not allow myself to have them.

"Ina, I have to tell you something." My heart was already breaking.

"That you love me?" she said, her eyes suddenly playful. Her moods had always been mercurial, but now they seemed to change with the swiftness of the spring weather.

"I do," I said, but I couldn't force a smile. "That's where this all began. You know I am more than mortal."

She nodded.

"There is more than that—more than what I do with the herbs and potions. I have a gift, one I was told never to share." I hesitated, terrified to reveal the darkest part of myself to someone for the first time.

"You can tell me anything. You know that," she said, her voice encouraging.

For just a moment I let myself get lost in the cool blue of her eyes, but I couldn't stop now.

"I can shape the future by writing it in my blood." Speaking the secret aloud felt like letting part of my soul go.

"You mean you could write the death of the king if you chose?" She gripped my arm, her eyes glittering.

"No. Gods, no." Even if it wouldn't be treason, the thought made my stomach churn. I could hardly believe she'd suggested it. How could she so quickly turn to killing as the answer, and how could she want me to bloody my hands, too?

"But why not?" A spark of anger lit in her eyes.

"Using my gift ages me before my time. And if I'm not specific enough about what the future should be . . . things don't go the way I expect. People get hurt. People die." Images of burned bodies flashed through my mind. I swallowed hard as bile rose in my throat.

"What do you mean?" she asked.

"You remember the drought when we were children? The one that had started to take over the southern part of the kingdom? I ended it," I said. Sonnenborne's curse had begun to spread north into our kingdom, creating a terrible drought of both water and magic. My blood had been the only way to stop it.

The memory twisted like a knife, even now.

"But how?" Her blue eyes were wide. "And why you?"

"After the boar king tried and failed to end it with his magic, he made a bargain with the gods. They spoke to me through Miriel, telling me I was the only one of my kind. The last like me had died hundreds of years ago. So I did what they asked. One simple sentence. One kingdom saved." I fought to keep my voice steady.

Her eyes widened. "But the gods never speak to anyone but their clerics or the king. They don't interfere in human lives."

"You're right, they don't," I said. "That's why they demanded I do it when the king's magic wasn't enough. Afterward, I aged at least a year in the span of an hour. I'm not sure exactly how much. For weeks I stumbled around, not feeling at home in my body." I tried to make her understand the agony. My knee still bore a jagged scar from one of the falls I'd taken, where I'd managed to split myself open enough to bleed buckets onto the forest floor. In that same spot, a cluster of red flowers still bloomed every autumn.

Ina put her hand gently on my arm.

"Eventually, news made its way to Amalska that the drought had indeed ended," I said bitterly. "A flood had destroyed every village along the river bordering Zumorda and Sonnenborne, killing at least a thousand people on both sides. I begged Miriel to let me rewrite the past, to make things unfold differently. She told me if I tried to change the past, it would kill me. The past is not so malleable as the future." My voice came out hollow, dark and distant as the painful memory. Miriel had assured me that the death of all those people wasn't my fault since I had been faithfully serving the gods, but I had still cried myself to sleep every night for moons, especially when I overheard the village elders telling Miriel how little the crown had done to help the survivors. I had been only nine years old.

"So then you never used your power again?" Ina asked, her voice doubtful.

"I refused to. I didn't trust myself to write something that wouldn't have dire unforeseen consequences. But then . . . I missed you so much all winter," I said, my voice careful and soft. "You were always in my mind. Always in my heart. So when you returned and told me about Garen . . . it hurt. I couldn't bear to watch you marry him, especially if you didn't feel certain about it. So the night before the bandits raided, I used my blood to write that you would find your manifest the next day. I wanted you to have the chance to choose your own path . . . and I wanted to give you a better chance of choosing me."

She withdrew her hand. The absence of it felt like a blow, but it was too late to turn back.

"While all I wrote was that you would find your manifest, everything came true, even the intention behind my words. As I wrote, I wished more than anything that you would choose me, not him. Now you never will marry Garen, because he's gone with all the others. I wasn't specific—I never meant to hurt anyone—but it was my fault for pushing the future in that direction. I should have known people might die as a result. I'm sorry, Ina. So sorry." My voice rose in pitch until tears stung the corners of my eyes.

"You have no idea what you've done." Ina's hands shook as she pulled her cloak tightly around herself and stepped away.

"Yes, I do," I insisted. "Everything that happened was my fault. I'm the one you should punish. The king is not owed your revenge. I am." Every word took effort to push past the tightness of my throat. Now that she knew what had happened, even if she couldn't forgive me, she'd stop her plans of regicide. She had to. I couldn't lose her when she was all I had left of home.

"He still could have sent help," she spat. "His negligence started it. You just made it worse."

The crushing weight of my guilt grew heavier.

"I can't believe you didn't tell me right away." Her voice trembled, the pain on her face raw as an open wound. "I can't believe you didn't ask me before you acted!"

"I know. I should have. I'm so sorry," I said, and then a sob tore from my throat. My chest felt like it was collapsing in on itself.

Ina made no move to comfort me. Her fists clenched and unclenched, her left hand finally coming to rest on her stomach.

"This baby has been robbed of a family and a community because of what you did. My child will never know love—because of you." Her eyes shone hard as gemstones.

"What?" I blinked at her in confusion.

The pieces of our history snapped into a new position.

Garen. Ina. The betrothal . . .

Ina's desperation to find her manifest had never been only about the village. It had been about the child she was already carrying before she came up to beg me for help. She would have married Garen, if for no other reason than to give the child a family and a community, because that was what was expected of mothers in Amalska.

She was pregnant, and I had killed her baby's father.

This was what she meant when she told me I had no idea what I'd done.

I stood, frozen, barely able to keep breathing. All this time I thought I was the one who owed her an apology for something she might never be able to forgive, but her knife had been buried in my back long before I made my mistakes.

She didn't even seem sorry.

"You loved Garen?" I asked, my voice weak. "You were intimate with him?

"Only once, the night of the midwinter festival. But you know what the truth is, Asra? I never loved either of you." Never once had her voice sounded so cold or cruel. "You were both supposed to help me become an elder, and instead both of you ruined that for me. If I live a thousand years I will never, ever forgive you." She turned and ran, then leaped into the air, her transformation almost instant. The white dragon screamed, something between a keen and a roar, then a burst of flame erupted from her jaws, blindingly bright even against the afternoon sky.

I cowered behind the boulders, waiting for the flames to hit, sure she was about to destroy me, but nothing came. I opened my eyes a few breaths later as she vanished into the clouds, carrying the shredded remains of my heart.

CHAPTER 14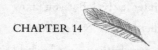

I STARED AFTER INA, CHOKING ON MY OWN TEARS AND a rising tide of anger. Never had I thought she could betray me this deeply. It would have broken my heart if she had told me the truth when she first came up from the village, but not like this—not the kind of heartbreak my body couldn't contain. She had seduced me already knowing Garen's baby was growing inside her. She had played with me like a toy, like it didn't matter that she knew she was already destined to have a family with someone else. She had left my cave after that first visit this spring and walked right back into his arms.

The thought made my stomach heave.

She was still going after the king, and now I had nothing left: no way to stop her, no home, no love, no idea who my parents were.

I had no purpose at all.

In the wake of Ina's flight, the wind picked up again. It was even stronger this time, blinding me with dirt swept from the ground and splattering me with droplets lifted from the stream. I needed to find somewhere to take shelter until I was collected enough to return to Hal and the Tamers. After that, I could figure out what to do next.

I forced myself to my feet and kept a hand on the side of the boulder, inching my way between the two largest ones in hopes of finding some protection from the wind. Instead I discovered a stone archway leading into a cave. It had to be the Sanctum Mukira had mentioned. Surely inside I would be safe from the curse of the cliff.

Moss had filled in cracks around the mouth of the cavern, but they deepened into intricate carvings farther in. I ran my fingers over the swirling grooves. Whoever had created them had had the luxury of time. The deeper I went, the more the outside world seemed like a nightmare I didn't have to face just yet. I used my Sight to navigate the tunnel, hoping it would be enough to see by once the entrance disappeared from view.

I needn't have worried. At the bottom of a spiraling set of stairs carved into the floor, the path opened into a breathtaking room with archways leading into others. I looked around with curiosity and wonder. Natural light streamed through windows embedded in the cliff side, the glass so clear it must have been crafted with magic. My Sight indicated that the other sides of the windows were enchanted to blend in with the face of the cliff; it would look like ordinary rock from outside.

Still, something about the space made me uneasy. The silence was thick enough to cut. I paced through the interconnected rooms. Every surface had been chiseled into something spectacular. Patterns of leaves twisted into animals so lifelike it seemed as though they might spring from the walls. Stone columns stretched from floor to ceiling, narrowing in the middle, some in the likenesses of creatures and others in the shapes of humans.

At the back of the cave closest to the entrance lay the pool Mukira had spoken of, the water an inky blue-black in the slanting light from outside. Beneath the water, old magic swirled and eddied, pulsing underground farther than my Sight could reach. I peered into the pool for only a moment, recoiling when my reflection gleamed back at me clearer than any looking glass I'd ever seen. It was hard enough to carry my sorrow inside, much less see it in my eyes.

A wave of emotion struck as I stepped back. I had tried so fiercely to hold together the pieces of my heart that had broken when Amalska burned, and I'd thought Ina was the only one who might help me stitch them back together. Now she was gone forever, leaving me with even deeper wounds—ones she'd salted well.

I slumped against a wall and hugged my knees to my chest as my throat tightened and tears spilled over again.

A baby. How could she not tell me she was going to have a baby? It changed everything. Her lie of omission made me question everything we'd ever had. Had I ever meant anything to her, or was the love we had no more than a fleeting summer romance? When she came to see me at winter's end, had it truly been for the village and because she missed me, or had she been using me all along? I never should have used my gift to help her. I never would have if I'd known it would turn out like this.

I sobbed into the folds of my cloak. What would I do now?

My grief swallowed me so completely that I failed to notice the breezes eddying through the cave with increasing strength until a gust hit me so hard my head smacked against the wall. I coughed and wiped my eyes, looking around in confusion for the source of the wind. When the stars cleared from my vision, a man was shuffling toward me, still partially obscured in the shadows.

"You trespass," his voice hissed through the cave. The chill in the words cut through me like jagged edges of broken ice.

He came into the light at a deliberate pace, his tattered robes rippling in the wind that swirled around him. In my Sight he glowed bright as a demigod, but dark tendrils laced through his aura like some kind of rot. What little hair he had left was white as fresh snow, his face lined with centuries of age. He hissed at me again in an inhuman way that froze me to the core.

I scrambled toward the path out of the cave. Gusts twisted around me and pressed on my chest, shoving me onto my back. Wisps of wind worked their way beneath my clothing and dug into me like teeth and claws.

"Get off me!" I screamed.

"Foolish child. This sacred ground is not for you." The malice in his baritone voice was as palpable as the force of his magic.

The pressure on my chest increased, and darkness began to creep in at the edges of my vision. The wind he controlled was stealing my breath. If I didn't do something, he would asphyxiate me. I might have welcomed death at Ina's hands; it would have been fair after what we'd put each other through. But being destroyed by the whims of a random monster wasn't.

My heart pounded in my chest, quick as the wings of a sparrow. I flailed desperately, only managing to scrape my wrist on a sharp rock. A hot trickle of blood ran down my fingers.

The man stopped moving toward me, the wind momentarily ebbing. I crawled backward, leaving a thin trail of blood. Some of my panic must have bled out with it, for everywhere my blood touched, it created grooves in the stone. He raised a hand again, his magic shoving me hard against the floor. My own gift pulsed at the edges of my open wound, urging me to write a way out of this situation. I held it back with all my remaining strength, no longer able to flee.

The man slowly bent down to where my blood had splattered on the floor. He touched the blood with a knobby fingertip, then brought it to his tongue.

A soft cry escaped his lips. The wind departed as swiftly as it had arrived, leaving dust to swirl through the sunbeams angling into the cave. Now that the man wasn't attacking me, he looked much weaker. Age had hunched his shoulders, and his hands trembled with some kind of palsy.

"You taste like him," he whispered reverently.

"Like who?" I clutched my injured wrist to my chest, terrified of what he might do next.

"Veric," the old man said. "This is his sanctuary in which you trespass."

"Who the Hells is Veric? And who are you?" I asked, scrambling to my feet to take advantage of the reprieve from his attack. I was getting very tired of being accused of trespassing when all I wanted was to be left alone to mourn what I'd lost.

"I am Leozoar, son of the wind and guardian of the Sanctum," he answered.

I started. He was one of Hal's brothers—or at least claiming to be.

"You don't look like a demigod." Nor did he behave like one. Not all of us were especially moral, but we generally didn't kill the way he'd apparently been doing for generations.

"Ah, so you have the Sight, do you? How useful." Leozoar edged closer. "The gods forsook me when I took the first life in protection of this Sanctum. But my vow was to Veric. He was my family, too. My love." His gaze grew distant, as if looking for a memory too far away to grasp.

"I see." Worry needled at me. Did all the death I'd caused in Amalska mean the gods had turned away from me as well? Or perhaps I'd been cursed and abandoned by them since birth. That would certainly explain a lot.

"Go to the dais and offer your blood." Leozoar's words sounded like a command, not a choice.

"No. I want to leave," I said, my voice weak. The day had been long enough. I didn't want anything to do with this wind wraith and his dark magic.

"But you have everything to lose and just as much to gain," he said. His dark eyes grew fierce and the wind picked up again. The meaning was clear: if I didn't obey him, he'd kill me. A tingle of fear zipped down my spine, then faded away. I barely had the energy to be afraid anymore. In a way, it was almost a relief.

"Tell me why I should," I said.

He huffed in frustration, sending another gust through the cave. "Because I am tired of waiting here and you might hold the keys to set me free."

I crossed my arms. "What's in it for me?"

"Everything. Your past and your future," he sputtered. "Do you dare dishonor the only other like you? The only one with your gifts?"

"Which gifts?" I asked, fear finally creeping its way in.

"Your ability to make the future what you wish, just as Veric could." His hands trembled more fiercely.

"Veric was a bloodscribe?" I stared at the man in shock. If that was true, Veric and I had to be related. Finally, I had a lead on my origins.

"It's like you haven't heard a word I've said!" Leozoar shuffled up until he was barely a handbreadth from me.

I backed away along the wall. If Veric had been a bloodscribe, that meant some secrets of my past might be preserved here. I had never expected to find any keys to my past. Then again, I had never known I needed to search for them back when I thought I was the daughter of wind.

I had to do it.

"Where's the dais?" I asked.

"Follow the stones," Leozoar said, raising his arm to send another burst of wind through the chambers. Dust blew aside to reveal a mosaic of polished granite winding a glittering path through the stone floor of the cave. Leozoar limped along beside me as I followed the intricate designs. We walked past the pool through an archway into another smaller room that also had windows on the cliff-facing side. The patterns on the floor twined toward the center, and I followed them as if tugged by an invisible wire.

A circular stone dais lay between two columns at the heart of the cavern. Text spiraled around its surface toward the center.

I gift you my blood so that I may serve my kingdom.
I take your blood so that I may know your intentions.
If my blood is your blood
And your heart is my heart
The past and the future will be yours to command
Until the blood of us both is but memory and dust.

A shudder passed through me. The similarities to the rite Ina had used to take her manifest stood out to me in sharp relief. Old blood magic had been practiced here. A handprint much larger than mine lay embedded in the center of the stone table. Perhaps it was Veric's.

I touched the indentation, the coolness of the stone seeping into my fingertips. Apprehension stirred, sending a shiver through me. I looked back at the old man, and instead of hostility in his expression, I saw something else.

Hope. For what, I didn't know.

"Offer your blood," Leozoar said, his voice fervent. A groove through the center of the handprint seemed made for just that. His dark eyes shone with intensity, freezing me in place.

Did I dare tempt fate by offering the dais my blood? Did I even have a choice? Ina had left me. Now I had to take care of myself. Perhaps the secrets of my past would help show me the way to a better future. I took a shaky breath, gathering what little strength I had left. I couldn't turn my back on something that might provide information about the only other demigod like me.

I squeezed the wound on my wrist to reopen it and let a few drops of blood fall onto the handprint. They dripped into the groove, tracing a red path toward the center. The earth trembled and groaned as the dais turned on an unseen axis until a chamber appeared. Inside lay a leather booklet containing a single sheet of folded vellum.

The binding was stiff and aged, but clean—safe from the grime that had overtaken the rest of the cave. On the outside of the vellum, a single line was written in an ornate and slanting hand. The ink was a deep scarlet that could only be achieved by mixing blood with midnight thistles. Even though the folio had to be centuries old, even now, the handwritten letters burned with magic in my Sight. My throat tightened as I read them.

The next bloodscribe born will find this before their eighteenth winter.

"You see?" Leozoar said. "Veric wrote that you would come here. His words shaped your destiny, just as you will shape others'."

My hands began to shake. My fate had never been entirely mine. Emotions assaulted me from every side. Anger that my future had been tampered with. Relief, because someone else might be partly responsible for the events that led me here. Guilt, for even momentarily trying to blame someone else for my failings.

"My time as guardian of this place is over. You'll send me to meet the shadow god—to be with Veric again." He grasped my arm so tightly it hurt, and a rapturous expression came over his face.

"What are you talking about?" I broke free of his grip and shied away.

"I want you to free me," he said, gripping my arm again. "This must be why you've come down from your mountain. To bring me peace. Do it. Do it now!" His hysteria intensified.

"How do you know where I'm from?" I accused him, gripping the strap of my satchel until my knuckles went white.

"I tasted it in your blood," he said, his voice taking on the hissing tone it'd had upon our first confrontation. "All you have to do is take my power. Make it yours. Do what you want with it—I don't care. Please."

Cold dread coursed through me. "You want me to kill you?"

He touched my wrist with trembling fingers, and memories broke over me like waves.

The first time I wrote with my blood.

The way Ina had looked at me those hot summer nights last year.

The smell of burning as Amalska was reduced to ash.

The expression on Hal's face when he'd woken up this morning and I was still there.

"Veric promised me you would," Leozar insisted. "His legacy awaits you. I'm no longer needed. Please have mercy on an old man. I'm ready to see Veric again. You know I've killed many—you could stop that right now." His tone grew wheedling as he tried to take advantage of my guilt.

I wasn't that easy.

"A death for a death does not bring absolution for either one," I said bitterly. Neither did the death of bandits make up for the loss of a village. Nor would the death of the king.

"Then help me because I am in pain. Everything hurts. I've already lived more than half a dozen mortal lifetimes. The wind is the only strength left in me."

I dropped into my Sight and studied the patterns of darkness curling through his aura. He was already a broken thing, slowly fading away. One day he might be little more than wind, slowly returned to the earth like all demigods. But what would it do for the poison in him to pass on that way? He might remain as a killing gust at the top of the cliff forever. He might continue to take lives long after his corporeal form disappeared.

"If I do this, it will be a true death, and you'll never hurt anyone again?" I asked.

"Never," he said fervently. His icy hands gripped mine.

I'd only used my power to kill when it was necessary to end the suffering of trees or animals too diseased or broken to survive. I tried to convince myself this would be no different.

Tentatively, I looked for the place inside me with its own darkness so unlike his. A false sense of peace washed through me when I found that nightlike river of magic. I loosed my hand from his and took his forearm to let the blood on my wrist smear on his skin, giving my magic a connection to grasp his. My heart beat in my ears like a drum.

An expression of peace and bliss came over Leozoar's face. My Sight made it easy to see the magic that comprised him, the strengths and the weaknesses, the threads I could pull to unravel it. He was held together so tenuously, and the darkness beckoned to him.

Carefully, I pulled on his power, drawing into myself the magic that wove together his very being. Absorbing his power felt like submerging myself in an icy lake. Remnants of his anger snatched at my conscience and tried to convince me his feelings were mine. The part of me ruled by him wanted to do terrible things. His magic surged wildly inside me. It took everything I had not to use his power to pull out my knife and make the future into a twisted nightmare as dark as the broken pieces of his soul.

But I could also feel what he had once been—a demigod with the same whimsical spirit as Hal. A person who had loved someone so completely he'd given centuries of life to protect his legacy. Someone who had loved Veric as I had loved Ina: without reservation or compromise.

I bent the magic to my will until it coursed through me quick as the wind, vibrant and powerful as the hum of life itself. Instead of holding on to it, I channeled as much as I could directly into the land, into the place that had belonged to him and Veric. The sunlight pouring through the windows intensified, and a final gust of wind swept through the cave, carrying centuries of dust and grime with it. The land itself seemed to breathe a sigh of relief, and the oppressive sadness of the cave relented.

My hands were empty and Leozoar was gone.

Without him, the Sanctum took on the peace of any other abandoned space. Channeling his magic left me refreshed and humming with energy, as if some of his power still lingered in me. I unfolded the folio from the dais and read the words within.

If you retrieved this letter, your blood is my blood. You found this place because fate led you here—fate written in my hand to lead you to the gift that will make it possible for your life to end in a better way than mine. Humans endlessly twisted and shaped my blood and magic to create enchantments for their own ends. They begged me to change their fates until I had nothing left to give, so I used the last of my blood to create the Fatestone.

Worn by a mortal, the Fatestone would be simply an amulet of eternal life, but it was not created for that purpose. A demigod with my powers is the only one who must use it—the heir whose blood is able to dispel the protections on these pages, the one who will lift the Fatestone from its place of safekeeping in Atheon.

The Fatestone protects against the cost our gift demands. It gives a bloodscribe the power to make right what has been wrong—to correct the path of darkness, to bring light to the world and life, all without the suffering of aging before one's time.

May it serve you well.

—Veric Pirov

I nearly dropped the booklet in shock. My throat went dry. I shouldn't have released Leozoar before I could ask more questions. The enchantments Veric spoke of—those had to be the same ones Miriel had taught me. How to use my blood to augment potions. How to paint a bit of it on her skin to give her some of my passive gifts. But the Fatestone? That I'd never heard of until Hal mentioned it as the amulet his sister was looking for. I pawed through the chamber in the dais, but it was empty. I reread Veric's letter. Where was Atheon? I'd never heard the word before, and although I'd never left home, I wasn't entirely unfamiliar with Zumordan geography. Even with so many questions remaining unanswered, all my paths of thought led to the same conclusion.

The Fatestone had been made for me. Veric was indeed my half brother, born and dead centuries before me. This letter and the Fatestone were the only true legacy I had.

But more important than that, if I found Veric's Fatestone, not only could I shape the future without succumbing to the ravages of age—I would be able to change the past without sacrificing my life.

I could make it so that bandits had never destroyed Amalska.

I could return Ina's innocence.

I could undo the mistake I'd written in my blood.

My anger and grief took a more powerful form: determination.

I had to find the Fatestone and start our story over.

CHAPTER 15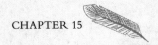

THE SUN SAT LOW OVER THE TREES BY THE TIME I exited the Sanctum. Instead of the sweeping gales that had greeted me when I first arrived, only gentle breezes teased at the grass on the escarpment now that Leozoar was gone. I worked my way back down through the cave with Veric's letter snugly tied in my belt sash. The booklet held my only shard of hope, and the last of the answers lay just beyond my fingertips. I only needed to figure out where Atheon was. And if I could get this far from my hometown and keep myself in one piece, conquer a corrupted demigod, and talk my way out of trouble with the Tamers—I could do it.

Hal must have heard me coming, for he stood outside the cave as I emerged, just out of reach of the waterfall's mist. The Tamers were nowhere in sight. The sun slowly impaled itself on the sharp tops of the trees, giving Hal's dark-brown skin a warm glow. Gratitude swelled in my breast. After what had happened with Ina, I suppose I had half expected him to leave me, too. He owed me nothing.

"You're back!" He rushed over and hugged me, but I winced as his arms put pressure on tender bruises. The battle with Leozoar had finally caught up with me.

"I'm sorry," he said, stepping back awkwardly when I failed to return his embrace. "You were gone so long. I was worried. . . ."

"It's all right. I'm just a bit sore," I said, trying to explain my reaction. Though he had startled me with the hug, and I truly did ache all over, the embrace provided comfort that had ended too soon. Thoughts of Ina rose unbidden, reopening the gaping wound of her absence and deepening the stab of her betrayal.

Perhaps it was remnants of Leozoar's wind magic calling to something like itself, or perhaps it was just my need for comfort, but I stepped back into Hal's arms and closed my eyes. I needed a friend. Hal's arms might help keep me from flying apart until I figured out how to go on alone. Everything depended on it now that my only hope was finding the Fatestone.

He held me gently, resting his chin on the top of my head. As he took a deep breath, I echoed it without thinking. Even though we barely knew each other, something about him felt warm and safe. He smelled clean and subtly herbal, like the soap Mukira had given us to bathe with.

Hal squeezed my shoulders gently when I finally pulled away. "What happened up there? I Heard the wind—that thing—speaking to you."

"What did you Hear?" I asked.

"Not much. My head still hurts and I can't Hear as far as usual. I just checked a few times to make sure you were still alive," he said.

I told him about entering the Sanctum, the magic pool, how I'd found the source of the cliff's curse. My explanation faltered only when I tried to explain how I'd destroyed Leozoar. It had been an act of mercy, not an act of violence, but it still bothered me how easy it had been.

"You didn't do anything wrong," Hal said. "If he was going to kill you, you did what you needed to." I had no idea how he could be so agreeable about everything. The guilt of not telling him the whole truth grew heavier, but I wasn't ready to share Veric's letter.

"I think he was once something more like you—a demigod born of the wind. Something happened to him after he was deserted by the gods. The dark parts of his magic took over."

Hal shuddered. "I hope nothing like that ever happens to me."

"I don't think it will," I said. Nothing about Hal was anything like Leozoar. He was too easygoing and lighthearted to end up like that. He seemed to love his family and the other children of the wind. He had people he cared for, and others who cared for him.

"Mostly I'm glad you're all right," he said. "You're much too interesting to lose when I've only just met you."

"Interesting is sometimes more of a curse than a blessing." I smiled a sad smile. Under any other circumstances I would have been flattered by his words. "Where did the others go?"

"After the dragon flew past, Mukira sent most of the hunters to track it to make sure it doesn't circle back. She just left the one hunter to watch us—and to shoot me if I tried to run off, I presume. He'll escort us back to their camp." He pointed into the trees. It took me a minute to locate the boy perched in the branches. He had an arrow nocked to his bow, and I had no doubt he could draw it and let the thing fly before we got more than a few paces away. A crow sat beside him, tilting its head at me with a keen intelligence in its eye.

"She won't come back," I said softly. That much I knew was true. If she did, surely it would only be to kill me for what I'd done. My skin crawled at the thought. I'd never expected to find myself doubting whether she cared about me, much less knowing her hate burned brighter than the fire from her jaws. And part of me was angry with her, too.

I tucked a loose lock of hair behind my ears, and Hal caught my hand as I dropped it back to my side.

"Your wrist," he said, his voice thick with concern as he examined the scrape.

"It's nothing," I said, but I liked the way he held my hand. It comforted me that someone could still be tender with me when I felt so undeserving.

The crow flapped off toward the camp, and the Tamer boy dropped down from the tree.

"Are you well enough to walk?" Hal asked.

"Of course," I said, not thinking to question it until we entered the trees and lost sight of the waterfall. With every step I took, the bruises and trauma of the day caught up with me until I wanted to curl up on the forest floor. My stomach rumbled, reminding me that I'd eaten nothing since breakfast.

"If you feel like sharing what happened with your dragon friend, I'm here to listen," Hal said, his voice pitched softly to keep the boy from hearing. "She didn't look happy when she flew off. You don't seem very cheerful either."

I thought for a moment, taking a deep breath of pine-laden air.

The familiar ache rose in me, tightening my throat so that I couldn't speak. The more time that passed, the angrier I became with Ina, but even as my rage grew, I couldn't shake my other memories.

The warmth of her lips.

Her eyes, lit with desire.

The way she'd made me hers, claiming every inch of me with kisses pressed in places no one else had ever seen.

Hal and I walked on in silence, but he didn't push. He gave me room to breathe and let me be until I was ready, and for some reason, that made me feel like I could tell him.

"Ina left," I said, my voice flat. "She's angry with me about something I did back home—something I should have told her sooner. I had tried to help her, but it all went wrong. Then it turned out there were things she hadn't told me either."

Hal nodded, not seeming to mind how vague and jumbled my explanation was. "Do you think you can work things out if you talk again?"

"I don't know." But I did. She would never come back and she would never forgive me. Ina always kept her word. I should have wondered sooner why she never promised me anything.

"So what now? Where will you go next?" Innocent curiosity shone in his eyes.

I wondered if he would look at me that way if he knew everything that had happened to lead me here—if he knew about the trail of blood Ina and I had left behind.

"A place someone told me about," I said. "But I don't even know exactly where it is, so I suppose I need to figure that out first."

"Oh?" He seemed intrigued. "I've traveled a lot of Zumorda in the past year. Maybe I've heard of it."

It couldn't hurt to ask. "Have you ever heard of Atheon?"

Hal furrowed his brow. "I haven't heard of a town by that name, no. But maybe it's in the northwest? I haven't spent much time there. It's mostly peculiar little villages. And sheep. Lots of sheep."

My heart sank. "What about someone named Veric?"

"I don't personally know anyone by that name." Hal tapped his chin thoughtfully. "But there's an old drinking song about a man named Veric. Why?"

"Do you know any songs that aren't about drinking?" I eyed him balefully, ignoring his question.

"Not really!" He grinned.

"How does the song go?"

"I only remember the chorus. 'Drink for a penny or drink for a crown, hunt with a smile and kill with a frown. Few things are certain and that's why we sing, but the blood of Sir Veric can make you a king.'"

"I hope that song is long out of fashion," I said, disturbed. If people still sang it, did that mean they knew what could be done with my blood—the things Veric had alluded to in his letter, perhaps even more dangerous than the spells Miriel had taught me? And if mortals knew of those things, why didn't I?

"I've only heard it once, on a trip to Kartasha. The tavern served a raspberry lambic meant to look like blood. Kind of silly."

"And awfully macabre," I added. "What about you—where are you headed from here?"

"Back to my sister as always," he said.

An uneasy feeling twisted in my stomach. She'd been looking

for the Fatestone, too, and surely she had more information about it than I did—maybe even some idea where Atheon was. But finding out what Nismae knew about the stone and its location meant walking right into the middle of a feud. The last thing I needed was the leader of a group of assassins chasing after me if I obtained the Fatestone and they found out. What hope did I stand of defending myself against trained killers?

Ahead of us, the Tamer boy whistled a greeting, and then a series of birdcalls echoed through the forest.

"We have a problem." The boy dashed ahead without looking to see if we would follow.

Hal and I exchanged a worried glance. We could have used the opportunity to escape, but I had no doubt the Tamers would be able to catch up with us no matter how far and fast we ran as long as we were within the borders of their woods. We broke through into a small clearing a few minutes later.

Mukira knelt over a Tamer who lay very still. I didn't need to get closer or reach for my Sight to know that she was near death. My gaze skittered through the surrounding trees, searching for signs to confirm my suspicions about what had happened. Broken branches littered the ground around a nearby pine. Bile rose in my throat.

I knew it had been Ina.

Elder Mukira used her staff to get to her feet, then turned to face us with a deep frown. "The fall broke her back. There is nothing we can do."

"Was anyone else injured?" I asked, my voice small.

Mukira shook her head.

I approached the fallen Tamer. An owl hooted mournfully in

the branches overhead, though the sun had not yet set.

The woman lying on the ground was Kaja, the Tamer who had captured me.

She'd already gone into shock, her skin clammy and cold with sweat. Her life was slipping away, back into the forest she'd spent her life protecting, but it wasn't her time. She hadn't deserved this. The remnants of Leozoar's magic surged up with curiosity, giving me an idea. Some good could yet come of that murderous old wraith.

I crouched beside Kaja and pressed both my hands into the earth, digging my fingers into the thick bed of pine needles and other shed foliage on the forest floor. Life hummed under my fingertips, glowing gently in my Sight. My senses blurred. It was almost as if the forest had a sound, like a chorus of bells so deep they were barely audible.

"May I?" I asked Mukira. I had performed smaller healings before and had an unusual amount of power at my disposal now. It couldn't make things worse to try.

The elder looked at me with a strange expression. "If you do no harm," she acquiesced.

I pulled my journal out of my satchel and flipped to one of the simpler blood spells Miriel had taught me. I nicked my finger and drew the symbol of the spirit god on Kaja's forehead for clarity of Sight. My magic melted into her, letting me see the broken pieces of her body.

Beyond Kaja's fading heartbeat and the acute pain of her broken back, I sensed the roots beneath the earth, the vegetation all around me, and the animals scavenging for food and nesting materials—all the things that came with the first breaths of spring. I let the forest consume me, and then matched it to the last of Leozoar's magic, weaving them together like a tapestry inside my mind.

I almost lost myself to the forest as the two powers merged. The bright white of Leozoar's power pulled at the dark river of my own. I felt like it would be all right to become part of the forest, to sink into it and embrace the slow pace of its life. But this wasn't my place, and these were not my people, so I held back my own magic and let go of the rest, funneling it through my blood into Kaja and the land around her. The forest took her pain and I realigned her broken back with my magic, reminding her body what it had been before her fall.

All around us, seeds lying dormant within the earth burst into sprouts that fought their way free of the ground despite its being too early for them. Ivy crawled over the trees until they were swathed in green. Vines twirled around Mukira's staff, bursting into fragrant bloom. The trees all around us put out bursts of pale green needles, gilding the forest with the colors of spring.

Kaja opened her eyes, blinking at me in confusion, and then a wave of exhaustion hit me. I swayed on my knees, too dizzy to stand up. No more of Leozoar's magic remained.

Hal rushed to my side, helping me over to a fallen log where I could sit. Platforms of new fungus jutted out of the wood, and tiny white flowers poked up from the moss growing in its crevices. The Tamers crowded around Kaja, murmuring with wonder at her recovery and the new life in the clearing.

I turned to Hal to thank him for helping me, but stopped when I saw the look in his eyes. It wasn't reverent, exactly, but admiring. Respectful. Maybe even a little hungry, in a way that made something warm blossom in the pit of my stomach.

"Well done," he said.

His compliment warmed me. I liked the way his eyes were locked on me, their deep brown soft and warm. I liked the pressure of his one hand on my arm, and the way his other rested on my lower back. But if I liked him, if I let myself care about him . . . all that meant was that it would hurt when he left. I couldn't get too attached.

Mukira whistled a sharp call, and moments later a tall woman with long braids and a rich dark umber complexion dashed into the clearing, calling Kaja's name. When she saw Kaja sitting up on her own, she fell to her knees beside her, and they clung to each other like they would never let go. Kaja gently kissed the tears from the other woman's face, whispering, "I'm all right. I'm here."

I looked away, feeling as though I'd witnessed a moment that should have been private. I didn't even notice Mukira approaching until Hal nudged me. She came to a stop in front of us, looking at me with new respect in her eyes.

"Thank you for saving Kaja," the elder said, "I have never seen magic like that before."

"You're welcome," I said. Because my confession had chased Ina off in a storm of rage and hurt, in a way, Kaja's injury had been my fault. Preventing her death was the least I could do to atone for that.

"How did you save her?" Mukira asked.

"With magic left over from destroying the curse on your cliff," I said. "There was a wind demigod living in the Sanctum—he was the one tossing people off the cliff to keep them away. He's now at peace," I said. She didn't need to know about Veric or how I'd destroyed Leozoar. I opened my satchel and pulled out a vial of water. It swirled in the glass, the pale blue of a summer sky.

Mukira's eyebrows rose. "That's water from the sacred pool!" She took the vial from me, gently touching it to the tip of her staff. She closed her eyes.

I let my Sight come to me and watched what Mukira was doing. Questing threads of magic reached through the network of life in the forest. The full extent of their reach wasn't visible to me—her connection to the forest must have broadened her ability to See magic far beyond what I could, even if she didn't recognize the nuances of it the way I did. If she had, surely she would have known what Leozoar was, not just that the cliff was cursed.

"The Sanctum is ours once more," she finally pronounced. Her eyes opened, now lit with joy.

"We can never thank you enough for this gift, Asra. Make haste back to the camp when you feel ready. We'll resupply you for wherever you are headed next. I must tell the others." She hurried away, gathering other Tamers, gesturing broadly as she showed them the water I'd brought back from their sacred pool.

"Look what you did," Hal said. "You got us out of trouble, defeated a deranged demigod, and saved a life, all in a day's work."

"I couldn't have found Ina without you," I said, uncomfortable with all the credit he was giving me.

"It was the least I could do. You saved my life." He smiled. "Besides, I like you."

The ache of loneliness I carried with me intensified. I didn't deserve his kindness, even if I longed for it. If I wanted to earn it, I needed to find the Fatestone and set things right—and that started with talking to his sister.

"Then perhaps I can get you to take me to your sister," I said.

I bit my lip nervously, knowing I'd asked him for a lot.

An odd expression passed over his face, too quickly for me to pin it down. "Why?"

"Now that I know my father isn't the wind god, I'm wondering if her research might contain any clues to which of the gods I might be descended from," I said. Also, she was the only person besides the king who knew anything about Atheon or the Fatestone, but I didn't know if I could trust Hal with my true motives.

"She's in Orzai," he said. "I had been planning to go there anyway, but it's quite a bit north of here . . . and it's not the safest place."

I mustered what little energy I had left and looked Hal right in the eyes. "Take me with you."

I had nothing left to lose.

CHAPTER 16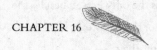

THE TAMERS STILL REGARDED ME WARILY AFTER I healed Kaja, but now with respect instead of distrust. Those who ventured to the Sanctum made me the most uncomfortable, treating me with reverence upon their return. Mukira asked them to supply us for our trip to Orzai, and they complied with enthusiasm. One of the Tamers stuffed my satchel with dried meat, and another offered me some string and a set of carved fishhooks. Kaja's lifemate turned out to be an extraordinary tailor, and the two of them gave me a knee-length tunic made of honey-colored doeskin so soft I never wanted to take it off. Mukira even gave Hal a new pair of boots and a set of fine hunting knives.

We rested until Mukira's hunters returned the next day with word that the dragon hadn't been sighted anywhere in the forest. In spite of their gratitude for Kaja's salvation, they still seemed as eager to see us go as they had been to kill us when we first arrived. I was more than happy to obey their wishes.

A band of Mukira's hunters guided us to the edge of their lands, no doubt to ensure we didn't trespass again. At least any city guards who might have searched for the two of us in the days since our escape had probably given up by now.

Eventually the trees began to thin, and the hunters left us when the cover could no longer hide them. Then they were gone, as invisible as ever, leaving the two of us at the edge of a plain that stretched as far as the eye could see. I breathed a deep sigh. While I feared what lay ahead of us, I had become too accustomed to my life on the mountain alone to enjoy much time in communities where solitude was so hard to come by.

Our boots crunched over rocks hidden in the grass—we'd left the farmlands far behind. This ground was too rocky to till, and too remote to make getting to markets in larger towns easy. Clouds scudded overhead, a mixture of white and gray that blocked the sun like a heavy blanket, breezes endlessly teasing them into new shapes that threatened rain in every leaden shadow. The farther we got from the forest as the afternoon wore on, the more the wind picked up, slowing our progress as we leaned into it. Birds flew overhead in small brown clusters, like seeds scattered against the gray sky.

Hal didn't talk much—at least not to me. A few times I caught him with a far-off smile on his face and an ear to the wind. I always looked away. It felt like eavesdropping, even though I couldn't hear a thing, and every time I witnessed his gift, it reminded me I wasn't who I'd thought. The ache of it grew bigger each time. I forced myself to turn my thoughts to the Fatestone, to fuel my determination. If I found it, I could have my people back. My life. Everything.

Still, my mood grew darker and more anxious the farther we walked. Conversations replayed over and over in my mind. Could I have said something different to talk Ina out of killing the king? Why hadn't she told me about her pregnancy, and how could she be willing to die trying to murder the king knowing she carried another life inside her? When those unanswerable questions weren't consuming me, intrusive thoughts of burned bodies and blood-spattered slush rose up unbidden, forcing me to relive the carnage I wanted desperately to erase from my past.

Now, more than ever, I felt lost and alone out in the world. I thought about saying a prayer for comfort, but which god was I even supposed to ask now that I didn't know who I belonged to?

"What's wrong?" Hal finally asked.

"Nothing," I said. Talking about it wasn't going to change anything.

"Tamer breakfast not sitting well with you? Cloudy weather bringing you down?" he guessed, even though he had to know it was more than that.

I didn't know how to communicate the mess of memories and emotions tearing me apart. He couldn't understand what it was like to be responsible for the deaths of countless souls. He had useful gifts, things that helped him get by in the world, not magic that left a trail of death and destruction in its wake.

"Talk to me, Asra. It's no good holding all of it in. The things that brought you here can't have been easy." His voice was gentle.

"I wish I could do something to get us to Orzai faster. I'm useless. Worse than mortal. I'm not even who I thought I was. All I have is the ability to mix herbs. What good is that?" The anger in my own voice surprised me. I'd never had such ugly thoughts about myself before, but in my other life, I'd known my place. I'd known who I was and how to help people. All that had been taken away.

"But you can mix herbs with magic," he said, as though that made any difference at all. "And you healed someone who would have died without your intervention."

"I was only able to heal Kaja because I'd drawn so much magic out of that dying demigod in the Sanctum. And anyone can learn to mix herbs and magic. Even mortals, if they study as clerics of earth like my mentor did. Your heritage gave you gifts—the Farhearing, the wind manipulation, the compulsion—some of which barely have a cost to you. I wish I were mortal. At least then I could take a manifest. Be like everyone else. At least have another form to use to flee or to defend myself."

"No mortal could have done all you did," Hal said. "You helped us get out of Valenko unscathed. You talked sense into your friend. You bargained with the Tamers and defeated a corrupt demigod, then used that power to heal. That's amazing."

I sighed. "Yet here I am, back on the road in search of yet another person who has a vendetta against the king."

"From what little I know of Ina, I'm pretty sure Nismae is nothing like her. Nis has an agenda, certainly. And always several irons in the fire, knives up both her sleeves, and half a dozen spies in every city. But she's never let that stop her from being a good sister," Hal said.

"Ina wasn't my sister," I said. She was both so much more and, in the end, so much less. Whatever I was to her, it wasn't enough.

"My point is that Nismae has her preoccupations, but she

wouldn't desert me. Like your friend, she has her secrets that she chooses to reveal only at her own discretion, but she would never let those come between us. She's forthright when it matters most."

"You're lucky to have her," I said. I didn't know what else to say. In his attempts to frame his sister as a source of hope, he'd only reminded me of what I lacked.

"Yes, I am. She'll help you, too, though. I'm sure of it. She has to know something that will help you uncover your parentage," he said.

"She'll probably tell me I'm descended from some forgotten god of dung." I kicked a rock and sent it flying across the road.

Hal chortled. "That would explain how well you fertilized those plants in the Tamers' forest!"

I couldn't help a smile. "Maybe for my next act I should see if I can conjure fewmets to use as a starter for our fire tonight."

"That's the spirit! We might as well enjoy the journey while we're on it," he said. "Here we are, free, out on the open road!" He stretched out his arms as though the dull, rocky landscape was something we should be thrilled to be a part of, as though he could see the sun shining from some far-off place beyond the clouds. "Look at us! We can shout obscenities about the king and no one can throw us in jail! For example, it would probably take an entire team of plow horses to dislodge the enormous stick from his rear!"

I covered my mouth with my hand, pretending to be shocked even as a smile crept onto my face.

"We can do dances that have been banned in Corovja!" Hal gyrated in a way that was both peculiar and suggestive in equal measure.

That time, I couldn't help giggling. He looked ridiculous.

"We can pretend to be feral Mynarian war steeds galloping for freedom from the oppression of idiots who wear tin cans on their heads!" He whinnied and cantered zigzags across the road in front of me.

"Stop it," I said, laughing. All the awful things that had happened should have outweighed my ability to feel any lightness or humor.

"Why? There's no one here to see us! No one to tell us what to do! We could keep going clear past Orzai and Corovja to the Zir Canyon and see who can spit farthest off the edge!"

I laughed so hard my cheeks started to ache.

"We can sing bawdy tavern songs inappropriate for a fine young lady such as yourself!" He broke into a song called "The Tavern Lamb," which involved a wide variety of intoxicating drinks, a woman who enjoyed them all, and several mentions of sheep's wool that were clearly metaphors for something else entirely.

"You're hurting me!" I gasped to catch my breath.

He walked backward in front of me, grinning. Despite my conviction that I didn't deserve it, the laughter eased the burdens I carried with me, unknotting the tangle of leaden feelings in my chest. Even my satchel felt lighter on my shoulder, and the part of me that Ina carried with her ached a little bit less.

"You needed that," Hal observed.

"Maybe I did," I replied. In that moment, my gratitude for him was overwhelming, but fear followed close on its heels. I liked him. His appearance in my life had been a blessing, but how long could I expect to have his company? Certainly not past the time it took to get to Orzai and introduce me to his sister. The moment I had a clue about the location of the Fatestone, I'd have to press on to Atheon, wherever that was.

Nothing was permanent, and the things we thought were solid could be ripped out from beneath us at any moment.

Perhaps that was why I felt compelled to take his hand.

It was warm, and his long fingers wove comfortably through mine.

His eyes widened in surprise, and then he smiled, a little more shyly than the playful grin he'd worn before. He didn't seem sure what to make of me. I wasn't sure what to make of myself, either, but I liked the steadiness of being connected to him. After spending most of my life alone, I was learning to be grateful for the opportunities I got for good company and easy companionship. I'd have to work on accepting that no relationship, and certainly no love, could last forever.

I could learn to enjoy my simple and temporary connection with Hal because it didn't have to last. I'd been a fool to hope for a lifetime with Ina. Perhaps love was only an ephemeral thing that existed for a breath or a heartbeat, there and gone like a sunbeam breaking through the clouds of a storm.

After a hard day's walk east, we found the northern road. There were not many signs of other travelers. A few pairs of wagon ruts cut lines through the road, none of them fresh. I tried to keep my mind on how light I'd felt in the few moments when Hal had made me laugh. I had to focus on the future, not the past, which meant I needed to know more about Nismae.

"That Fatestone your sister is looking for—why does she still want it?" I asked. "It makes sense to me that she left the king's service after he sent her on a suicide mission, but why keep chasing the artifact that nearly got her killed?" If I didn't have problems I needed the Fatestone to solve, I would have run as far as possible in the other direction.

Hal snorted. "My sister laughs in the face of the shadow god. She's as competitive as a gladiator, and she doesn't suffer betrayal. She'll probably sell it for as much money as she can to whichever buyer lives farthest away from the king. Or see if she can figure out some way to use it against him."

I thought about telling him that Veric was my brother, the Fatestone was meant for me, and the letter was the proof, but it would pose a thousand other questions I didn't want to answer. I didn't know if I could trust him with knowledge of my powers, or the admission that I barely knew the scope of them beyond the simple enchantments logged in my journal. There were too many secrets in my past unknown even to me that I needed to unravel first. The thought of them made me ache. I hated how rootless I felt.

"Do you think your sister will expect anything in exchange for her research?" I asked Hal as we crossed a wooden bridge over a stream rushing with spring snowmelt.

"It's hard to say," he said.

"What does she care about?" If I needed to offer her something, I wanted to know what I might be able to trade her for the information I needed.

Hal looked up at the sky for a moment, then ticked off a few things on his fingers. "Achievement. Knowledge. Success at any cost. Me."

I raised an eyebrow. "In that order?"

He sighed. "You have to understand why Nismae is the way she is. Things weren't easy for us growing up. Our mother was a cleric sworn to the wind god. She joined the temple after Nismae's father died, several years before I was born."

I pushed aside the prickles of envy that he knew where he had come from and who he belonged to. Now that I knew the wind god wasn't my father, my connection to Veric was the only evidence that I might be related to anyone, but it didn't do much good for my only known sibling to be several hundred years dead.

"Nismae never cared for the temple much, in spite of growing up there. So she spent a lot of time getting the farm children in trouble for shirking their chores, or hiding from my mother in the temple library, reading. So it was no surprise that she manifested as an eagle and turned out to be a scholar—one as respected for her knowledge as she was for her sharp eyes and quick right fist."

"So you grew up in the temple as well?" I asked.

He shook his head. "Our mother died before my third winter, when Nismae was fourteen. Nismae had no desire to stay, so we left for Corovja, where she could further her studies. But the crown city was a more challenging place to navigate than she expected. It's a hard place to stay alive, much less keep a little brother safe. So she started training to become a Nightswift. All that time she'd spent hiding and sneaking and fighting with the farm children at the temple came in handy."

"But what did you do?" I asked. "How did you survive?"

"I grew up on the streets, learning to make a living stealing this and that and talking my way out of trouble. It's much easier when you're small, let me tell you. Once they stop seeing you as a child . . . well, you know how we met. You know where we would have ended up if we hadn't managed to escape and if you hadn't given those drunk guards a little extra help to forget us." He stated it calmly, like a fact, but his tense fists betrayed him.

"It must have been hard to grow up like that," I said. I wondered how, in spite of that beginning in life, he'd turned out to be so kind.

"It was," he admitted. "I've never liked to fight. Even if I were mortal and given the choice, I never would have wanted to be a Nightswift."

I understood that sentiment all too well. Neither one of us had ever wanted to deal in death. It seemed to be all I did lately.

"But Nismae . . . she had high hopes when she started working for the king. She wanted to be his chief adviser, and as it turned out, the fastest way into his inner circle was to serve as one of his elite assassins." He frowned a little, like there was some part of the story left untold.

"What about you, though? Did you work for him, too?" I didn't know why the idea hadn't occurred to me before.

He shook his head. "No. Sometimes I helped Nis, but I never worked for the king directly. It's convenient to have spies who don't need to get very close to eavesdrop on secret conversations."

"How did you feel about that?" I asked. Having been told never to use my gift, it seemed a foreign idea that Hal would be expected to use his at the insistence of anyone, especially a mortal—even if she was his sister.

"Truthfully? I hated it. I stopped doing it a few years ago. It made me feel awful to listen in on people's secrets. By then, Nismae had plenty of others to do her dirty work anyway. And more lining up in the wings. She had quite a devoted following in Corovja."

I pondered his comments for a moment. Would I have been as good as him if I'd been raised the same way? How did he know the difference between right and wrong when those kinds of expectations were placed on him as a child? And what about his own wants and hopes and dreams?

"What would you do if you could earn a living any way you chose?" I asked.

"I'm not sure." He shrugged. "I haven't ever had much choice in the matter."

Sympathy welled up. I knew what that felt like.

"Maybe I would have been a messenger, or gone into service with the crown someday if Nismae hadn't broken away from it. I like to travel. I like to move fast—and I'm good at it."

I could see it even in the way he'd behaved since we had left the Tamers' forest. He liked to be moving, and it put a spring in his step to be headed somewhere new.

"You would be good at that," I said.

"What about you?" he asked.

"Honestly, I never thought I would leave home. I was a good herbalist. I liked helping and healing people. I just wanted a family someday, even if I had to cobble it together." I thought also of Miriel's dark warnings, of her promise to the wind god. It was too late to hold to any of those now. I hoped that someday I'd be able to help people again, maybe even to have a community where I belonged.

"You aren't doing so badly at the adventuring," Hal pointed out.

I smiled weakly. He didn't know how terribly I'd failed, to end up here in the first place.

A few fat drops of rain slapped down on us, warning us of a spring shower about to come. We pulled up our hoods, ending the conversation, keeping our heads down as we hurried onward.

We stopped for the night long after the fierce ache of my feet had faded into numbness. As twilight fell we came upon an abandoned farmhouse and decided to make camp. The fields around it lay as fallow as the others we'd passed earlier in the day. Water glistened in the few furrows remaining in the dirt and reflected the gray and purple of the dimming sky. Weeds sprouted haphazardly throughout the field, having grown quickly after the recent rain.

The two of us trekked down the overgrown path to the house, only to find that most of the roof had burned away and caved in several moons ago. A family of skunks peered out curiously at us from a den they'd built in the fireplace. The copse of trees behind the house suddenly seemed like a far better option.

"I'll hunt if you can put camp together," Hal said.

I nodded, surprised he'd made the offer before me, but grateful that my sore feet wouldn't have to trek any farther. "Will a lean-to be enough?"

"Should be. The winds are most likely to come from the north or the west, but I can wake you up if that changes." He disappeared into the field as soon as I'd nodded my acknowledgment of his words.

I gathered branches and fashioned us a rustic shelter, thinking about the way he'd tipped his ear to the wind before he had answered me. I closed my eyes and tried to listen. Perhaps, like my ability to unravel Leozoar's magic, the Farhearing was simply a gift I hadn't yet discovered. I needed guidance to know what else I could do. My ability to repurpose Leozoar's magic for other things surely represented some connection to the wind, didn't it? Maybe a chance still existed that I could be the wind god's daughter. But all I heard were the last soft chirps of nearby birds returning to their nests. The hollow inside me grew deeper and darker, as vast as my uncertainty about who I really was and who I might belong to.

Hal returned with two lean hares already skinned and gutted, then quietly went about the business of preparing them for the fire. I got the blaze going as he worked, then sat beside it, chilled in spite of the dancing flames. All at once the world felt so large and so empty. My anger hadn't relented, and still I missed Ina. I longed for a shoulder to lean my head on, for something familiar. For the intoxicating peals of her laughter or the way her eyes sparkled when I knew she desired me.

I wanted to know that none of those moments had been lies.

I hung my head.

"Asra?" Hal said, putting a gentle hand on my shoulder.

"I'm all right," I said, pressing the palms of my hands into my eyes. "I'm just upset about what happened with me and Ina."

"I thought you two were . . ." He gestured, and if I hadn't still been trying to gather up the shattered pieces of my heart, I might have laughed at his awkwardness.

"Not anymore," I said softly. Definitely never in the future that stretched forward from this moment. When I remembered the hatred in her eyes, I found it hard to believe that anything—even the Fatestone—could make things right between us again. I ran my fingers over the black ribbon of the courting bracelet still on my left wrist. The time had come to take it off, but I couldn't do it. I deserved the painful reminder of all I'd destroyed. Maybe if I kept it, it would remind me never to be such a fool again.

"I'm sorry," he said.

The simple words made me tear up. Hal let me lean my head on his shoulder until my sobs eased. He never offered any false condolences. He simply existed beside me and let me be and did not ask any more questions. I wished I'd had someone like him in my old life—someone who joked with me, who wasn't afraid of me, who liked me for exactly who I was. Someone who didn't lie to me. He always just pointed out the facts, reminding me that I had done more good than I realized.

That night I slept fitfully beside him, periodically keeping one eye on the horizon. But when the birds began to sing and dawn cracked the horizon with her silver hands, there was no sign of the dragon or the girl.

CHAPTER 17

IT TOOK US NEARLY HALF A MOON TO MAKE THE journey to Orzai, even with the help of a few hitched wagon rides. The sensation of being watched haunted me whether we were alone or with others. Perhaps the shadow god had left the spirits of Amalska behind to keep vigil until I rescued them from the past. The Fatestone was the only way.

As we traveled, I got used to the pressure in my chest, constant headache, and nausea that came from not sleeping well. Even my tinctures of lavender and valerian did nothing to help. Every night when we stopped, I swore I'd sleep as though I were dead, and every night I ended up lying awake with thoughts racing through my mind as swiftly as the wind lashed through grass and trees.

Many of our fellow travelers warned us of bandits, and we were grateful to lend them a helping hand with their animals or goods in exchange for the protection of numbers. Small towns and farming communities lined the road north, most of them little more than clusters of houses and fields waiting to be tilled. Hal's way with words meant we always managed to find a place to rest—he made friends no matter where we landed.

Sometimes we heard rumors that made me think Ina had passed through these areas before us. One farmer had found a pair of his sheep torn to pieces at the back of his pasture, deep gouges in the earth around them. A merchant's young son talked our ears off for an entire half day's ride, telling stories of all he'd seen, insisting that just last week he'd seen a white bird big as a house. The stories made my skin crawl and my stomach turn. Where was she? How close was she to mastering her manifest and attempting regicide?

I wished she could know that, even now, I was still trying to save her and those she'd loved.

The hills became greener by the day as spring grass pushed up through last year's dead and flattened growth. Hal grew facial hair that accentuated his high cheekbones, and the strength in my legs increased until I wasn't nearly so sore after our long days of walking. Storms passed through, and we found ourselves running for cover, only to realize that surrounded by nothingness, we had nowhere to take shelter. So we walked on, even as ditches rushed with water and the road turned to muck that sucked at our shoes.

When the downpours became intolerable, Hal created a bubble of air around us that kept the rain at bay. Every time my mind started to storm with thoughts and memories of Ina, he told me silly stories or sang his favorite tavern songs to make me laugh. I never forgot my reasons for hurting, but they always hurt a little less because of him.

When we made camp at night, I took up singing vespers again.

Hal listened with closed eyes as I let the wordless songs of prayer temporarily wash away the soul-deep ache of Ina's betrayal—and her absence. My only moments of peace came then, as the music sank into my bones and Hal's attention warmed me, gentle and comforting as spring sunlight.

Eventually the road curved east along the Vhala River, which tumbled with the muddy water of spring snowmelt. The river cut deeper into the land as we traveled, until the road climbed so high up on the cliffs that the rush of the water could no longer be heard. Every night mist curled into the canyon like a sleeping animal, dissipating only when the sun hit the top of the sky, growing thicker and more lingering the farther north we traveled.

"We should arrive in Orzai tomorrow," Hal told me one night as we sat picking the last of the meat from the bones of our dinner. He'd been quieter than usual that day, which worried me. Perhaps asking him to bring me to his sister had been too much to demand. He hadn't even made much conversation with the farmer who had given us a ride out of the last town.

Granted, the farmer had held up both ends of the conversation just fine. His chatter had even eased my fears about Ina being too close—apparently his cousin's town many leagues to the west was all stirred up about the appearance of a dragon. The people there had never seen one and thought she was some new kind of god. The offerings of livestock, honey, and other foodstuffs must have made Ina very happy. Perhaps she'd settle there for now, leaving me free to get the Fatestone and correct the past. Then I could decide what I wanted—if the life I had thought was enough still would be.

The next morning, I saw nothing along the road to indicate that we were approaching a settled area, much less a large city. From Hal's descriptions, I had expected Orzai to be visible from some distance away. He'd told me it was almost entirely built of stone—a city of towers so tall the tops couldn't be seen from the bottoms. All I saw were mountains looming on the horizon in the northeast, and the cliff dropping off sharply on the northwest side of the main road.

"Shouldn't we be getting close?" I asked him. The sun was nearly to the midpoint of its journey now, though the mist below us still showed no signs of dissipating.

"Orzai is a city you won't see coming," he said.

Soon enough, I discovered what he meant. As we crested a steep incline, the peaks of watchtowers appeared along the side of the cliff, jutting into the sky like the uneven teeth of a predatory animal. The spires went on almost farther than I could see. Some smaller buildings clustered on either side of the road near the towers ahead, businesses set up to house those who needed a waypoint outside the city. Though the road continued to hug the cliff side, ostensibly heading northeast to Corovja, before the first tower we reached a fork that seemed to drop right off the edge of the cliff.

Hal stepped to the edge alongside the path. He teetered there with his toes hanging off, his arms spread to the wind. The sight made my heart rise into my throat, though I knew with his gifts, he wasn't likely to fall.

"It feels good to be home," Hal announced when he turned back to me.

"I thought you said you lived in Corovja, not Orzai," I said, confused.

"Home is where my sister is. Home for me has always been family, not place," he replied, his expression serious.

"You don't miss Corovja at all?" I asked. It seemed strange he could leave the city he'd grown up in with such ease.

"I don't belong there anymore." He turned away from me and walked on. "I don't ever want to go back."

Home felt so distant to me now. For a moment I let myself sink into the past, remembering the familiar walls of my cave, imagining sitting down at my table to a spring meal of warm bread rubbed with garlic, salty cheese, and fresh greens on the side. And to my surprise it was Hal I pictured there sharing it with me, smiling at me over the table and telling me about his latest adventure. A coil of nervousness tightened in my stomach. That scene would never come to be. I couldn't let myself want it.

We continued along the main thoroughfare toward the watchtowers. Turrets of varying sizes peeked over the edge, each one manned by guards who stood still as statues, their expressions unreadable beneath solid metal helmets with ornamental plumes. Behind them, arched doorways led into the narrow towers.

He stopped at the fourth turret, one of the narrower ones built into a stone building that looked as though it was held together with little more than spit, hope, and cracking mortar. A heavy wooden door covered in peeling black paint stood closed behind a man who had both the stature and evident personality of a boulder. He scowled at us—at least until Hal made eye contact.

"Nice to see you again," Hal said. "We're special members. You can let us in without a token. We know the boss, and she won't mind."

I sensed Hal's magic enveloping the guard, surrounding him in a soft haze.

The man's gaze grew glassy, and he nodded, opening the door to let us pass.

"You aren't supposed to do that. You might hurt yourself like last time!" I whispered to Hal as I slipped into the room behind him. He'd barely used his gift since we'd left Valenko, but if he overextended his abilities and left me to deal with him being unconscious again, I couldn't count on being able to bargain with other people the way I had with the Tamers.

Predictably, Hal ignored my scolding. "Welcome to Death's Door!" he said, gesturing expansively with a wide grin.

"It better not be," I muttered, smiling at Hal in spite of my nerves. We entered a large room, its windows darkened with grime. Lanterns cast dim light over heavy tables of unfinished wood, polished smooth by the passage of many drinks over their surfaces. The booths were separated by thick partitions that gave each one a sense of privacy, and the hum of conversation was quieter than I would have expected given the ill-reputed look of the place. Only the minstrel in the corner looked up when we walked in, giving us a cursory glance as she tuned the strings on her instrument.

My heart started to beat more quickly, even though I didn't know what was coming next. Hal led me to the back of the pub down a hallway lined with dark wood. At the far end, a lantern hung, casting a dim pool that barely seemed to penetrate the darkness. The moment we crossed the threshold into the hallway, it felt like a vise had closed around my lungs. Had I been human, I might have chosen to align with the wind god and manifest as a bird. I couldn't live without the open sky.

As if he sensed my discomfort and the cold sweat about to break out on my neck, Hal subtly flicked his fingers and sent a breeze circling around my head. Then he took my hand. I closed my eyes and let him lead me blindly down the hall, imagining wide skies above me and remembering all the distance I'd covered since home. It was enough to get me to the end, even though anxiety about meeting Nismae was quickly rising.

My discomfort with the enclosed place was about to reach a fever pitch when Hal plunged his hand through the stone wall at the end of the hallway as if it weren't even there. My eyebrows shot up. Somehow I hadn't expected to encounter this kind of magic in Orzai, so casually used, so much a part of daily life. It hadn't been like that in Amalska. Magic was for my tinctures, or for mortal manifests. Not for invisible walls, human convenience, or secret entrances to a city. I'd spent my life so sheltered, and it made me angry and ashamed to learn that now.

"Sometimes it's easiest to do this backward the first time," Hal said.

"Do what?" I asked.

"Jump." He tugged me through the stone wall. Magic tingled over my skin as we passed through, raising goose bumps on my arms. Someone must have enchanted the wall, perhaps one of the earth god's children. The king wouldn't waste his time installing secret doors in alehouses.

We stood at the edge of a tiny platform barely wide enough for the two of us. Below us, darkness gaped like an open mouth. I couldn't see the bottom of the shaft.

Hal tugged a bell cord hanging beside the platform, and a chime rang through the tower. A few moments later, the sound echoed from below.

"The way is clear," he said, and gestured for us to move forward. "There's a net below. I recommend pulling your knees to your chest. It's most comfortable to land on your back."

Even though my hands still trembled a little, it wasn't the height that frightened me, but the closed-in space. The whole room smelled musty and dank. I needed some fresh air.

"There's a way out at the bottom?" I asked.

Hal nodded. "A short ladder and a tunnel into the alley. Do you want me to go first?"

"I'm not afraid of heights," I said, then pulled my cloak tightly around myself and stepped off the edge.

CHAPTER 18

"ASRA!" HAL'S VOICE TRAILED OFF AS I DROPPED LIKE A stone. Though the fall was longer than I expected, the light at the bottom of the tunnel came up in a rush. I hit the net less than just a few heartbeats later, then sprang up, gasping for breath. As I grabbed the ladder leading up to a narrow door, the chime sounded from the top of the tower again, and then the ground-level one echoed close by to signal that the way was clear.

Hal flew down behind me, using a gust of upswept air to soften his fall. He grinned at me when he stood.

"Sometimes you take me by surprise," he said. I could barely make out his eyes in the dim light cast by a single gas lamp near the exit, but I could see the admiration in them.

"I wouldn't want you to get bored," I quipped.

He laughed, and the sound warmed me a little. Thankfully, the tunnel to the outside was short, and moments later I pushed through a swinging door to emerge in an alley. Fog swirled through the streets, limiting visibility to only the adjacent buildings. With how bad it was during the day, I wondered how anyone could navigate the city at night, when the light of even the brightest lamp would be dampened by the thick fog.

I dropped into my Sight. The life energy of the molds and mosses that grew in every crevice of the stone towers provided a dim outline of all that surrounded us. The buildings closest to us were so tall I couldn't see the tops—they had been carved directly into the face of the cliff. Everything was made of stone save the doors and shutters.

"Be careful—the cobblestones are slippery. Do you need my hand?" Hal asked.

"No, that's all right," I replied, ignoring my desire to accept anyway. Soon he'd be reunited with his sister and I would have to continue on to Atheon. The sooner I could accustom myself to doing without him, the better. I could get by just fine alone.

"All right." He turned away too quickly for me to catch his expression, but I might have heard a trace of disappointment in his voice—that or the fog was playing tricks on my ears as well as my eyes.

I followed Hal through the sloping streets, the mist swirling around us in ever-changing shapes. Most of the buildings were connected to one another, forming solid walls of stone on either side of us in a variety of heights and widths. Many walkways dropped off into staircases or ramps. The absence of any trees made it feel as though we'd entered a castle the size of a city, and the other street traffic felt strangely distant, shrouded in the fog, even as we passed shoulder to shoulder or a cart rattled slowly by.

Finally, we entered a narrow alley beside a cobbler's shop. Water dripped down the brick buildings on either side, gathering to form a rivulet that trickled through the center of the alley. Halfway down the dead end, a door stood in the stone side of the building. It had no handle, only a keyhole. Both the door and the side of the building were devoid of any markings or decorations, anything that might give an indication of what the place was. Hal put his ear to the lock, and I recognized the serene expression that came over his face when he used his Farhearing.

"They're here!" he said, his face breaking into the grin that had become so familiar and so warming throughout our travels. A pang of some confused emotion stirred in my breast. Somehow during our journey I had come to enjoy being the cause of that grin, and it was strange to see it painted on his face by others.

"How do we get in?" I asked.

"Like this." He grabbed a pebble off the ground and dropped it into a tiny hole near the door. A few breaths later, a click sounded and the door swung open.

"Come on," he said, and vanished into the stairwell.

I took a deep breath and plunged in after him.

Thankfully, the door led up another stone staircase instead of farther down into the earth. At the top of the third flight, we went through a creaky wooden door into an octagonal turret with a ceiling that arched to a high peak in the center. Muted conversations hummed from somewhere nearby. Windows of leaded glass in lacy patterns sparkled like gems in the light of an enormous chandelier hung from the center of the ceiling. The fixture seemed ordinary enough until I realized it was composed of several dozen glass orbs in varying sizes that burned with bright light in spite of being self-contained. In my Sight, the orbs shimmered almost as brightly as Hal, and seemed to be drawing energy from some low place in the earth that I couldn't fully see or sense.

"What is that?" I asked, staring in wonder at the chandelier.

"A prize of the crown—a magical artifact created by one of the former monarchs using the gift of the gods' magic," Hal said.

"How did it get here?" I never would have guessed I'd see a prize of the crown anywhere outside Corovja. Miriel had told me pieces like the chandelier were often presented to the revelers at midsummer and midwinter festivals in Corovja as a reminder of the monarch's power and abilities—some decorative and others deadly.

"The west wing of the palace in Corovja was redone about five years ago. One of the Swifts was able to rescue this piece for Nis before the entire wing was demolished. The lights weren't working, but her research allowed us to restore it."

Another surge of anxiety made me bite my lip. Nismae's research was deep enough to somehow give her—or one of her people—the ability to work with magic directly. It was easier to meddle than to create, and certainly possible for them to do simple enchantments, but repairing something as sophisticated as a prize of the crown wasn't something ordinary mortals should have been able to easily do. I hoped that meant she was that much more likely to know something about my abilities and which god they had come from.

"Are you ready to go in?" Hal asked.

"Of course." I nodded, squeezing the strap of my satchel with both hands where it crossed between my breasts. We were about to rejoin his people, including the sister who had raised him. Would he be the same person around them? Hal had become entirely familiar to me. We could set up or take down our camps without exchanging more than a few words, the tasks routine and companionable. I'd come to rely on our easy familiarity and was suddenly frightened it might be snatched away.

What if Nismae didn't like that he'd brought me here?

And what if she didn't know anything about Atheon or the Fatestone after all? Knowing the secrets of my origin wouldn't help me if I couldn't fix my mistakes.

Hal tugged open a heavy wooden door so we could enter the adjacent room, a rectangular chamber filled with people conversing over food and hot tea. The windows along the west-facing wall stood open, though some unseen barrier kept the fog and the chill of the air at bay. A potted plant in the corner grew wildly over one windowsill, its heart-shaped leaves turned toward what little light filtered through the mist.

"Hal!" someone said, and then everyone in the room surged to their feet, surrounding Hal, hugging him and clapping him on the back. I scanned the room, looking for Hal's sister, but I didn't see anyone who shared his features or who carried herself like a leader.

"Where have you been?" an older man asked.

"We thought maybe you finally encountered something you couldn't outrun," one of the younger girls joked.

"Just took an unexpected detour on the way home is all," Hal said, basking in the warmth of their affection. The younger people jostled Hal, showing him all sorts of improbable places they'd figured out to hide their weapons in their clothing. Was this what it felt like to truly have a family? Things had never been this way with Miriel, or even with Ina. The camaraderie in the room was so much bigger than anything I'd ever experienced.

"Yeon, where's Nis?" Hal asked the older man who had spoken first.

"Said she'll be back by the end of the week," Yeon answered.

"She didn't say where?" Hal asked.

Yeon shrugged. "Sometimes it's better not to ask."

"Well, at least we have a place to stay until she returns," Hal said. He didn't seem concerned, but of course he wouldn't be—he didn't understand the urgency of my quest.

I looked at him uncertainly, not sure how I felt about staying in this cold stone tower with all these people for days on end. He finally gestured for me to move up alongside him as soon as the others gave him a little space.

"This is Asra," Hal introduced me.

Everyone stared at me, their expressions ranging from curiosity to distrust.

"Nice to meet you," I said, even though I wasn't sure yet that was the case.

"Where'd you pick this one up?" the oldest man asked. "Not that special massage parlor in Kartasha, I hope. Remember that?" He guffawed and elbowed a slim person beside him, nearly sending them flying. They gave him an indignant look and elbowed him back even harder.

Special massage parlor? *That* story hadn't come up on our travels.

"Yeon! That was Nis's job and you know it," Hal said, shooting me a panicked look.

I raised an eyebrow.

"I was with Nismae on a mission to bring a lord's daughter back from Kartasha, and it turned out she was working in a special massage parlor there where the people provide their services . . . unclothed." He rushed through the explanation, clearly mortified.

"The kid was only twelve at the time!" Yeon slapped his knee, beyond delighted by the whole thing.

"It was very . . . educational," Hal stammered.

"You northerners are so prudish, probably because it's too gods-damned cold to take off your clothes ten moons out of the year," Yeon said with a chuckle.

A few of the other Nightswifts—also from the north, I presumed—gave him dirty looks.

I couldn't help a laugh at Hal's red cheeks.

"Asra isn't from Kartasha, nor does she work in a massage parlor. She saved my life when we ran into trouble in Valenko," Hal said, doing his best to change the topic.

"Wondered how you were gonna get out of there without a manifest, but you always manage it." Yeon shook his head.

"No thanks to you," Hal teased.

"Not my fault you can't fly like a proper Swift. Let's give thanks to Asra, who helped our Hal escape!" Yeon said, raising a mug of tea from the table.

The rest of the room toasted me as well, and though I wanted to melt into the floor to disappear from the intensity of their attention, it still felt better than the skepticism with which I'd initially been received. They beckoned us to join them at their tables, sharing their bread, cheese, and bittersweet preserves, and caught Hal up on the humorous mishaps from their latest missions. I didn't know what to say to anyone, so I kept quiet, smiled when it seemed appropriate, and stuffed myself with warm, crusty bread slathered in a thick creamy cheese veined with salty blue.

After nearly falling out of my chair the first time a bird flew through a window and took human form beside me, I soon became accustomed to the way the Nightswifts came and went—always through the window, always in and out of manifest form. They all seemed to have an affinity for the wind god. By the time we retired for the night, I'd met at least two dozen Swifts. They'd come from every part of the kingdom and every walk of life, now united by their purpose and their leader.

The accommodations turned out to be nicer than I would have guessed, largely because Hal gave me his west-facing room instead of one of the windowless guest chambers.

Besides a practical lantern, the table beside Hal's bed bore a tiny set of chimes made of hardwood—a symbol of the wind god. A painted portrait of a woman who shared Hal's deep brown skin and long-lashed eyes hung on the wall; she could only be his mother, because she fitted no description he'd ever given me of Nismae. Her hair was worn free of any braids or twists and framed her face in a halo of spiraling curls. She sat poised on a stone bench with a cluster of blossoms in her hands, but she had the slightest mysterious smile on her face—one I'd often seen on Hal. She even had the same single dimple in one cheek. I wondered who had painted it, if that person had loved her, and if the painting was something Nismae had stolen, perhaps from the temple of wind where their mother had been a cleric.

Because the Nightswifts spoke about things in a veiled way with me in their midst, it took a few days before I realized that many of the missions they referred to in passing or joked about over meals were still ones of death. Now they worked solely through Nismae instead of on behalf of the king. The lives and magical objects they stole made a lucrative business from the sound of it, though I couldn't quite make out if Nismae's goal was to obtain riches, knowledge, or something less specific. I didn't know how she managed to serve in the role of contractor, researcher, and black market merchant, all without the king's spies or soldiers catching her.

The scholars and craftsmen were a smaller and quieter group than the rest of the Swifts, from a young red-haired girl named Poe who couldn't stop looking at Hal and blushing to a man about Yeon's age who called Hal "son" even though he clearly wasn't. Hal explained that the scholars and craftsmen didn't participate in missions, but were a supporting force to help design weapons and patch up anyone who came back injured. The scholars were eager to hear what I knew of herbalism farther south, and we passed many hours in conversation. Meanwhile, the craftsmen showed Hal some enchanted blades specially designed for the Swifts. When Hal passed his hand over the bone handles of the daggers, an iridescent eagle appeared over them for a moment.

"These are very fine," he said, hefting one of the larger blades and weighing it in his palm.

A blond woman with powerful arms who had to be their smith passed him another. "I've developed a new forging technique that allows us to imbue the blades with magic. It's even better than the ones used by the king's craftsmen. The weapons respond best in the hands of someone who can sense the energies."

"Asra, feel this knife," Hal said, handing the smaller blade to me.

I shook my head. I didn't want it. The magic in my blood stirred uncomfortably at the thought of what I might be able to do with an enchanted knife. I'd done enough damage already without a weapon at my disposal.

I sighed as the conversations continued to go on without me, half wondering if I should give up on Nismae and start doing research of my own. Corovja might be a good place to start—if I could get there. But before I could start to follow that line of thought to a conclusion, Hal stood up and inclined his head toward the window, a slow smile blossoming on his face.

"What is it?" I asked, hope fluttering in my chest.

He leaned over to me and whispered in my ear so that no one else could hear.

"She's back."

CHAPTER 19

NISMAE'S RECEPTION WAS DIFFERENT FROM HAL'S, though no less enthusiastic. Admiration and respect radiated from the other Nightswifts as they greeted their leader.

I never could have mistaken her for anyone other than Hal's sister—she had the same broad shoulders, high cheekbones, and strong jawline. Her eyes were almost hazel and her skin a warm shade of amber. A long glory of box braids cascaded over her shoulders, the top half of them pulled into a twist at the back of her head. Both of her forearms were laced with scars below her rolled-up sleeves, and ornate iron cuffs adorned her wrists. The cuffs appeared strangely dead in my Sight, as though magic could not touch them.

Her serious expression softened as soon as she laid eyes on Hal.

"About time you turned up," she said, pulling him into a tight embrace.

"About time *you* did!" Hal replied, matching his sister's smile as they pulled apart.

"I see you had to do your twists yourself," she teased, reaching out to ruffle his hair. "Only about a three on the ten-point disaster scale this time."

"Hey!" He ducked, his voice indignant. "We don't all have teams of people to spend hours braiding our hair before heading out on a mission."

"You rarely even have enough hair to braid, you loon." She laughed.

Hal pouted, but his eyes still held a spark of amusement.

"And what did you drag in with you this time?" she asked, finally taking a look at me. Her eyes traveled up over my body in critical assessment.

"I'm Asra," I said, standing up straighter, trying not to worry about what else Hal had brought back with him in the past. Did she mean other things? Or other people? The thought sent a prickle of jealousy through me. It had felt special to be let in here, to meet the people he was closest to.

Her gaze didn't waver as she waited for further explanation. Fortunately, Hal cut in.

"After the attack in Valenko, the two of us got caught. Asra helped me escape, but I got sick after overextending myself tricking the guardsmen into setting us free."

"You shouldn't take risks like that," she scolded him. I could tell it wasn't the first time they'd had the conversation.

"Asra dosed the guardsmen with something and it's the only reason they didn't come after us. She could have left me after I got sick, but took care of me instead." Hal was clearly playing up what I'd done to ingratiate me to Nismae, but she didn't seem particularly moved.

"I'm an herbalist," I added. If nothing else, she should appreciate the knowledge I'd shared with her medics and craftspeople.

"I knew one of those in Corovja," Nismae said. Her dark tone of voice did not invite questions.

"Actually, Asra was the one who asked to come to you," Hal said. Then, lowering the pitch of his voice, "She's a demi, like me."

A spark of interest finally lit in Nismae's eyes. "You always manage to bring home the most interesting souvenirs from your misadventures." She turned back to me. "Let's talk about it at my table."

Everyone parted as she moved toward a table in the corner. Hal gestured at me to follow. I did so reluctantly. What did Nismae mean by "interesting souvenirs"? Maybe Nismae saw me as another useful magical object, like her stolen prize of the crown. The thought made my tension rise further. Still, I wanted to impress her if I could. Getting her help to find the Fatestone depended on it, and I needed it to change the past to save my village. I took a seat at the table, trying not to let my uncertainty show.

"Tea?" Hal asked me.

"Yes, please," I said. He poured Nismae a cup without asking her, and then filled mine. The strong aroma of bergamot wafted from our earthenware mugs.

"Your cuffs," I said tentatively. "What are they?" I couldn't figure out why they looked so empty in my Sight.

She raised an eyebrow, impressed. "They neutralize magic," she said. "Helpful when working with volatile energies. Even more useful if something magical and unpleasant is attacking."

"She won them in a game of dice in Kartasha," Hal added.

"How did you know they were something beyond ordinary?" she asked, intrigued.

"I have the Sight. I can see magic more clearly than most."

"Perhaps we can put your skills to use," Nismae said. "What can you do besides keep my brother out of trouble?"

I glanced at Hal, nervous about what might constitute "useful" by Nismae's definition. Hal gave me an encouraging look. I took a deep breath. She already knew Hal and I were demigods, so what else did I have to lose?

"I can infuse tinctures with magic to make them more powerful." I thought of Kaja. "And I didn't know it until recently, but I can draw magic from other beings and repurpose it for healing or growth." I thought back to how I'd pulled Leozoar apart. How easy it had been. How powerful it had made me feel and how some of that energy had lingered all the way until I gave the last of the magic to Kaja. I twisted my mug in my hands.

"Fascinating," Nismae said. She looked at me as though she could dissect and examine all the ways I worked.

"There might be some other things," I mumbled. I could destroy a village. Make a dragon. Create a flood that killed thousands.

The memories burned like brands.

"Asra is still exploring her powers," Hal said.

"I haven't had much training in anything beyond herbalism. I don't have any family, and I don't know who my parents are," I admitted. The farther I got from home in search of answers, the clearer it became that I knew very little about myself or anything else.

"Well, we Nightswifts care for our own," Nismae said. "Perhaps you'd like to join our family, learn the art of our trade, and exchange a bit of work for information that might help you discover the full range of your gifts? My research into those like you and my brother has been substantial, if not my primary focus. It sounds like you have skills that could be useful to us, especially with further development."

My stomach dropped as I tried to match her sharp gaze. Become an assassin? Of course an herbalist's knowledge included poisons and their antidotes, weapons like nightshade powder . . . but I couldn't. I had never wanted to hurt anyone.

"I don't think I could do that," I said. All I'd ever wanted was a quiet life as part of a community. I wanted a family, and to know I belonged, but not with those who dealt in death.

"Don't pressure Asra," Hal said.

"I'm not. I only take those who join out of loyalty and passion, not those who are coerced. Though she may regret turning down the opportunity, given what I've brought back from my latest excursion," Nismae said, a sly grin on her face. "I finally have what I need to take care of my unfinished business in Corovja."

A shock ran through me. Her plans to exact revenge on the king were already in motion?

"Are you going to challenge the king for the crown?" I asked tentatively. Or had she already found the Fatestone and figured out how best to use it to make him suffer?

"I'm not stupid enough to want the crown," Nismae scoffed.

"My family is too important to me." She gestured to Hal, then the rest of the room. "Monarchs don't get to have this. I do."

I looked around, knowing she was right. Family meant vulnerability—too many pathways to hit people where it hurt most: their hearts.

"I could have been the king's second. His top adviser. He could have had my knife and scrolls in exchange for his ear, but he chose to betray me instead." Her expression hardened so subtly it was barely visible. She'd obviously cultivated the art of restraint.

"I wish he'd made a different decision," Hal said.

"You and me both," Nismae said. She turned back to me. "So if you don't want to join us, what can I do for you?"

"Hal told me how broad your research was, so I thought you might know of a place called Atheon." I kept my voice very careful, studying her response. I couldn't bring myself to show her Veric's letter. I wasn't yet ready to give up the only extant piece of my past—and I didn't want to know what she'd make of my blood gift. No good could come of her knowing I could shape the future, or that my blood could be enchanted for mortal use.

"Heard of it, yes. Know where it is, no. It's a name that refers to one of the ancient Corovjan royal crypts," Nismae said.

Hope rose in me. "So it still exists?"

"Exists? Certainly. But most of the crypts are in interconnected tunnels beneath Corovja. Nearly all the entrances have caved in or been built over. I doubt anyone besides the shadow god knows where it is. Good luck getting her to talk to you." Nismae laughed.

"What do you mean, only the shadow god knows where it is?" I asked.

"About one hundred and fifty years ago, the fox king decided he wanted to be buried with all his monarchal treasures. He burned all the crypt maps and burial records during his reign so that no one would be able to take his riches from him, even in death. Historians and cartographers may never be able to re-create them," she said with disgust. "Greedy bastard."

"I remember you complaining about the fox king before," Hal said.

"He had very little regard for the history of his kingdom, which is probably why he only managed to rule for five years before the hawk queen took the throne. But the damage to the records was done before they laid him to rest. He planned well."

"So there are no maps of Atheon or the other crypts . . . but are there lists of what might be in them? Or other clues to where they might be?" I asked.

Nismae shook her head.

Despair wormed its way in, crushing the air from my lungs. How was I ever going to find Atheon and the Fatestone now?

"Why are you looking for Atheon, anyway?" Nismae asked.

I refocused on her, trying to gather myself.

"It's the only clue I have about someone who might be part of my family. He died a long time ago," I said glumly. I didn't want to tell her it had anything to do with the Fatestone—not yet. I didn't know if I could trust her.

"I'm sorry," Nismae said. "Family is important. It's the only thing you can count on in this world." She looked at Hal with love in her eyes, and he smiled back at her.

I tried to smile, too, but the expression wouldn't quite come.

"So tell me what happened after Valenko," Nismae said.

Hal launched into our story, with Nismae asking questions to methodically extract all the information she could. The only time she broke eye contact with him to glance at me was when he told her about how I'd chased the dragon out of the Tamers' forest. He left out my history with Ina, perhaps because he understood it was only mine to reveal.

As for Ina, I hoped she was far, far away, still in that town to the west where the merchant's cousin had seen her. Even though she was the one who had declared she never wanted to see me again, the longer we were apart, the less certain I was that I had any desire to face her either. I wanted to fix our history, but now more for myself than her. The guilt I carried might still be possible to ease if I could restore Amalska. But once that guilt was gone . . . I wasn't sure what would be left.

Now that I knew Nismae couldn't help me, all I wanted was to leave. It didn't seem like she knew any more about the Fatestone than I did, and the longer we stayed, the more uncomfortable I became. These weren't my people. I couldn't see myself becoming a part of their community.

In that moment, I wondered if Hal might leave with me if I asked him to. Perhaps seeking the Fatestone alone was a foolish quest. The subtle ways he was considerate comforted me and gave me strength to go on. The ways he'd made me laugh had filled me with the only happiness I'd known since leaving Amalska. I wasn't sure I could stand to lose him yet. But I didn't know if his sister would let him go—or if he'd even want to leave.

As it turned out, I didn't get a chance to ask.

CHAPTER 20

THE FOLLOWING NIGHT I WAS TALKING WITH POE AND the other medics and herbalists in the common room when the door swung open. I raised my head, startled, having become accustomed to the way the Nightswifts entered and exited only through the window as birds.

Nismae swept into the room with another person behind her. The figure wore an ivory robe that looked like a death shroud, the hood pulled up to obscure their face. Nismae called for silence in the room.

"Nightswifts, rise!" she commanded.

Everyone leaped to their feet.

"We have a new member. One who will make our betrayer bow before us. Meet my champion." Nismae's eyes glittered with pride.

The figure reached up to pull down the white hood of the robe, and the sleeves slid down to reveal slender wrists I would have recognized anywhere.

Ina.

I inhaled sharply, feeling as though the floor had dropped out from under me. It had been nearly a moon since I'd seen her at the top of the Tamers' cliff. She pulled down the hood of her white robe, a slow smile blossoming on her face. But this time, it wasn't the friendly smile that she'd favored me with in our past life together. This smile was small and dark and triumphant.

"This autumn, she will challenge the boar king for his crown. One day she will be your queen," Nismae continued.

I waited for someone to question Nismae's proclamations, but no one did. I could hardly breathe. How had this happened? Beneath Ina's robe I could barely make out the gentle swell of her belly. In the time since I'd last seen her, her pregnancy had begun to show. The reminder of how she'd hurt me twisted like a knife already buried deep in my flesh. I hadn't been ready to face her yet—not until I knew I could rewrite our past. Not until I'd found the Fatestone.

"Show them what you can do," Nismae said, eagerness shining in her eyes.

Ina looked around the room, seeming to enjoy the way the audience hung on her next move. I shot a panicked look at Hal, hoping to silently communicate the magnitude of the situation. Then Ina opened her palms and sent columns of white-hot flame bursting up toward the ceiling.

This time, the Nightswifts reacted. They sank to their knees with wide eyes, Ina seeming to grow taller and more fierce as they bowed before her. She fed on their worship, letting the fire surround her until she blazed bright as the sun. When the last head had bowed, she drew the fire back into her palms. Twin black marks remained on the ceiling.

"Isn't her gift extraordinary?" Nismae asked. "With a few moons of training and practice, she'll be unstoppable." Pride blazed in her eyes.

I felt faint. How had they met, and when had this training begun? Nismae's knowledge honing Ina's power would considerably even their odds against the king. I'd never given thought to what might happen if she actually won. She wasn't bound to the gods. What would that mean for the battle and the aftermath? It couldn't be good either way. I had to get the Fatestone and stop it—save Amalska, prevent any of this from coming to pass.

"I will be proud to serve as a champion for the people of Zumorda," Ina said. "We deserve better than to have our villages destroyed by bandits, to be taxed into poverty, or to be turned away after years of loyal service to the king."

The Nightswifts murmured their agreement.

"Leave us for now and return at sundown," Nismae said. "I'll have new assignments for you then." She waved a hand to dismiss her people.

Squawks and screeches filled the room as the Nightswifts took their manifests and bolted for the windows, feathers flying. In mere seconds the room stood empty save for me, Ina, Nismae, and Hal, the last feathers still drifting to settle on the floor.

In the emptiness left by the Nightswifts' departure, Ina faced me. If she was surprised to see me, it didn't show. She pointed a graceful finger at me, then looked at Nismae. "That's her. The one with the ability to change the future with her blood."

"No," I said, panic choking off any further words.

Nismae shot a look at Hal. "Why didn't you tell me?"

Hal looked at me in confusion. "I've never seen her do that. Asra . . . is it true?"

Nismae walked toward me slowly, like a puma stalking its prey. Her friendly demeanor was gone, replaced with calculating tranquility.

"Don't touch me!" I leaped to my feet and backed up against the door that led back to the street-level exit, but it didn't budge when I tugged on the handle behind me. If only I had wings like the others.

"Don't bother trying to run," Ina said. "Even if you refuse to write for us, we can still use your blood. Painted with it, I'll have as much power as a god." She still wore the same cruel smile.

"Please don't do this," I begged.

"I'm sorry, but there is no choice," Nismae said. "From the moment Invasya told me about your gift, I knew your blood could be the final key to seal the king's fate."

Hal took a step forward. "Wait a minute, Nis. You can't just hurt my friend. She doesn't even know the full extent of her powers. She should be given a choice to join the Swifts if she wants—"

"I gave her that choice already," Nismae said.

She reached for me and I screamed.

I scrambled away, but not fast enough. She slammed into me like a battering ram, sending me sprawling. My satchel fell open and vials scattered, clinking over the stone floor. My journal slipped out and fell open to a page written in Miriel's angular script.

Ina folded her arms and watched with satisfaction.

"Nis, stop it!" Hal grabbed his sister from behind, but she tore her arm easily out of his grip. His height advantage was no match for the strength she'd honed over years of working as an assassin.

"There will be time for friendship after this battle is over. Family comes first," Nismae said. She moved toward me again.

The only nonliving magical thing close enough to draw power from was the chandelier just on the other side of the wooden door. In desperation, I twined my own magic together with that of the light fixture and pulled, hard. Glass shattered in the adjacent room. I flung the stolen magic out in front of me like a shield.

"You didn't," she said coldly. She lunged, only to be repelled. "What the—"

I stood up, feeling stronger, but even as I pulled the magic closer and tried to weave it together more tightly, I knew it wouldn't hold forever. There wasn't any more energy to draw on in this prison of stone.

Instead of attacking me again, Nismae stepped back and swept Hal's feet out from under him without so much as an apology. She snatched the blade he held—one of the enchanted ones her craftsmen had forged. In one fluid motion, she whirled around and thrust the knife toward me.

The blade cracked my shield of magic in half, and as her enchanted cuffs passed through the fissure, the whole thing disintegrated. Threads of power recoiled on me like the smack of a hundred bent branches, making stars dance in front of my eyes.

Before my vision cleared, one of Nismae's hands closed around my throat.

"This would have been less painful if you'd told the truth right away," she said, and plunged her knife through my forearm into the door.

I choked on my own breath as pain shot up my arm. The agony of it obliterated my ability to string together a single thought. Blood trickled from the wound and dripped off my fingertips. Where it hit the floor, fissures formed in the stone, red cracks scattering in lightning patterns like broken ice.

"Stop moving," Nismae said, so close I felt her breath on my cheek and the brush of her braids on one of my legs. My heart pounded, echoing in my ears.

"Hal." My voice came out a weak cry. I could barely see him over Nismae's shoulder, registering the horror of what she'd done and starting to move toward me. Behind him, Ina's face remained in an impassive mask. She raised her hand and Hal's cloak ignited.

Fear for him lanced through my pain.

He tore off the burning garment, but then she set his shirt ablaze, forcing him to drop and roll to put out the flames. Nismae craned her head around to see the cause of the commotion. As he stumbled to his knees, Ina gestured to him in warning.

"Don't hurt my brother," Nismae said.

"Oh, I won't. As long as he doesn't make a nuisance of himself," Ina said, raising her hand and lighting another ball of fire in her palm. She hurled it in his general direction, forcing him to scramble out of the way. She scattered sparks to herd him toward the open window. "Can you fly like the other birds?" she asked, her voice dripping with venom.

I couldn't believe this was the girl I had once loved. What had the dragon done to her? Or was she always this way and I'd been too blinded by love to see?

"Nis!" Hal pulled a hidden knife from his boot, but Ina used her fire magic to make it blaze with heat. He dropped the red-hot metal with a cry.

Nismae's grip on me didn't waver.

"Let Asra go. I'm begging you," he said, clutching his burned hand. "We can talk about this."

"Stand down, both of you," Nismae said to them.

Ina shrugged and lowered her hands. Hal obeyed, staring at me, shifting his weight, a muscle in his jaw clenching. How could he let this happen? Was he just going to back down from his sister? And then the truth dawned on me . . . family came first for him just as it did for Nismae. Despair swallowed me whole.

Nismae whistled sharply, and two birds flew in through the window, a tiny sparrow and a red-tailed hawk. One transformed back into a large warrior, and the other was Poe, the mousy scholar girl I remembered talking to about some of my healing potions. The girl trembled when she saw Ina.

Ina grinned and snapped her teeth at her, and the girl shrank away.

"Take him somewhere quiet. I'll talk sense into him later," Nismae said, pointing to Hal. The warrior grunted something inaudible, then pulled a pinch of powder out of a bag on his belt and blew it into Hal's face.

"Hal!" I said. It came out like the yelp of a trapped animal, high and pathetic.

Hal's eyes glazed over and Ina took several steps back. They must have dosed him with peaceroot—an herb that silenced a magic user's ability to wield any power. If I had been able to think through the pain, I might have jerked my arm free of the door and hoped to bleed out. Peaceroot was rare in Zumorda but grew abundantly in the kingdom of Mynaria to the west—if Nismae's reach in work and trade extended that far, there was no telling what other horrors she had on her side.

"Damn it, I didn't mean you needed to do that!" Nismae said to the warrior.

"I'm not taking any chances after the last time he caught me unaware," the warrior grumbled. "Ended up having to fetch my weapons from the bottom of a latrine."

Nismae let out an exasperated sigh. "Fine. Poe, get over here and help me with this."

As the warrior heaved Hal to his feet and shuffled him out of the room, the girl approached us and removed a set of glass vials from her belt pouch.

"Stop," I said, my voice weak. "Don't do this." It terrified me to think what Nismae would do with my blood.

"I'm sorry," the girl whispered softly. She jerked the blade out of my arm and blood gushed from the wound. I nearly blacked out, only aware enough to dimly note that the wound wasn't spurting, which meant the knife had missed any major arteries. The wrap bracelet Ina had given me fell away—it had been cut clean through.

Nismae held me pinned against the door while Poe funneled my blood into glass vials. I stared at Ina, cycling between pain and rage. She watched the whole time as if my suffering was a show put on for her amusement. Somewhere deep inside, the cinder of anger born of her betrayal smoldered. I had never hurt her intentionally. Now she'd done it to me twice.

I deserved better than that.

They drained me until I could barely hold on to consciousness, until Nismae declared it enough. Then Nismae let me fall to the floor. I had no energy to try to fight them off or to run.

The needle pinched as Poe stitched me back together with confident hands. Nearby, Nismae flipped through the pages of my journal, her excitement growing as she read. The pit of dread in my stomach deepened. If she and her people had the ability to restore something like the chandelier I'd destroyed, I had no doubt she'd figure out how to decipher the notes Miriel and I had spent years compiling. She'd learn how to use my blood to enchant Ina and make her powerful beyond all reality—and like all enchantments, only their creator could break them.

"This is the last bit of luck we needed," Nismae said, her face glowing with satisfaction as she shut the journal and gathered my vials.

"No," I whispered, knowing it was futile. If Nismae hadn't known how to enchant my blood before, the journal would give her all the information she needed. Combined with her own research, who knew what horrible things she'd be able to achieve?

"The king won't know what hit him until I tear out his throat with my teeth," Ina said.

I weakly turned my gaze to Poe.

"Let me die," I whispered to her. If I bled enough, I could die like a regular mortal. In this state I would never be able to fight my way free of them. If they had enough peaceroot, they could keep me captive for a long time. They wouldn't care about the vicious headaches caused by use of the herb. They could drain me as many times as they wanted. Perhaps they could even figure out a way to use my own blood and potions to force me to write for them. I prayed they wouldn't use enough peaceroot to cause me to suffer the worst effects—necrosis of the fingers and toes.

Poe ducked her head and kept stitching, refusing to meet my eyes.

Nismae came over and crouched beside me.

"I wouldn't dream of letting you die." She brushed a lock of hair from my face, tucking it behind my ear as gently as a lover. "This is just the beginning."

I shuddered, and a tear traced its way down my cheek.

"This is the least you can offer after the way you lied to me," Ina cut in. "Your gift is what got us into this situation in the first place. Now it will make me queen." The iciness of her voice froze me to the bone.

Poe bandaged my arm and tipped some liquid into my mouth. The bitter tang of it numbed my tongue, making my insides feel as though they were stuffed full of clumps of raw wool. My Sight faded into nothingness until my eyes were as ordinary as any mortal's. By the time Nismae's soldier returned to the room, I couldn't even sense the second soul of his manifest in his body. I was blind.

"Put her up top by herself in one of the one-way chambers," Nismae said. She pulled a loop of keys out of her pocket and unhooked an ornate one with a green stone mounted in the center of the bow. "Bring this back to me after you leave her."

The large warrior took the key, slung me over his shoulder, and headed for the door through which Ina had come in. I tried to claw at him, to fight, to do something to get him to let me go. It took mere seconds for me to realize the futility of it. I couldn't move the fingers on my left hand. The knife must have severed tendons. Without my magic, I had nothing.

The warrior carried me up flights and flights of stairs. My arm throbbed with every step he took, and I fell deeper into shock. When I thought we could surely ascend no farther without reaching a level of the building the same height as the top of the cliff we'd come down, the warrior inserted the key into a lock in the wall and then stepped through into a tiny turret room. It had only one notable feature—an empty archway that opened to the outside. The room stood so high that I could see the far side of the canyon. We'd risen above the fog. Night had begun to fall in halos of peach and purple that cut through the sky from the west like broken promises.

He set me on top of a ratty straw-stuffed pad through which I could feel every uneven spot on the stone floor, then manifested into a red-tailed hawk and winged out into the dying light. I lay on my side, staring through the archway with tears blurring my vision. When night finally fell, the stars glittered like vicious sparks in the velvet dark, reminding me that everything that had happened tonight was just like them—unchangeable and true.

 CHAPTER 21

DAYS PASSED IN A HAZY STRING AS THE NIGHTSWIFTS let me heal. They took me to bathe often, no doubt to reduce the chances of infection in my wound. Meager portions of food were delivered twice each day, accompanied by tea that was syrupy with peaceroot and a substance that dulled my pain and left me too exhausted to do anything but sleep. I tried to avoid the tea, but they offered me no other liquid. Those who delivered it were never familiar and always left through the window by manifest as birds. My pleas to see Hal and questions about what they were doing with my blood were met with silence. Eventually I gave up speaking.

Wind eddied in the tower room, leaving me always cold. During my wakeful moments alone, which were few, my head pounded from the peaceroot and anxiety prevailed. I feared Nismae would come back for more blood, or worse, with a way to make me write the future for her. I searched every crevice of the room one-handed for some sign of the door through which we had come in. No evidence of it existed. The room was completely empty except for the chamber pot in the corner. They'd taken my satchel and cloak, leaving me with nothing but the clothes I'd come in wearing—and Veric's letter, still tucked between my bodice and skin.

My arm slowly healed but brought no function back to my hand. I mourned its loss, and in my coherent moments raged that if I'd been free, I might have been able to do something about it. There were stronger poultices for the wounds. Fire-flower tinctures that would have better dulled the pain.

The few times I was awake at sundown, I sang vespers to try and calm myself. If Hal was anywhere nearby, he had to hear them. At first I thought the songs might lead him to my prison, but it was a foolish hope.

Sometimes I dreamed of him. In those dreams he had golden wings, and we flew away from the tower, from everyone, all the way to the end of the earth. There I no longer had to worry about Atheon, the Fatestone, royal vendettas, or stolen blood. At the end of the world we lay on a bed of stardust in the empty black of the sky. He surrounded me with the light and magic of those golden wings and held me close, telling me this had all been a mistake, a bad dream, and he would never leave me again.

I woke up hating him for the lies my own mind told me, and angry with myself for longing for a fantasy that could never come true. The more time passed, the more furious I became. Why hadn't he tried to listen from afar to discern Nismae's latest plans instead of walking me right into the arms of the enemy? Perhaps he'd known all along what she was going to do or how quickly she'd turn on me if she saw a way to use me. I tried to fight the way the anger twisted my insides, begging me to turn into something as dark and vengeful as everyone who had hurt or abandoned me.

Some days the anger lost. Some days it won.

One morning in the pale light of dawn, I stood in the archway with my toes hanging over the edge. The scent of green and growing things came in on the breeze, and I knew spring had come without me. Below, the brume lay soft and white as a blanket. It almost looked as though it wouldn't hurt to fall. I spent several long minutes there, weighing whether it would be better to let Nismae take more of my blood, or to jump. I didn't want to die, but the thought of her using me as a weapon was worse. *All life is precious*, Miriel used to say. In the end, I went back to my pallet, turning to face the wall. My abilities were the only hope to change the mistake that had begun this story—the fall of Amalska. If I died, all hope of that would be lost.

When Nismae finally came, it was only to check on my wound and to declare me healed enough for her to take more blood. When she examined me, I struck at her with my other hand, succeeding only in leaving a long scratch down the soft flesh on the underside of her arm.

"I see what Hal appreciates in you," she said.

Anger flared in my breast.

"You're making a mistake," I told her.

"No, I'm getting what I want and what this kingdom needs. You'll be free to go as soon as my goal is achieved. Hal doesn't seem to think you'll be inclined to stay nearby."

So Hal was on her side, was he? Why had I ever trusted him?

Nismae stood up, indicating for the man accompanying her to bind my hands and feet so that I wouldn't be able to attack when they returned for my blood.

No apology came for what she was doing to me.

With my meal the next morning, I received water instead of the drugged tea. With no use of my hands, I was forced to lap it from the cup like an animal. Over the course of the day my headache receded and my magic began to come back to me again, but so high in the tower and surrounded by stone, I couldn't reach anything other than my own power. I only once made the mistake of trying to pull apart the enchantment concealing the door, but something made the threads of magic too slippery to hang on to. I tried everything I could think of until I had thoroughly exhausted myself—everything but pulling the life force out of the people who came to deliver my second meal. Even now, I couldn't sink that low.

Poe was the one who came to take the second batch of blood. She took it more gently than last time, using a thin slit on my already wounded wrist, carefully delivered where it wouldn't do any damage. Still, I trembled in the hands of the two warriors who held me—but this time it was with fury, not pain. How could these three look me in the eyes after I'd spent nearly a week before being imprisoned learning their names, hearing their stories, sharing with them pieces of my past? How could their loyalty to Nismae be stronger than empathy for someone who had never done them any harm?

By the time Poe moved to the fourth vial, my head had begun to swim. "Why are you taking so much?" I slurred.

"Nismae's orders," Poe said, her voice shaky.

"What is she doing with it?" I asked.

Poe shrugged, unable to meet my eyes. "Giving gifts to Invasya," she murmured.

By the time I woke up, I was alone and unbound again, and then the next morning I was served another batch of tea thick with tranquilizers. I drank it, grateful for the oblivion. I didn't want to remember Ina. I didn't want to think about where I was or what would come next.

Nismae looked happier the next time she visited me several days later. "We're so close," she told me. "You're going to be the reason for change in this kingdom."

Resentment burned in my breast as I stared at her, wishing I could tear her apart the way I had Leozoar. But her iron cuffs blocked my ability to steal her life force, and so instead she left me with a cup of water and a stronger urge than ever to walk out the open window.

Later that night, someone whispered my name in my ear.

It sounded like Hal. Another dream. Another betrayal. Another lost hope.

"Go away," I mumbled to the dream phantom.

"Wake up, Asra!" Hal said more insistently.

"Leave me alone!" I struck out with my good arm, and my fist connected with solid flesh.

"Gods!" Scuffling followed, along with several more curses.

I cracked an eye open. Hal stood silhouetted against the moonlight streaming in through the window. Even after all these hours, days, weeks, I still recognized the breadth of his shoulders, the angle of his jawline, the way he moved.

"I suppose I deserved that, but you could at least warn a person," he said.

"Why are you here?" I asked. I wasn't in the mood to be teased. The rescue I had dreamed of was too good to be true.

"To get you out. I'm so sorry, Asra. I didn't know where she had put you. I could Hear you, but I couldn't find you. There's some kind of enchantment on this room."

I wanted so badly to believe him.

"How did you find me?"

"I eavesdropped on Poe, since I knew she'd be helping Nis," he admitted. "I never would have found you otherwise."

I sat up on my pallet, my injured arm burning and prickling in the way that had become familiar as it healed. I didn't trust him. He was part of the reason I was here.

"You let her do this to me," I accused him. "You led me straight to her, knowing she might be dangerous. I thought we were friends." I never would have let anyone hurt him.

"We *are* friends," he said. "But Ina could have killed me. Would have if Nis hadn't stopped her. I saw it in her eyes. What use would I have been to you then?"

I didn't want to believe that it was true, but I had seen it, too.

I hated her.

I touched my bandaged wrist where Ina's courting bracelet had once lain. For the first time, I wondered if things would truly be better or different if I rewrote the past. Had Ina ever loved me? I thought she had, but the moment everything had fallen apart, she left. The moment I had confessed to her, she admitted to betrayal. The only person who kept coming back for me was Hal . . . and I didn't know if I could trust him either.

"I'm sorry for hitting you. I didn't think you were real," I said.

"It's all right. Like I said, I deserved it. How is your arm?" The sadness in his question was as palpable as the lumpy mat I sat on.

"My hand doesn't work the same way anymore," I said. "They've kept the bandages clean and changed, no doubt because they don't want to risk me getting a case of blood poisoning. Might inhibit them from draining me again."

"Yes, they're planning to do it again tomorrow." His voice took on new urgency. "That's why I need to get you out tonight. There's more—but I'd rather talk about it somewhere else." For once he didn't sound like he was joking.

I stood up and brushed the straw and dust from my rumpled clothes. He didn't have golden wings like in my dreams, but any place was better than here.

"Lead the way," I said.

He walked over to the window and beckoned me to the edge. We faced each other, feet no more than a hand's width from the edge. "Do you trust me?" he asked.

I shrugged. I didn't, but it wasn't as if I had any choice. I could always take off on my own after I regained some strength and got far enough away from Nismae to disappear. I didn't have to trust him to do that.

"I need you to for just a few minutes, because we're going to fly," he said. "My life will be in your hands as much as yours will be in mine."

"All right," I said. Nervousness fluttered in my stomach.

"Put this on," he said, grabbing something off the floor that looked like a cross between a vest and a harness. He helped me secure the buckles in the back, then unhooked a bundle of lines from somewhere outside the window and clipped half of them to me and the rest to himself.

"Stand behind me as close to the edge as you can get. Once we get moving, keep your legs straight out behind you and follow the motion of my body if you can. If you can't, just try to stay steady and straight." He waved his hand and called a gust of wind. A winged contraption in the shape of a wide inverted triangle dropped from the tower wall to hover before the window. It was made of pale blue fabric stretched taut over a frame made of some material I didn't recognize. A straight bar hung from the middle of it.

"What is that thing?" I asked. I had never seen or heard of anything like it.

"Meet the Moth, one of the few things I helped Nismae craft," he said. "She's made of fabric and dragon bones, and she's our way out of here."

"How did you get it from her?" I asked.

"She sent me out on a mission with it tonight. I came here instead. They won't look for it—or me—until morning," Hal said. "Are you ready?"

I nodded, not sure how to respond to the knowledge that he'd betrayed her for me. I didn't imagine Nismae reacted well to incomplete missions, much less her own brother turning on her.

Hal pulled me closer, the scent of him so clean and pure I felt as transported as I'd been in my dreams. In spite of my new uncertainties about him, the familiarity of his closeness brought such solace that I struggled not to cling to him, to bury my face in his back, to hold on and never let go.

"On the count of three, we jump," he said.

"All right." I held on to him one-handed, hoping it would be enough. I no longer had the ability to grip anything with the other, and likely never would again.

He stretched out both arms in front of him and counted to three. His muscles coiled before he sprang, and I moved intuitively with him so that we took the leap in perfect tandem. He caught the bar of the Moth, and it glided away from the tower.

For one perfect moment I felt nothing except the wind in my face and a heart-pounding surge of energy as we swooped through the sky. Was this how Ina felt when she flew? The cool night air whipped loose strands of my hair and slipped into the gaps in my clothing, but I barely noticed, too caught up in watching Hal manipulate the wind in my Sight. It was a little like dye being gently stirred into water, the way he pulled the thermals toward us to give us altitude. We glided left and then banked right as he shifted his weight, floating over the city in a serpentine pattern that allowed us to lift through the turns. After a few weeks of near blindness thanks to the peaceroot, having my Sight back made me feel alive again.

When we lost enough altitude to almost sink into the fog over the city, Hal called a more powerful gust to lift us closer to the dome of stars overhead. I never wanted to stop flying. No one could reach me here, and even without the bed of stardust, I felt as safe as I ever could have wished in my dreams.

Like all good things, it came to an end too soon, when the opposite side of the canyon came into view.

"We're going to hit the ground hard," Hal shouted. "Try to run with the momentum if you can."

We barely cleared the far side of the canyon before our feet hit the ground. We ran, stumbling over the rocks and grass, coming to a crashing halt when the Moth slammed into the ground in front of us and pitched us both into the dirt. I barely muffled a cry as I caught some of my weight on my wounded arm.

Hal unhooked me from the Moth and helped me slip out of the harness. I lay on my back for a moment, trying to ignore the buzzing of damaged nerves in my injured arm. My heart still raced from the flight, and a swell of fierce gratitude made my breath catch. Never in my life had I been so thankful to feel earth and grass underneath me. I was free. Thank the Six, I was free.

Hal bundled up both our harnesses, tying them securely to the Moth's navigation bar, then teased the contraption back into the air with conjured gusts of wind, sending it out across the canyon and over the fog to the south.

I sat up. "Why did you do that? Couldn't we have flown farther?"

"The Moth is too difficult to travel with—my magic can only carry us so far, and if I were to exhaust myself in the air and lose consciousness . . . well." He didn't have to finish the sentence. "It will be more useful as a decoy to keep Nismae off our trail. She'll notice me missing, and she has spies everywhere in this city. There isn't anywhere safe to hide in Orzai. Might not be out here either," he said grimly.

I sighed, brushing the fingers of my uninjured hand gently through the leaves of a dandelion. My satchel was gone, probably forever. Nismae had all my notes, precious years of Miriel's work and mine, details about how to enchant my blood. I had no doubt she'd succeed in doing great things, or that she'd come after us as soon as she noticed our absence. Hope seemed very small and far away, but at least outside the confines of the tower, it existed.

"I need to sit down for a minute," Hal said as soon as the Moth was out of sight.

"Help yourself," I said, still sitting on the ground.

He collapsed beside me. "I know you're probably angry with me, but you need to know what's going on. Nismae read that journal of yours and figured out how to enchant your blood to give Ina some of your powers. The shielding. The magic draining. She saw you do both those things when trying to defend yourself from her, so it wasn't hard for her to replicate. Now that she has another batch, she might be able to do more."

My stomach clenched. Everywhere I turned and everywhere I went, my blood led only to further doom and destruction.

"I should have unhooked myself from the Moth somewhere over the city," I said.

"Don't say that," Hal said firmly.

"You don't get to tell me what to say," I replied.

"No, I don't. But maybe there is a safer way to use your true power. I can take care of you if it comes down to having a headache, like I get with mine—"

"No." I interrupted him. Power always had a cost. I knew what the price of my gift was. It wasn't so much aging or pain that frightened me, but the unexpected collateral damage that always seemed to result. A flood that killed thousands. A village destroyed by bandits just so one girl could find her manifest. What would happen next?

"There's one other thing. Nismae plans to try to use the other demigods to help her. She wanted to start with me. She asked if she could have some of my blood, too, to see if there is a way to bestow my powers on a mortal." He looked out over the horizon. "I said no."

I studied his features in the moonlight—the gentle curve of his nose, the shadows beneath his cheekbones, the bold and curling eyelashes that gave his face a constant air of innocence. I couldn't tell what he might be feeling. My heart tugged me in directions at odds with my mind. It would be so easy to scoot closer to him, to rest my head on his shoulder, to lull myself into believing he'd be there when I needed him. He'd rescued me, hadn't he? But how could his loyalties lie with anyone other than his sister? How could he have led me to her in the first place? I didn't know what to believe.

"Is that why you betrayed Nismae to rescue me tonight? Because she wanted to use you?" I asked.

"No. It was that thing I Heard at the top of the cliff in the Tamers' forest." He shuddered.

"His name was Leozoar," I said. As terrible as the old man had been, I understood him. He deserved to have his name remembered by someone.

"He didn't speak to me like my siblings might have, though I suppose he once was one. More like he was muttering to himself, lost in his own mind. It was mostly nonsense, but there was so much suffering and agony in the words. If Nismae finds a way to pull the magic out of us and use it, or if we let our abilities be used by others for evil, who's to say we won't end up just like that—some twisted thing, barely more than a wraith?" Fear shone in his eyes.

"So it's selfishness, then? Self-preservation?" It was too much to hope that he'd come for me because he cared, but still, I did. I longed to mean something to him. I wanted to matter to someone—something I was less and less sure I ever had.

"No. Not just that. I don't think what she and Ina are planning is right. I don't believe in hurting innocent people like you, even if they think it's for the greater good." He spoke softly.

I swallowed hard against a surge of guilt. I wasn't as innocent as he thought.

"Do you think killing the boar king is for the greater good?" I asked.

"No. But coming for you was." He looked at me, finally, sadness in his eyes.

It took everything I had not to embrace him, to thank him for caring enough to come for me. But if there was one thing I knew, it was that I couldn't trust anyone but myself ever again. And with only myself to rely on, there was only one thing left I could do, now that I was free.

"I have to go to Corovja," I said. "I have to go to the Grand Temple and try to talk to the shadow god myself."

"That's daft," Hal said. "You can't. Nobody can enter the Grand Temple without permission from the king, even demigods. And even if you could get in, how could you get the gods to speak to you?"

"I have to at least try," I said. "I'll tell the clerics I just want to enter the temple to see if my parent will answer me. Besides, if I go to Corovja, I can warn the king so he can stop Ina and Nismae. He's the only magic user with enough power to do it. Maybe if I get on his good side, he'd speak to the shadow god on my behalf—if I can't gain entry myself."

In spite of my resolutions, guilt still ate at me. In stopping Ina and Nismae, the king would no doubt kill them both—two people who had more history with me and Hal than anyone. We both stared vacantly at the fog swirling in the valley below, the silence strangely comfortable between us. Everything had a sense of finality, until Hal spoke.

"Can I come with you?" he asked.

I looked at him, startled.

"I thought you said you never wanted to go back to Corovja." I'd half expected him to try and talk me out of what I was about to do, but not to ask to go with me.

"If the clerics won't let you into the Grand Temple, how are you going to get to the king?" he asked, his voice flat.

"I thought anyone could petition the crown for an audience," I said. Honestly, I'd hoped I wouldn't have to. If I could get the Fate-stone right away, I wouldn't need to speak to him at all. He'd never know his story had been written over.

"They can . . . but it takes time. Some people wait moons to be granted one." He sighed and looked down. "But I could get you in much faster."

"How?"

"The royal alchemist. He owes Nismae a favor that I might be able to collect on." The expression on his face told me that it might be best not to inquire how that had come about. I'd never thought about the people Hal had known and left behind in Corovja—about the whole life he'd lived before we met. The thought of him being forced to beg and steal to survive there made my heart ache. I just hoped the friends he'd made along the way weren't dangerous ones, the royal alchemist included.

"But Ina isn't your problem, and Nismae is your sister. Are you sure you want to help me?" It had to be impossible for him to take sides in this and feel good about it. Still, I wanted to take what he'd offered me. I could go to the Grand Temple and the king on my own, but it would be better with Hal by my side.

He took my uninjured hand and squeezed it just once. "Ina is clearly dangerous. And well . . . Nismae taught me that we protect people we care about. So I'm not going to let her hurt you."

This time I couldn't talk myself out of the feelings of warmth that pooled inside me.

"You're sometimes awfully moral for a thief," I said, and returned the squeeze. He grinned at my jab, then stood up and helped me to my feet.

I scanned the sky until I found the constellation of the huntress, following her lines to the tip of her arrow, bright in the northern-most part of the sky.

After a long pause, I said, "Thank you."

"For what?"

I thought about all the things I was grateful to him for—helping me out of Nismae's grasp, trying to protect me, and most of all, not standing in my way when I needed to stand up for myself. He hadn't been perfect, but he had always done his best, and done it honestly. I could forgive him for standing down when Nismae had attacked me. What other choice had he had? Forgiveness was the only thing that would keep me from leaning into the darkness and letting it become part of me. I didn't want to be like Ina, consumed by grief expressed as rage. I didn't even want her in my life anymore, not the way she was now. I wanted to continue to be a healer, not a fighter.

"For doing the right thing," I finally said.

"I'm sorry I didn't find you sooner. She'll come after us, you know." His voice was gentle, but sure.

"I know." If Nismae and Ina considered my blood part of what they needed for overthrowing the king, they would not stop hunting me until they got it.

Perhaps the shadow god truly was the only one who could help me now. I shook off a shiver and started walking toward the huntress's star.

 CHAPTER 22

WE TRAVELED NORTHWEST, CUTTING OUR OWN PATH
across the wild land, with spring keeping us company. Rainstorms
brought forth more flowers until orange, pink, and blue blossoms
dusted the rolling hills. Though Hal Farheard no signs of Nismae,
with her at our backs the road wasn't an option until we were well
clear of Orzai. I got used to being cold and to sleeping curled up
against Hal for warmth while he kept watch. Some part of me was
never able to stop looking for Ina, for flashes of light peeking out
from the shadows. During the days we mostly walked in silence, Hal
with an ear tipped behind us, and me always scanning the horizon
for white wings.

A few nights after our escape, I sat stirring the meager coals of
our fire, not quite ready to go to sleep.

"It's quiet out there," Hal said, almost as if he could hear my
thoughts.

"I know." But the truth was that silence didn't offer me any comfort either. What if the quiet came from Ina stalking us through the woods, frightening away the wildlife? The pit of dread in my stomach deepened the longer I thought of it. If we saw her, we'd have to run. And while I was afraid of her returning me to Nismae, I was also angry—and that frightened me more. She had the right to be upset with me for what I'd done, but she hadn't needed to hurt me at every turn after that. Part of me wanted to strike back, too.

"It makes me feel like Ina could be nearby when it's quiet like this," I said.

"Has she always been . . . so ruthless?" Hal asked, adding a few more small sticks to the fire.

I pondered his question. Ina's desire to be elder of Amalska had started long before she met me. She'd always wanted more for her village and herself but never had the means—until she took the dragon as her manifest.

"I suppose she's always been ambitious," I said. I touched the bandage on my wrist where her courting bracelet had once pressed comfortingly on my skin. Thanks to her revealing my gift to Nismae, my hand would never work the same way again.

"Is her ambition why you love her so much?" he asked, his voice soft, the low flicker of firelight reflected in his eyes.

I might have thought the question rude if not for the innocent way he asked it, like the notion of love itself was an utter mystery to him. Ina's ambition was part of her, but certainly not what accounted for the way she used to make me feel. Every moment with her had been charged with desire. Close had never been close enough. She made me feel light and alive. Colors were brighter, food tasted better, and the world was full of possibility with her beside me.

Now, the memories were bittersweet, tainted by the darkness of all that had come after.

I had been a fool.

"I don't love her anymore," I told him. And while I hadn't known it until I spoke the words, they were as true and firm as the earth beneath our feet. I could never go back to that kind of innocent devotion.

Hal scratched at the dirt with a stick, taking a few moments before asking his next question. "Do you think you'll ever feel that way about anyone again?"

"I don't know." I wanted to love again, but never wanted to be so in thrall to someone that I couldn't see them clearly. I never wanted to be so close to a person that I couldn't hold on to my convictions when they were near. That was what Ina had done— obliterated any ability I had to think, to feel in anything other than extremes, robbing me of the wisdom to use my magic only for the greater good and fear the consequences of doing otherwise. So here we were.

"I hope I might," he said so quietly I wasn't sure I'd heard him properly.

Our eyes met and locked for a moment, heavy with all we'd suffered together. Part of me wanted to believe the spark that had jumped between us when we first touched had meant something. More of me wanted to be careful not to feel too much.

I looked away first.

"I'll take first watch." He stood up and left the fireside instead of settling into his usual place beside me.

I sighed and lay down, pulling my cloak more tightly around me. The nights had grown shorter, and I needed what sleep I could get before Hal woke me to take the second watch. I tried not to think about what he'd said earlier about wanting to fall in love. He didn't know how terrible it could be. Still, unwanted thoughts kept rising—the crisp, fresh smell of him after we'd found a good place to bathe; how contagious his laugh was; what it might feel like if he touched me as tenderly as Ina used to.

Spindly trees reached for the sky, providing little shelter around us. I'd already sung my vespers at sundown, and now a creek murmured nearby, its susurration a delicate counterpoint to the sounds of nighttime insects and calls of other animals. Even though I was grateful to be outdoors again instead of trapped in Nismae's miserable tower, trying to fall asleep never seemed to go well for me.

At least I no longer dreamed of Ina or woke with her dream kisses tingling on my skin.

We were safe. We had escaped. We were headed for Corovja with the hope of locating the Fatestone. The chances of Nismae or Ina finding us with someone as canny as Hal keeping watch were very, very small. I could sense him nearby and was comforted by his presence.

I closed my eyes and breathed deeply, trying to dredge up memories of safety and warmth. Standing with Miriel over a potion, watching the practiced way her fingers drew the symbols of the gods to enchant it. Lying alone in a meadow on my mountain as the afternoon shadows grew long, listening to birdsongs and the sounds of animals readying for sleep. Singing vespers that no one else was there to hear, my heart taking flight on the notes.

Just as I found the quiet place between wakefulness and dreams, an owl hooted.

I huffed and turned over, annoyed that it had broken my brief moment of peace. I didn't know anything was wrong until echoes of the owl's hoot sounded in the distance, followed by a chorus of two-note poorwill calls, then the fluttering of what sounded like a hundred sets of wings as they fled the area. Familiar footsteps hurried through the underbrush toward me.

Hal.

I scrambled to my feet, suddenly wide awake.

"It's the dragon," he said, his knife drawn.

Fear crackled through me like lightning. Once she saw us, she wouldn't have trouble catching us. "We have to leave. Now."

It appeared that when it came to Ina and me, one of us would always be chasing the other.

Now it was her turn.

Hal and I hastily scattered the coals of the fire, then hurried deeper into the forest.

The heavy beat of wings sounded over the trees.

"Run," I choked out, trying to pitch my voice low. The words had barely left my mouth when fire lit in the treetops, illuminating Ina in dragon form.

"Go!" I shouted, and took off.

Hal dashed alongside me, leaping over obstacles in his path as nimbly as a deer. Overhead, Ina's wings blotted out the moon, and then cinders showered from the treetops and the smoke thickened. Green spring growth was not meant to burn.

"We have to find shelter," I said, coughing. "Somewhere she can't follow."

It seemed completely futile. The forest was thin and scrubby, the ground rocky between the trees. Even the smoke of the burning saplings provided little cover to obscure her view of us. I followed the creek, stumbling over fallen branches and rocks in the dark, hoping that the water might have carved out some small place we could disappear. Hope rose in my chest like a soaring bird, and then fell away as I burst through a final line of trees and onto the rocky shore of a lake.

I cast a glance back. Behind us, owls gathered on the bottom branches. They dropped to the ground, shaking off their manifests and drawing blades from their belts as soon as they were in human form.

We were trapped. There was nowhere left to run.

Ina swooped in front of us, hovering over the water. Her beating wings sent ripples of moonlight dancing across the glassy surface. Another plume of fire bloomed from her jaws, close enough that it warmed my cheeks and left scorch marks on the rocks just a few paces away.

"Fine! Kill me!" I screamed. "Take your revenge!" I didn't want to die, but I was tired of this game—and death would be preferable to being returned to Nismae.

She roared in response, a vicious sound that split the night.

"She's not going to kill you. You're only of use to them alive," Hal said from behind me.

He was right. She didn't advance, but the group of Nightswifts slowly tightened the circle around us.

"Don't come any closer," Hal warned them, drawing his hunting knives.

"You shouldn't have betrayed us," the leader of the group said.

I didn't recognize him—Nismae had been wise enough to send people who would have no sympathy for us. These weren't the Nightswifts with whom I'd broken bread and shared stories; they were people who had been on missions during the brief time when I'd visited their headquarters.

Hal kept his chin up. "It's not betrayal to protect the life of someone who did the same for you."

"Then we'll take you both down," another one snarled.

Ina landed on the shore of the lake, her neck arched and ready to strike.

"Give me a knife," I said to Hal. I wasn't going to let the Nightswifts hurt Hal because of me. Together we'd fight back.

Hal handed me one of his blades without question. The gesture of trust galvanized me, and I raised the weapon to stand my ground.

Hal lifted his arm and a gust of wind burst out of nowhere, kicking gravel and dirt into the eyes of the Nightswifts. They shouted and staggered back, but one of them recovered quickly enough to pull a throwing knife from the strap across her chest and take calculating aim. Hal shifted the direction of the wind and threw her off balance, but the others were already regrouping and drawing new weapons. He wouldn't be able to hold them back for long.

A few of the Nightswifts broke away from the group, aiming blows at me meant to disable and threaten, not to kill. I staggered backward, splashing clumsily into the edge of the lake, realizing too late that they'd managed to separate me from Hal. More and more of the Nightswifts gathered, pushing me back until I stood knee-deep in the water. They'd cornered me, leaving Hal to face off with Ina. As powerful as he was, he was no match for her. His magic was enough to hold off the Nightswifts, but not a dragon.

My heart raced. I didn't know what to do. I couldn't be in two places at once. I couldn't stop Ina, and I didn't have time to write our way out of trouble.

Ina advanced on him, withholding her fire in favor of using brute strength. She rose onto her hind legs and slammed into his chest, knocking him to the ground.

"Hal!" I yelled. I knew Nismae would want them to capture me alive, but I wasn't sure Ina felt the same way about Hal.

The circle of Nightswifts around me tightened.

I dropped to my knees and clumsily pricked one of the fingers on my right hand with Hal's knife. Blood began to drip and my magic surged. I opened myself fully to the Sight, barely able to hold back as my magic writhed in its eagerness to pour out and shape the future. I didn't want to risk writing anything, but I had to somehow use the power of my blood to get us away.

All around me the life of this remote place pulsed, from the gentle glow of the trees to the swirling depths of the lake. I wished it was a river and that we could jump in and be swept away. I wished the water god might put their arms around us both and carry us west to Corovja, but that was not the way water ran from here. I wished that I belonged to the water god, so that they might treat me as family.

The cut on my hand throbbed. I was out of time. I stumbled to the edge of the lake and let my magic pour into the water along with my blood.

I had never done magic this way before, directly from my body. Without the precision of ritual.

Without control.

I sketched the symbol of the water god beneath the lake's surface, trying to still my panic and weave into the magic a sense of calm, of promise, of good things—even as the battle heated around me.

An arrow splashed into the water beside me. The Nightswifts drew closer.

My hold on the tendrils of magic streaming out of me broke, taking with them the power of wind and water and all my wishes for something—anything—that would get us out of here.

"What the Hells is that?" one of Nismae's warriors shouted.

They backed away from me as the ground began to rumble.

"Fly!" another said.

The air filled with beating wings as the warriors took their manifests.

Even Ina launched into the sky.

"Asra!" Hal turned to me in surprise, his eyes widening as he caught a glimpse of something behind me. I followed his gaze. The surface of the lake rippled and rose, swelling into a wave. It rushed toward us, building into a wall that loomed high enough to block out the moon hanging full and round over the horizon.

He ran toward me, and I barely had time to grab him with my uninjured arm before the wave crashed over us. We tumbled under the water in the dark until I had no idea which way led to the surface. A powerful current tugged us down until my lungs felt as though they might burst. How had this been the result of my cry for escape? Just as I began to choke, certain I would drown, we broke through the surface atop another wave, both of us gasping for breath.

Water surged beneath us, mingling and reshaping until we sat astride a massive horse made of liquid and darkness, its mane bleeding shadows into the night. The magic of my blood held the constructed creature together, giving it form and strength. Hal held me from behind with one arm wrapped around my waist, grabbing a fistful of the horse's mane in his other hand.

Ina roared behind us, and a plume of flame scorched over our heads. My heart rose into my throat.

The horse's powerful hindquarters gathered, then launched us into the sky. Ina gave chase, spouting fire. Her wings carried her swiftly, and when I cast a fearful glance over my shoulder, it was just in time to see her snap at the water horse's tail only to come away with a mouthful of empty shadows. We needed to go faster.

I shut my eyes tightly. All I had to draw on was my own magic—or Ina's.

There was no time to be moral.

I yanked power out of her, hard. With a yelp of surprise she faltered, tumbling several lengths down until she righted herself.

I used the stolen power to feed the water horse more energy, and we ascended to a dizzying height. Behind us, Ina roared, but she couldn't keep up. Just before she vanished from sight, she turned back toward Orzai while the horse galloped northwest with great beats of its shadowy wings. Relief washed through me, quickly followed by an ache that spread through my bones until all I could do was hang on.

"It's so beautiful, Asra," Hal murmured, his breath warm on my cheek. I opened my eyes to a dark world painted by the moon. Our altitude was far too great to see any signs of life below, but a river glistened beneath us, a silver ribbon of reflected light. Soon the horse cut to the north and hills began to gently roll beneath us. But the farther away we traveled from the lake, the smaller the horse became. We sank in the sky until its watery hooves skimmed the treetops, and then finally, it set us on the ground and faded away into nothing. Its wings were all that remained, the shadows mingling and whirling around me until I could barely see Hal. They re-formed into a cloak that settled around my shoulders—a cloak made of darkness.

I fell to the ground, trembling.

"Asra!" Hal sank down beside me and put his hand on my forehead.

"I'm fine." My teeth chattered. Fever had already taken me, as it always did when my magic caused me to age. I'd hoped it wouldn't happen since I hadn't written anything, but apparently any use of my blood for powerful magic was going to shorten my life either way.

"You don't seem fine," he said, concerned. "And this cloak . . . what is it?" He took his hand from my forehead and ran his fingers curiously over a corner of the black fabric. "My Sight isn't anywhere near as strong as yours, but it looks a little like Nismae's cuffs. I can't really sense you while you're wearing it."

"I don't know," I said. "It somehow formed from the last of the water horse's magic."

"No sense looking a Sight-blocking gift cloak in the mouth, I suppose!"

I laughed weakly, which quickly devolved into a cough.

Hal sat back on his heels and thought for a moment. "What can I do to help?"

Somewhere beyond the shivering and the ache and the warm cloak of shadows closing around me, I was more grateful for him than I had ever been for anyone. He always asked. And listened. It was more than Ina had ever done. More than Miriel, either.

"Find us somewhere safe to rest," I said. "Then help me get there."

"I can do better than that. Put your arm around me." He knelt beside me so I could hook my uninjured arm around his neck, then picked me up as though I weighed nothing.

"I hope we aren't going far," I mumbled into his chest. But I couldn't help closing my eyes and giving in to the security of being carried. I felt safe in his arms and warm in the cloak. If I could just stop shaking, I'd be able to rest.

I slipped in and out of consciousness until he set me down. He settled me on the ground and tucked my cloak more carefully around me to keep out the wind, then lay down near me. Though the night wasn't terribly cold, I continued to shiver as the fever tried to burn its way out of my body. I had felt better when Hal was carrying me, but now that comfort was gone.

"Hal?" I whispered.

"Hmm?" He reached over and laid a cool hand on my forehead.

It felt so good. I took a shuddering breath. "Can you keep me warm?"

"Of course." He turned on his side and wrapped his arm around me, pulling me close.

I told myself I didn't feel anything when he did.

I lied.

 CHAPTER 23

I WOKE UP TO BIRDS HERALDING THE DAWN WITH their songs. Hal lay pressed close beside me. My fever had broken, but my bones still ached. Even my hand throbbed dully when I finally sat up, though an examination of the wound in my wrist revealed no signs of infection. I thought the cloak of shadows might disappear as the horse had, but when the sun rose over the hills, it remained on my shoulders. In the light of day it looked like ordinary fabric, if unusually fine for someone as bedraggled as me.

"Your hair," Hal said, touching the end of my long braid.

"It's a mess, I'm sure," I said. Riding a flying water horse half-way across the kingdom had probably turned it into an impossible tangle. Hal looked a little windblown himself, but he seemed to have at least had the presence of mind to pull up his hood during our ride.

"It's not that. The color is changing." Confusion was evident in his voice.

I pulled my braid around to examine it, and sure enough, several new silver hairs wound through the brown. How many years had I lost? Was there even a way to know? As for Hal, the time for anything other than honesty between us was over. He already knew what I was and what I could do.

"This is what happens when I use my blood magic," I told him.

"It gives you fevers and silver hair? I can't decide if that's better or worse than my headaches," he said, looking worried. He didn't fully understand.

"It ages me. It steals years from my life. I don't know how many." I didn't bother trying to hide my bitterness. I had no regrets about using my blood when it was the only thing I had in my arsenal, but this had only confirmed what I already knew—I needed to find Atheon and get the Fatestone before I ended up like Veric, or worse.

Hal stared at me. "Wait . . . you're telling me that every time you use your gift, it *kills* you?"

"That's about the shape of it." I looked away and wound my fingers through a tuft of grass, trying to hide my vulnerability from him. If he asked more questions, it might force me to examine a part of myself I couldn't make peace with, no matter how hard I tried. I didn't want Hal's pity.

"But—" he started.

"Come on." I cut him off. "Let's move before the sun is too high and it gets harder to tell which way is north." Thanks to the water horse, we had a lead on Nismae and Ina that we couldn't afford to waste. Judging by the lengthening days, summer solstice couldn't be far away, which meant we had no more than three or four moons before the birth of Ina's baby. Dragons healed quickly—it might take her even less time to recover from childbirth than most mortals.

I hurried to clear our meager camp in an attempt to avoid further conversation, but once we were trekking over the hills, Hal couldn't help himself.

"Asra . . . shouldn't we talk about this? Your gift making you age like that? What I wouldn't give for an antidote to my headaches . . . or even something to make them less incapacitating . . . gods. But the price of your gift—it's not reasonable."

I pulled my cloak more tightly around my shoulders. I didn't know how to have a conversation about my gift and the relationship it had with my mortality. Most demigods lived for centuries. I wouldn't—unless I found the Fatestone. I sighed, resigned. He might as well know that there was more to finding Atheon than unearthing family secrets.

"There is a way to stop it from happening," I said.

"How?" he asked. "If there's something you can do, you have to do it!"

"The Fatestone," I said with finality.

Hal stared at me wide-eyed, grabbing my sleeve and pulling me to a stop. "What?"

Without further explanation, I pulled Veric's letter out of my shirt and handed it to him.

When he looked up after reading, his eyes were filled with shock.

"This is why you want to try and speak to the shadow god. This is why you asked me about Veric, isn't it?" he asked.

I nodded. "He's the only half sibling of mine that I know of."

"'The blood of Sir Veric can make you a king,'" Hal recited. "That stupid song was true—mortals sought his blood for the same reasons Nismae took yours." He cursed a few times under his breath.

"I may not be able to do anything about my blood that's already been stolen. But if I get the Fatestone, I can use my power without worrying about how many years it takes off my life. I have to find Atheon." It was the only way to rewrite the past without sacrificing my life. The only way to stop Ina from killing the king. Most important, the only way to bring back the people of the village I had sworn to protect.

"I should have done a better job defending us at the lake. Maybe I could have called on one of the other children of the wind. Or even my father. If I'd known what it would cost you to get us out of there . . ." He trailed off, anguish in his expression.

"Ina had you cornered. You did everything you could," I said. "And compared to what I've done, that escape of ours was relatively without consequences. My gift isn't a thing that happened to me—it's part of me and always has been. Nothing will change that."

Hal handed Veric's letter back to me with a furrowed brow. I met his gaze with a challenge in my eyes, daring him to feel sorry for me.

"Thank you for getting us out of there. You were amazing and I'm grateful," he said.

An unexpected smile bloomed on my face, and for a moment I forgot the way my bones ached with every step.

"You're welcome," I said. The pain would fade—at least this time. A few strands of silver hair wouldn't kill me. Not yet. And he knew that too.

"So, onward to Corovja?" he asked.

"Yes," I said resolutely.

We crossed many hills and valleys, ignoring the rumbling in our stomachs, both of us glancing over our shoulders as though we expected Ina or Nismae to swoop in at any second, but the skies stayed clear and the sun grew warmer until we reached a town. It was little more than a few weathered houses alongside a narrow dirt track, far enough off the main trade route that it felt like a safe place to stop for a couple of days to regain our strength before pressing on to Corovja. The people greeted us with trepidation until we clarified that we were just travelers, not bandits or tax collectors—apparently their village had experienced problems with both. The more of the kingdom I saw, the less certain I was of the king's objectives. Was he as negligent as Ina seemed to think based on his treatment of Amalska's plea for help? Or was his answer to banditry taxing his people so that there was nothing left for the bandits to steal? And why did he want an amulet that would grant him eternal life?

Hal traded two days' work in the fields for the things we needed—some soap, packs, and a few warm meals. The villagers thought the two of us were married, and though it made me blush scarlet the first time someone made the assumption, I found that I didn't mind. I liked that it meant we shared a bed, chaste but close, his familiarity keeping me grounded. He was there to soothe me when I woke one night from a nightmare, murmuring gentle words to me and brushing the sticky hair out of my eyes. I clung to him like he was the only person who mattered, then tried to forget the intimacy of it in the morning, when daylight reminded me that we were only temporary allies.

With each day, the aches in my body slowly faded back into something more normal. While Hal spent a few days planting spring crops alongside the villagers, I occupied myself by teaching the children where to find herbs and what could be made with them, replenishing my supplies of the most basic poultices and tinctures that might be useful. The children's incessant questions kept my mood from souring with the knowledge that Nismae had my satchel, journal, and silver knife—the only three material things that mattered to me. Dread raked its claws down my back every time I thought about what she'd do with them.

By the time we moved on from the little village, I was glad to be alone with Hal. We fell easily back into a rhythm of chores and routines as we traveled; he hunted dinner while I gathered herbs for seasoning and built our fires or shelter. He fixed breakfast and I cleaned up our campsites to erase all evidence of our passage. Knowing that Nismae had spies everywhere, we stayed clear of the main road even once we found it, exchanging the quicker pace of road travel for the shelter of the ever-taller trees so that it was harder to see us from the sky.

Deep in the mountains with Corovja only a day's walk away, we made camp in a meadow full of swaying grass and bright wildflowers. After our night there, silver light had barely kissed the horizon when I woke to Hal stirring the coals back to life for our breakfast. Waking to the rush of the river brought a certain kind of bliss, the music of water singing me into the day.

I rolled onto my side and watched Hal from beneath lashes still heavy with sleep, admiring the strength of his arms as he nestled two large stones into the embers of last night's fire. He readied a rabbit with confident hands, slicing and adding spices to the meat while the rocks warmed. As the rabbit cooked, he tossed horseroot with other greens and herbs. Finally, he arranged the meal on a leaf as large and round as a plate. Our food may have been scavenged from what we had at hand, but his care with it turned it into something truly special. The knowledge that he'd done it for me made a warm feeling spread through me, enough to counteract the morning chill.

The intoxicating smell of the rabbit had me half sitting up, but before I could call to him, Hal turned away from the fire and strode over to a patch of yellow clover blossoms just opening to greet the sun. He murmured something inaudible over the flowers and then severed a single stem. I lay back down and closed my eyes, turning my face into my cloak to hide the smile threatening to give my wakefulness away. His footfalls hissed through the dewy grass to where I lay, and then he crouched down beside me with the leaf plate in his hands.

I opened my eyes as if seeing him for the first time.

"Good morning!" The words were the same as every other time he'd spoken them, but when I looked at the plate he'd brought me, with the single yellow flower alongside my food, I knew that this time it was different.

Until this moment I hadn't let myself see the way he had begun to look at me—as though my dirty face on the other side of our campfire in the morning was dawn breaking over the edge of his world.

I held his gaze. His eyes were so warm, so soft, so dark—as

comforting as a starry summer night on the mountain. They were now as familiar as the place I had grown up and thought I would always call home.

I picked up the flower between my fingers and twirled it, the yellow center bright with pollen. A pointless thing, that tiny yellow flower beside my breakfast, but I knew when he cut it that it was meant to be a promise.

He smiled. Even on someone who had been raised a criminal, love looked so innocent. I smiled back, though somewhere in the dark recesses of my mind, Ina's ghost rose unbidden, pressing the jagged blade of betrayal into my back. I pushed the thought away.

"Thank you," I said. Then I traced the flower down his nose, leaving a trail of yellow dust on his brown skin.

It felt good to be loved.

It felt good, for once, not to be the one who loved more, who loved too much, who loved until she lost herself in something beautiful and reckless and dangerous that could only end in blood and death.

CHAPTER 24

WE REACHED COROVJA THE NEXT MORNING, AND FOR the first time in days I felt the tiniest bit of hope. The Fatestone was somewhere here—I just had to find it and the key to changing the past would be mine. The city began in the bottom of a valley filled with farmers' fields, growing more densely populated as it angled up the side of a mountain that Hal and I had only just begun to climb. The sun shone down on us and a cool breeze nipped at our heels as we walked. Big fluffy dogs with tails that curled over their backs trotted alongside most of the people passing by. The road carved a wide path through the city until it made a sharp switchback to the palace at the top, a castle made of white marble that glistened in the sun almost as brightly as the snow-capped peaks beyond it. The Grand Temple stood not far from the castle, its stained-glass windows glimmering like gemstones in the sunlight.

"I'd almost forgotten how spectacular the views are," Hal

remarked. Tall trees, green hillsides, and patchwork farmland seemed to extend for leagues in the valley below.

"They'll be even better from the Grand Temple," I said. The promise of finding the Fatestone put a spring in my step, and I kept a keen eye on my surroundings, as if clues to Atheon's location might suddenly appear. Along the road, narrow shops pressed tightly together, advertising everything from jewelry, books, and crystals to food and herbal spirits—anything a person could want. The smell from a bakeshop wafted over us, making my mouth water.

"How does anyone get around in the winter?" I asked. Even though it was summer, the altitude was high enough that old snow still lingered in shadowy nooks the sun couldn't touch.

"Snowshoes, ice cleats, dogsled, and, if it gets really bad, tunnels." Hal ticked off each one. "Sometimes it's deep enough that the smaller houses get buried."

The homes and storefronts grew taller the closer we got to the top of the mountain. Instead of simple A-frames like the homes in Amalska, these were built with roofs angled only on one side, pitched to the south to deflect the worst of the wind. Even the most humble of buildings bore snow cleats tacked into them. Glittering prisms hung from the eaves, catching sunlight to cast rainbows on the whitewashed walls of other structures nearby.

"What are the crystals?" I asked.

"Festival decorations," Hal said. "They're put up during solstice week to celebrate these longer days, and to spread and reflect that light across the land to show that it is what makes all things possible."

"Back home we decorated with flowers," I said. My throat

tightened at the memories. In Amalska, our midsummer celebration had been about the bounty the land gave us. This year flowers might still have sprung from the ashes, but they would have only had empty houses and burned rubble to grow on. No one would have trained vines to climb over trellises so they could burst into fragrant bloom for solstice. No one would be there to weave wreaths of blossoms to crown the heads of those ready to be married. There would be no feasts or stories—only silence, and the animals and land reclaiming the structures that remained.

I tried to close my heart to the sorrow. We had other tasks at hand—ones that might change the fate of Amalska. The shard of hope that I might find the Fatestone was all I had to hang on to, so I clung to it with all my strength. I fondled the edge of the bandage on my arm. I still couldn't grip anything. The injury was a constant reminder of what the world wanted from me—my blood—and what I needed to fight against.

"There were flowers at the solstice festival here, too," Hal said. "See?" He pointed to a low stone wall decorated with garlands that had begun to wither.

"If solstice has already passed, our time is running out. There's no telling when the first autumn snow will fall and Ina will be able to challenge the king." I frowned, trying not to give in to the growing dread in the pit of my stomach. There wouldn't be much time to come up with a new plan if I couldn't get into the Grand Temple or Hal couldn't get what we needed from the royal alchemist.

Also, I couldn't help worrying about Ina's child. If it was solstice week now, Ina's pregnancy had to be entering its final moons. How would Ina take care of a baby while preparing for battle? What would happen to her baby if I couldn't change the past—or if I could?

"Fair point. Let's go this way. I still don't think they'll let you into the Grand Temple, but I know a shortcut to it if you're determined to try," he said, tugging me into an alley.

We climbed up the alley stairs and emerged onto another street that soon joined the road leading south of the palace toward the temple.

As we drew closer, I began to appreciate how truly staggering the Grand Temple was. A high stone bridge with towering archways led through the castle wall to the temple. Some kind of ordinance must have prevented any of Corovja's wealthy citizens from building homes too close to it, because a public park filled with trees, flowering bushes, and verdant grass decorated the hillside beneath it. It extended all the way up to the thick walls of the castle.

As Hal and I passed through the park, we cut through a grove of apple trees covered in pink and white blossoms. Hal playfully nudged their branches with a breeze so that the petals rained on us like snow. I couldn't help but come to a stop, closing my eyes to let the falling petals brush over my cheeks for just a moment.

"I like it when you do that," Hal said, his voice warm.

My eyes snapped open. "Do what?"

"Disappear into that place you go sometimes." He plucked a few petals from my hair. "It's like you've found a place or a moment where you're at peace with the world and know you belong, and you're happy."

Warmth crept into my cheeks. In the moments of stillness when I felt most at peace, Miriel had scolded me for daydreaming, and Ina had often grown impatient to carry on with whatever we were doing.

That Hal saw more and appreciated it . . . that meant something. Part of me wanted to follow where it led, to take his hand—not because I needed it but because I wanted to, because maybe a spark would leap between us again, just as it had the first time we met.

"The entrance is ahead," Hal said, interrupting my thoughts. He pointed to a path of cobbled flagstones leading to wide stairs climbing up the hill at least two stories to the entrance.

At the top, a cleric stood between two heavily armored guards. Behind her stood the closed double doors, with large, ornate hinges stretching across them.

"It's a pity I can't use my compulsion on those sworn to the spirit god," Hal said.

"Why can't you?" I asked, not that I wanted to risk him passing out on me again.

"Those with vows to the spirit god are attuned to emotions and feelings. They can sense truth and lies. And in a way, my compulsion is a sort of deception—a way of getting people to lie to themselves."

I knew spirit users could turn people's minds against them, but I hadn't thought about truth sensing or that Hal's gift was a kind of lie.

We climbed the stone steps until we stood before the temple doors. My mouth was dry with nerves. The cleric carried a staff of knotted wood, and her hair was braided into an intricate arrangement adorned with golden beads and bells to symbolize her devotion to the spirit god.

"Hello, my children," the cleric said gently. "The temple is closed to visitors without permission from the crown."

"But I'm a demigod," I said. Shouldn't that give me some right to speak to the gods? One of them was a part of me. "The woman who raised me said my father was the wind god, but that has since been proved untrue. Now I know nothing about my history or parentage. This is my only hope of finding out the truth."

The cleric's gentle expression grew firm. I remembered a moment too late what Hal had told me about the spirit god and those who followed them.

She knew I wasn't telling the whole truth.

"Without the king's permission, you may not enter alone. If you are in Corovja for winter solstice, you may enter at that time to make offerings," the cleric said.

"I don't have that long," I said. Winter solstice would be far too late. The more time that passed from Amalska's destruction, the more complicated it would be to unmake history.

"Asra, come on," Hal said, tugging the sleeve of my cloak.

"But—" I couldn't give up this easily. "Isn't there some other way to gain official entry? Please, if there is any way at all . . ."

"No. Not unless the king gives you permission," the cleric said. "Guards?"

The guards standing on either side of the door moved up to flank her.

"We need to go right now," Hal said, pulling me harder this time. The nervous expression on his face made me give in.

Reluctantly, I turned away from the cleric and followed Hal down the stairs.

"Maybe we can come back later," I said. "Sneak in."

Hal shook his head. "Look back."

I glanced over my shoulder and saw why he'd wanted us to leave.

The number of guards had multiplied, and the cleric was speaking to them.

"They can't have thought we were a threat," I said, incredulous.

"It's the most sacred place in Zumorda. Everyone knows no one is allowed in, so when someone tries to go against that . . . it draws attention. The king will probably already know about what just happened long before we make it to him, but I didn't want us to end up getting an audience with him as criminals rather than petitioners."

"He would treat us as criminals just for asking to enter the Grand Temple?" That seemed extreme.

"It's better not to push our luck," Hal said. "We should talk to the alchemist. He'll be able to get us in to see the king."

"Onward to the alchemist, then," I said. Convincing the king to speak to the shadow god was now my only hope.

I hoped he wasn't as monstrous as Ina and Nismae thought.

CHAPTER 25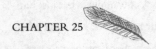

THE GATE TO THE CASTLE SAT IN A WALL SO THICK
that the tunnel beneath it took us at least twenty paces to walk
through. The stones of the wall had been polished smooth so that
it would be almost impossible to climb, and the top was crowned
with a sharply slanted roof studded with snow guards sharp as the
heads of pikes. Soldiers stood evenly spaced along the walls, swords
buckled at their waists and small knives sheathed down one side of
their chests. Though they stood still as statues, their eyes sharply
watched all the foot and horse traffic heading in and out through the
yawning gate.

The closer we got to the building itself, the more troubled Hal's
expression became.

"Are you worried the king will recognize you?" I asked.

"More that he might think I'm complicit in what Nismae and
Ina plan to do to him." Hal's voice was grim.

"He might make that assumption." I wasn't going to lie.

"And then what?" he asked.

"I vouch for you," I said, holding up my bad arm. "She hurt me. Given that, there's no reason he shouldn't trust my word. I'm not going to throw you at his feet and run to save myself. That's not what friends do."

"You don't really need me, Asra. You're strong on your own. Once you get your audience with the king, you won't need me. You have a gift that can make anything possible. You don't even seem afraid of what it might cost you. The future is yours." His eyebrows drew together with worry.

I tugged him to the side of the road. "Is that what you're worried about? That I'll abandon you?" The thought was ludicrous after all we'd been through together. His sister might never forgive him for stealing me from her. He'd made that sacrifice for me.

"Maybe a little," he admitted.

"I want you with me," I said. Of course I could survive without him, but that didn't mean I wanted to. Not now, not yet—not unless I had to when I used the Fatestone to rewrite the past. I'd grown too used to sleeping with my back pressed against his, to waking up to his smile, to the way he made up nonsense words to popular tunes to make me laugh and our hours on the road pass faster.

"You have me." He smiled a little, and his expression reminded me of the look in his eyes yesterday morning. We approached the castle doors. I felt no bigger than an ant in front of the building. A line of people spilled down the front steps, winding back and forth and continuing around the circular drive nearly all the way to the entrance we'd just come through.

I stared in dismay. "This is how many petitioners there are?"

"Yes, and their names have likely been on the ledger for a moon. This must be their scheduled day. Follow me." Hal led me toward a smaller gate leading into one of the gardens surrounding the castle.

The palace garden had just blossomed into summer. Rhododendrons of every color burst with flowers, and butterflies hovered around daphne bushes that carried a scent so intoxicating and rich I slowed my footsteps to linger in the perfume. Hal and I passed by a wall of green that twisted into a hedge maze filled with shadows. I hoped the king paid as much attention to protection as he did decoration.

Ahead of us a stone walkway lined with columns led to a set of double doors into the castle. A uniformed woman stood guarding the entrance, her hand already drifting toward her weapon when she saw us coming.

"This entrance isn't for petitioners," she said.

Hal stood up straighter and smiled warmly at the stony-faced guard.

"We are here to clean the king's commodes," he announced with extreme formality.

I barely held back a snort of laughter.

"Of course," the guard said, giving in as the tendrils of Hal's magic seduced her. "Right this way." She ushered us through the door and then waved a casual good-bye.

"The king's commodes?" I whispered, stifling a giggle.

"Why not? Soldiers are so easy. They're used to being ordered about," he said, grinning. He led me through the hallways with the ease of someone familiar with the layout of the grounds, making me wonder how much time he'd spent there when he was younger. How close had he been to the king?

Our footsteps echoed on the stone floors, which were tiled with intricate mosaics made of different kinds of granite. A short flight of stairs at the end of the walkway led down into the cavernous main atrium.

"Not much has changed," Hal said, smiling as my jaw dropped.

I looked around in awe. "I've never seen anything like this."

The ceiling towered over us, supported by dark-stained beams. The walls and floor were smooth, white polished marble laced with copper except for one notable exception—what looked like a huge pool of blood that spanned the center of the room, edges splattering out toward the walls. As we came closer, I saw that it was an illusion—just a different kind of stone. But strangely, it wasn't inlaid. The rock was simply white and then red, with no discernible break.

Pages, nobles, and other members of the castle staff hurried about their business, paying no mind to the two of us. Calls rang out from various chambers around the edges of the room, and benches were lined with petitioners awaiting their turns to enter.

"How did they get the floor like that?" I asked Hal.

"You recall the first monarch?" he asked.

"The bear queen?" She had been the founder of Corovja, the first to raise her banner over Zumorda.

"The earth god took a particular liking to the bear queen, long before Zumorda was a unified kingdom. She led the queen to this very spot and gave her the power to wield earth magic to carve the rock out of the mountainside. When the bear queen did so, a perfect slab of white marble was revealed, and the bear queen declared it the future crown city of Zumorda. But before she and the earth god could so much as put walls up around the site that would one day be this castle, a challenger came for the crown—just as the first flakes of autumn snow began to fall. A snow leopard challenged the bear queen, one who not only believed this territory to belong to her but also wanted to keep the kingdom the way it was, with separate regions governed by different rulers.

"At first it seemed like the bear queen would lose. The snow leopard called on two champions to fight before her—one who manifested as a snowy owl, and the other a ram. The snowy owl pecked out the bear's eyes, and the ram gored the bear almost through the heart. By the time the bear finally faced the snow leopard, dawn was rising. The bear was exhausted, her fur matted, her eyesight gone so that she had to rely on her other senses. But she had the favor of the gods, and that made all the difference.

"So as the sun rose, not only did the earth god lend her support, but the wind picked up and lent his hands. The fire god split the clouds with his sunlight. The water god gave the bear queen a pool in which to cleanse herself before the final ritual. The spirit god healed her wounds and gave her strength to go on, and the shadow god waited for the snow leopard with open arms. When the bear tore out the leopard's throat and she bled onto the floor, the earth god sealed the leopard's blood into the stone to remind all future challengers how the kingdom of Zumorda would be won forevermore—by the one with the greatest gods-given strength."

I had heard the story of our kingdom's origin, but not like this. Not with the evidence right in front of me. It was a stark reminder of the power of the gods, and how much they gave to a ruler. How could Ina and Nismae ever hope to stand against this without a god at their backs? It was madness. An uneasy feeling crawled through me as I wondered what they were doing with my blood. Would it be enough to make Ina equal to the king in battle?

Hal pointed to a splatter near the edge of where the red stone met the white. "Doesn't that look like a bear print to you?"

I looked down, and sure enough, the marking looked just like the imprint of a bear paw tracking fresh blood onto the white floor.

"It does," I said with terrible wonder. I had always known our kingdom was ruled by the strong and that the crown was taken by battle to the death, but seeing it here, having it be real, it hurt. In the deepest place in my heart, I wanted the world to be a place of kindness, not brutality. Maybe Ina was better suited for the crown than I had ever imagined.

"This site is almost sacred now," Hal said. "It remains intact to remind us of the first battle—the first stone upon which our kingdom was built."

"A kingdom built on blood," I murmured. How apt.

CHAPTER 26

THE DEEPER WE WENT INTO THE CASTLE, THE QUIETER it became. Fewer servants hurried past us, and the patrolling guards changed from pikemen in heavy armor to those wearing a variety of smaller weapons and lighter armor for mobility. The maze of passages seemed as though it would continue forever, until Hal led me down a narrow hallway. An unmarked wooden door stood at the end, shrouded in shadows.

Hal knocked in a careful rhythm.

We waited, the silence stretching out. I fidgeted uneasily. Hal hadn't told me much about the alchemist, only that the man owed Nismae a favor Hal intended to collect on. What if he refused to help us?

"Are you sure he's here?" I asked a few moments later.

"I'm sure. Sometimes he gets too absorbed in what he's doing to answer the door. Other times, he falls asleep over his work." Hal tested the door, but it was locked. "Well, I suppose I'll have to handle this like I used to." He pulled out a thin tool with a curved end and inserted it into the lock. After a few practiced twists of his fingers, the door swung open on silent hinges.

I cast a nervous glance over my shoulder, but the hall was empty behind us.

"Come on." Hal gestured for me to enter.

The sun slanted in through a wall of arching windows on the south side of the room. I squinted until my eyes adjusted. In front of the windows stood a series of workbenches covered in an astonishing array of plants, vials, and substances, many of which I recognized. My heart lifted. Something about the place gave me comfort—perhaps the familiarity of so much of what surrounded us. I knew what to do with these things.

"I'll go see if he's in his rest chamber," Hal said, pointing to a different door than the one we'd come in through.

"I'll wait here," I said, curious to explore more of the workshop.

Shelves spanned from floor to ceiling on the wall opposite the windows. The contents seemed entirely random. Some books stood vertically and others were stacked haphazardly on their sides, all interspersed with empty vials in every size, baskets filled with dry herbs, and other relics I didn't recognize.

I moved closer to the shelves, intrigued by something purple and sparkly. My breath caught when I saw what it was. A dried fire flower lay preserved in a glass tube, the petals in far more ragged condition than the ones I'd carried in my satchel before Nismae stole it. A pang of longing struck me. I missed my cave, my flowers, my herbs. I missed home, but it felt so distant now.

"He must be somewhere in here," Hal said, reentering the workshop.

Something screeched overhead, and I nearly jumped out of my skin. An enormous raccoon peered down from a high shelf, squinting at us. He stretched, yawning as though we'd woken him from a nap.

I backed up swiftly to Hal's side. The raccoon clambered down, knocking over a couple of empty bottles on his way. He scurried across the room, already transforming before he reached the workbench, taking the form of a tall man wearing simple robes, the sleeves carefully bound to keep them out of his potion work. He had salt-and-pepper hair shorn close to his head and facial hair of a similar length and color. As soon as he donned the spectacles sitting on the table, his expression changed from one of sleepy confusion to shock.

"Eywin," Hal said, his tone neutral. Only a twitch in his jaw betrayed his feelings.

"Phaldon!" The man walked toward Hal slowly, adjusting his glasses as if to be sure his eyes told the truth. Sentiment swept over his features until he seemed near tears. "I can't believe you returned."

Hal glanced away, like he couldn't stand to see the genuine emotion on the man's face. "I'm here to collect on the debt owed for Nismae sparing your life." His voice was flat.

Eywin looked genuinely confused. "What debt?"

"Nismae told me you chose the king over us, but she spared you when we left because you're our blood." Hal's brows drew together.

A shock traveled through me. "Wait, you're related?" I'd thought Nismae was the only mortal family Hal had.

Eywin peered at me over his spectacles. "I'm sorry, we haven't been introduced."

"My name is Asra," I told him.

"Very nice to meet you, dear. Yes, to answer your question. Hal and Nismae's mother was my older sister."

"It doesn't matter now," Hal said bitterly. "Not when you were partly responsible for sending Nis on a mission meant to kill her."

Eywin sighed. "That was a misunderstanding."

"How was it a misunderstanding to let the king send your niece on a deadly mission you knew about?" Hal asked, his voice rising. "You're part of the king's council. Only a monster would send his own niece to die."

I touched Hal's arm softly, trying to steady him. His life in Corovja had been far more tangled up with the crown than I'd ever known. Hopefully there weren't any darker reasons why he'd kept this from me, but now I understood why he hadn't wanted to come back. Guilt made my heart heavy. He'd returned only to help me.

"That's not quite what happened," Eywin said, rubbing one of his temples. "I had no say over anything Nismae was being assigned to do outside this workshop. I never wanted any harm to come to her."

"She worked for you. She said you knew about the mission," Hal accused.

Eywin took a slow breath, looking up as he exhaled. "I knew about the mission, but I don't believe it was intended to kill her. The king is no fool—he would never have tried to do away with his best assassin, or an assistant he knew I needed to continue my research. The king has always valued my work, especially the advances Nismae and I made together. He's been good to our family. She didn't have to turn against him."

I glanced between them, wondering what research and advances Eywin was talking about. I pulled my shadow cloak more tightly around my shoulders, grateful for the magic shielding it provided. There was no telling what this man could see in me, and like Nismae, he seemed to be someone who would know how to use my blood if he could get his hands on it.

"So you weren't part of the group that sent Nismae to the Zir Canyon," Hal said. His voice faltered. "She said you were. She said that's why she left—because everyone she trusted had turned against her."

"Oh, Nismae." Eywin shook his head sadly. "Always with the secrets. Always with the story that suits her."

"What are you talking about?" Hal asked, confusion and hurt battling in his eyes.

"Your blood," Eywin said. "The thing your sister so foolishly abandoned the crown to protect."

A wave of horror flooded through me. Why had they wanted Hal's blood?

Hal stared at him, equally aghast. "But . . . why?"

"While seeking the Fatestone, we discovered its creator was able to use his blood to temporarily bestow his magical gifts on mortals. We hoped to see if it could be done with other demigods, since there hasn't been a bloodscribe in hundreds of years."

I swallowed hard, my throat tight. As far as I knew, my blood was the only kind that could be used that way, but I wasn't about to volunteer that information. Thankfully, neither was Hal.

"The king has the power of the gods. Why would he need those abilities?" I asked.

"Channeling the magic of the gods drains the king's energy. If someone used demigod blood to give him additional abilities, he wouldn't have to use his own magic to sustain those enchantments or waste his own capacity on channeling those gifts from the gods. Thus, his power would be augmented. An enchantment is sustained by the caster, not the person or object imbued with magic," Eywin explained.

I knew that last part from my work with Miriel, but I hadn't thought about what it would mean in the heat of a battle between Ina and the king. Dread made my stomach heave. Nismae would use my blood to strengthen Ina, while the enchantments themselves would be tied to her. That meant the only way to break them would be to kill or disable Nismae during the battle. Would the king know to do that? Could Hal stand aside and let that happen? Could I?

"So we decided to see if we could replicate those kinds of enchantments using the blood of other demigods," Eywin continued. "Naturally, the king's councillor Raisa was happy to lend hers. Nismae was sent to the Zir Canyon to obtain a vial of blood from an earth demigod the king had known as a child, which is where she was ambushed."

"You're saying the king had nothing to do with that ambush?" Hal said doubtfully.

"I'm saying that *I* didn't," Eywin responded. "That snake who used to train the guard corps was part of it. He had the king's ear more than I did. But what's important is that the last demigod we knew of—"

"Was me," Hal said, his understanding dawning.

"Yes. I had planned to discuss it with you and ask your permission before Nismae returned from her mission," Eywin said.

"But I was in the city those days, down in the Miners' Quarter...."

"Yes. We couldn't find you, and then Nismae came back early with a few more scars and a lot less loyalty to the king. Then she found out we planned to ask for your blood. That was the end of that," Eywin said, his voice weary. "I'd hoped she'd always be a loyal servant to the crown. And you, too. You could have had whatever you wanted if you'd stayed."

When I'd worried about trouble catching up with us in Corovja, I hadn't imagined anything as complicated as this. From the expression on Hal's face, I guessed he hadn't either. He'd clearly never known what Nismae had sacrificed to protect him from being experimented upon.

"Nismae didn't offer me that choice," Hal said.

"No, she didn't. She should have told you the truth and let you make your own decision," Eywin said. "Maybe you could even have talked some sense into her. But she'll never be pardoned now—not after killing the other members of the group who sent her on that mission."

Hal paced back and forth, struggling to absorb everything Eywin had said. "But why did she lie to me? Why did she try to turn me against the king, too? Why did she tell me you owed her a debt for letting you live?"

"I'm sure she believes a debt is owed, just as she believed she was doing the right thing by hiding things from you," Eywin said.

"As for the debt, I got Nismae the job here because she's smart and she's family. It was the least I could do for my sister's children, and I know she would have done the same for mine if I'd ever fathered any. I wouldn't trade the years I spent with you, or even Nismae, for anything. There is no debt to collect. If you want my help, all you have to do is ask."

"I want to believe you," Hal said, his voice wavering.

"Then do. You're still family. You're the closest thing to a son I'll ever have." Eywin opened his arms.

I stood frozen. Somehow I'd ended up in the middle of a moment that should have just been between them.

Hal stepped forward and hugged Eywin.

I sighed with relief, ignoring the familiar prickle of envy that always came from seeing the closeness of other families. Not having my own never ceased to sting.

Eywin looked at me over Hal's shoulder, favoring me with a gentle smile. "Now, please let me properly speak to this lovely person you've brought with you," he said.

Hal stepped back and swiped at his eyes, pulling himself back together.

"Asra's an herbalist, like you, and a demigod, like me," Hal said.

Eywin broke into a grin. "It's always a pleasure to meet someone interested in the herbal arts."

"It's a pleasure to meet you," I said, grateful that he seemed less interested in my parentage than my skills.

"We came because we urgently need an audience with the king. Nismae is planning to come for him," Hal said.

"We're here to warn him what he's up against," I added.

Eywin sighed heavily. "I trained Nismae myself, at least in the preparation of herbs and enchantments. There's nothing she can pull that I won't expect."

I decided to cut to the chase. "Have you ever seen a dragon?"

Ewin looked at me more intently. "Not since I was a little boy."

"That's what's coming for you. A dragon with no allegiance to the gods—a dragon who wants to take the throne," I said. "Ina destroyed an entire bandit caravan in the space of fifteen minutes. It was as easy for her as breathing." My stomach heaved as the memories came roaring back. We weren't safe yet. We might never be—not until I found the Fatestone and made things right.

A flicker of uncertainty passed over Eywin's face. "I heard about that."

"I saw it happen," I said, swallowing bile as the memories came back.

Trees sending tongues of flame into the sky.

Ina's wings, shimmering silver in the flickering light.

Snow, red with blood.

"There were no survivors," I said. "But we know what Nismae and Ina are planning. We can help the king prepare."

"Then you certainly do need to speak to him," Eywin said. "I'll see that it is arranged."

Eywin scheduled a meeting with the king for the following day and saw that accommodations would be prepared for us in the castle for the night. He and Hal made plans to catch up over supper, which I declined, and then a page arrived to escort us to our rooms.

Hal and I followed the page in silence, as my worries ate one another, each larger than the last. Hal had been reunited with his uncle, we had obtained an audience with the king, but so many unknowns still hung over us. We didn't know exactly when Ina and Nismae would arrive in Corovja. I didn't know if the king would heed my warnings about them. And I still didn't know how to find Atheon. Worst of all, I had begun to worry that the Fatestone might not be able to solve the ever-deepening web of problems I felt trapped in the center of.

"Your room, my lady." The page stopped in front of a door.

I paused at the door, casting a glance at Hal.

"I will escort you to your room at the far end of the hall, sir," the page said, turning to continue down the corridor.

"I'm sure I can find it myself," Hal said. "Thank you for your help."

The page bowed and hurried off to his next errand.

"Asra, can we talk for a minute?" Hal asked.

I nodded and pushed the door open.

Hal followed me into my small room, which was simply but thoroughly furnished. I collapsed into a chair, no longer sure how I was going to make it through the rest of the day.

"Do you think we can trust my uncle?" Hal asked.

I looked up, startled. "You'd know better than I."

"Apparently not," he said, frowning. "I wish I understood why Nismae lied to me. It's so unlike her. She keeps secrets, yes, but she doesn't usually lie."

"She thought she was protecting you," I said. But I knew how he felt, what it was like to find out someone close to you had withheld the truth, only for it to end up shaping your life forever. If not for Nismae, he might have stayed in Corovja, his life entirely different, and in the end, she too had asked for his blood. "It would be nice if people were always honest."

"That's the gods-damned truth," Hal agreed.

"If the gods had told me where I came from, I would have known how dangerous my gift could be. I might have known how to protect myself and my people. I could have stopped the bandits from killing everyone." The gods still could have dumped me on the mountain and left me in Miriel's care, but they could have also told me the truth. My hands trembled as guilt for all the destruction I'd caused rose up to drown me again. I could still smell the burned flesh of the people I'd meant to care for. I could still see the smoldering embers of Amalska when I closed my eyes.

"Asra," Hal said. "Stop. I wish you knew more about your history, too. But you can't change the past."

My heart froze. The look in his eyes was so open and earnest. He believed in my goodness. And while he seemed to be more the sort to offer a helping hand when it was convenient and then be on his way, I knew it wasn't like that with us. For some time now, he'd been offering me somewhere to fall. Somewhere to be safe. But I couldn't be. Not with the fate-twisting blood that ran in my veins.

"But that's the thing," I whispered. "I can."

"What?" He looked at me in confusion.

"That amulet your sister and the king have been seeking—the Fatestone—gives a bloodscribe the ability to use their gifts without cost, by preserving life instead of draining it away." I took a deep breath. "Because the Fatestone offsets the cost of my power, it will also give me the ability to rewrite the past. I can undo the mess I've created from the very beginning."

Hal stared at me in shock. "That's why you want the Fatestone . . . not to be able to safely shape the future, but so you can rewrite the past."

I nodded. "I have to. I could stop all of this before it starts. I can save the king without a battle ever having to take place. Nothing else will stop Ina now. With Nismae behind her, what other choice do I have?" I begged him to understand.

"But . . . if you rewrite the history of it all, I never would have found you," he said, his voice soft.

"But the kingdom . . ." My voice trailed off.

The sorrow in his expression gutted me—the way he couldn't quite meet my eyes. We had known each other only a few short moons, and yet I was important enough to him that he didn't want things to change. He didn't want to let go.

The knowledge cut like a knife. I so desperately wanted to be able to give him what he wanted. Sometimes all I could think about was how it might feel to put my arms around him, to bury my face in his neck, to find out what his lips tasted like. But I couldn't have that. Not when death seemed as tied to my gift as my own shadow was to my body.

I stood up and crossed the room to him.

"I wouldn't like that part either, but would it be so bad? All I've managed to do is get you into trouble. First we get detained by guardsmen, then nearly killed by Tamers, and you had to betray your own sister all because of me. Now you're back in Corovja, when you never wanted to be." I had to get him to understand that changing the past was for the best.

"Betraying Nismae was a choice I made. Don't you understand? I chose you." He met my gaze then and took my hand, his expression fierce.

"Hal . . ." I liked the warmth of his hand in mine. I didn't quite understand why he was so upset, or how choosing me now meant we shouldn't do what we could to save the kingdom at any cost. Wasn't that why he'd saved me—because he knew I was the best hope of stopping Ina?

"I should go," he said, dropping my hand.

Fear fluttered in my chest like a caged bird. I didn't want to be separated from him, much less when he was upset with me. We'd been together for so many weeks. It would be strange to wake up alone.

Hal looked into my eyes, and for the first time I saw a hint of the same worry line Nismae had between her eyebrows.

"I make my own decisions," he said, his voice firm.

"I know you do." I understood that, but it didn't mean that helping me hadn't hurt him.

"It is my choice to be here with you right now. In this room, in this castle, in this city I didn't think I ever wanted to return to," he said.

"I know," I said, my voice smaller. I swallowed hard.

He moved toward me, so close that energy crackled between us. I longed to close the last of that gap, to ask him to stay in my room with me even though it was a terrible idea. I wanted to fall asleep with him, but not like we had on the road, back to back for warmth and safety.

Now I wanted to learn the planes of his face by tracing his

jawline and cheekbones with my fingers.

I wanted to learn his body by meeting it with every curve of mine.

I wanted his dimpled smile to be the first thing I saw when I woke up.

He cupped my cheek in his hand. My eyes fluttered closed as I leaned into his touch, my heart hammering so loudly I couldn't think. His other arm wrapped around my waist, tugging gently until I stood pressed against him. The moment our bodies connected, heat burst in the pit of my stomach.

I opened my eyes, hoping it might help me fight what was happening, but I might as well have tried to dam a river with a handful of pine needles.

All I could think about was how badly I wanted him to kiss me.

He whispered my name, then traced his thumb over my lower lip. I trembled in his arms, searching his dark eyes for some evidence that he understood why we shouldn't do this, something I could latch onto and use to fight my own feelings.

All I saw was tenderness, and a hot flame of desire that mirrored my own.

"Asra, you need to understand that I will always choose you."

Without waiting for me to respond, he turned and walked out the door.

CHAPTER 27

AFTER DINNER, WHEN I HAD MY EMOTIONS BACK UNDER control, I searched for Hal. Something had to be done to ease the tension between us—some acknowledgment of what we felt, or an agreement made as to what to do about it. How was I supposed to respond to his declaration that he'd always choose me? I couldn't give him that in return—at least not until I atoned for the mistakes I'd made and the deaths I'd caused. Couldn't we work together to help the kingdom first and put other things aside?

In spite of an hour of checking all the places I thought I might find Hal, and enlisting the brief help of a page, I wasn't able to find him. I spent the night barely able to sleep in my comfortable bed even after a warm bath. In the morning I knocked on Hal's door, but if he was there, he didn't answer. I didn't get any more time to look, thanks to being chased down by two palace servants sent to do my hair and provide appropriate clothing while my travel garments were laundered.

I didn't see Hal until a page gathered us both to meet with the king.

On our way we walked in awkward silence, hardly looking at each other. An extension of the red marble in the great hall led us all the way from the atrium through a set of gilded doors to the dais where the king's throne sat, flanked by a heavily padded chair in which his chief adviser rested, an old woman introduced to us as High Councillor Raisa.

The king's robe swept the floor, the exact color of the blood-splashed stone. He was a man of medium build with iron-gray hair and pale eyes almost the same shade. His guards hovered nearby like twin shadows. One bore two long knives tucked in her belt, the other a short sword. Between the two athletic guards, the king appeared rather unremarkable. I don't know what I had expected, but it wasn't this. He didn't look like someone who held the power of all Six Gods at his fingertips. I could sense the second soul in him, but not any indication of the gods' magic.

In contrast, even without sinking fully into my Sight, so much power radiated from High Councillor Raisa that it was almost impossible for me to look away. A few wispy strands of white hair escaped from beneath the hood of her robe, which was lined with thick fur in spite of the mild temperature. Her eyes were clouded over and milky, almost a pale violet, with no pupil showing at all. She had to be blind, but she still seemed to know exactly where Hal and I stood. It had to be the Sight. Like me, she could sense the magic all around, and she didn't need her eyes to do it. I wished I had my shadow cloak instead of the floor-length dress I now wore.

Hal and I both fell to one knee in front of them and bowed our heads.

"Rise," said the king. We stood up, Hal letting me brace myself on him with my uninjured arm.

The king's gaze landed on Hal, and he smiled. "Ah. Phaldon. Welcome back. I don't suppose your sister is likely to follow your example?"

Hal stared at the floor. "I imagine not, Your Majesty."

"A pity. She's missed around here—there was so much more good we could have done for the kingdom together. I miss her voice on the council."

My eyes widened in surprise. After everything I'd heard, I had expected the man to be vicious. Brutal. Uncompromising. Instead he was soft-spoken and welcoming. Regretful that he'd lost Nismae—not vengeful like she was.

Hal didn't say anything, but his jaw clenched. I had to redirect the conversation away from Nismae before it could turn antagonistic.

"Your Majesty, we are here to warn you that you are in danger," I said.

The king sat back, seemingly unperturbed by this news. "Who are you, and what leads you to believe that?"

"I am Asra of Amalska, Your Majesty," I said.

He raised his eyebrows. "We were not aware anyone had survived the double massacre there."

"I'm not the only one." I took a deep breath. Yet again I would have to detail my failures and be judged. Worse, I had to do it in front of Hal, which was somehow more terrible than confessing to the king alone. I could already anticipate the emptiness that would come when Hal's affection for me slipped away as he understood that I was responsible for even more death than Ina. He knew about my gift, but he didn't know how many I'd killed using it.

I told the king my story from the very beginning—how it had all started when I'd tried to help Ina, how our village had been destroyed, how Ina's manifest had been born solely for revenge. He listened as I spoke of my confession to her, and how it had done nothing to slow her mad quest to kill him.

At that point, the king held up a hand to stop me. "Anyone who challenges me will die. No one can hope to defeat me without the backing of a god, and from what you describe, your dragon friend does not even have a gods-blessed manifest. I am the one who wields their power. Even if by some miracle she did manage to kill me, it would destroy all of Zumorda. She'd have nothing left to rule."

Shock kept me silent and frozen as Raisa nodded in slow agreement.

Nothing left to rule? That couldn't mean what it sounded like. My knees went weak.

"What do you mean, Your Majesty?" I asked.

"The bond with a god that allows a challenger to take on the reigning monarch is the same one that gives the winner the power to rule the land when all Six Gods grace him with their power. It is that power which gives me the ability to conjure fire out of air." The king raised his hand and a column of white flame roared from floor to ceiling, far more powerful than the ones Ina had produced in Orzai.

I grabbed Hal's hand, needing his solidity to help stand my ground.

"It is the power that allows me to call storms." The king raised his other hand and a rumble of thunder sounded overhead.

"It gives me the ability to bring forth anything I want." He opened his palms and a gray dove fluttered into the throne room, desperately seeking some way out.

"It gives me control over life and death itself." With a gesture from the king, the dove fell to the floor and then a sprout burst out of the dead bird's open mouth, leaves unfurling in search of sunlight.

With each of his acts my fear heightened. Even with Nismae's help, how could Ina ever expect to take on someone with powers granted by all of the gods?

"If an imposter took the crown and broke the bond between the monarch and our deities, the gods would abandon our kingdom. They would take the gifts they've granted Zumorda with them. Manifests. Magic that imbues all living things with power. Demigods like you would no longer be able to live here. Zumorda would end up like Sonnenborne—a godless wasteland." The king gestured at a servant to clean up the body of the bird lying in the middle of the throne room.

Horror flooded into me until I thought I might be sick. If the king won, Ina and Nismae would both surely die for their transgressions. If by some chance Ina defeated the king, the entire kingdom would be destroyed.

This was so much worse than I'd ever imagined.

Nothing I could do seemed like enough to help—except

stopping the battle before it could start. I needed the Fatestone to change the past.

"As you see, there is no way your friend will be a threat to me, dragon or not," he said, clearly misinterpreting the dismay on my face as fear of his abilities.

"Your powers are formidable, Your Majesty, but I'm afraid it's not that simple," I said.

I explained Ina's recent alliance with Nismae, and what had happened in Orzai, tugging back my sleeve to show the scar where Nismae had stabbed me. Both sides of the wound had healed into an angry red line that had only just begun to fade.

"Ina has a gift of fire somehow bestowed by the dragon she took as her manifest," I continued. "With the notes in my journal and the blood stolen from me, Nismae will be able to give some of my powers to Ina. There's no telling how powerful those enchantments will make her, and they can only be removed by the person who performed the enchantment."

The king leaned forward. "And do you know how to perform these same enchantments?"

"It would be easier with my notes, but yes. I can probably anticipate some of what she might come up with. But I don't know what else she's capable of," I said. Nismae had devoted her life to research of magic and magical objects. All I had was Miriel's training, and I didn't know how comprehensive it had been.

"Raisa, tell me what you see in this girl," the king said.

The High Councillor stared through me as I trembled beneath her otherworldly gaze. The energies surrounding me shifted, as though disrupted by an eerie caress.

I shuddered.

"It is as she says," Raisa finally said in a voice creaky as old wood. "She speaks the truth, and the power of fate runs in her blood."

"If a challenger is coming, we must prepare," the king said. "And if they have your blood, there is only one way to avoid any unpleasant surprises your dragon friend might have in store." He paused.

My stomach turned inside out.

"You want my blood, too," I whispered. This wasn't why I'd come here. How could he ask this of me?

"Yes." He nodded gravely. "It would be wise to match them enchantment for enchantment. Use your knowledge and blood with Eywin's research to ensure that nothing they come up with is more powerful than the protections placed on me. Together we can ensure that the dragon will be defeated, and Nismae will be punished for her betrayal."

A sliver of doubt worked its way beneath my skin. If his magic was as powerful as he claimed, why would he need my blood, too? I thought of the dove he'd conjured, alive for only a moment before the sprout burst out of it.

Perhaps I was meant to be the dove. My sacrifice for his gain.

Hal edged forward as though he intended to stand between me and the king. I grabbed his hand to stop him.

"It's not only for me, Asra. Your kingdom is at stake," the king said, almost as though he had read my mind.

I didn't want to do it.

Thinking about giving away my blood dredged up memories of being locked in Nismae's tower room. If I never had to use my blood or my gift again, it would be too soon.

"Let me be clear, Asra," the king said. "I don't want to see you hurt. You would be helping of your own free will. You and Eywin could work together on the enchantments. You'd have food and lodgings provided—everything an esteemed guest of the crown could expect. Perhaps you might find that you like it here. Eywin could use a new apprentice." He steepled his hands and waited for my response.

I waited to feel reassurance, but it didn't come. I looked at Hal, whose stormy expression made his feelings very clear. He didn't want me to do this, either. But with a battle looming that I'd have a part in whether I wanted to or not, the only thing I still had control over was my search for the Fatestone. If I pledged myself to the king, perhaps I could get him to speak to the shadow god on my behalf to find out where Atheon was. He wouldn't have to know why. The only hope of preventing the battle was to get the Fatestone and fix all this before it came to pass.

"Your Majesty honors and humbles me with this offer. I pledge my service to you for the battle to come," I said. If finding the Fatestone later meant an unwelcome sacrifice now, so be it.

Hal looked at me as though I'd lost my mind.

"The royal scribe will make a record of your acceptance," the king said.

His words settled on my shoulders with weight almost too heavy to bear. "Thank you, Your Majesty."

Hal and I bowed and were escorted out. I left the throne room with sweaty palms, my heart racing. Hal walked ahead of me so quickly that I could barely keep up.

"Wait! We need to talk," I said. I needed him to weigh in on my plan. I wanted to discuss what had happened between us the night before.

He sighed, and walked faster. "I'm tired."

"Like the Sixth Hell you are," I said. It was only midafternoon. "What's wrong with you?"

"Nothing!" he said, but he didn't look at me. I followed, trying to figure out how to confront him. It would have helped if I'd had any idea what was wrong. All I knew was that by the time we entered the hallway that housed our chambers, I couldn't bear everything that lay unspoken between us any longer.

"Come into my room," I said, still searching for the right words.

"Why?" He folded his arms.

"Please," I said. After what we'd just been through and the risk I'd just taken, I was too exhausted to argue with him.

"Fine." He marched into my room and I followed, closing the door behind us. He took a seat at the vanity beside the bed, looking comically gangly atop the ornate stool where I'd sat to have my hair done that morning.

"I need your advice. I don't want this to just be about me. I want this to be about what's right for the kingdom," I said.

"It looks like it's going to dragon dung either way," Hal said. "Maybe we should get out of here while we can. Head for Havemont or Mynaria. Some of my demigod siblings seem to think that's a good idea—a few of them have left for Havemont already."

I quashed the anger threatening to rise.

"Could you try to be helpful even for a minute? Is that too much to ask?" Running away wouldn't solve anything, not when the fate of people we cared about hung in the balance. Not when the entire kingdom could be at stake.

"I didn't bring you here so you could sacrifice yourself to the king. So he could bleed you out worse than my sister did," Hal said.

"I have no intention of allowing him to do that," I said. "Nismae said to ask the shadow god where Atheon is. If I make myself useful to the king, I can get him to ask the shadow god for me. I can still find the Fatestone and rewrite everything."

"You're out of your mind. You've just pledged yourself to his service. That gives you no leverage at all." Hal's voice rose.

"What other choice do I have left? I have to at least try." I threw up my hands in frustration. "Ina can't be reasoned with. The king has a plan, and honestly, I'm a little more comfortable helping someone who isn't going to stab me out of nowhere—especially if it means there is a chance I can stop the battle from ever happening in the first place. If you have a better idea, speak up now or stand by my side."

Hal hung his head, massaging his temples with his hands. "I don't have any ideas. All I can think about is what will happen if you rewrite the past."

"You mean, when I fix things to prevent the king from killing Nismae and Ina or our kingdom from going up in flames?" I asked, not bothering to rein in my sarcasm.

"You don't understand!" Hal leaped to his feet. "Yes, I want those things, but I don't want a world to exist in which I didn't meet you!"

I stared at the floor, the frustration shocked out of me.

"Have you thought through that possibility?" he asked. "I suppose you have, if you're so certain this is what you should do.

Maybe you even have some half-baked plan about how we might stop everyone who lied to us from doing so in the first place. Restore harmony, birds, butterflies, all that nonsense. Make the world all perfect and pure the way you think it should be." He gestured broadly, rolling his eyes.

A fresh surge of anger made me rise to my feet. "Stop it. I never said that!"

"Stop what? I'm telling the truth. You have this rosy vision of what the world should be, and it just isn't like that. You can't make everything perfect. That isn't how the world works. Where there is light, there must be darkness. Goodness only exists in contrast with evil. Until you accept that, life is only going to disappoint you."

"Life has already disappointed me," I said bitterly, trying to flex my injured hand. The fingers barely moved.

"So what are you going to do about it?" He stepped closer. "What are you going to do about the fact that life is terrible and unfair?"

"I need the Fatestone. If I can get the Fatestone, I will have the power to decide." The more I thought about it, the more certain I was. I didn't know exactly what the version of the past was that I wanted to write, or how to mitigate collateral damage, but I knew I could change the past to create a better present than the one I lived in now, even if evil and darkness still existed in the world.

"Giving your blood to the king was really the only way to do that?" he said darkly. "And now you're definitely going to write a new past?"

"Stop pushing me. I don't have everything figured out yet," I said. I had done the best I could under the circumstances.

He stepped nearer, almost as close as he'd been to me last night. "I need to know. Your fate is tangled up with mine now. At least until you rewrite the past."

I stood my ground and met his eyes. They were warm and liquid dark, looking for answers I didn't have. I took a deep breath and then another, feeling the tension between us crackle like sparks from a fire. Part of me wanted to throw him out of my room immediately so I could think clearly again. Another part longed to close the distance between us.

"I don't want this," I said, deflating.

"Don't want what?" His expression grew colder, more guarded.

"To be at odds with you," I whispered.

Some of the tension ebbed out of his body, and an emotion flickered over his features that I couldn't quite put a name to.

"I missed you last night. I could hardly sleep," I admitted. A tingle of nervousness raced through me.

I saw a shock travel through him. Then he smiled sadly, just the smallest upward quirk of his lips. "I missed you, too."

We sat down side by side on my bed, tentatively renegotiating the closeness that had once been so comfortable and easy between us. His body was coiled, not like he wanted to spring up, but as though all he wanted in the world was to be closer, and when he got closer, it still wouldn't be close enough.

I knew that feeling well, and had never thought it would find me again.

"This is hard," he said. He looked away, and seeing him was like gazing into a mirror of how Ina had made me feel sometimes.

"Hal," I said. Just his name, a simple thing. I let the fingers of my uninjured hand wander down his jawline, then brushed my thumb over his lip like he'd done to me the night before. His breath hitched in a way that made a dangerous wave of desire rise in me.

This time, I couldn't help but give in.

I leaned forward and tentatively pressed my lips to his—and then my breath caught, too, as he tenderly kissed me back. We explored each other with the familiarity of friends and the strangeness of new lovers, delighting in the ways we could make each other feel with even the lightest touch. Eventually he laid me down on the bed, his deepening kisses waking a slow-burning hunger in me that I thought had died forever after Ina broke my heart. And just as surely as Ina had shattered me, he put me back together piece by piece until the fire he ignited burned brighter than any she had ever called.

For the first time since leaving Amalska, I felt like I was coming home.

CHAPTER 28

THE NEXT DAY, AFTER A BRIEF TALK WITH EYWIN about my abilities and what we hoped to accomplish, he sent Hal and me into the forest to collect some of the rarer ingredients he hadn't managed to cultivate in the castle gardens. I took the opportunity to steal kisses from Hal all afternoon as we walked hand in hand through the woods, though the Fatestone was never far from my thoughts. The sounds of the city faded into a distant hum the farther away we went.

"So what's your plan for the battle beyond what you've discussed with Eywin?" Hal asked.

"To make sure it doesn't happen," I said. I'd have to endear myself to the king quickly if I wanted him to speak to the gods on my behalf. I doubted he'd do so for any random person who asked, but I was the only bloodscribe. His inkmistress. I wasn't dispensable, and that gave me power.

"But what if you can't find the Fatestone? What if you can't stop it?" He frowned. "I don't like all the ways this could go wrong."

"I at least have to try." I had to stop Ina from killing the king—especially now that I knew the kingdom would fall apart if she did. "If I try, there's still hope of bringing back the people of my village. It's my fault they're gone."

"You can't know that for sure," Hal said.

"No, I know I'm responsible. I can feel it," I said, my voice resolute. But he'd seeded doubts. What if I changed the past and the bandits destroyed Amalska on a different day? What if Ina found the dragon on her own, and some other series of events led her to embark on the same murderous quest she'd ended up on now? Could I truly plan for all those potential paths?

"If you're sure this is the only way, then I'll help you if I can." He kissed me again, and a little stab of guilt went through me when I pulled away and saw some of the levity gone from his eyes. I knew he was thinking again about what changing the past might mean for us.

"Either way, it isn't a bad idea for me to work with Eywin and start using the smaller aspects of my gift again." I'd given it some thought. The king was right. I needed to be able to match Nismae enchantment for enchantment, whether the battle came to pass or not. This was my blood. My gift. I had to be its greatest master. I had to be the most powerful, not because I wanted to hurt anyone, or needed to win, but because this power belonged to me. Only I could make sure that it was used for good and not evil.

"What kind of tinctures do you think will be helpful in the battle?" Hal asked.

"I'll show you," I said, tugging him to a stop. A little rush went through me. I could give him the ability to see the world through my eyes. I could give him another little piece of myself. I'd never really shown him the smaller things of which I was capable. I'd spent so much time hiding, so much time fearful, that my power had been only a dark, blurry thing hanging over us. Not something useful or real.

"Show me what?" he asked, puzzled.

"Everything. Close your eyes." I pulled out the little knife Eywin had lent me, dredging up memories of how I'd done this for Miriel. It was the spell we'd used most often—the one that gave her the ability to use my Sight.

I nicked my finger, then traced the symbol of the spirit god on Hal's forehead, freeing a few tender threads of my magic. I opened myself to the Sight, letting my blood form a pathway from him to me.

"Look around," I told him.

He opened his eyes and gasped.

The magic twisted like vines through every living object, rising through trees to meet the sky in cascades of light. It lived in the souls of the people of the castle, whom I could barely sense as more than moving pinpoints in the distance.

"This is incredible," Hal murmured. "My Sight is nothing like this. Is this how you see the world all the time?"

"When I choose to." I shrugged, but a little thrill ran through me just the same. I liked sharing this with him.

"Can't you use this to help find the Fatestone?" he asked. "It's like you can see anything."

"Probably, if I knew what I was looking for." I sighed. We were barely any closer to having clues about Atheon than when we'd arrived.

"So you think asking the king to speak to the shadow god is the only way to get more information?" Hal asked.

"It's all I can think of. Nismae had access to the palace archives for years. If there had been any evidence pointing to the Fatestone's location, she would have found it," I said. Nismae was many things, but she wasn't stupid.

"True. Nis was always very thorough in her research. It was more of an obsession for her than a job," he said.

That was what I was afraid of. What other things had she figured out how to do with my blood since we'd last seen her?

We walked through the forest, Hal using his temporary Sight to more quickly find herbs, marveling at everything around us.

When dusk began to fall and Hal's Sight began to fade, we turned back toward Corovja with full packs. I let my own Sight wander over the hills, hoping against reason that I might glimpse a clue that would lead me to Atheon. But the woods were quiet around us, and ahead, the city lay in a mess of magical life that I couldn't even begin to untangle.

"That's odd." Hal stopped me as the trail we followed skirted the edge of a meadow.

"What?" I scanned the trees for signs of trouble, my hand already on the hilt of my knife.

"There's something in the meadow," Hal said.

He was right. A figure stood facing us from some distance. Even though she had somehow made herself invisible to my Sight, I would have recognized her broad shoulders, long braids, and heavy wrist cuffs anywhere. Nismae.

I gathered some magic from the forest, ready to put up a shield. Hal drew his knife. I followed suit with the small blade Eywin had given me to harvest herbs.

Beside Nismae, Ina gracefully rose from the swaying grass in dragon form. My chest tightened. She still stole my breath, but the reasons were different now.

Now I was afraid.

Now I was angry.

"Should we run?" Hal asked.

I shook my head. They wouldn't be here if they didn't want something.

Hal and I stood our ground as the two of them approached. Nismae held up her hands to show she carried no weapons. Ina remained a dragon, fierce and radiant. I kept my knife raised, every muscle in my body prepared to fight.

"You'd better have an explanation for what you did," Nismae said to Hal by way of greeting. "Asra." She nodded at me, and I narrowed my eyes.

"First, promise me you won't hurt Asra," Hal shot back. "Then maybe I'll explain."

"I'm not promising you anything. Not when you broke your promise to me by taking her from me in the first place. Not when you gave Eywin the very thing I left Corovja to protect," she said.

I stepped back, shocked. How did she know all this?

"First, you never told me what Eywin wanted. You never even

told me he was part of the reason we left. I never wanted to turn my back on you, Nis. You know I never would have, but then you hurt Asra. You acted before taking the time to explain what you needed. You could have had us both on your side. You hurt me as much as you hurt her when you did that," Hal said.

"She refused to join us," Nismae stated.

Ina arched her neck in agreement. I met her serpentine eyes with a steely expression of my own.

"Just because I didn't want to become a killer didn't mean I wouldn't have heard you out about what you wanted to do," I said to both of them.

"We're not here to fight." Nismae sighed.

"Then what do you want?" I tightened my grip on my silver blade. I trusted her less than I would a poisonous snake. At least snakes were happy to leave people alone if you gave them a wide enough berth.

"I was informed that you've pledged your services to the king. We're here to tell you what a mistake you're making. Join us instead," Nismae said.

The reach of her spies was truly staggering. The news was barely a day old and she already had it in hand. My skin crawled as I realized that meant she'd been right behind us on our journey to Corovja all along.

"What in the Sixth Hell makes you think I'd do that?" I asked. Nismae had never given me reason to trust her, and knowing what I did now, I had even less interest in joining their side of the fight.

"We'll give you any position you want. You can help us rebuild the cities ravaged by bandits. You could open a school to train herbalists for villages that need them." She'd clearly been coached by Ina, but her words had no effect on me.

Nismae ran a hand fondly along the dragon's neck, but Ina's expression remained unreadable, the moon reflecting eerily in her sapphire eyes.

A bubble of anger burst in me. "Or you could consider giving up this mad crusade against the king. He's been nothing but kind since our arrival."

Nismae snorted. "Because you gave him exactly what he wanted. You've only seen one side of him—the side he wants you to see. He only cares about himself and what benefits him. Try asking him for something *you* want and see how well that goes."

I scowled. I wasn't going to let her bully me into doubting my choices. I'd done what I had to. "No matter what you say, I'm on the side of this fight that will protect Zumorda. Have you even thought about what Ina taking the crown will do to the kingdom? The land? The gods? The demigods, including your brother?" The pitch of my voice increased until I was nearly shouting at her. "This battle could destroy all of Zumorda if Ina wins."

Ina tilted her head at me and Nismae frowned. "What are you talking about?"

"If a challenger for the crown wins without the backing of a god, the geas between the monarch and the gods will be broken. All six of them will forsake us, tearing apart the magic that holds our kingdom together. It will destroy manifests. It will drain the life from our kingdom. Ina will have nothing left to rule." I kept my shoulders squared even as fear rose. What would it feel like to have my magic ripped out of my body? Would those like Hal and me even survive it? Perhaps we'd become mortals without manifests, the lowest of the low.

Nismae's face betrayed no reaction, leaving me unsure if we were telling her something she already knew. "I'm surprised you're in favor of letting him continue to reign, given what he's so intent on doing to those like you," she said.

"Using our blood?" I asked. It wasn't anything I didn't already know.

"Trying to use it to give himself your powers. It's all part of his plan. Get the Fatestone—live forever. Take on the powers of the demigods—become a god in his own right."

"And you're so much better," I snapped. "You stole my blood and are using it for the exact same thing."

"I believe in the greater good—it's more powerful than any monarch, and more important than any one person. Our kingdom belongs to its people, not to a king who rules from a castle where he gets to feast every day while bandits destroy people's homes or children starve in border cities. Perhaps Zumorda will be more peaceful without the gods. We all have some small magic—our manifests, the training that clerics receive. Those things don't require divine blessing or intervention."

"It won't matter if there isn't any magic left for anyone to draw on," I said, my voice rising.

"We will not let what you're talking about come to pass," Nismae said. "If the gods leave, we will find another way to maintain our kingdom. Ina is the first nonmonarchal mortal to possess the gift of fire magic. She can see it and knows how to access it—she can teach others to do the same. You could become a teacher or a mentor, work to make sure that the magic of the kingdom remains stable. Collaborate with us to develop new ways for all people in the kingdom to contribute to the magic that links us all together."

"If that is the plan, I want to hear it from Ina," I said. "She's the one who will be queen. She's the one who will have the power, not you." I had no intention of being swayed by their mad ideas, but I wanted to know if any of the Ina I knew still remained inside.

Nismae's expression darkened. "The queen trusts me to serve as her voice."

"Well, I don't," I said. Nothing she'd done had ever given me reason to trust her. At least I had once had trust with Ina, even if we'd both broken it repeatedly since then.

Ina hissed, sending a plume of smoke blossoming into the night air.

"She stays in this form now," Nismae said, clearly growing frustrated. "People rally behind the dragon. She is the symbol of change and revolution and will soon be our queen."

"I don't care about your revolution, and if you want me to join it, you'll let me speak to Ina. Alone," I demanded.

"Just let her, Nis. We should talk, too," Hal said.

Her facade cracked for only an instant, and then she was composed again. "You made your choice, and I will respect it."

"If you respect it, then talk to me about it for a minute," Hal said.

"Fine." Nismae finally relented, though she didn't look happy about it. "Talk to Invasya if she'll agree to take human form. But keep in mind that if you make any move to hurt her, I will find a way to destroy you."

Anger and resentment flared in my breast. "I'm not the same kind of monster you are," I said. My gift was dark and dangerous, but I would never hurt Ina or anyone else on purpose.

"You know nothing about me," Nismae said. She kissed the scar on the dragon's cheek, and then she and Hal walked away.

"I won't have a conversation with you like this," I said to the dragon.

She hissed in reply. She was used to getting her way.

"I am not afraid of you," I said. "If you want me to discuss joining your cause, you have to be in a form with which I'm not obligated to hold up both ends of the conversation."

She snapped her tail in irritation.

I sat down and pulled up some long strands of grass to braid and waited for her to give in. Ina was not the patient sort. I could outlast her by days.

Finally, she shrank in on herself, more slowly than usual, until she stood over me. She still wore white as she had in Orzai, the luminous cloak a sharp contrast to my own mantle of shadows. Her white hooded robe hung from her shoulders, her white dress girded with silver rope beneath her breasts. Below that, her belly was large and round. Though I had expected it, the reminder was still a blow.

"What do you want to talk about? Nismae already told you everything."

I stood up. "It looks like the baby will be coming any day."

"One hopes. It's much more comfortable to stay in dragon form right now." She gestured at her belly with irritation.

"You won't have that option when the time comes." I said, wondering what they planned to do when she went into labor. I doubted many of the Nightswifts had given birth. It wouldn't be convenient in their line of work.

"Don't remind me." She sighed. "Nismae is always by my side, but the Swifts' most experienced medic is so timid."

"You're afraid," I said. She was trying to be flippant, but I could see the truth in her eyes. Taking on the king didn't frighten her, but giving birth did. She wanted someone with confidence and experience to be there when the time came—someone like me.

She didn't respond to my statement. She'd never admit weakness.

"Tell me the point of defeating the king if there is no kingdom left to rule over?" I asked.

"We'll save the kingdom from that fate. Nismae has studied magic for long enough that she'll find a way. Right now we have to stay focused on our goal—it's time for change," she said. "Perhaps the gods will see what we're trying to do for the kingdom. We want Zumorda to prosper, so our people don't have to live in fear of bandits or excessive taxation. Surely the gods will see our side."

"But you don't have a plan. You don't have a way! And in the meantime, the people will suffer. The demigods will suffer. The landscape of our kingdom will be changed forever."

Ina scowled. "I thought you would see that our cause is better for the people." She paused. "And I thought you cared about me." She looked at me with an imploring expression I now recognized for what it was—manipulation.

"I didn't just care about you. I loved you more than reason," I said.

I'd loved her more than anything, even myself.

That had been my first mistake.

"Then come with me. Do what's right." Her voice had the same seductive lilt she'd used on me a thousand times before. But she wasn't Hal—she didn't have the power of compulsion. And now that I could see her clearly, I wasn't going anywhere with her.

"I can't put my faith in someone who betrayed me. This time, I choose reason. Not love." I would never choose love again. I spared Hal a guilty glance, trying to tamp down the warm feeling that welled up when I looked at him.

"I still would have put my faith in you," she said with a little half smile. "You would never hurt anyone on purpose, Asra, and that is both your strength and your weakness."

Before I could answer, she changed form and launched herself into the sky. As the dragon passed over the trees, Nismae rose as an eagle to join her.

CHAPTER 29

IN THE DAYS AFTER I REFUSED INA AND NISMAE'S offer, my anxiety continued to grow. Now that I knew they were already in Corovja waiting for the right time to strike, it was that much more important to win over the king so he could ask the shadow god about Atheon. I had to find the Fatestone.

I spent most of my time in the following days with Eywin, working on blood enchantments meant to empower and protect the king. I threw myself into the work, knowing that every successful enchantment meant impressing the king enough to get him to speak to the shadow god. Soon my fingers were nicked all over, making me almost grateful that I wasn't able to use my left hand for much anyway. Still, I fought the scarred tendons in my arm, attempting every day to make a fist, and every day failing.

Hal was my only source of levity: Hal who winked at me across Eywin's workshop, Hal who often got himself thrown out after distracting me one too many times. When our experiments failed or became frustrating, he sometimes gave silly voices to objects in the workshop and acted out scenes. The forbidden love story he'd conjured up that involved a preserved baby bat in a jar that sat high on a shelf above the door and the lemon balm plant that lived on one of the windowsills was a particular source of amusement. Hal and I didn't tell Eywin what was going on between us romantically, but we weren't exactly subtle. Sometimes Eywin looked back and forth between us and smiled, shaking his head. He had to know.

With Eywin's help I was quickly able to reconstruct most of the notes I had lost to Nismae with my satchel. Combining those with his research meant soon I was doing more powerful enchantments than I had ever mastered with Miriel. A twinge of fear came with the rush of every discovery—I hoped none of the enchantments would be used to harm the innocent. With a smudge of my blood I could now lend the ability to shield, draw magic from other living things, or, most terrifyingly, tear someone apart as I had Leozoar. I even figured out how to replicate the enchantment Nismae had cast to make herself and Ina invisible to my Sight when they'd ambushed us in the meadow.

It was after that last discovery that the king finally came to the workshop to check on our progress one afternoon. Informal armor of leather and dark-red cloth hugged his body closely, showing off an impressive physique. Only one guard accompanied him, but the woman was half a head taller than me, with enough ice in her gaze to freeze a lake with a glance.

"How goes the work?" the king asked us.

I set aside the pain-relieving tinctures I'd been working on, grateful that he hadn't interrupted us in the midst of more difficult or volatile work. This was my chance to impress him and to ask for the favor I so desperately needed.

"Asra has been a gift from the gods themselves, Your Majesty." Eywin smiled approvingly in my direction.

Hal watched the king with a warier eye from where he sat on the floor, cleaning vials for us. Though he hadn't expressed any opposition to what we were doing, he always frowned at the mention or sight of the king.

"May I have a demonstration?" the king asked.

"Of course, Your Majesty." A rush of anticipation hummed through me. I couldn't wait to show him what we'd developed.

I beckoned him to the section of the workbench I'd taken over and uncorked a vial of my blood that had been mixed with an anticoagulant and infused with other herbs for stability and preservation.

"Asra, let's show him the true magnitude of your power," Eywin said.

The king raised his eyebrows in curiosity.

"First I'll enchant you, Your Majesty. Then Asra will do the same. You'll see the difference."

"We are going to give you my Sight," I explained.

Eywin performed the enchantment first, carefully tracing the spirit god's symbol on the back of the king's hand. I watched Eywin with my Sight as I had many times before. Since he wasn't a magic user himself and didn't have the amount of power I did, he relied on what already existed in the blood. He also had the disadvantage of working blind without having my gift of Sight. It was a wonder that mortals had ever figured out how to manipulate magic at all.

"Ah! I've seen the world this way before," the king said, taking in the workshop with new eyes. "Raisa is a daughter of the spirit god and uses this gift often, and I've borrowed it from the gods a time or two."

"Wait until you see what Asra can do," Eywin said.

It took only a few moments to perform the same enchantment again on the king's other arm. Soon I was tethered to him with thin strands of magic that drew from my power, far stronger and more solid than those Eywin had cast.

The king opened his eyes, blinking as though in bright light. As soon as his eyes adjusted, he walked to the windows and laughed—a booming sound too large for the room.

"This is astonishing," he said, awestruck. "It's so far beyond what I've been able to do before, even with the help of the gods. I can See everything."

I knew what he meant, because I could too, though this was normal for me. The gardens outside glowed with life and magic. I sensed people everywhere in the city, like sparks in the streets. The Grand Temple also had its own energy, power so deep I couldn't imagine where it ended.

I tore my eyes from the view to glance at Hal. His frown had deepened. When he caught me looking, he turned away to line vials up on a shelf.

The king continued to survey his kingdom, gently tugging at the magic I'd shared with him. How long could we sustain this? It had been easy with Hal because he had a vast well of his own power to draw on, but the king was mortal. And it was easier for him to use me than the gods, since channeling their power took more energy from him. With me in control of the enchantment, he didn't have to think about it. The Sight was effortless.

Finally, he turned toward me again.

"You're a wonder, Asra. Your service to the crown will be remembered for years to come. Perhaps centuries." He smiled warmly.

"Thank you, Your Majesty," I murmured. I wasn't sure being remembered was anything I wanted. Not if it meant being remembered for the same things as Veric—or worse.

"I must reward you for all this astonishing work," the king said. "Are you finding your accommodations here satisfactory? Is there anything else we can do?"

My heart leaped. This was my chance. "Actually . . . there is. Might you be willing to speak to one of the gods on my behalf?"

A flash of surprise crossed the king's face. "I'm afraid that's not possible. I only speak to the gods on the high holy days—solstices or equinoxes. Perhaps at the autumn equinox we could revisit the subject?" He smiled again, but this one was a veneer compared to the last. I had asked for too much.

My heart sank as quickly as it had risen. The autumn equinox would be too late. This far north, the first snow of autumn would probably come weeks before then.

The king must have seen my disappointment, because he said, "But in the meantime I would like to extend an invitation to my feast table. You deserve a seat there. And please take this token—it will allow you access to nonpublic areas of the castle, including the Grand Temple. You may go there to pray and offer to the gods if you wish."

"Thank you, Your Majesty." I bowed to hide my frown. Getting into the temple myself was better than nothing, but I didn't feel sure the gods would deign to speak to me.

We dispelled the enchantments while the king chatted amicably with Eywin until the two departed for a council meeting with the king's bodyguard trailing after them. The moment they exited the room, I sat down and slumped over the workbench and laid my face on my hands, trying to breathe as I sank further and further into a pit of despair. He'd refused to help me. The equinox was too far away.

"What am I going to do?" I asked.

Hal walked up and gave my shoulder a gentle squeeze.

"Are you sure finding the Fatestone is the only solution?" he asked, his voice soft.

"The only other choice is to continue this." I gestured around the workshop. "Help the king. Let him kill Ina."

"But that's not what you want," Hal said, a little wariness in his voice.

"I don't want anyone to die. I'm responsible for enough death. And even if things aren't quite right with you and Nismae, I don't want to watch you lose a sister, too." There was no way the king would let her live if he defeated Ina, and she couldn't possibly escape Corovja quickly enough to escape him.

"So rewriting the past is truly the only way we can avoid something horrible from coming to pass," he said.

I turned and gazed up at him, even though it made my heart ache to see the pain and worry in his eyes. I couldn't promise him that things would be all right, but there was one promise I could make—one I had been thinking about since he'd first noted that changing the past meant we'd lose each other.

"With the Fatestone, there's no limit to what I can reshape, or the number of words I can use. I can make sure the kingdom stays safe and preserved." The amount of detail it would take to write all of it out made me nervous, but it seemed like a sacrifice worth making. If I had the Fatestone and didn't have to worry about aging, I would be able to much more carefully dictate the changes to prevent any other collateral damage. I paused, considering my next words, weighing the promise I was about to make. "When I change the past, I can try to make sure I still meet you."

"Why would you do that?" he asked. "Not the part about the kingdom. The part about me." Hope gleamed in his eyes.

I stared back at him, weighing honesty and vulnerability against each other.

"Because I don't want to lose you." I caressed his cheek. In some other version of the present, the future ahead of us might be amazing.

"But if you created a past in which Nismae never left the crown and you never left your mountain, I might have been a messenger for the king instead of my sister's hunting dog. How would we have met then? There would have been no search for the Fatestone or the only living bloodscribe." He sounded like he had it all mapped out better than I did.

Then I realized what he'd just said.

"Wait. What do you mean, a search for the only *living* bloodscribe?" I asked.

"I meant the Fatestone. Nismae's research. Veric." He fumbled the words.

He was lying to me.

Everything started to snap into place.

His willingness to stay with me when we first met even though we'd been complete strangers.

How easygoing he'd been about leading me back to his sister, who was otherwise incredibly secretive about everything she did.

The knowing look in his eyes when I'd channeled Leozoar's magic to heal the Tamer huntress.

The way he'd stopped fighting back when Nismae stabbed me.

"You knew what I was all along," I said, my voice shaking. "Did she send you to look for me? Is that what really happened?"

Hal winced and looked at me with anguish in his eyes. "I didn't know," he whispered.

"You didn't know what?" My anger surged. "Because you had to know she intended to hurt me." I held up my left hand, demonstrating the feeble way the fingers moved.

"I didn't know I would fall in love with you," he said, and hung his head.

For the briefest moment, my heart soared, only to come crashing back to earth seconds later.

I stared at him, reeling. How could he tell me he was in love with me? Was that supposed to make up for leading me to Nismae? Were lies and deception his idea of love? All his actions had ultimately been for his family—something I couldn't understand because I'd never had one. Nismae could still be behind all this, waiting for a chance to strike as part of a master plan I'd been too naive to see. Maybe that was what they'd been talking about in the meadow.

No one had ever loved me. Not my parents, not Ina, and not Hal. I had never known love.

"I'm so sorry, Asra. I wanted to tell you, but there was never a good time. . . ." He trailed off, looking as stricken as I felt.

"So what's your secret mission now? To seduce me so I'll be distracted from what I'm supposed to do? To kill me before I can get the Fatestone? To let me get it, only to turn it over to Nismae?" The fury made my veins feel like they ran with fire instead of blood. New possibilities of his ulterior motives sprang up like weeds, choking the tender feelings I had for him.

"There's no secret mission," he said firmly. "I betrayed Nismae when I set you free. I meant it when I said I would always choose you." He looked me in the eyes.

"I can't . . ." I didn't even know if I could believe what he was saying. How could I, with all the lies between us I'd never known about until now? There were no words. The pain was too great, too complete, too unbearable.

I never should have trusted him in the first place. Stupid, stupid Asra. Always wanting to believe the best of everyone, even Ina. The world was full of monsters, and my isolation had raised me to be blind to them.

"Go back to your sister. Go back where you belong." I flung the words at him like weapons. I had survived almost entirely on my own for years, and there was no reason I couldn't do it now.

"But Asra—"

"No." I grabbed my cloak of shadows from the rack on the far side of the room. When I got the Fatestone, it would be so much easier to change the past knowing I had nothing to salvage from the present.

I wished I'd never met him.

"I'm sorry," Hal repeated, his voice cracking.

I headed for the door. No footsteps sounded behind me, but a breeze rose to caress my cheek.

"Stop that!" I whirled around and threw a shield up to repel the wind into Hal's surprised face. "Don't touch me. Don't follow me. I never want to see you again, and I will never trust another word you say." My voice came out so cold I barely recognized it.

The world had made me a monster, too.

CHAPTER 30

ANGER MADE MY FEET SWIFT AS I FLED THE CASTLE. IF the king wouldn't speak to the shadow god on my behalf, I would try and do it myself. I had to. The notion was completely mad, but hurt and fury obliterated my ability to think about anything else. All I knew was if I got the Fatestone and rewrote the past, I could change the moments that had led me here.

I could make the pain stop.

I fled into the gardens, hurrying toward the six turrets of the Grand Temple. They stood bright against the southern horizon, stained-glass windows reflecting the late-afternoon sun. I didn't know how to get to the covered archway that led from the palace to the temple, but a winding set of stairs led from the back of the garden across a lower bridge to the clerics' entrance on the side of the building. I jogged until my lungs burned, ignoring stares from others I passed who were moving through the gardens at a more dignified pace. I didn't slow down until I reached the last long set of steps.

When I reached the doors and showed the clerics the king's token, they invited me in. When I told them I wanted to try and speak to the gods, they walked me through a purification ritual. I was shepherded through a series of warm pools until not a speck of dirt remained on my body. The attendants adorned me in light-gray robes like those the temple clerics wore, anointed me with oil that carried the faint perfume of mountain roses, and braided my hair into an intricate crown. They admired its length but said nothing about the silver streaks. I tried not to cry when they touched me with their careful hands, tried not to remember the way Ina had once run her hands through my hair, tried to forget the way Hal's kisses had turned my insides to stardust.

The clerics escorted me to an antechamber lined on each side with small partitioned booths in which to rest or pray, telling me they'd have me enter once the temple was empty of mortal visitors. I settled my cloak of shadows over my shoulders, needing its familiarity. My prayers were unfocused as I waited. I had no sounds of nature from which to draw music to sing, no way to limit the direction of my thoughts. Instead I was left with words rattling around inside my head in a jumble.

Death.

Loss.

Betrayal.

Love.

I tried to set aside the simmering anger I felt toward Hal, but every time I thought of him, it surged up anew. I prayed for answers, for guidance, to somehow know that I was doing the right thing. I prayed for the shadow god to deign to speak to me to tell me where Atheon was.

I prayed for the Fatestone, and the chance to start my story over.

When the sun had shifted far enough west that the stained glass made luminous pools of colored light on the floor, two clerics returned for me. They led me through gilded double doors into the heart of the temple, both signing the symbol of the spirit god before closing the doors behind me. My footfalls echoed in the vastness of the empty room. Chandeliers hung from the peaks of six turrets, illuminating intricate mosaics covering the walls from top to bottom. The whole building hummed with magic, like a pool into which all the streams of life gathered. I opened myself to the Sight just enough to sense the undercurrents swirling around me. They all led to the same place—an inlaid star on the floor with designs in the color of each god spiraling away from its tips.

My heart raced as I knelt at its center. The time had come for me to ask what I needed to know. But how would I get the shadow god to answer?

"Please speak to me," I whispered, tracing her symbol in the air. "I need your guidance."

I bowed my head and waited, but my request was met only with the deep silence of the temple. My knees ached. All I saw when I finally looked up were dust motes dancing through the beams of light slanting in through the western windows. My Sight showed no shift in the energies around me.

"Tell me what I must do. Please!" My voice rang through the space, echoing back from the apses. Tears stung the corners of my eyes, but I refused to let them fall.

When I looked down, a small silver knife had appeared in front of me. I stared at it in confusion. What did it mean?

A few breaths later, understanding dawned. A pit of dread slowly expanded in my stomach.

The shadow god wanted a sacrifice.

I had only one thing to offer.

My blood.

Dread and sorrow warred in my heart. My blood would always hold the answers I sought. It always came back to this, no matter how hard I tried to escape it.

This time, I would do this on my own terms.

I needed all the gods to give me strength.

I rose to my feet and went first to the altar of the earth god. Her steadiness would still my shaky hands. I nicked a finger and pressed it into the dip in the stone worn smooth by the thousands of hands that had come before mine. Invisible magic twined around my arms, familiar and comforting. She had accepted my offering.

"Please say hello to Miriel," I whispered.

I circled the rest of the temple to the other gods. The wind god was the only other one to answer me, with a sourceless breeze that whispered across my cheeks.

My stomach churned as I faced the shadow god's altar. She might not answer my call. Some would say it was madness to try to speak to a god when I didn't have a crown and wasn't pledged to a temple. I didn't even know which of the gods had fathered me. None of them appeared to be willing to claim me and my dark gifts.

The shadow god's turret was darker than the rest, the mosaics depicting death and mystery, shadows swirling throughout the other images.

She had taken so much from me.

Or perhaps I had given too many lives to her with my mistakes.

I offered a drop of blood to the empty space beneath a hollow box studded with gemstones. But instead of asking about the Fatestone, an entirely different question slipped out.

"Why did you let this happen?" I whispered. "Did you really need to take everyone from me?"

The light in the temple grew richer as the sun sank to the west.

"At least tell me how to make it right!" I shouted.

I collapsed in front of the altar and finally let the tears fall.

Everything was hopeless. Perhaps I would have to find Atheon on my own, or Nismae would kill me before I could even try. Perhaps the Fatestone was lost forever, and I would have to live with the tangled mess I'd made of the future—both my own and that of the kingdom itself.

I sobbed into my shadow cloak, not noticing at first that black smoke had begun to pour from beneath the shadow god's box. I scrambled backward, clutching the silver knife so tightly that the base of the blade nicked one of the fingers on my uninjured hand. A trail of blood droplets followed me to the center of the room.

The black cloud finally drew in to become a tall, hooded figure, wisps of smoke retreating until it became solid. It moved toward me, shrouded in a cloak of darkness that shifted restlessly about its body. The figure leaned forward, and terror choked off the last of my tears.

Only in moments when I had used my blood power and felt it

steal the years from my life had I ever felt as mortal as I did kneeling before the god of death.

Hope and fear battled inside me, shifting and tumbling until I couldn't tell which was stronger.

"I am both sorry and glad to see you." Her voice was gentler than I expected, almost soothing. It had the low quality of a bell, and held the promise of a quiet place to rest. A white hand with long, slender fingers emerged from the sleeve of her robe.

"Look up so I can see you, child," she said. Her hood left her own face shrouded in darkness.

Frozen in place like a frightened rabbit, I obeyed the nudge of her hand when she tipped up my chin. I swallowed hard, grasping to find words to ask for what I needed.

"You have his eyes," she said, and her voice faltered. She withdrew her hand, leaving me staring at her in stunned shock.

"Whose eyes? My father's? You know who my father is?" Though I'd come here for other reasons, my desperation to know consumed everything else. My mouth went dry and tremors continued to rack my body as I waited for her to answer.

Instead, she drew back her hood.

Hair the deep red of dried blood cascaded over her shoulders. Her eyes were empty and black as a starless night, but that wasn't what frightened me. It was the long arch of her eyebrows, her high cheekbones and delicate nose, the angle of her jaw and the pensive pout of her lips. It was that her face, in spite of bearing the terrifying exquisiteness of a god, was so similar to the one I saw when I looked into a tranquil pool of water and saw my own reflection.

My tears finally spilled over.

My father was not a god.

My *mother* was.

The abandonment I'd known about all my life cut down to the dark heart of my soul. How could a mother leave her child? How could she have let all this happen to me?

"Asra. My child," she said. The sorrow in her voice made my chest grow even tighter.

"Why did you leave me?" My voice cracked. Even as I asked, some part of me knew that no answer would be satisfying. I couldn't imagine leaving a baby in the hands of strangers without so much as any idea who she was—or how much destruction she could cause.

"Amalska was supposed to be a safe place to keep you out of mortal hands. Who would look for you in such a small and unassuming place, especially if your gifts were never used?" The lack of emotion in her voice made it impossible for me to tell how she felt about it. Did gods even have feelings?

"Where is my father? Why couldn't you have left me with him?" It would have meant something just to know I had family. That someone loved me without conditions or because they were hungry for the dark power I possessed. Even Hal's friendship hadn't been free of ulterior motives, much less his love.

"Your father passed away before you were born," she said. "He was sick for a long time, with a wasting illness that slowly destroyed his body."

"Why didn't you help him? Why didn't you save him if you loved him?" If I could heal someone's broken back, surely a god could heal someone from an illness. She could have at least given me a father if she wasn't going to be there for me.

She blinked slowly, her black eyes unreadable. "That is not my role."

Anger raced through me, fierce and wild. "So you left me with no family? If you couldn't save my father, why did you bother getting close to him?" What was the point of falling in love if it was doomed to end from the start? I never would have let myself grow so accustomed to Ina's arms around me if I'd known they would one day be torn away. I never would have kissed Hal if I'd known how he had betrayed me.

"I didn't mean to. But your father composed the most beautiful music. He had the sweetest voice," she said distantly, remembering. "I spent so many hours hovering close by, waiting for the right time to welcome him. I fell in love with those melodies—and with the man who made them—even though I didn't want to. Not after what happened to Veric."

The way I heard music in all of nature, in the chirp of a cricket, the whisper of leaves in the wind, the sound of a stream running over rocks—that had been my father's gift. The vespers were a far kinder one than my mother had given me.

"But how could you leave me all by myself?" My voice trembled. My life would have been so different if I had grown up with someone who understood my powers, with someone who would have told me I was dangerous. My decisions in life would have been so different. Would that not have been better for everyone?

"Asra, my days and nights are spent at the edges of battlefields, by the bedsides of the sick, or hovering at the edges of an accident just before it happens. I am sometimes the only witness when a mortal chooses to take their own life. I am fed by the last heartbeats of the dying, and my duty is to unmake their souls and deliver them back into the magic that exists all around us. What way would that have been for a child to grow up, seeing death at every turn? Even if it is part of the cycle that sustains our world, love cannot grow where grief and sorrow reign."

Resentment smoldered in my breast. She'd never even given me the chance to be loved. "It might have. You could have at least shown me how to use my gifts. Told me who you were. That you existed. That you cared!"

"Your gifts are those of blood, fate, and death. And like all gifts, they have their prices. No one has ever survived the blood gift long enough to master it. You know what happened to Veric. . . . I thought if you never used it, perhaps you might have a chance at a more normal life." Her voice was deep with sorrow. Perhaps she did have feelings after all.

"Nothing about my life has been normal." I failed to keep the bitterness out of my voice.

"But a life with me would have been no life at all. I left you because you deserved the chance for a quiet and beautiful life, and if that meant I could only watch you from the shadows when you cut the stem of a plant or took the life of an animal for food, so be it."

"I would rather have known who I was," I whispered. "I would rather have known that someone loved me." Tears streaked down my cheeks.

"I have always loved you, sweet girl." She pulled me forward and kissed my tearstained cheek, the brush of her lips cold and tingling. In that single kiss the pull of darkness and final endings called to me. "I did not want to repeat the mistakes I made with Veric. He was ambitious. I visited him often when he was a child, and sometimes I took him places I thought he needed to go to understand the gravity of his power. The problem was that he never could keep it to himself—he wanted to make the world a better place, and to use his gift to accomplish that. When he was still quite young, he used his gift to destroy the serpent king at the behest of the Six, much like you ended the southern drought."

I remembered the story. The serpent king had been the most evil leader Zumorda ever had. While it was true that Zumordans favored power, and the strong would always rise to leadership, once he got there the serpent king had twisted the power into something evil. He hadn't cared for his people. His rule was one of bloodshed and death, as venomous as the enormous black snake he'd taken as his manifest. Entertainment at his court was always something that ended with spilled blood.

"When the serpent king turned away from the Six Gods, refusing their guidance or their magic, we asked Veric to write his death."

"So the mouth rot . . . and the respiratory infection that killed him . . . you're saying that wasn't natural? The gods were responsible?" I had never heard this version of the story.

"Yes, Veric wrote the king's fate in great detail, and it came to pass. The use of his power aged Veric into a feeble old man. He retreated with his partner, Leozoar, to the cave in his territory, hoping no one would find him. But he was too well known and had done too much work documenting how his blood could be used for various purposes. Mortals were desperate for what he had to offer—desperate to get it from him before he died. So they hunted him. Only by the grace of his lover's protection did he escape. But he knew he could only hold them off for so long. He decided that if he couldn't do good for his own generation, he would do it for the next."

"The Fatestone," I said. My birthright.

My mother nodded. "It was made from the last of his blood, and enchanted with his dying breath."

"If I can't find it, all is lost," I said. "Please tell me where I can find Atheon."

"First, tell me why you seek the power of the Fatestone," she said. "I know much of your story as told to me by the dead, but I want to hear it from you."

"The boar king is expecting a challenger," I said. "She does not have a manifest bound to the gods, and it is all because of me." The story of Ina and me poured out, of how I'd selfishly tried to change our future and destroyed everything instead. "It's my fault she doesn't have a bond to one of the Six. I must correct the mistake that made her a monster."

The shadow god considered my words. "I have felt the boar king's soul calling to me in the distance from time to time. It would not take much to push him close enough for me to grasp. Perhaps you will be the one to decide his fate."

"What does that mean?" I already carried too much responsibility on my shoulders.

"Whether you change the past or the future, the ripples will be felt throughout all of time. Are you prepared to take on that power?" my mother asked.

"Yes." I wasn't ready in the least, but what other choice did I have?

"Then let me tell you how you will find Atheon. First, look for a thread of magic that feels like yours. Like calls to like. Second, listen to your heart. Third, know that your blood is the key. Remember—fate is a slippery and changeable thing. You are one of the few with the power to change it. Be wise and be well, my child." She touched my cheek with a gentle hand.

"But wait—where do I find the thread of magic?" I asked. She'd left me with a riddle, not an answer.

The darkness surrounding us gathered until a new cloak formed around her body. She pulled up her hood and the shadows fell to pieces and dissipated into nothingness, taking her with them. The emptiness of the Great Temple felt vast enough to swallow the world.

I wiped the last tears from my face. Fate had led me to live up to my birthright, even without intending to. Now I had to embrace it no matter how much it hurt.

 CHAPTER 31

I ARRIVED BACK IN MY ROOM TO FIND TWO MAIDS waiting for me in a state of near panic—they'd been sent an hour before to prepare me for supper with the king. The two of them stuffed me into a borrowed formal dress, used the braids done by the clerics as the basis for a more complex arrangement, then fussed and fretted over my tearstained face, powdering me until I sneezed. I spent the whole time lost in my own mind, haunted by memories of my mother's face.

I was seated next to Eywin for the meal as usual. An empty chair on his other side vanished before the second course, but I knew it had been meant for Hal.

"Where is he?" I asked Eywin.

He looked at me strangely. It wasn't as if Hal and I had often been apart in the past weeks.

"He said he was leaving. He didn't say why or for how long,"

Eywin said, seemingly unconcerned.

Worry crept in at the edges of my anger, but I tried not to give in. I'd told him I never wanted to see him again. What did I expect? I hated the way he'd lied. That was what I needed to hang on to. I couldn't let myself think of how he'd made breakfast for me day after day, how he'd taken care of me in fights, or the way he'd made me laugh in Eywin's workshop. I couldn't dwell on how it had felt to trace the angular line of his jaw or to kiss the dimple in his cheek. I needed to stay focused on finding Atheon.

Still, I couldn't help needing to confirm what Eywin told me. I knocked on the door to Hal's room after dinner, but there was no answer. And when I tested the knob, the door swung open to reveal a chamber that showed no signs he'd ever been there.

That empty room crushed my heart like a vise.

I told myself I didn't care.

Every day after that, the battle between Ina and the king felt more inevitable. Though I did not see Ina again, her presence in Corovja was palpable even in the castle. Outsiders poured into Corovja in droves. No one spoke about the challenger in polite company, but rumors spread quickly among the servants. I even caught one of my maids tugging her sleeve down to cover a white ribbon tied around her wrist. Without asking, I knew exactly what that meant and who she supported. She'd gazed at me with panic in her eyes, but I shrugged and said nothing. I had sworn to support the king, but that didn't mean my choice was right for everyone.

Sleep stopped seeming particularly important. My days were spent in the workshop, and at night I used the king's token to sneak out a side gate and stalk the streets of Corovja in my shadow cloak.

No matter how deeply I probed with my Sight open, I couldn't find the thread of magic my mother said would lead me to Atheon. I didn't know what my mother had meant when she said to listen to my heart. If the magic I was following felt like my own, shouldn't it have been one of the brightest things in my Sight?

The ache of Hal's absence grew the longer we were apart, showing no signs of healing over. Still, I refused to allow myself look for him. Instead, every time he crossed my mind, I let the feeling burn to galvanize me. I would fight him, Ina, and Nismae that much more fiercely knowing they all deserved it.

But at night, when I put on my cloak of shadows and left the palace to follow random threads of magic in search of Atheon, I remembered him in other ways. In the palace gardens, I remembered how he'd rained petals over us. In the woods outside the castle walls, I remembered the way we'd slept next to each other, his warmth radiating through me. In city cemeteries I remembered running through the streets of Valenko with him, and the spark that had jumped between us the first time we touched. When I returned to my room, I remembered the way he'd kissed me and it felt like coming home.

In those moments of weakness, I would have given anything to have him back.

With less than a moon remaining until the autumn equinox, the king summoned me to the coliseum to exercise my enchantments and strategize for battle. He had never seemed to notice Hal's absence, and I had never felt compelled to explain.

The coliseum lay on a plateau carved into the side of a sheltered valley in eastern Corovja. A tingle of magic made me shiver as Eywin and I passed beneath the arched entrance. As soon as I was inside, I knew what that feeling had had been—a ward. Apparently the battle was meant to take place in a protected area. Neither the king nor Ina would be able to draw on the magic of anything outside the coliseum. The barrier was so strong, it had even protected the inside of the coliseum from my Sight, so I was surprised to find the king already waiting when we arrived.

He stood in the center of the coliseum, wearing practical armor for fighting. He'd brought four guards—two who stayed close, and two others who patrolled the edges of the ring in case anyone decided to preview what was going on here today. An even greater surprise than the coliseum itself was who he'd chosen to be his champions. Until now, he'd been secretive about his choices, no doubt to keep rumors from spreading.

"Raisa?" I asked Eywin, surprised. She sat on a portable chair heavily laden with cushions. Could she even fight at her age?

"Don't underestimate her," he said with a glimmer of something unreadable in his eyes. A warm wind from the south gently tugged strands of hair free from my braid. The sun shone brightly, forcing me to shield my eyes from both the sky and the white sand under my boots. I was grateful for the mild day—my injured arm always felt better when it was warm out.

As we drew closer, I saw that the other champion was Gorval, the king's steward, a wiry man with a hooked nose, and eyes so dark I could barely see the pupils. He had a pasty face and a balding head, his shoulders perpetually stooped. Something about him had always felt off to me, something to do with his manifest, but since I'd never seen him take animal form, I didn't know what it was.

"Welcome, Asra, Eywin," the king greeted us.

Gorval gave us a curt nod, and Raisa stared silently as she always did.

I shuddered beneath her sightless gaze.

"Let's begin," the king said. "I'd like to enhance each of us in a way that complements our own abilities."

"First it may help to give you the Sight again, Your Majesty," I said. "That way you'll be able to See with the clarity I have and make your own decisions about which are the most useful."

The king regarded me with appreciation. "Clever thinking," he said.

"I have three gifts to offer today," I said, addressing the broader group. "First is the Sight, which I'll give the king. Raisa would not need it anyway, as it's something she already possesses."

I turned to Gorval. "The second gift is that of healing—to restore injuries. But it can be costly if you don't have the energy of another living thing to draw on." Or a dying demigod, as in the case of Leozoar. "The third enchantment allows you to conjure a shield. It can deflect magic or reflect it back at your opponent, but again, it will require my energy or the energy of something else to sustain."

The king frowned. "Are you sure you can hold all these enchantments together at once, or will Eywin be providing one of them?"

I glanced at Eywin where he stood quietly beside me. We actually hadn't practiced that. Without Hal, we didn't have anyone else to test things on. We couldn't risk word of what we were doing spreading far enough to reach Nismae—and it wouldn't have to go far to do that.

"I think it's best if Asra places these enchantments. She is far more powerful than any human attempting to wield the same magic." Eywin's long robes fluttered in the wind, the silver frames of his spectacles glimmering in the sunlight.

A little burst of warmth for him swelled up in me. Eywin believed in my strength. He trusted me. At least one person did.

The king smiled. "That is what I'm counting on."

"Of course, in battle only one of you would be fighting at a time. That would make these enchantments easier to manage." I drew a vial of my blood from the bag of supplies I'd brought and carefully painted the symbol of the spirit god on the king's forehead. Because of his geas with them, the spirit god's symbol seemed most likely to give him strength.

To Raisa, I gave the shield. With so much power of her own, she probably wouldn't need much assistance from me during the battle, but better defense seemed like a useful thing to provide her if nothing else. When she brought the shield up before her, her manipulation of the energies tugged at my own life force, my own magic. And it was strange to watch the dark river of my magic be unwound and re-formed into the blinding glitter of hers as she crafted a wall of power. She made it look effortless, as easy as breathing. She needed no coaching at all from me once I'd shown her what to do, though her power was so great that my head swam after she was done.

Finally, I used a last dab of blood to trace the symbol of the earth god on Gorval's hand and bestow the gift of healing.

I didn't dare test it by drawing my own blood and creating an enchantment loop, so Eywin nicked his wrist. I coached Gorval through using the power, and magic knitted the flesh back together until it looked as if nothing had ever happened.

The king hurled fireballs at Raisa, delighted when they dissipated against her shield. He increased his attack, pelting her with bolts of energy and spikes of ice. Every blow that landed on her shield reverberated through the connection she had with me until my head felt like the inside of a clanging bell. Raisa figured out how to use her shield as a weapon, pushing it away from herself to knock Gorval off his feet. They all marveled at their new powers, but the longer I helped maintain their enchantments, the more my own energy faded. The sun made my skull pound. Or maybe it was lack of sleep and the constant thread of desperate anxiety about not having found the Fatestone. I felt pulled in too many directions as each of them played with the abilities I'd given them. Soon I was on my knees in the sand, the sky spinning above me.

"Asra, are you all right?" Eywin asked.

"I need them to stop now," I said, my voice coming out weakly. "It's too much chaos. . . . I can't manage this many at once."

Eywin crossed the sand to them, waving his arms to get their attention, but it was too late. Darkness was already closing in.

My sacrifice for his gain.

I woke up hours later back in my room at the castle with Eywin at my bedside. Twilight hovered outside the window in gloomy colors as clouds rolled in from the west.

"How are you feeling, dear?" he asked.

I propped myself up in bed, trying to ignore the pounding in my skull. "What happened?"

"The enchantments broke when you collapsed," he said, handing me a steaming mug of tea.

The sharp, herbal scent of it sent a pang of longing for Hal through me, and I made it through only a few sips before having to set it aside.

"I suppose this means I can't enchant all three of them for the battle," I said.

Eywin shook his head. "It was decided that you'll reserve your powers for the king. Gorval and Raisa are both very powerful on their own. If they can't match Ina, at least the king will be prepared to soundly defeat her. He's defeated his last challengers with very little trouble. This shouldn't be any different."

"Right," I said, a creeping thread of unease winding through me. Could I watch Ina die if that was what it came to?

"As for me, I should be off to the workshop. I have a few more calculations I'd like to run to see if there's any way to prevent what happened today. You missed the evening meal, but I can have something sent to you if you like," Eywin offered.

"That's all right," I said. Night had almost fallen—it was time for me to go out in search of Atheon again. Now that I knew what the battle might do to me, I wanted more than ever to find the Fatestone. I didn't want to fight at all. I didn't want to be anyone's sacrifice.

After Eywin left, I pulled on my cloak and sneaked out to the city. As I crossed the palace gardens, the night smelled of dry grass and stones still warm from the heat of the day. Insects chirped and night birds called to one another. I picked up their melodies and hummed a few bars of a tune for comfort. My head still ached. Could I even do this tonight?

I took a deep breath. I had to.

After passing through the wall surrounding the castle, I stopped to look up at the stars. All I could think of was where I'd been a year ago. Back then, Ina and I would have been lying side by side somewhere remote, a blanket of wool spread beneath us and a blanket of constellations across the sky. She would have buried her face in my neck and kissed me there until I turned away from the stars and into her arms. Last summer I had two equally functional hands with which to touch her, and innocence that had not yet been broken.

Longing overcame me. I missed the person I used to be and the person I had hoped to become. I missed the version of myself that knew how to love without fear. I missed a time when I hadn't felt like love was cursed to go hand in hand with betrayal.

I closed my eyes, trying to remember what it felt like to have a heart in one piece.

I couldn't.

"Psssst," a voice whispered.

My eyes flew open, and I had my knife drawn in seconds. I was no longer the fearful child I'd been before I left home.

"Asra?" the person said, his voice tentative.

The sound of it almost stopped my heart.

Hal.

"Why are you here?" I asked, my voice clipped.

He sighed. "I told Nismae this was a bad idea. She sent me to get you." He sounded like a kicked puppy.

"So you did run back to your sister after all," I said bitterly.

He shook his head. "No. But she knew where to find me, and she knew I'd be able to get to you. It's not as though she can walk up to the front doors of the castle."

"What does she want now?" I hadn't changed my mind since I'd spoken to her and Ina. The questions I truly wanted to ask danced through my mind. Where had he been? Was he all right? The dark circles under his eyes seemed to indicate he'd been sleeping about as well as me, unless they were just cast by the moonlight.

"It's Ina. The baby is coming and she asked for you," he said.

 CHAPTER 32

I STARED AT HIM AND CROSSED MY ARMS AS THOUGH I might be able to hold back the feelings of hurt and confusion that swam in my breast. How could he be the one to fetch me, and how could Ina possibly be asking for me to help her?

"This feels like a trap," I said. There was no upside for me in this situation. If Hal was back on their side, they were surely using him to lead me straight to Nismae. She'd drain the rest of my blood to keep me from helping the king. And if Ina's baby was about to be born, that meant my time to find the Fatestone was dwindling.

"It's not a trap." He looked at me with troubled eyes, a mirror of everything I felt.

"I know what your word is worth," I said. A stab of guilt followed.

He looked at me as though I'd struck him, then took a slow breath and tried to pull himself together.

"This isn't about me and you," Hal said. "There's a baby about to be born, and nobody down there knows what to do."

Unbelievable.

"Nismae couldn't possibly find a competent midwife in the entire city of Corovja?" I gestured broadly. "She couldn't just let nature run its course and leave me out of it?"

"Nismae wants what Ina wants, and Ina wants you." He held out a pair of objects that glinted in the moonlight.

Nismae's cuffs.

"She gave me these to lend you as a promise of her intent," he said. "Without them, she's as vulnerable as any other mortal. You're more powerful than her and you know it."

"And what about Ina? How do I know she's not waiting for me in dragon form, ready to tear off my head because I refused to join her?" I challenged him.

"She gave me this," he said, pulling the dragon charm from my wrap bracelet from his pocket.

I took a sharp breath. She'd saved it. Why? Because it was from Garen, or because she'd given it to me? My resolve faltered the slightest bit. Maybe they really did need help. What if I turned my back on them and something terrible happened to the baby? It would certainly make things easier for the king if something befell Ina, but I couldn't handle being the one responsible for it.

"Then what about you?" I couldn't follow him anywhere with things like this between us. Hurt sparked between us the same way love once had.

"I'm still sorry for everything," he said. "I know you can't forgive me right now, and that's all right. For what it's worth, I haven't forgiven myself yet, either."

He was right. I couldn't forgive him, not now.

He waited for my answer, not pushing.

I still loved that about him, even though I didn't want to feel anything but anger.

Resigned, I held out my hand for the cuffs and the charm. "Show me the way."

We raced down the mountain through alleyways and staircases, shortcuts and back roads, until we reached an old mining area where the Nightswifts had apparently set up camp. Lights winked amidst the trees, and when the wind shifted, I smelled cook fires.

As we drew closer, I pulled my knife from my belt with my uninjured hand. Nismae needed to know that I wasn't going to be toyed with, regardless of any supposed promises she'd made. With my injured hand, I drew my cloak of shadows more tightly around my shoulders, ready to disappear at the slightest provocation.

Nismae broke through the tree line to greet us, alone. It was strange to see her without her cuffs—I'd come to think of them as a part of her, as much as her strong stature and the keen intelligence in her hazel-brown eyes.

I held up my knife.

"I still don't trust you," I said.

She nodded, accepting that without argument. "You don't have to. Ina just needs your help. We may be on opposite sides of the battle to come, but that doesn't have to matter tonight."

"How do I know you aren't just trying to get more of my blood?" I asked.

"Because I swear on my own blood and life that all we need is help delivering this baby," she said.

I edged closer, trying to get a better look at her expression. She held herself as proudly as usual, but I could sense the fatigue in her now that the bracelets weren't muddying her aura in my Sight.

"Promise me," I said. "Promise me that you will not hurt me, that I will be free to go as soon as the baby is born. Promise me you won't reach out to me after this or send Hal for me like some kind of errand boy."

Hal looked at the ground, not meeting either of our eyes.

"I promise," she said. "Please help us."

I hesitated a moment longer, but it was the *please* that broke me. Nismae didn't seem like the kind of person who used that word often.

"All right. Show me where Ina is. I don't want to spend any longer with you than I have to."

"Thank you," Nismae said. "Come this way." She turned and led us toward the Nightswifts' camp.

Hal followed us, wisely keeping his mouth shut.

Nismae led us through the camp to a cave. Warmth enveloped me when we stepped in; it must have originally been a bathhouse for miners. My eyes slowly adjusted to the dim lantern light as Ina let out an agonized—and quite human—moan from the back. As I'd warned her, she had to labor in human form. Poe crouched near the fire, anxiously folding and refolding blankets and minding a kettle of boiling water.

"What have you given her?" I asked Poe.

"Nothing," the mousy girl said. "She won't take anything from me. She shouts if I go near."

"Is there anything in this that will help?" Nismae asked, flinging my satchel into my arms.

"Yes," I said, hugging it to my chest and feeling a quick burst of gladness. I never thought I would see it again. I dropped to the floor and started rummaging through it. "How long has she been in labor?"

"Since early this morning," Nismae said. "Is this normal? Should she be like this?"

"She should be all right unless the baby is breech or something else has gone wrong," I said. "I'll have to examine her."

Ina moaned again from the back of the cave, where she was submerged in a pool of water. I hurried to her side and tested it with my hand. Not too warm. At least they'd had the sense not to let her get into one of the hotter pools.

"Hal, set aside some of that boiling water and let it cool a little so I can wash my hands."

He obeyed as quickly as if we'd been back in our easy rhythm of setting up camp. My heart squeezed uncomfortably at the memories.

"What can I do?" Nismae trailed anxiously behind me.

"Get over here and help her out of the water. If she has another contraction, support her under her arms so she can squat," I said. "You've got two working hands, unlike some of us."

Nismae ignored the jab, seemingly grateful to have something to do. She helped Ina out of the pool and wrapped her in a blanket, then lowered her over the straw they'd laid beside the pool.

"You're here," Ina said. Tears sprang to the corners of her eyes. She grasped my hand, sending uncomfortable twinges up my injured arm thanks to the damaged nerves. For the first time since leaving

Amalska, she looked like the Ina I remembered. One who relied on me, who had a sweet side to balance her ambition and fierceness.

I felt nothing.

The vulnerability in her eyes didn't sway me as it once might have. I wanted to help her, but I wasn't enslaved by that desire. I left the job of hovering and soothing to Nismae, who stroked Ina's brow and whispered comforting things in her ear, only to earn a glare and a yell during the next contraction.

"These contractions are coming close together," I said. "Poe, heat more water and make tea." I flung several sachets of herbs at her and listed out the proportions of each. She rushed to do it, looking more confident now that someone else was in charge.

As soon as the contraction subsided, Nismae helped Ina lie down, propping her up with stuffed cushions and folded blankets to support her back while I washed my hands in the hot water Hal had prepared.

"Is it all right if I examine you and check on the baby?" I asked Ina.

She nodded, breathing heavily, strands of her sable hair sticking to her face.

I examined her, trying to ignore the strangeness of revisiting such an intimate part of her for such different reasons.

"Ina." I returned to her side. "It's time. Push when you feel ready."

"All right," she said, her voice a raspy whisper.

Poe rushed over with swaddling blankets and fresh rags. Nismae helped Ina into a squatting position again, even as Ina moaned and cursed and gnashed her teeth.

After fifteen minutes of Ina continuing to labor to no avail, Nismae spoke up. "Is this supposed to take so long?"

"Be quiet and hold her up," I said, and Ina and I bestowed her with matching glares. "The baby will come when the time is right."

Ina's contractions continued to intensify until she couldn't get comfortable. She alternately cursed us and demanded we do something about her situation. I stayed steady, familiar with this phase of childbirth, while Nismae looked half-panicked.

A few minutes later, I held Ina's son.

"Look at you!" I said to the baby.

He let out a good healthy cry.

I couldn't help but smile at the miracle of him—his tiny hands, his angry scrunched-up face, so unhappy to be out in the world. While I no longer felt anything for Ina, looking at this baby flooded me with emotions I didn't entirely know how to manage. I wanted to hold him close and keep him safe, to tell him every day how perfect he was.

Instead I enjoyed the few minutes I had, humming him a lullaby as I carefully wiped him clean. I swaddled him, then moved to put him on Ina's chest, where he could rest until she delivered the afterbirth.

Ina put up her arm. I thought she was reaching for the baby—until she spoke.

"No," she croaked.

That one word cut me to the bone.

"What?" I asked. Stupefied, I knelt beside her with the baby in my arms, instinctively holding him closer to myself.

"I don't want to touch him," Ina said. "Get him away from me."

This couldn't be happening. She wouldn't do this.

"You have to. He needs to nurse. He needs his mother!" I pleaded with her to understand, to look at how tiny and helpless he was. How could she not see how much he needed her? How could she deny him the comfort of resting on her chest, of hearing her familiar heartbeat to welcome him to the outside world?

"I'm not his mother." She turned her head away.

"But—"

"No," she said firmly. "I cannot be both a mother and a queen. Raise him as your son. You'll be a far better mother than me." She closed her eyes. Labor had exhausted her.

After everything we'd been through from Amalska to here, she expected me to keep him.

A wave of anguish hit me. I thought about setting him down on her chest anyway so that she could feel how soft and small he was. So that she could hear his cries and feel compelled to give him some nourishment, some love. How could she refuse him? How could a mother turn her back on her own helpless baby?

But I knew it was possible, because my own mother had done this—turned away from me the moment I was born, leaving me to be raised by someone else, abandoning me to never truly know who I was. I couldn't let that happen to this little boy.

In the wake of my empathy for the baby, rage swiftly followed. I hated her.

I looked for Hal, only to realize he was right behind me, peering over my shoulder at the baby. He looked just as horrified and dismayed by Ina's words as I felt. We exchanged a look of understanding that temporarily bridged everything that was broken between us.

"Can you hold him for a minute while I gather my things?" I asked softly. I trusted him to do that much, at least.

He nodded, and I nestled the baby in his arms.

"He's so tiny," Hal said with wonder.

Moments later, he was already walking around having an animated one-sided conversation with the bundle in his arms. "Can you smell the cook fires? I can. But no rabbit for you. You don't have any teeth yet!"

I slung my satchel over my shoulder. As angry as I was with Ina, she'd get what she wanted. If he couldn't have his mother, he would at least have me.

As for the next time I saw her, it would be from the opposite side of a battlefield.

"Wait," Ina said, weakly reaching out a hand.

I paused, wondering if the threat of my departure had finally changed her mind, but all she said was "Call him Iman."

His name meant "faith."

She'd chosen to put hers in me after all.

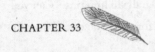

CHAPTER 33

HAL'S NETWORK OF FRIENDS AND ACQUAINTANCES helped us find a wet nurse for Iman, which was how I ended up with a sweet, freckled girl named Zallie sharing my little room at the castle. As cramped as we were with both of us and two babies, she didn't quite seem to believe the luck of receiving free food and shelter in exchange for her services. The boy who had been courting her had disappeared as soon as he found out she was pregnant, and her parents had thrown her out shortly thereafter.

I hadn't forgiven Hal, but he kept showing up anyway. His draw to Iman could not be denied, and between me, Zallie, and Hal, Iman never lacked for food or a loving pair of arms. I tried to stay angry with Hal, but it was increasingly difficult. Hal brought me and Zallie food and herbs. He told the babies stories that were so ridiculous it took all my self-control not to laugh until I cried. He shared openly with me what he learned in the city. At night when Iman was safely asleep under Zallie's watch, he accompanied me on my walks in search of the Fatestone and its elusive thread of magic, even though I never told him about meeting my mother or what we were looking for. I didn't want to admit it, but his presence helped keep my despair at bay enough so I could stay focused. Now that Iman was here, time was running out. The only thing standing between now and the battle for the crown was the first snow.

On one such excursion, after another futile attempt to locate Atheon, Hal and I climbed the stairs to K'vala Falls—the largest waterfall on the mountain. Though exhaustion weighed on my bones, I thought it might be worth venturing up above the city to see if that provided my Sight with any additional information.

Together we continued up the stone steps that wound their way toward the waterfall. Long before we reached the bridge that passed in front of it, the crash and rush of it soothed me. If we got close enough, the sound would be deafening, perhaps enough to drown out the endless loop of thoughts in my head.

The night air was cold and wet after an evening rain. Winter weather would be coming soon. I recognized the smell of it in the air, and the equinox was only a week away. That meant snow was coming, and not long after, the battle for the crown. Anxiety lanced through me every time I thought of it.

I sighed, feeling the weight of responsibility on my shoulders more heavily than ever. We stopped early on the bridge, away from the part sprayed with continuous mist from the falls. If I couldn't find the Fatestone, what would my future hold? What would Hal's?

"What are you going to do after all this is over?" I asked him.

He leaned over the stone railing of the bridge, peering at

moonlight reflecting on the ripples of water below. "I don't know. I suppose it depends on whether we survive."

"But what would you want if you knew anything was possible?" I asked.

He looked at me with sadness in his eyes. "I'm afraid to let myself dream of that."

I was too. The future seemed impossible to plan for when I didn't know what would happen if I found the Fatestone and changed the past. In a different version of our lives, Hal and I certainly wouldn't have been standing on a bridge in Corovja right now.

"I'm afraid of losing Iman," Hal added.

A pang of something fierce tightened my throat. "Me too," I admitted. The thought of it gutted me. And Hal loved Iman as much as I did. I could see it in his eyes every time he held the baby. Maybe in another life, we would have been a family.

Perhaps the time had come to forgive Hal for what he'd done. Did his recent loyalty outweigh one betrayal? Was there even such a thing as anyone who was truly honest?

"Asra . . . I think we should talk about what happened," Hal began. "I should have told you the truth from the beginning. You have to understand that I grew up here in the city. On the streets you can't afford to trust strangers. It can get you killed."

I almost laughed. Trusting strangers—including Hal—had certainly come close to getting me killed every step of the way since leaving home. "Truer words may never have been spoken."

He nodded. The only acknowledgment of my jab was the flicker of hurt in his eyes, but he soldiered on. "The only person I could trust was my sister, who protected me from the time I was young.

She was my hero. She could do no wrong. I didn't understand until recently that her protectiveness wouldn't extend to people I cared about. And . . . there was never someone I had feelings for like the ones I have for you." His expression was so raw, so vulnerable. The wrong reaction from me would surely break him.

Seeing him unbox his heart crumbled the walls I'd tried so hard to maintain. All I wanted now was to cradle his cheek in my hand, lean into his embrace, seek out the familiar planes of his body and find safety there. Most of all, I wanted to take what he was offering me and protect it with all the fierceness I had.

When I didn't say anything, he kept going. "If I had your gift and could do it without harming others, I would rewrite the history of us. I wish I could give us another beginning, one in which I had told you the truth from the moment we met," he said, his voice firm.

"Oh, Hal . . . ," I whispered.

"I wish I could rewrite taking you to Orzai. I wish we could have taken the Moth and flown past there. I wish we could keep going forever. See the world. Us, Iman, and the open sky."

"I understand that wish." If it hadn't been for the sorrow I'd left behind in Amalska, the fear driving me forward, and the knives always at my back, traveling with him might have been the happiest time of my life—until he betrayed me.

"I knew when I heard you sing those vespers that they would change my life. I just never knew how much." His voice was so tender it broke my heart.

"I knew when I heard you sing 'The Tavern Lamb' that you were the most ridiculous person I'd ever met," I said, teasing.

He smiled, the slightest upturn of his lips.

I missed that mouth. I missed that smile.

"I just . . . I never expected . . . you," Hal said. "I didn't expect how special you are."

I leaned on the railing of the bridge, burying my face in my hands. Heat rose in my cheeks, and I wanted to push it back down. The compliment was so bittersweet.

"Special is why your sister took my blood," I said. "Special is why the king keeps me close and puts up with me having a girl and two babies in my room. I would give anything to not be special. I would give anything to be just like you or, better yet, to be human. Even one without a manifest. Someone simple. Uncomplicated. Someone who hasn't been chased across half a kingdom for the power that runs in her veins." Now that I knew what the world would do with someone like me, I longed to be something, anything, other than myself.

"I didn't mean anything to do with your abilities. I meant the way you watched over me when I was unconscious in the Tamers' forest. Mukira said you never left my side. I meant the way you look at Iman like he means the world to you, like he's your own. I meant the way you've kept fighting even when it seems like all is lost. Even now. Most people aren't like that. That's what makes you special. Not your blood."

Hal reached for my left hand, and I jerked it away before he could touch me. Letting him touch the broken part of me was still too intimate, still too much.

"How is your arm?" he asked quietly.

"There are some things magic cannot repair." I tried to close my hand and was rewarded with the usual stab of pain through my wrist.

"I'm sorry," he said. "I know it will never be enough, but I am so, so sorry."

"If it had been my writing hand, perhaps Nismae would have done me a favor," I said bitterly.

"No. There is no light in which it was a favor," he said.

"It's fine. It's just more damage to someone who was already broken, and a lesson in whom not to trust." I couldn't stop lashing out at him. The pain was too much.

"You aren't broken, Asra."

"I don't need you to tell me what I am!" I said.

"You're right, you don't, but I wish you could see yourself the way I do. You are all goodness and light. You're as bright and beautiful as a star—one I feel like I've been searching the sky for my whole life. I felt pulled to you from the very first time I heard you singing." He could have used his compulsion to try to make the words more moving, but he didn't. They were delivered raw and unpolished, simple as an ugly truth.

"Feelings are a terrible reason to do anything," I said, but the fight was starting to seep out of me. I tried to cling to the knowledge that feelings were what had started the avalanche of disaster that got me here. It had started the moment I put pen to paper to help Ina find her manifest, and that had been about nothing if not feelings. Selfish, stupid feelings.

"I know I made a mistake," he continued. "When we met, I didn't know that you were the kind of person with whom I could have been honest from the very first breath and you still would have helped me. I didn't know you would stay by me even when I collapsed in the middle of the woods and you could have left me behind. And while I knew you were the one my sister wanted me to find, I didn't know that your gift was something she would injure you for, and I am so sorry for the suffering that my actions and choices have cost you. But I want to do better. I want to be better. Maybe I don't deserve that chance, but I'm asking you for it because if I don't, I know I will regret it for the rest of my life. And I know you now, Asra. I know you. I trust you. Please give me another chance."

Somewhere in the middle of his speech, I met his eyes, daring him to try to use his compulsion on me, to try to touch me uninvited, to do anything to undermine his own words.

He simply waited for me to say something, his face tight with fear, but his eyes holding the smallest flicker of hope. I couldn't cling to my anger with him looking at me so humbly. I let the last of it slip away like a bird released into the wild. It would still exist. It would still be part of our past, but it didn't have to define our future.

In spite of it all, I had to face the truth I'd been denying for moons.

I loved him.

"Sing me that song about the tavern girl and the sheep again and maybe I'll forgive you," I said.

A slow grin emerged on his face. "Really?" He stepped closer, still cautious.

I slipped my hand into his and laced our fingers together, unable to help the sigh that escaped when I did. It felt so good to be connected to him again, and though the peace between us was still fragile and new, the rightness of it was undeniable.

"I missed you so much," he said. "Every day, every hour, every minute—"

"Oh be quiet," I said. Then I kissed him.

A spark leaped between us as it had the very first time we touched. I let my arms wrap around him, giving in to how good his mouth felt on mine.

When he broke away from me and smiled, this time his smile was my dawn, the sun returning after too much darkness.

He sang me "The Tavern Lamb" on the way back down to the castle. I tried to sing with him but always ended up laughing too hard to go on. And when we crossed the threshold of my room to find Zallie awake and more than ready to hand off Iman, I finally understood what my mother had been telling me when she said, *Listen to your heart.*

I knew how to find the Fatestone.

CHAPTER 34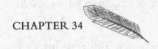

IF LISTENING TO MY HEART WAS THE KEY TO ATHEON, my heart led me to Hal. That meant it was Hal who needed to listen with his Farhearing. Veric had been a bloodscribe like me, and Leozoar had been a wind demigod like Hal. Of course they'd have worked together to hide the Fatestone. Of course it would be impossible to find the Fatestone without both gifts. Once I understood that Hal was the answer, it all made sense.

Why hadn't my mother just told me? It chafed a little that it had taken this long to figure things out when she could have given me stronger direction. But whose fault was that? I was the one who had stayed angry at Hal. I was the one who had been slow to forgive, and slow to admit my own feelings. My mother must have wanted me to find my own way to the answers, to be sure of my own heart. I understood.

"You're the key," I told Hal, who had sat down to hold Iman.

"What?" he asked.

Zallie nursed her own baby, Nera, not minding us. By now she was more than used to our odd conversations and arguments.

"It was something the shadow god told me that only makes sense now. I need you to listen. That's how we'll find the Fatestone. Listen for something out there that sounds like me."

Hal closed his eyes, and I recognized the tilt of his head that meant he was reaching beyond his normal range. At the same time, I reached for the well of dark magic in me that I now knew had come from the shadow god. It wound through me in its familiar way, and I gently drew on it to brighten my Sight.

"I don't hear anything unusual," he said. "I listen to the city all the time. If I heard something that sounded like you, but wasn't actually you, I would have noticed long before now."

My heart sank. Maybe my theory was wrong.

"Aw, don't frown like that," Hal said. "Here, hold Iman for a little bit. That'll cheer you up. We can keep thinking about the answers. We'll figure it out."

I took the baby from him, grateful that lack of dexterity and grip in my left hand didn't affect my ability to hold Iman. Even though the knowledge that Iman was Ina's child nagged at me from time to time, he felt like my child, not hers. The way he felt pressed to my chest was already so familiar and natural, like he had always been meant to be there. I hummed him a lullaby made of memories of my mountain.

"Wait," Hal said.

I stopped humming.

"There's an echo. How did I never hear it before?" He stood up and paced to the window.

My breath caught. "Where?" I asked.

"Sing that tune again," he asked.

I hummed the simple melody.

"It's not far away. It sounds like it's coming from the center of the hedge maze."

"I have to go, then. Right now," I said, reluctantly handing Iman back to Hal.

"You can't seriously go looking by yourself," he said, gently rocking Iman in his arms.

"Why not?" I asked. But I already knew.

Hal looked down at the baby sleeping in his arms. He didn't have to say a word.

"I know." I deflated. "Every time we leave him to go out, I worry. And the thought of leaving him to go somewhere that could be dangerous . . ." I bit my lip. But everything relied on it. How could I turn down the first solid lead we'd had on the Fatestone?

"You're a good mother," Hal said softly.

I wasn't prepared for the tears I had to suddenly blink back. I had never thought I would hear those words, or that they could belong to me. I recognized that for all the importance Nismae placed on family by blood, Hal wanted a family built on choice, with the person he loved and trusted most: me.

I had always thought if only I knew my parents, I'd be different. Better. Whole. Right. But they hadn't chosen me, and they hadn't given me the chance to choose. Now I got to decide what kind of family I wanted.

I knew the answer.

"I have to go," I said. "Promise me you'll stay with Iman until I return. If something happens to me . . ." I couldn't finish the sentence.

"I will. But I wish you didn't have to do this." Hal looked at me sadly.

"Me too, but I promise you that I won't do anything with the Fatestone without talking to you about it first, all right? I want this to be a decision we make together," I said. The relief of sharing the weight of it with him made it so much easier to bear.

His expression relaxed a little. "I'd like that," he said, then smiled at Iman, who was just waking. "Should I tell you a new story?" he asked the baby. "Once there was a sheep named Shep, who liked to swim. . . ."

After leaving Iman safely in Hal and Zallie's care, I took a lantern from near one of the castle doors and slunk outside. In the dead of night, the palace gardens were empty other than the occasional guard. I used my Sight to avoid them without any trouble. My shadow cloak protected me from anyone else who might be using the Sight. The hedge maze towered over everything else and was devoid of the fragrant and colorful blossoms that decorated most of the other gardens. A few turns into the maze, the barest thread of something shadowy tugged in my Sight. The deeper I ventured, the stronger the pull of the magic became and the more wild the hedges. I followed the trail of power through the empty maze until I reached the hush in its center, where tangled walls of greenery blocked out all sound.

All that stood in the center of the maze was a small fountain, old and stained, with vines crawling haphazardly over it. Water burbled from the mouths of three stone birds on top to cascade down tiered sides into a basin. The pulse of the magic beneath it was as sure and steady as my own heartbeat.

I sighed and took out my knife. I already knew what it would take to unlock the secrets of this place.

As soon as a few drops of my blood fell into the water of the fountain, the earth groaned beneath my feet. An archway burst out of the earth on the far side of the clearing, showering soil as it rose. Dirt and knotted roots clung to the damp stone, beneath which a dark hole opened to reveal a stairway.

Dread crawled slowly down my back, but I couldn't turn back now.

As I entered the cave, the scent of must and earth hung in the stale air, making it hard for me to breathe. At the bottom of the stairs, a narrow tunnel continued farther into the earth. The lantern cast a pool of light around me that felt far too small for the enclosed space.

While it seemed as though the walls had once been smooth and polished, fissures now ran through them and the edges crumbled at the seams where they'd been tiled together. The tunnel wound into the ground, branching out in dozens of directions. I followed where my magic led. The deeper I traveled, the more the tunnel narrowed. Several times I had to duck to avoid tree roots that had punched through the passageway from one side to the other, leaving piles of rubble all over the floor.

Finally, the tunnel opened up into a large room. Something about it made the hairs on the back of my neck rise as I entered. I held up the lantern to look around, and immediately wished I hadn't. The ward in this room had taken more than one enchanter to create—and they were all still here.

Skeletons hanging from the walls with arms outstretched and fingers entwined encircled the room in a bony embrace. Jeweled charms dangled from nails hammered through their foreheads. Their jaws were wired shut, the metal holding them together rusty. I couldn't imagine why it had been done, but the horror of it made my mouth go dry.

A twining rope of power moved through their linked hands. They had cast the same kind of ward on the room that the coliseum had—one that prevented seeing any magic within it from the outside. That was why I hadn't been able to find this place with my Sight.

At the center of the room, a stone tomb protruded from the floor. A statue loomed at one end of it, the folds of her marble cloak cascading in a canopy over the grave. Like the dais in Veric's Sanctum, the surface of the tomb bore a handprint on the top with a blood groove. The stone of the handprint was cool to the touch, and my fingers came away smudged with dust.

My heart beat so loudly in my ears that I could hardly hear my own thoughts.

I reopened the cut on my finger and let my blood drip into the handprint as I had in the Sanctum. Slowly the flat stone atop the sarcophagus slid away. I tried not to think about the layers upon layers of earth above me, or the bones waiting for me below. They were just remains, just one more thing I had to face to get what I needed.

Inside, a skeleton lay on its back with its arms crossed over its chest. The bones carried an unmistakable aura of magic that matched my own. The Sight of it sent an unexpected wave of sadness through me. This had to be Veric. Now I knew where the echo of my magic had come from. Inside his rib cage, something golden glimmered, untouched by the passage of time. I leaned in to get a closer look while my heart raced even faster. Etchings of twining vines adorned the golden parts of the ring, so precise that they had to have been created with magic. They reminded me of the carvings I'd seen in Veric's Sanctum. Through the middle of the band ran a channel of dark red that swirled and glittered in the torchlight. Veric's blood.

I had found the Fatestone at last.

Joy flooded through me. The battle didn't have to happen. I could change the past. But right on the heels of my joyous realization, darkness encroached. Did this mean I would lose Iman? And Hal? And even Zallie, whose sweetness had grown on me every day as I watched her tenderly care for Iman?

There were so many things to weigh. It was too much to bear.

But I had Hal. He would help me carry these burdens if I needed him.

I sketched the symbol of the shadow god, then reached carefully between Veric's ribs and picked up the ring. It seemed unfathomable that one tiny object had created so much strife, especially one that wasn't even a weapon. The lengths mortals would go to in order to set aside their own mortality staggered me. They didn't seem to realize that a long life could be a curse more than anything else. I shuddered as I remembered Leozoar and the creature of darkness he'd become.

The ring had more weight in my hand than I expected, and as I slipped it over my finger, it shrank until it lay warm and perfectly fitted. I felt different the moment I put it on—like it held back everything in the world that might pull at the threads of my own life, what little held me together. I doubted any mortal would feel what I did once the ring was on. It might prevent them from aging, but it wouldn't do for them what it would for me. For the first time, I felt powerful.

The future was mine.

There would be no more gray hairs.

No more lives sacrificed due to my mistakes.

Everything was fixable now, the past and the future flexible in my hands.

I swore to myself I wouldn't take advantage of it, but it was still a heady rush.

"Thank you, brother." I hoped he would rest peacefully and that wherever his soul was, he knew his wishes had been carried out.

I knelt before his tomb, then sketched the symbol of the shadow god again. I owed her thanks as well for leading me here. And perhaps even the wind god, who had given me Hal.

Then I heard footsteps.

"Who's there?" I stood up, my heart racing wildly.

An arrow flew through the cave, shattering my lantern. Oil poured onto the floor, and then the flame winked out.

I sensed nothing at all with my Sight, smelled nothing. The

footsteps drew closer at a deliberate pace. I fumbled back along Veric's tomb, trying to take shelter behind the statue.

A strong arm locked around my neck and a burst of acidic powder exploded in my face.

Peaceroot.

It stole my abilities even as I struggled in the person's grip, bit their arm, tried to grasp at magic that slipped away as the herb took hold.

My vision blurred, silver sparks warring with the comfort of absolute darkness. They'd mixed something else into the peaceroot. My entire plan had unraveled before I could even begin. Whoever had me this time would surely bleed me to death. Soon my mother would welcome me into her arms, which might have seemed like a better place if not for Iman, whose face was the last thing I thought of as consciousness slipped away.

CHAPTER 35

I WOKE IN DARKNESS, WITH NO IDEA HOW MUCH TIME had passed. It could have been hours or days. Cold and soreness crippled my body. When I shifted my weight, hard, lumpy objects dug into my thigh and arm.

The Fatestone was no longer on my finger.

Panic lanced through me and I struggled to keep my breathing even. Who had taken it? The darkness made me feel shut in. It was hard to stay calm or to think. I grasped at fragments of memory, but all I remembered was my lantern shattering. Everything was hazy after that. I felt around, trying to see if there was anything I could grab onto to help me stand up, and realized with horror that the smooth objects digging into me were bones. I raised my arms perpendicular to the ground and encountered a slab. To the sides, the same.

Someone had shut me in with Veric.

I screamed and clawed at the stone in futility, but nothing happened until the tips of my fingers grew raw enough to bleed. As soon as my blood made contact with the stone, the lid of the tomb slipped aside. I scrambled out as quickly as I could with only one useful hand.

The skeletons on the walls weren't visible to me now, but somehow I still felt like they watched me, judging me for my failure. I'd had the Fatestone no more than five minutes before it had been stolen. My chance to rewrite the past was lost. I wished the skeletons with their wire-tied jaws could tell me who they'd seen come after me.

But really, who else could it be besides Nismae? Anger bubbled up through the pain. The only others who knew about the Fatestone were the Nightswifts. If Nismae had used Hal to get to me . . . the thought filled me with fury. But I didn't believe he'd help her with something like that now. Not after how I'd seen him looking at Iman. Not with the way he looked at me.

By the time I exited the tomb, the sky had just begun to lighten east of the mountains. A biting wind gusted through the gardens, chilling me to the bone. I didn't make it far beyond the maze before spotting a guard. I sneaked around him and several others until I got back into the castle. I kept the hood of my shadow cloak up to hide the filth on my face from pages and servants moving through the castle halls.

I didn't so much stumble back into my and Zallie's room as fall against the door, which Hal opened a few moments later.

"Asra! Gods, I've been looking everywhere for you!" He caught me in a hug so tight I could barely breathe. "Is this blood on your hands?" he asked, examining them with concern.

"I'll call someone to draw you a bath," Zallie said, her green eyes round as saucers.

"Iman?" I asked the moment Hal got me settled in a chair.

"He's been fine," Hal assured me. "He's missed you. We all have. The king has had his soldiers scouring the city. Eywin's been trying to enchant your blood to create a way to track you, but hasn't been successful yet."

"How long have I been gone?" I asked.

"You disappeared into that damn hedge maze the night before last. I couldn't even find the middle of the maze when I went looking for you. I couldn't hear you. I thought you were dead. I thought . . ." He trailed off, the worry on his face as plain as day.

The truth was that I would have been dead if I wasn't half god and able to withstand things no mortal could—like a day and two nights sealed inside a tomb.

"I found the Fatestone," I said. "Then it was taken from me."

"What happened?" he asked.

"Your sister." Rage burned in my chest again. I had to get the Fatestone back before she sold it or managed to find a way to use it for something more nefarious than its intended purpose.

His expression darkened. "Are you serious?"

"I had it on my finger no more than a few minutes before someone attacked. It had to be one of the Nightswifts. They blew peaceroot into my face, laced with some sort of powerful opiate. I woke up inside Veric's tomb, sleeping on his bones."

Zallie gasped so dramatically it was almost comical. Sometimes I forgot she hadn't been through the kinds of things Hal and I had.

"Peaceroot isn't easy to come by here," Hal said, frowning.

"And there are even fewer who know how to process it," I said. All the evidence pointed to Nismae.

A page arrived to take me to the bathing chambers. I scrubbed until not a speck of grave dirt remained, but I still felt dirty. Violated. By the time I went back to my room, I knew I had to confront Nismae about what she'd done. I was more powerful now, more confident than the last time I'd faced her. I still didn't want to hurt anyone, but I would if I had to.

I pushed open the door to my room. "Hal, I need to go—"

I froze after crossing the threshold. Hal rushed over from the other side of the room with Iman in his arms. A small woman perhaps twice my age stood near Iman's bassinet—I recognized her as one of the king's guards. One of the maids who had often attended me stood by my bedside, looking nervous. A spill of red fabric lay across the bed—some garments I didn't recognize. I scanned the room in confusion, trying to figure out what this was all about. Zallie had a grim expression on her face that quickly changed to concern as Nera gave a little cry.

"Asra, look outside." Hal pointed to the window.

"Oh no," I whispered, my heart plummeting.

In the pale morning light, snow had begun to fall.

The king's guard crossed the room to my side with the athletic grace of a mountain cat. "My lady, the king has assigned me for your personal protection and to escort you to the coliseum for the battle," she said.

I went hot and then cold. How could I fight like this? I hadn't had any time to recover from my injuries—and more important, to confront Nismae about her theft of the Fatestone.

"These vestments were sent for you, my lady," the maid said, holding up a simple dress in shades of crimson and a bloodred wool cloak lined with brown fur.

"As long as I can wear my own cloak as well," I said. Red was the king's color, not mine. I belonged dressed in shadows—in my mother's legacy. I wanted her protection for the battle to come.

The maid put my hair into a braided crown, then helped me into the crimson dress and placed the red cloak over my shoulders. All the while, I shot Hal a series of desperate looks he seemed to understand. He regretfully gave Iman to Zallie and pulled on his boots, subtly stashing his weapons in the hidden places where he always carried them.

"Keep them safe," I told Zallie. "If the unthinkable happens, run. Go as fast as you can. One or both of us will meet you where we agreed."

She nodded her understanding, her face pinched with worry. It wasn't far to the Switchback Inn, our rendezvous point, but it might seem that way with two babies and the chaos that would take over the streets after the battle regardless of who won.

I kissed Iman and Nera good-bye, and then Zallie's cheek, too. She blushed.

Then the king's guard led us away.

We met with the king's procession and paraded through the streets surrounded by onlookers. The Nightswifts' stream of white pennants made its way through the city on a lower street, flooding in the direction of the coliseum. Thick flakes of snow pelted our faces as we walked. The noise of the crowd was deafening. I gripped

Hal's hand like I was trying to crush the life out of it.

"What are we going to do about Nismae and the Fatestone?" I asked. It was the only way I could have stopped this day from unfolding as it had.

"I'll enter the coliseum with you and then go to Nismae. She and Ina will be settled in the challenger's quarters soon." His voice was resolute.

Nervousness raced through me. As if crossing lines between the challengers wasn't bad enough, I hated the idea of him leaving now. If something went wrong, we'd be separated during the battle. I'd be occupied managing the king's enchantments, but it would have felt better doing it with Hal by my side. But what choice did we have?

"She isn't going to give it to you," I said. The chances of Nismae parting with it now seemed very small. I'd have to make a trade I wasn't willing to, like giving up helping the king. Could I make that sacrifice? If he won, he'd surely kill or imprison me for treason. I shuddered. I couldn't spend the rest of my life locked away in some dank cell. I couldn't let Iman be abandoned a second time.

"As you once pointed out, I'm a thief. I'll find a way to get it," he said.

The coliseum loomed before us. Some of the Swifts had chosen not to walk, and instead swooped down from the sky to line up outside the gates. Gone were the subtle vestments of trained killers and thieves. Today they dressed in white to honor their champion for the crown.

"I don't want you to go," I whispered.

"I don't either," he said.

These might be our last moments together before the battle. I hadn't expected them to come so soon.

"Go now, before I change my mind and decide I can't do without you," I said.

He smiled. "I'll be thinking of you every moment," he said.

His words sent a thrill through me—the only reprieve from my anxiety.

He kissed me, and I let myself get lost in it for just a few heartbeats until he reluctantly pulled away.

"Be swift and be safe," I said.

He nodded, and then he split away from the group at the coliseum's entrance.

Once inside the king's quarters, I turned back to watch the end of the procession.

Ina was last to appear, and I shuddered when I saw her. She winged through the low clouds, white against white, until she finally burst free with a roar that seemed to shake the very foundations of the city. Onlookers pointed and screamed, some of them fleeing. How long had it been since anyone had seen a dragon in Corovja? Or anywhere?

Those who had come to Corovja in the past moon were finally going to get the show they'd been waiting for.

Ina landed in front of the escort that had preceded her, and they saluted her with their white flags. She roared again, then loosed a plume of flame. Steam rose from where she'd melted the snow, leaving the cobblestones scorched black.

The challenge had begun for the crown of Zumorda.

CHAPTER 36

THE COLISEUM WAS ALREADY FILLED FROM TOP TO bottom upon our arrival, thousands upon thousands of people waiting for the show to begin. I tried to ignore the dull roar of the crowd and the impossible level of fatigue in my body as I set up my work area in the king's preparation chambers.

Eywin greeted me with a warm hug when he arrived. "We were so worried," he said. "Where were you? Hal seemed to have some idea, but he didn't have any luck tracking you down."

A swell of gratitude for Hal rose in me. It must have been hard for him to keep from Eywin what I had been up to, but I was grateful that he had. I didn't know if Eywin could be trusted not to tell the king what we knew of the Fatestone, and the last thing I needed was another complication in getting it back from Nismae.

The king strode in just as I set out the last of my vials.

"All ready?" he asked.

"Yes, Your Majesty." I turned to face him. He wore simple leathers meant to go under heavy armor—breeches, a fitted vest, a black shirt. Some of my blood would go on his temples, but I also planned to paint a few symbols where they couldn't be seen. Ina and Nismae would have a hard time telling what I'd done without using the Sight.

I did not hold back as I drew the bloody symbols on his skin and armor. Once the battle began, there wouldn't be any opportunity to add more. With each symbol I drew, more and more threads of magic connected us until a web of power lay between us, initiating a gentle exchange of energy that would become fierce when the time required it.

"The final ones will go on your hands, Your Majesty," I said.

He held out his hands to me.

The Fatestone adorned his ring finger.

I felt dizzy. It wasn't Nismae who had stolen the Fatestone from me.

It was the king.

The truth slammed into me like a battering ram. I stared at him, frozen. "You took it from me," I finally said.

"Only for your protection. It's very sought after, you know—it would not have been safe for you to carry around such a powerful artifact. Someone might hurt you to get it, and I couldn't risk losing my most important battle asset right before the challenge." He spoke with the calm and rehearsed manner of someone who expects to be believed.

"Yes, you could." My voice rose. I'd dispensed with formality. "Whoever attacked me left me there to die!"

He chuckled, like it was all some sort of joke to him. "I wouldn't have allowed that to happen." He glanced at Eywin, and I knew then that he hadn't expected me to survive my ordeal in the tomb. That was why Eywin was here today—because the king hadn't known I would come back.

"But you did," I said coldly. "Why do you think my fingers look like this?" I held out my hands. The ends of my fingers were still scraped and tender from clawing my way out of Veric's coffin.

He shrugged. "It's not important now. Finish your work. You can't turn your back on me without risking Zumorda losing its magic. You're half made of magic, so that seems unwise at best."

"You . . . you betrayed me," I said. And it seemed perhaps Eywin had, too, though I didn't know to what extent.

"I did what's best for my people," the king said. "We have a fine and prosperous kingdom. Now with the Fatestone I can rule it forever."

Forever. Even demigods didn't live forever. Mortals were certainly not meant to.

"Prosperous . . . so that your people are driven to banditry to pay their taxes? Fine . . . when you have multiple massacres in the space of days?" I asked him. I'd only sworn my services to him because I thought it was the path to the Fatestone. What was I supposed to do in battle now that he'd made the truth about himself clear?

Annoyance finally cracked his facade. "I don't have time for this right now. I don't have to defend my rule to you. You are but a subject who serves me for the greater good. Remember that." He walked away to where Gorval and Raisa made their own preparations on the other side of the room.

None of my words had meant anything to him.

I felt sick to my stomach. I didn't know what to do. My blood already painted his skin. I could wait until he entered the arena to break the enchantments and let Ina make short work of him, but what then? The kingdom would collapse. The same would happen if I tried to tear him apart myself, and since he was bound to the gods, it might incite their rage. Then what? I doubted they would give me the chance to rewrite history under those circumstances.

No good choice existed.

There was nothing left to do but see the battle through—if not for myself, then for my kingdom. I had to survive so that I could get the Fatestone back from the king and rewrite the past. It was the only way.

I went out to the royal viewing box and waited for the battle to begin, casting glances into the audience, looking for some sign of Hal. I shivered with nerves even though the snow had stopped.

In keeping with tradition, as the challenger, Ina entered the battlefield first.

When the doors on her side opened, the crowd shouted a mixed chorus of cheers and boos. She wore white again, fitted pants that would allow her to move without getting caught on anything and a white shirt that floated around her like silk. Only the faintest swell of her belly indicated that she'd had a baby just one moon ago. I doubted anyone else noticed.

It was hard to look away from her face, which was painted with my blood. She could have put the symbols anywhere, but I knew why she'd done it—to strike terror into people's hearts. To make sure they remembered her whether she lived or died in the challenge.

Even in human form, she looked fierce and feral, more animal than human.

Three red streaks were smeared vertically down one of her cheeks, and two horizontal ones adorned the other. At the center of her forehead, the blood had been painted into a circle. The markings glowed with magic in my Sight. Nismae had grown masterful with her enchantments in the time she'd had to practice. I caught a glimpse of her just inside the entrance to the challenger's quarters, waiting at the ready to manipulate the energies of Ina's enchantments.

Where in the Sixth Hell was Hal? My anxiety was reaching a fever pitch. I wanted to talk to him. I needed his help figuring out what to do. How could I support the king after his vile betrayal? Had he hurt me more or had Nismae? I didn't even know anymore.

Ina stopped about a quarter of the way into the coliseum, looking very small in the middle of the battlefield, but that illusion was dispelled the moment she took her manifest. As she changed into the dragon, the crowd stomped their feet and roared. She leaped straight into the air, breathing a plume of flame that showered the audience with sparks. Then she landed and stalked around the ring, making a display of herself. No one dared to defy the boar king by carrying Ina's flag into the king's coliseum, but everywhere I saw people with white ribbons tied around their wrists. She was not in this alone. Most of her supporters seemed to have come from outside Corovja. They were the people of small towns, of overtaxed cities, those who had felt distant from the crown for far too long. Ina was their champion and their voice. Now she had to fight for them.

Gorval emerged from the king's side of the stadium as the first champion of the king. He walked out in human form as Ina had. The crowd murmured in confusion. People asked each other who would pit this shrew of a man against a dragon. I knew he'd been hiding something, but I didn't understand until he took his manifest.

Gorval's body rippled and expanded. When the magic stopped distorting the area around him, I gasped. His manifest had the body of a lion, the wings and head of an eagle, and the scaly tail of a serpent—a chimera, someone who had taken multiple manifests. I had never seen or heard of anything like him before, not outside of legends. He screamed his own challenge, a sound so high and sharp the entire audience collectively winced.

Then both challenger and champion took to the sky.

The chimera wasted no time, using his ear-piercing scream to his advantage. But Ina had both size and speed on him. She dodged his attacks with ease. My body trembled with memory watching her—she was even more deadly than the reckless creature she'd been when she killed the bandits outside Amalska. Nismae wasn't even going to have to touch the powerful enchantments she'd set.

Guilt tasted bitter on my tongue. Even if I could tell Nismae now that the king had the Fatestone, it wouldn't change anything. He'd already achieved what both of us hoped to prevent, and the amulet was no use in battle anyway. All it would do was ensure that whoever won and wore it never had to age again.

When Ina tired of letting the chimera chase her, she snapped off his tail in one bite. She spat it at the feet of the king, and it rolled through the sand toward us, oozing blood, still writhing.

I gagged.

Then she used a burst of flame to torch the chimera's wings, and tore out a mouthful of pinion feathers while they still burned.

My stomach heaved again.

Gorval's shrieks now were not of challenge, but of agony as he clumsily flapped back to the ground, barely managing to stop his fall. The sound of his pain cut me to the core. If I could have done anything to help him, I would have. I didn't care that my instructions had been explicit—save my power for the king if the battle came to that point. But in my weakened state, there was little I could do for Gorval without having enchanted him before the battle. I had to save my power whether I wanted to or not.

When Gorval hit the ground, Ina was already there with a swift strike to the neck to end him. He collapsed into the sand, but she wasn't done. She picked up his dying body in her claws and flew a victory lap around the coliseum, showering the spectators with blood and sand as they screamed and cheered. I pulled up the hood of my red cloak, shuddering as Ina passed overhead—and for the first time, grateful for the color of the wool.

Ina finally dropped the carcass in front of the door to the king's side of the coliseum only a few lengths from where I sat. Her nearness made me shiver with nerves. If she knew how much support I was supposed to lend the king, would she pluck me out of the audience and kill me for fun? It was against the rules of the challenge, but I wasn't sure that mattered.

Ina paced through the ring while attendants cleared the body and raked up as much of the blood from the sand as they could. She lashed her tail, eyes still glittering with bloodlust, impatient for the second challenger to arrive. She didn't look the slightest bit winded, and the chimera hadn't managed to land a single strike on her. The only blood on her was mine, and she hadn't even needed to use the magic of it yet. Nismae still stood waiting in the wings, biding her time for the battle that mattered.

The longer they went without using the enchantments, the more nervous I became. It was true that the strength of my magic was more than a match for Nismae's, but she had time and experience on her side. I was exhausted from spending two nights in a tomb.

High Councillor Raisa ascended the stairs next. She moved unsteadily, using the railing to support and guide herself. But once she entered the ring, she straightened, the years seeming to fall away as she skimmed power from the thoughts and feelings and emotions of everyone in the coliseum, all of which still ran high from the battle. Her magic stung, like thorns or nettles working their way into my skull. As she did so, her body unbent itself until she stood steady on her feet, looking closer to forty winters of age than the many centuries she'd lived.

Ina roared and it sounded like laughter. She wasn't the least bit afraid. I clenched my cloak so tightly I thought my hands might go numb. What none of us knew was how many of my gifts Nismae might have been able to impart to Ina with my blood. If she had figured out how to use the most dangerous of my powers, all it would take was a tug on the threads of Raisa's magic to pull her away into nothingness, to hand her over to the shadow god.

Part of me wanted to make a break for it—to race across the ring to the challenger's side and find Hal. Get Zallie and the children and leave now before the worst of the battle could come to pass. I didn't know how to help the king who had betrayed me so deeply, who had left me to die. But how could I switch to Ina's side when she and Nismae had done things just as terrible?

Unlike the ill-fated chimera, Raisa was not going to let Ina make the first move. She flicked her hand and a cloud of magic floated toward Ina, who snapped at it, only to freeze in place when it hit her. She backed up quickly, shaking her head, trying to free herself of the misty shroud following her. She screamed a roar of frustration and hurt.

And then I remembered what spirit users could do: give other people emotions and feelings that didn't belong to them. All Ina's worst fears were coming to life inside her mind. Raisa was not a fighter with weapons, but with emotions.

At first, Ina shrank back, but as soon as she realized she couldn't escape the illusions Raisa had woven into her mind, her fury boiled over. She thundered around the ring, roaring, shooting out random bursts of flame. The audience shrank back from the edge, some of them only narrowly avoiding incineration. Raisa wove a spell around herself like a luminous golden shield, separating herself into two people, then three, then four. The illusions kept splitting until a dozen of her circled Ina.

Would Nismae do her part to stop this?

Ina turned in a panicked circle in the middle of the arena, then leaped into the sky. All the Raisas raised their hands, and Ina crashed to the ground as her equilibrium was thrown off by Raisa's spell. Then the illusions closed in.

The crowd surged to its feet. This had never been how we expected this battle to end, with Ina cowering in the center of the ring, keening from the psychological torture wrought on her by a person centuries older than her. Only Ina's tail twitched, sweeping through one of the illusions, and then her head snapped up.

Something about the feel of the magic as her tail passed through it must have reminded her of the Sight. One of my gifts. A gift she could now use thanks to my blood.

She caught Nismae's eye, and one of the streaks of blood painted on her face lit up with magic. With growing horror I watched it glow more and more brightly, saw Ina begin to distinguish reality from illusion. Perhaps I had underestimated Nismae's skill and power. She seemed to be using the strength of Ina's fire magic to give more power to the enchantments she'd set with my blood.

With an unfamiliar gift like Ina's, there was no way to know how much energy she'd have left to use against the king. How deep did that well run? Would I be able to help him enough to hold them off? And did I even want to after what he'd done? I tried to tell myself that anything I did had to be for the best of the kingdom, but if I was honest with myself, all I wanted was the Fatestone and my family. I wanted to take them, run, and never look back.

The moment Ina locked eyes with the real Raisa, she and Nismae pulled the next of my tricks. In a way that was sickeningly familiar, she began to unthread the magic that held Raisa together. I felt it keenly as she reached in, absorbing the power from Raisa and winding its threads into her own until she glowed more and more brightly in my Sight.

Watching someone else do it, knowing the gift had been bestowed with my blood, made my stomach turn inside out. At least Leozoar had asked to die.

As Raisa weakened, so did the illusions, vanishing one by one. The psychological torment must have quieted too, because soon Ina was rising, arching her neck, drinking in Raisa's magic like it was water. She didn't even bother going for blood. The audience had already seen enough of that.

Raisa screamed as her body was stolen from her again, aging back into its previous form and then further, until her skin shrank over her bones, her eyes became empty sockets, and then her bare skeleton crumbled into dust.

Ina roared in triumph, kicking Raisa's ashes into the sky, and then making another lap of the ring. The crowd screamed, still on their feet.

The time had come for Ina to face the king.

The time had come for me to enter the battle in his support.

At this point, it was the last thing I wanted to do.

CHAPTER 37

THE CROWD TOOK THEIR SEATS BUT RAGED ON AS INA
retreated into the challenger's quarters for her final preparations. I
descended from the audience and hovered near the king's entrance to
the coliseum, my nerves jangling as I waited for Ina to return. Cold
wind battered me, making the red cloak whip around my ankles.

Ina emerged still in dragon form, her face painted even more
ornately, the enchantments so bright she was hard to look at with my
Sight. Then a familiar shape moved into place beside Nismae: Hal. A
jolt ran through me, equal parts relief and desperation. What was he
doing still over there? I needed to tell him what the king had done. I
wanted the security of his hand in mine.

The people of Zumorda cheered as their king entered the arena,
perhaps for him, or perhaps for the hope of his blood being spilled.
I was no longer sure which I hoped for. The dragon's eyes narrowed
when she saw the bloody armor, and then she glanced to where I

stood. This wasn't something she'd expected. Her surprise was satisfying, but no match for my despair. I'd helped my betrayer, and it was too late to turn back now. If I did, the kingdom would be destroyed, and there was no guarantee I could get the Fatestone from Ina if she won.

I had no doubt Nismae would be more than happy to claim the Fatestone as proof of her revenge on the king. And even if she handed it over, my powers would drain away along with the magic as it left Zumorda. I'd have to flee to Havemont, where the gods would still be worshipped and nothing had been done to upset the order of their kingdom.

Ina reached for the magic of the king's life force immediately, attempting to rend it into pieces. She tugged at it as if to snap the neck of a small animal. I felt her magic pulling at me, too, but it was easy enough to push it off. The king's enchantments held strong, and the magic slipped away from her. She couldn't use my powers against a person enchanted the same way—especially with me at his back.

The king was slow, but calculating. Ina was fast and filled with fury. Few sounds made it above the shouts of the crowd—the awful sound of teeth on metal when Ina landed a strike, then her roar as he shocked her with lightning that burst from his fingertips, borrowed from the storm clouds brewing on the horizon. Ina retreated, head low, tail whipping.

I felt every jolt of magic, even the fierce shocks as he drew on the powers of all six gods.

The king advanced. I saw him try to draw on her magic as she had attempted with him, but the power slipped away. Though she was bigger, he was more experienced at using magic. He also had the gods on his side, and Ina had only Nismae.

The king took his boar form and charged across the coliseum. The crowd roared incoherently, their screams a demand for blood.

Ina didn't keep them waiting.

She lunged toward him, breathing a storm of fire into the face of the boar. He waited, unperturbed as the flames scudded around a magic shield he threw up as though it was nothing. What he didn't realize was how Ina had closed in behind the fire until she stood only a pace away from him. The moment the flames subsided and he dropped his shield, she snapped for his neck. He tore away with a squeal and her jaws closed around his shoulder instead. He struck back immediately, attempting to gore her with a tusk.

I trembled as they fought, unable to do anything to help with the physical aspect of the battle, but still feeling the king's pain resonate through me. Ina whirled out of reach and reared up on her haunches, never taking her eyes off her prey. The crowd stomped its approval until the earth felt as though it might split in half. In some of the rows near the front, people had begun passing around a container of carmine, painting their cheeks to match the streaks of my blood on Ina's face.

There were no words for the depth of my horror at that sight.

The king returned to his human form to more easily manipulate magic, giving little indication in the way he moved of the deep wound she must have made in his shoulder. I saw it as he turned to the light—the slow drip of blood from beneath the shoulder piece of his armor. Ina saw it too and took her advantage, pressing him back toward her side of the coliseum. He threw up another shield, this one pulsing with red light. Ina's flame rippled around it, sending smoke into the sky. He was going to need more power to maintain these kinds of shields, much less heal. And more yet to put himself back on the offensive.

I felt it coming before the king's magic touched me. He tried to reach through our bonds of blood and drain my magic to use for his own. I whispered a prayer of thanks for my shadow cloak hidden beneath the red wool to protect me from that kind of magic. Ina and Nismae were the ones I'd expected to need protection from. Not the king.

Fury rose, hot in my chest.

How dare he?

With the gods to channel and my blood enhancing him, there was no reason to steal my magic unless he wanted me dead.

Perhaps he did.

I couldn't trust him—not when he'd left me for dead in Veric's tomb and now was trying to end me a different way. I'd already sacrificed enough to help both sides of this battle.

I wasn't going to help him anymore.

I looked around, trying to guess what else he might draw magic from, realizing that only one other person in the entire coliseum glowed brightly in my Sight.

Hal.

The king reached for Hal's power and began to tug.

"No!" I screamed, but my voice was lost in the crowd.

Wispy threads of magic unwound themselves from Hal as the king drew them in to use as his own. Through my connection with the king, I felt the wound in his shoulder begin to close. Hal stumbled a few steps into the coliseum, like a puppet pulled by strings.

Shimmering threads of magic joined the two of them, and the audience gasped in awe. Even the mortals were able to see the transfer of power.

Nismae sprinted into the arena, and then grabbed Hal in an embrace as though to drag him back into the challenger's quarters. The moment her arms closed around him, the king's magic exploded against her iron cuffs. The threads snapped loose and recoiled on both of them, sending a shock all the way back through the king to me. Hal and Nismae fell to the sand, unmoving.

It took everything I had not to bolt out of the doorway of the king's side of the coliseum and straight to Hal, but it wasn't safe. Ina was still on the move. She arched her neck and opened her wings, roaring with fury, falling on the king more savagely than ever.

Even with Ina's rage fueling her, the king had drawn enough power from Hal that he was not going to be easy to destroy. He nimbly shielded himself from her and flung magic back into her face, battering her until she slunk backward around the edge of the ring. He was playing with her like a toy. Nismae's enchantments on Ina had weakened or broken. She had to be unconscious, if not close to death, for that to happen. My heart pounded with fear for Hal. I only knew he was still alive thanks to his aura in my Sight, but it was weak. Too weak.

The entire audience was on their feet again, the floor trembling as they stomped.

It seemed the king was going to defeat a dragon—something unheard of.

I couldn't let that happen.

The king disgusted me. He'd used me; Nismae had been right.

He only cared about himself. In the space of two days he'd shown willingness to sacrifice me for his cause, and now Hal. Neither of us had ever done anything but support him.

The time for loyalty was over—I had no one to be loyal to but my family and myself. I knew what I had to do to save Hal—and my kingdom.

I needed Ina to win.

As volatile and dangerous as she was, she wasn't as selfish as the king. A chance of recovering the Fatestone from Ina was worth avoiding letting the king achieve his goal of virtual immortality. If the kingdom was destroyed in a few days by Ina's win, I could run for Havemont and rewrite it. If the king had the Fatestone and destroyed the kingdom over a hundred years or more . . . that future was far too vast to tame and shape.

First I broke all the enchantments on the king. A few murmured words and the magic faded, leaving him painted with nothing but ordinary blood. The only sign that he felt it was the way he paused in his advance on Ina, just for a heartbeat. He believed he'd already won. He still had the power of the gods, and he switched to channeling theirs with barely any sign that I'd inconvenienced him. My blood was of help to him, but not a necessity.

He wasn't counting on what else I was willing to do to take him down.

I pushed past my exhaustion and reached for the dark river of my magic. I let it flood through me and sent questing tendrils out toward the king. He was so absorbed in sending waves of water crashing over Ina to douse her fire magic that he didn't notice me.

I didn't touch the magic of the gods, but instead wove my power through the very magic that gave him life.

Then I pulled. Hard.

That stopped him in his tracks.

Ina raised her head. She knew something had changed. The predatory gleam in her eye was back, and she wasn't going to waste an opportunity.

I waited to feel guilty, but the feeling didn't come. All that came was a rush of energy flooding in as I stole it from the king, making me feel more alive than I had in weeks.

His face contorted in fear as Ina slammed him to the ground. She tore off his armor piece by piece, giving the audience time to crescendo into a deafening roar.

Between me and Ina, the king was helpless, pinned to the ground with nothing between him and death but cloth and leather. Ina slowly dug in the claws resting on his chest. The king's scream rose to join that of the rest of the crowd.

Ina's fangs closed around his throat to choke off the sound. She tore out his windpipe, spattering her white scales with his blood. A pool of red spread beneath him.

Zumorda had its new queen.

CHAPTER 38

I IGNORED THE OVERWHELMING SHOUTS OF THE CROWD and ran into the combat arena.

My focus was singular: I had to get the Fatestone.

Ina still stood over the king's body, both of them now in human form.

When she saw me coming, she stepped in front of his body like an animal defending her kill. Then she saw where my focus lay. She bent down and tugged the golden ring from his finger.

I came to a stop before her, staring her down in a way I'd never done before. My place had always been to accommodate her, to please her, to love her.

My days of subservience were over.

"Give me the ring!" My voice cut through the roar of the audience.

Ina behaved as if I hadn't spoken. She cast a nervous glance at

Nismae, who still lay in the sand, unmoving. Hal wasn't far from Nismae, but I could still sense the brightness of his life force in spite of what the king had drained.

"I just helped you win the crown," I said. "Give me that ring."

"You did that?" Ina hesitated. She had to have sensed the transference of power. It was too big to ignore if she had the Sight activated at all, and I knew she had.

I was out of patience, and power still coursed through me. "I did it to him and I'll do it to you if you don't give me that ring right now." I let my magic slip into hers and tugged just enough to be a warning.

She fell to her knees. The audience gasped to see their new queen on the ground.

"I don't want to hurt you, but I will if I must," I said. She undoubtedly knew how priceless the Fatestone was, but not necessarily what it would allow me to do or how badly I needed it.

Her gaze flickered to Nismae. Worry creased her brow.

"Only if you agree to help Nismae," Ina said, raising her chin. Her eyes flashed in a way that once would have frightened me.

"You're in no position to bargain with a daughter of the shadow god," I said.

Ina's eyes widened. She only knew the version of my story that had long since been proven untrue.

"Demigod or not, I'm still your queen." She didn't back down, even on her knees.

I crouched beside her. "Queen or not, I can tear you apart."

Our eyes locked.

"I'd like to see you try," she said, but her voice faltered. She was tired from the battle, and maybe she could see the truth in my eyes—that I no longer loved her like I had back home.

"Give me the ring and you'll have your crown." I held out my hand.

She pulled off the ring and threw it into the dirt, then scrambled to her feet and fled toward Nismae.

I snatched the ring and put it back on my finger.

Hal.

I hurried to where he lay.

"Hal," I cried, checking for a heartbeat. It was faint, but it was there. Without hesitation I threw most of the king's magic that I'd stolen into him. Power flooded through him, pulsing and twisting wildly until the glow of his energy brightened in my Sight.

His eyes flew open and he sat up, gasping for breath.

I threw my arms around him, so grateful that he was all right.

"Nismae doesn't have the Fatestone," he said.

"It's all right," I murmured, burying my face in his neck. "I got it."

He kissed me softly and then looked to where his sister lay.

"Oh no," he said, scrambling through the sand to her side.

Ina fixed him with a look fierce enough to melt rock, but he paid her no mind.

Hal checked Nismae's pulse and listened for breath.

"She's barely breathing," he said. "She's going to die all because she saved me. Oh gods . . ."

His pain cut through me as Ina's once might have. I wanted to help Hal. But Nismae had never done me a single kindness, unless not killing me counted. But she'd saved someone I loved.

"Do something!" Ina looked at me. "You fixed him. Now fix her!"

On the far side of the coliseum, a palace attendant was approaching with the crown in his hands.

"I can't do this without you," Ina whispered to Nismae.

Hal hung his head.

Their combined suffering was too much. I poured the last of the king's magic into Nismae.

A few moments later she coughed weakly.

"Nis!" Ina said, hugging Nismae as she sat up. "Oh, thank the gods."

"My blade is yours, Invasya. So are my scrolls. Now and always," she said, her voice gravelly.

Ina's eyes softened and a shaky smile came over her face as she looked at Nismae in a way she'd never looked at me. Nismae gazed back with equal intensity in spite of her weakened state. What passed between them in that moment—I couldn't help but notice it looked a little bit like love.

"We need to go right now," I said to Hal.

He nodded. "Good luck," he said to Nismae.

"Don't be stupid out there," she said. They embraced, fiercely, with the tightness of two people who know they are unlikely to see each other ever again.

Then we turned and fled.

I looked back only once, just in time to see the intricate silver wreath of the Zumordan crown placed on Ina's head. As we passed beneath the arches leading out of the coliseum, the flags around the edges of the building changed from red to white in a burst of magic.

In my Sight, something cracked. Or perhaps it was the sound of the Grand Temple breaking under the pressure of the magic rushing toward it. The ground trembled as the Great Temple began to slide off the side of the mountain. Chunks of rock and shards of stained glass tumbled down, sending up clouds of dust.

The king hadn't lied about one thing—the gods were leaving Zumorda with him. They wouldn't tolerate a ruler who had a manifest outside their gifts, who didn't need them in order to be strong. Magic sank slowly into the ground in my Sight. Though the collapse of the kingdom had barely begun, I could already feel how it wanted to take me with it. It was like sinking into deep and paralyzing mud. None of the demigods would last long under Ina's rule. Not with the bond between the monarch and the gods severed.

"We have to go. Now. My Sight is already fading, and I don't know how long we have. Can you spread word on the wind to all your siblings? Tell them to gather everyone like us. Tell them to flee," I said. We had to get to Havemont, where my power would still be reliable, for there to be any hope of changing the past. I needed time to sit, to think, to figure out how to unravel the series of disasters since Ina and I had left Amalska.

Hal nodded. He whispered to the wind, to the ears of all who were listening. He whispered of the change about to come, of how magic would leave the land under Ina's rule now that the bond between the gods and the crown was broken. I hoped they could feel it already, the way power was draining out of us, crackling out across the landscape like untethered threads whipping and sparking in the wind.

I hoped they had the sense to go and the speed to outrun the death that awaited them if they didn't.

CHAPTER 39

WE MET ZALLIE AND THE CHILDREN AT THE SWITCH-back Inn and headed north for Havemont that same day. There was no time to waste. Hal's Farhearing and my Sight had already faded to almost nothing before we even reached the outskirts of Corovja. I had my satchel and my herbs, but without my gifts I felt much less sure of my ability to protect our group. Hal's worries were just as clearly written on his face, and almost everything startled him because he was so unused to being without his Farhearing. We had to get to Havemont, where the gods would still be in power—somewhere our gifts would work, the children would be safe, and I could rewrite the past.

As for the Fatestone, I kept it on a strip of leather tied around my neck, tucked under my clothing where no one would see it.

We were hardly the only travelers on the road. Many mortals chose to flee Zumorda, hoping they could escape before losing their manifests. Others chose to stay in spite of the risks. Word of the ancient blood rite Ina had used to take her manifest had spread, and some had successfully rebonded with their animal forms by using it.

Storms ravaged the kingdom as we traveled to Havemont, slowing the brutal pace we tried to keep in our haste to escape. Rivers eroded their banks and swept away homes. Farmers lost their final harvests of autumn. Trees seemed to be curling in on themselves, warping in strange ways that shouldn't have been possible. In the few times I got a glimpse of the Sight, it was easy to see why. Magic was funneling away, just as the gods had threatened.

Five days after leaving Corovja, we crossed the Havemont border in the back of a farmer's wagon with Iman and Nera both crying. Zallie and I tried to rock and soothe them, but the journey had been hard on us all. I had done my fair share of crying too—over the loss of my kingdom, the devastation I hadn't been able to prevent, and the fears I had about what was yet to come.

The change on the opposite side of the Zir Canyon bridge was instant. Suddenly the grass was greener, the skies brighter, everything more peaceful. My Sight came back so quickly it was almost hard to use due to its strength.

The border town of Fairlough appeared before us in the afternoon as crickets began to hum in the grass. A stone keep sat high above the settlement. Farmland led right up to the heart of the town, but the main street was still sizable enough to boast a series of shops and a large inn. The buildings were far more permanent and well kept than some of the rickety markets I'd seen in smaller villages during my travels with Hal. Something about the town felt off to me, and then I realized it was the people. The Havemontians worshipped the same gods we did, but unlike Zumordans, they did not take manifests. The people appeared strangely empty in my Sight compared with those who carried a second soul inside their bodies.

In a way, the difference was comforting. The gods still watched over Havemont, which meant we would retain our powers, and because the mortals had no manifests, we could blend in as long as we kept our magic secret.

Before our first afternoon in town was spent, Hal earned a basket of fresh fruit and vegetables from a farmer whose cart he helped load at the market square. Iman and Nera turned out to be the key to finding a place to stay. The innkeeper's wife, the last of whose three sons had moved out not so long ago, was instantly smitten with the babies and offered us two rooms in exchange for light work. After all of us being crammed into one room in Corovja, the two plainly furnished rooms still seemed luxurious by comparison. I felt guilty that we might not be there very long, but I needed enough time to recover from the battle to properly rewrite the past—to map out the way things should have gone. If I succeeded, everything would be different anyway.

Even once all our arrangements were made, I found it hard to shake the feeling that I needed to keep moving. At this point, I was used to it, and every time I looked at Hal and felt a burst of affection for him, I remembered what he'd wished for us—that we could take to the road as a family of explorers, not refugees.

But someone would always be hunting me for the power that ran through my veins, and carrying the Fatestone made it doubly likely. I wasn't fool enough to think that would stop just because Ina had finally gotten the crown she wanted. That didn't mean there wouldn't be others, either. I kept my shadow cloak close, taking comfort in its warmth and ability to hide me from anyone who might be able to sense magic.

All I had ever wanted was happiness for those I loved and a place to live where I could be an herbalist and help people quietly as I had before. Yet my journey had changed me.

Lying in bed beside Hal a few nights later, I asked him the impossible question.

"What should I do?" I whispered into his shoulder. The difficult thing was that lying beside him with Zallie, Iman, and Nera in a room just on the other side of the door felt so right. I feared what might come chasing me, but if not for that, perhaps I could learn to be happy here with this patchwork family of mine.

"You're going to change the past, right?" His voice was a little guarded, as it always was when we talked about the past or the future and the ways I could shape them.

"That's why we did all this—that's why we got the Fatestone," I said.

"But?" he asked.

In another version of my past, I might have met Hal anyway. Perhaps Iman could still have his own mother and father if I hadn't interfered with the fate of his parents. Ina could be a village elder instead of a bloodstained queen. I might have stayed on my mountain and grown old in the slow way that demigods normally do.

But I had to write for my kingdom, not for myself—for the land I had sworn to protect that was now falling apart. The land itself would give up on life, slowly becoming a desert instead of the verdant mountains, valleys, and plains that existed now. There would be nothing for people to eat, no resources from which they could build their homes or pay their tithes to the crown. Without my intervention, people would struggle to survive in the barren landscape Zumorda would become.

I couldn't let that happen.

"I need to save Zumorda and its people. That is the biggest thing. But I'm afraid if I rewrite the past to change their fate, I'll make things worse in some unexpected way. And if I'm honest about what I want . . . it's right here. With you."

He turned toward me and kissed my collarbone, making warmth blossom in my stomach.

I ran my fingertips down his bare arm, then buried my face in his neck.

"Your nose is cold," he murmured, a smile in his voice, and then he took my arm and wrapped it around his waist. I kissed his shoulder, and his hum of contentment sent desire racing through me.

"I love you, Asra," he said.

Our mouths met, his arm wrapping around me to pull me closer. I loved him too. I loved that when he deepened a kiss, he did it like it was a question. When he held me, it was with the care he took with any precious thing, but never with any restriction that would bind me. I loved the way he talked to Iman, as though the baby could understand every story and song and joke he told him.

It would be so difficult to say good-bye to that.

"I love you, too," I whispered.

"Surely there has to be a way to fix the past that might give us a similar future?" he said, hope and sadness warring in his voice.

"I don't know. The past is so hard to change. The past we have is what led us here. One tiny change could send everything spiraling in any of a thousand different directions. Every moment is full of possibilities for a different future that would become our present," I said. I wished I could show him what it looked like in my Sight, all the complicated nuances of time and fate.

"Is the future any easier to shape?" he asked. "At least there is more choice involved in that. The future is something more than fate. It's filled with choices. It's a collaboration with those you love. Or that's what I hope our future would be, anyway."

My obsession with changing the past had blinded me to the other option—changing the future. Guilt and grief still racked me every time I thought of Amalska and its people, but changing the past might not protect them. Even without my interference, Ina might still have resorted to the blood rite to take her manifest. Bandits might have still attacked. She still might have gone after the king. Could I truly write the past with enough clarity to prevent any of those things from coming to pass?

"What if I changed the future instead?" I asked Hal, trying to keep the excitement out of my voice.

"In what way?" He propped himself up on an elbow.

"Fix the kingdom from here forward. There are things that wouldn't be made right—the destruction of Amalska, mostly. That loss and those memories will never stop hurting."

"It could have happened anyway," Hal said as he had a hundred times before.

"I know. And that's what I'm worried about. What if I rewrite the past and it turns into a multi-village massacre? Or those bandits don't die and instead loot their way across the entire kingdom? I can try to prevent those things from happening, but I can't possibly think of every disaster scenario. I certainly didn't realize Ina would take a dragon as her manifest when I first wrote that fate for her."

"So what happens if you change the future?" he asked. "How can you possibly undo the destruction Ina's reign has already caused?"

"What if I create a feedback loop to sustain the magic of the kingdom?" I asked.

"I don't have any idea what you're talking about," Hal said.

"It would be similar to how Ina's manifest works. She's tied to the land. So the land would be tied to the people, and as the people die, their energy would go back to the land. It becomes self-sustaining. The Tamers would probably like it because it would make it difficult for Zumordans to do any damage to their land without suffering for it. Many more people would probably end up with affinities for certain types of magic like Ina has for fire, but as long as the affinities don't get out of control . . ." I muttered a long list of probable outcomes.

"If this future means I can go to sleep now knowing you'll still be next to me when I wake up in the morning, then it sounds good to me," Hal said. "And if I could have the chance to reconcile more fully with my sister someday . . . I'd like that, too."

"I think I can do this," I said, springing out of bed with a fresh wave of energy.

"Don't stay up too late," he said, sleepy contentment in his voice.

I rolled out of bed and tucked in the blankets around him, envious of how quickly his breathing grew deep and even as he drifted off to sleep.

I sat down at the little desk in the corner of the room and put on my shadow cloak. It enveloped me like an embrace, and I thought of my mother and her own mantle of darkness, wishing that she and I could have had a different story, too. She should have trusted me to grow up close to death in all its incarnations. Perhaps if I had grown up knowing it, I would not have dealt so much of it by mistake.

From my belt pouch, I took out an eagle feather stolen from one of Nismae's brethren and a sprig of midnight thistle I'd gathered along the side of the road on the way out of Corovja. I took the Fate-stone from its place around my neck and slipped it over my finger.

I pinned the feather to the table with my wrist, then sharpened the feather with my silver knife until the quill was fine and true. My left hand bore too many scars to count, but this one would be the last. I pricked my finger with the silver knife and let my blood drip into a small bowl bearing the thistles, and then I stirred, remembering Ina.

What I knew now was that the love I had for Ina had not been love at all. I had been chasing her before we left Amalska, from the first day we met, from the time I noticed that the blue of her eyes matched all my favorite flowers on the mountain. In all that time running after her, I'd raced on the ground, but she'd had wings long before she took the dragon as her manifest.

I dipped my quill into the ink.

Magic had always held our kingdom together, and it still needed to do that. The people themselves could be the key. The magic could be tied to the people instead of the monarch and the gods—rather like what Nismae and Ina had hoped for the future. Perhaps given the right set of circumstances, Ina wouldn't be a bad monarch. Her ambition might serve her well in the end.

I put my quill to the paper, carefully scribing the first words of a new story for Zumorda—not of the past, but the future. The magic poured out of me and into the words as I wove our kingdom back together. I dictated that the people, land, and power of Zumorda would be bound in a way that would sustain them all. The ability to wield magic would be given to the people with aptitudes and affinities for it, those who felt something extra when they built a fire, plucked a flower, or stood outside in the rain—those who loved the land and the kingdom.

Instead of manifests being tied to a god, they would be tied to the elements that often went with those gods—a simpler, more primitive magic. Each person with even the barest hint of ability would have an affinity connected to the god who had once blessed their manifest, like Ina's for fire, Hal's for wind, or mine for blood and shadows. The people would use their powers to defend their kingdom instead of relying on the divine.

Ina was the only person I wrote of by name—that she would strive to be a good ruler. That she would respect those she ruled. And one day, she would face one of Iman's descendants, who would help her learn the true nature of love.

When I finished writing, it was strange to put down the quill and not feel pain. After I sanded the pages, it was time for the last thing I needed to do. I murmured an apology to Veric and then unraveled the magic of the Fatestone itself. The blood channel through it slowly stopped moving, then turned black.

Now it was nothing but an ordinary ring.

Perhaps my days would be lived here in Fairlough with Hal, Iman, Nera, and Zallie, or one day Hal and I would take to traveling again, this time without missions of blood and vengeance following us. Either way, I wanted to spend my life with the people who had finally given me a home and a community. No one needed to know of my gifts—I didn't intend to use them again. I would only be known as the town herbalist, someone people could come to in need.

I crossed the room and slipped back into bed with Hal. Our future would be shaped as we willed it. Together.

Because love was a heart filled with kindness, eyes a deep brown that warmed me from the inside out, and a hand I could count on to hold through the next adventure. Love was the way he made me laugh when I least thought it possible, and the way our voices came together to sing a tavern song inappropriate for most company. Love was the way he kissed me until I knew without doubt that anywhere he was would be home. And love was the way Iman looked when he smiled, filling me with contentment that lasted long after I'd put him down to sleep.

Love was what would last through this winter—and many more to come.

When our story began, I thought I knew love.

In the end, I finally did.

 ACKNOWLEDGMENTS

I have no idea how I survived writing my second book except that it had everything to do with the people supporting me.

Alexandra Machinist, thanks a billion for making such a wonderful match by selling my books to Balzer + Bray. You are a superstar and I'm glad to have you on my side. Thanks are also due to Hillary Jacobsen, who is now a fantastic agent in her own right. Not once during the creation of this book did I ever have to worry about things being handled on the back end thanks to the diligent work of Alexandra and her team at ICM. You all rock!

Kristin Rens, thank you for slogging through this book with me and for your patience when I was struggling most. You may claim working on this book wasn't as painful for you as for me, but I know it wasn't easy. Having an editor who works so hard and is thoughtful, responsive, and kind is a blessing beyond belief. Many thanks also go to Kelsey Murphy, who makes sure all sorts of things run smoothly and does an outstanding job stepping in when Kristin is out of the office. Michelle Taormina and Jacob Eisinger—how do you keep giving me such incredible covers? Thank you from the bottom of my heart. The whole team at Balzer + Bray is one I'm lucky to work with. I'm so grateful to Audrey Diestelkamp and Caroline Sun and their teams for their contributions and support as my manuscripts travel through the cube maze that is book publishing.

Without my critique partners, I would be sobbing into a drink somewhere instead of having two finished books to my name. Elizabeth Briggs, you are a first-class mentor and friend, and I'm forever grateful that Pitch Wars brought us together. The ending of this book would still be a hot mess if not for your input and wisdom. Ben Chiles, thank you for your boundless encouragement and genuine friendship no matter how much our daily lives get in the way of staying caught up. Helen Wiley, thank you for being my primary plot wizard, reader, and rereader, always willing to lend a hand when I'm in a panic. You've saved me more times than you know. When your book is published someday, I can't wait to cheer you on and support you with the same steadfastness you've always offered me. Kali Wallace, thank you for being the source of logic, common sense, and reminders not to overwork myself, even if I don't always listen. Thank you also for your helpful plot suggestions, which mostly involve murder or finding dead things in the woods. Your thoughtful comments and careful consideration as a reader make you a wonderful critique partner, and it doesn't hurt that I'm always disgustingly eager to read whatever you're working on. #WallaceTrashForever

Paula Garner, what am I even supposed to say? It's still not clear to me how or why we met, connected like we did, and built the friendship we have, but it's one of the few things in my life that make me believe in some kind of higher power. You've immeasurably improved every book of mine you've read and critiqued, and you always leave me in awe of your diligence and talent as a writer. I may be the one who saved you from falling into the Willamette, but you're the one who regularly saves me from drowning in my own life. When I'm sad, you make me laugh. When I'm upset, you comfort me. When we have hard conversations or disagree, you always listen and respond with honesty and respect. When I procrastigloom, you're there with a swift kick to the ass. And when we write together, we make the most incredible magic. Never leave me!

A massive debt of gratitude is owed to the sensitivity readers who gave me thoughtful criticism of a number of aspects of *Inkmistress*. Dahlia Adler, thank you for your careful eye and wise notes regarding bisexuality. Vee Signorelli and Tiff Ferentini, I'm so grateful for the insightful comments you provided regarding the representation of genderfluid characters. Lastly, though I don't know your name, thank you to the moon and back to the reader who gave me their perspective on the black characters in *Inkmistress*. Your feedback was delivered matter-of-factly and generously, even when I had screwed up in ways that were hurtful. Your patience as I struggled to get things right was deeply appreciated. My representation of black characters in this book may not be perfect, but it is a damn sight better because of you.

Thank you to my day job keepers of sanity, Allison Saft, Katie Stout, and Elisha Walker. Without you as members of my team, I might have collapsed into a heap of overwork years ago, never to emerge again. I am so grateful for the way our team supports each other through both good and bad times. Go Team Awesome! Speaking of coworkers, Gretchen Flicker, for someone who doesn't write novels, you're awfully good at plot and character motivation. Thank you for your help making the boar king who he is today, for the loan of your convection oven when I was in the mood for basque cake, and for the splendid visits to the central coast.

Thank you also to the Sweet Sixteens and the Class of 2k16, groups in which I found some wonderful friends and critique partners. Many thanks also to the Fight Me Club, who are an ongoing source of discussion, education, and righteous ass kicking. Yay YA and Team Briggs are also places I can always go for support and advice—thank you to all members for your generosity and helpfulness.

And where would I be without fellow writers? Thank you, Traci Chee, Jessica Cluess, Corinne Duyvis, Mercedes Lackey, Rebecca Leach, Malinda Lo, Jessica Love, Adriana Mather, Mary McCoy, Kathryn Rose, Gretchen Schreiber, Rachel Searles, Amy Tintera, and members of the Austin Java Writing Company. Events, blurbs, meetups, swag, moral support, getaways, plot ideas, or commiseration—you have me covered. I'm lucky to know all of you and am deeply grateful for our friendship or acquaintanceship as the case may be.

And of course a big thanks is owed to the blogging community— you played a huge role in the success of *Of Fire and Stars* and you were also some of the first *Inkmistress* enthusiasts. Thank you for doing all kinds of hard work purely out of love for books and reading. Your passion is a joy to behold, and authors are lucky to have you as cheerleaders.

And finally, there are no words large enough to sum up my appreciation of my sweet wife, Casi Clarkson. You are always so supportive and encouraging, and I'm grateful for the many times you've recommended my book to others. You also took on many heavy burdens and accepted being essentially widowed for a year while I wrote *Inkmistress*. Without you, this book never would have come to be. Thank you for making it possible and for loving me along the way.

Read on for a sneak peek at the
sequel to *Of Fire and Stars*:

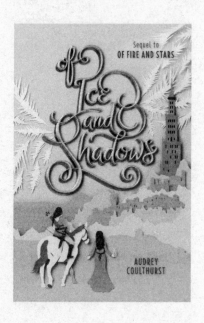

WHEN I LEFT MY KINGDOM FOR THE FIRST TIME, IT WAS on a mission to serve the crown I'd never given half a damn about pleasing. My horse, Flicker, carried us at a brisk walk that quickly left the wide stone bridge and border guards behind. The red road we'd already been on for leagues stretched out ahead, flanked by evergreen trees identical to the thousands we'd already passed, and the chilly wind that had chased us out of Mynaria continued to gust relentlessly.

"I expected Zumorda to look different from home," I said to the girl riding behind me.

"Why?" Denna asked.

"I don't know," I said. "People talk about this place like it's some kind of mysterious death trap." I thought the landscape would reflect that somehow—or at least justify the uneasiness that knotted my shoulders. After all, I was a girl without magic who had entered a kingdom where nearly everyone else had it. Coming here willingly made me about as sharp as a bag of wet barn mice.

"People like to exaggerate," Denna said. "This is a trade road, and the horse merchants cross here all the time."

"It seems too quiet." My saddle creaked with the rhythm of my horse's strides as the wind whispered through the pines. All else was silent.

"After that fuss at the bridge, anywhere would seem quiet," Denna said.

"You're right." Perhaps the frustrating half-day struggle with the border guards to let us cross the bridge had made me forget the hush of the open road. Perhaps it was that we'd so recently left behind the steady rush of the river dividing my homeland from this place—a kingdom I'd grown up hearing was full of magic-using heretics. Or perhaps I was just waiting for something bad to happen.

The frigid late-autumn wind pushed us forward, sending a bone-deep chill through me. I urged Flicker to extend his walk, hoping to leave my anxieties behind. I focused on the press of Denna's body against mine, a reminder that I wasn't alone. Without question, she was the only thing that had made the long, cold ride to Zumorda tolerable. The way her eyes danced when she smiled lit me up like nothing else in the world. I loved her fierceness and her intelligence and her ability to find her way out of almost any situation with her wits.

I didn't love that everyone believed she was dead, or that her presence with me made both of us traitors.

"I'm starting to think going on a quest in winter wasn't my brightest idea," I said with a shiver.

"We should have run away moons ago and gone to Trindor and

the sea," Denna replied.

I smiled at the thought, knowing it never would have happened. Denna had been much too concerned with doing her duty for both our kingdoms, and if I was being honest, I'd never especially wanted to leave Mynaria. "If I'd been the heir to the throne instead of my brother, we wouldn't have had to run away at all."

"True," she said. "But you would have hated that role."

"Also true," I said. Minding my manners and paying attention to my studies hadn't ever been my best skills, and expertise with horses would only take a princess so far, even in Mynaria, where horsemanship was a strong measure of rank. Still, I felt a little stab of guilt about the choices Denna and I had made that had ended her betrothal. In the past year my brother and I had lost our father and uncle, but at least I still had Denna. All Thandi had was a crown and the aftermath of a foreign coup to contend with.

"Either way, I'm sorry this is what it came to," she said.

"Don't apologize. It's not your fault I'm not used to the cold. Besides, I'm the chowderhead who got my brother to send me to Zumorda to open a dialogue with them. I should have just told him I was going to join the Sisters of the Holy Wineskin or some other made-up nonsense. If I'd told him I was off to run barefoot through the woods and become a vintner surrounded by other wild women, he'd probably have believed it with no questions asked." The thought amused me in spite of the accompanying twinge of guilt at the thought of lying to my brother. We'd rarely gotten along, but we'd mostly been honest with each other—usually to the point of brutality.

Denna laughed. "I'm glad you're with me instead." She tightened her arms.

"Me too," I said, lifting a gloved hand to squeeze her arm in return. Strangely enough, I was even a little bit glad to be doing something important for my kingdom. After years of being pushed to the sidelines by my father, who had only expected me to marry and run an estate somewhere, I'd managed to convince my brother to send me, the least diplomatic person in our kingdom, to lay the groundwork for an alliance. If we couldn't get Zumorda to work with us, war breaking out with Sonnenborne on our southern borders was all but inevitable.

Somehow I had to convince the Zumordan queen that Sonnenborne posed a threat to both our kingdoms. They'd assassinated my father and uncle, using magical means to throw suspicion on Zumorda. If I could just open a dialogue with the queen, then Thandi could send in the real ambassadors and I'd be free to focus on helping Denna find someone to educate her about how to use the magic she'd been hiding all her life. Getting it under control was our only hope of being able to have a normal life together, especially if we wanted to live in Mynaria, where those with magic were often punished or exiled. Even if my brother's reign helped make magic use more acceptable, attitudes would be slow to change.

Still, I questioned whether I was up to the task of engaging foreign queens and nobles. My rank as princess made me worthy of the assignment, but my background wasn't exactly in diplomacy—it was in training horses, sneaking out of the castle to spy in the city, and drinking cheap ale in seedy pubs. Moreover, Mynarians hardly ever went to Zumorda. The kingdom was full of magic users with the very powers we'd condemned—Affinities for fire, air, earth, water, and gods knew what else.

"We should be getting close to Duvey now," Denna said. "The trees are thinning, and the border guards seemed to think we'd reach it by sundown."

"The trees look like they're mostly dead," I observed. Skeletons of evergreens stood everywhere amidst the live trees. They creaked against each other in the wind, and their bleached bones littered the forest floor.

"It does seem awfully dry here, which doesn't make much sense, given that there aren't any geological reasons for the climate to be different on this side of the border," Denna mused.

"I'll take your word for it." I'd studied the maps well enough to know which way to point my horse, but my knowledge ended there. "All I know is when we get to Duvey I want five tankards of ale and to sleep past sunrise for once."

"I could go for something with more kick than ale," Denna said. "I wonder if Zumordans have a midwinter festival with liquor. In Havemont we have a competition for the distillers. Mother would never let me and Ali taste any spirits besides the winners, but the people-watching was always good." She spoke of home with a regretful fondness, a feeling I had a hard time understanding.

Home for me had never been somewhere I felt entirely comfortable. Not in the castle, anyway. In disguise out in the city? Somewhat. The barn? Definitely. But my tendency to escape my maids and royal duties to do barn chores or play cards with liegemen meant I'd fit in with the other nobles about as well as a jar of horse farts at a parfumerie.

"Well, I hope by the time we visit Havemont that your sister is the one in charge of the festival. I doubt she'll stop us from tasting all the spirits we want," I said, already picturing sitting in front of a roaring fire with Denna on a cold winter's night, both of us a little light-headed from good liquor and laughing too much. The thought of tasting sweet brandy on her lips instantly counteracted the chill of the crisp autumn wind.

"She'd encourage us for sure," Denna said, and I could hear the smile in her voice. "She's always had a mischievous streak. Did I tell you about the time she wrapped me up in furs and tried to convince a tradesman at a party that I was a cat he should purchase?"

I snorted. "That sounds like something I would've tried to do to Thandi. Although mostly I just threw him in the manure pile anytime he made me angry."

"If only his subjects knew he'd once been King of the Dung Heap." Denna laughed.

"More than a dozen times over." I smirked, but a twinge of unfamiliar regret needled me. My relationship with my brother had always been antagonistic, but maybe it hadn't needed to be. If we had tried harder to overcome our differences in opinion instead of taking opposite sides of every argument, would the rest of our family still be dead? It was pointless to think about, but still rose up in the back of my mind to taunt me.

The twilight shadows deepened as we rode over gently rolling hills past fallow fields carved out of the forest. All the houses we saw were closed and dark, their windows shuttered. There were no lanterns hung outside front doors, no other travelers on the road. It felt empty in a way it shouldn't have. Even Flicker seemed ill at ease, his head up and ears swiveling back and forth worriedly.

"The keep should be over the next rise. Where are the people?" Denna asked.

"Something definitely doesn't seem right," I said. "Let's get off and approach on foot through those trees over there." I pointed to a copse of evergreens at the top of the next hill. "We need to make sure it's safe."

When we reached the trees, I drew Flicker gently to a halt and braced my arm for Denna to use as an assist to dismount. We left Flicker tied to a tree and crept into the woods. On the other side of the copse we had a clear view down into Duvey Keep, a stone fortress inside a high wall with dwellings scattered all around it.

"There are riders down there," Denna observed.

"Those horses don't look like they're from our trade strings." The merchants hadn't ridden out that long before us, but most of the animals we'd sent out on trade were too young to be ridden.

As I spoke the words, a horse cantered down the narrow path between our hill and the exterior wall of the keep. It had the distinctive convex profile and high neck set typical of a Sonnenborne desert-bred, and the sight of it made my heart pound with fear. In one smooth motion the rider nocked an arrow and stood in the stirrups, preparing to let it fly.

My stomach heaved and I grabbed Denna by the sleeve, tugging her behind a thick tangle of bushes.

"What's going on?" she whispered, looking equally shaken.

"The keep is under attack by Sonnenbornes. The attackers' horses look just like the ones Kriantz had with him in Mynaria. That snake had bigger plans all along." Grief rose to choke me. Speaking

Kriantz's name consumed me with memories of the night my best friend Nils had died—the night I'd been abducted from the castle and Denna had chosen to forfeit her crown to come after me. In some ways, that night had broken us both forever. In others, it had made us both whole for the first time.

"His people must be more united than we thought," Denna said.

"But why in the Sixth Hell are they here?" It was true he'd given the impression that several tribes had only recently joined together beneath his banner—that they wouldn't do anything without his signal. But for the Sonnenbornes to be here now spoke of a plan far more complex and organized than he'd made it seem like they had.

"They could be trying to take an outpost at the Mynarian border," Denna said, her voice grim. "The keep would make a perfect settlement to fortify for attack."

"Six Hells," I said.

"Perhaps they plan to retaliate for Lord Kriantz's death," Denna continued, fear making her voice rise. The Sonnenbornes didn't know who had killed their leader—only that it happened on Mynarian soil. Denna had dealt him a swift and fiery death by calling down the stars with her magic. Though she'd saved my life, I knew it still haunted her.

"Hey," I said, taking her hand. "You did what you had to. You saved me." I leaned over and softly kissed her cheek. The fear in her eyes eased a little bit, so I pressed my lips to hers just long enough to feel familiar warmth blossom in the pit of my stomach. The truth was that the terrifying memories haunted me, too. Sometimes the smoke of the campfires along our journey had reminded me of that night, the scent of forest and flesh burning, the way the earth had shaken as flaming stones rained down from above.

"Or what if their plans are more elaborate than we thought, and they're trying to cut off one of Mynaria's most lucrative trade routes?" she said, always ten steps ahead.

"You're right," I said. "They'd be positioned to do either of those things. We need to get out of here." Keeping Denna safe was the only thing that mattered to me, but I also doubted my brother would approve of his sister—or his envoy—getting murdered by Sonnenborne raiders. That would start the very war we'd set out to prevent.

Denna's brow furrowed. "If the Sonnenbornes are already this far into Zumorda, there are two things we have to do: tell Thandi, and get you to the queen as soon as possible." She spoke with the kind of authority I'd heard her use back when she'd still been my brother's consort.

"I like it when you talk queenly to me," I said with a flirtatious wink.

A brief smile broke through her distressed expression. "Truly, though. The queen will be on your side if they've attacked her people."

"Let's ride north," I said, already walking back toward Flicker. "I doubt they'll send scouts until they've secured the keep."

"We need to make sure the Zumordans win this battle first." She grabbed my hand to stop me. "I can use my magic to help them."

I looked at her like she'd lost her mind. "Getting involved in this could get us killed."

"What better way to win allies?" she asked.

Fear flickered in my chest. "We can't. What if something goes wrong?" As much as I loved her, I'd be lying if I didn't admit that her magic sometimes scared me. Ever since she'd summoned the stars to save me from Lord Kriantz, her powers had become less predictable, and they'd only been steady as a green-broke colt in the first place. Less than a week ago we'd gone hungry one rainy night because Denna couldn't start a fire and it was too wet for the sparks from my flint and steel to catch. A few days later, she had a nightmare, and before I could wake her up she'd set her bedroll ablaze, charring it past salvation.

Frustratingly, Denna ignored my objection and carried on. "We could climb that tree by the wall. That first building looks like it might be the stables." She gestured to a stone building abutting the wall. Half doors lined the side, and a second-story window stood wide open as though no one had made it to close up the barn for the night. "There should be a good view from the hayloft."

"Hay is flammable," I said. "Your Affinity is for fire."

"Then we'll make that useful," she said, and before I could stop her, she was on her feet, sprinting toward the stables.

I cursed and took off after her.

If I had an Affinity, it would definitely be for trouble.